By Lantern Light

Michael Manosca

ISBN:

978-1-969915-07-9 (paperback)

978-1-969915-04-8 (electronic)

978-1-969915-05-5 (hardcover)

Library of Congress Control Number: 2025923580

First Edition.

Los Angeles, California, United State of America

Some lights guide us forward.
    Others warn us of paths already taken.

— Anonymous

A Note from the Author

This novel explores themes of love, identity, and belonging, but it also touches upon serious matters including suicide, homophobia, depression, and the struggles faced by LGBTQ+ youth in less accepting times and places. While nothing is graphically explicit, there are emotionally intense and potentially disturbing scenes, particularly involving characters contemplating or choosing self-harm as a response to societal pressure and internalized shame.

If you or someone you know is experiencing thoughts of suicide, struggling with their identity, or feeling isolated and without hope, please know that help is available. You are not alone, and your story doesn't have to end in darkness.

The Trevor Project (LGBTQ+ youth crisis support)
- Call: 1-866-488-7386
- Text "START" to 678-678
- Chat: www.thetrevorproject.org

988 Suicide & Crisis Lifeline
- Call or text: 988
- Chat: 988lifeline.org
- Available 24/7, free and confidential

Crisis Text Line
- Text "HELLO" to 741741
- Free, 24/7 support

If you're not comfortable seeking professional help yet, start with a trusted friend, family member, teacher, counselor, or any adult you feel safe talking to. Taking that first step toward asking for help is an act of courage, not weakness.

Like the characters I've written about, there is hope—even when it feels like there is no lantern to light your way.

I promise.

— Michael Manosca

Chapter 1

Ghosts

The lantern swung like a pendulum in the darkness below.

From the widow's peak, he gripped the railing, splinters catching against his palms. The night pressed close—thick with August heat that hadn't broken, the moon looming just above the horizon, almost full but not quite, swollen and amber in a way that felt wrong. Frightening. Yet impossible to look away from.

Below, the country road stretched pale between fields of corn that rustled and whispered. Two farmhouses faced each other across that distance—this one beneath him, perched on its hillside, and another smaller one half a mile down the road, its windows dark except—

Light.

A door opened in that smaller farmhouse, warm and yellow against the darkness. A boy emerged, maybe sixteen or seventeen, wearing what looked like a nightshirt, the kind from old photographs. In his hand, the lantern swung, its flame steady despite the breeze.

He tried to call out. No sound came. Dream logic—his throat worked but produced nothing.

The boy began walking up the road, the lantern lighting his path. Bare feet on gravel. He moved with purpose, as though he'd made this walk a hundred times before, knew every stone, every rut.

The light drew closer. He leaned forward, trying to see the boy's face, but shadows and distance kept it blurred. Only the lantern remained clear—its glass panels catching that strange amber moonlight, the flame inside dancing but never guttering.

At the base of the widow's peak house, the boy stopped. Slowly, deliberately, he tilted his face upward.

Their eyes met.

The gaze held. Held longer than was comfortable, longer than made sense. The boy's face was still indistinct, features blurred like watercolor left in rain, but those eyes—dark, desperate, pleading—burned clear. He was trying to say something. Trying to—

Wait.

The boy below wasn't looking at him.

He was looking beside him.

He turned, sudden and sharp, to find another boy standing there—taller, wearing similar old-fashioned nightclothes, no lantern in his hands but moonlight caught in his hair. When had he arrived? How long had he been standing there?

He opened his mouth to speak, to ask, to understand—

Jason Reynolds jerked upright in bed, gasping, his whole body seized by the kind of violent muscle spasm that comes from nowhere—like his leg had kicked out in sleep, only this was everywhere at once. His t-shirt stuck to his chest with sweat. The alarm clock on his nightstand blinked red: 6:47 AM. Three minutes before it was set to go off.

Tuesday, September 5th, 1989.

His heart hammered. The third time in two weeks. The same dream. The same boys. The same amber moon and swinging lantern.

He pressed the heels of his hands against his eyes, breathing hard. The dream clung to him, sticky and impossible to shake.

The alarm shrieked. Jason slapped it silent and stumbled out of bed, feet hitting worn carpet.

In the bathroom, he turned on the tap and splashed cold water on his face. The dream flickered behind his eyes—the lantern, the boy walking, that moment when he realized they weren't looking at him. He grabbed his toothbrush. The bristles scraped across his teeth while his mind replayed the taller boy standing beside him, silent, appearing from nowhere.

He spat into the sink. Rinsed. The dream.

He peed, flushed, turned on the shower. Steam filled the small bathroom as he stepped under the spray. Water beat against his shoulders while he worked shampoo through his hair. The dream. Why the same dream three times? Why those boys? Why did it feel less like dreaming and more like... remembering?

He dried off roughly, hair sticking up in damp spikes. Grabbing the cheap cologne his mom's boyfriend had given him last Christmas—some drugstore brand in a blue bottle that tried too hard to smell expensive, He dabbed it on his neck. The dream.

Jeans from the floor—clean enough. A black t-shirt from the drawer, the Def Leppard logo faded from too many washes. He shoved his feet into worn Nikes, the left one split slightly at the toe. Tied them without looking, muscle memory.

The dream.

He stood in his small bedroom, backpack slung over one shoulder, and stared at nothing in particular.

Who were those boys?

In the kitchen, his mom was already moving—keys jangling, purse over her shoulder, that harried look she got when running late. She glanced up as he came in.

"First day. Good luck, honey." She was halfway to the door before she stopped, turned back. "Oh, wait—"

She dug through her purse, fishing past receipts and loose change, finally pulling out a crumpled five-dollar bill. She pressed it into his hand.

"Lunch money. Make it last the week, okay? It's all I've got right now."

"Mom, I can—"

"Jason." She squeezed his hand around the bill. "It's fine. Payday's

Friday." Then she was gone, the screen door banging behind her, her car coughing to life in the driveway.

Jason stood there holding the five dollars, listening to her pull away. He folded it carefully and shoved it deep in his front pocket where it wouldn't fall out.

The kitchen was quiet. He pulled the cereal box from the cabinet —generic corn flakes in a bag, the kind you bought at IGA when name brands cost too much—and poured it into a chipped bowl. Added milk. Sat at the small table by the window.

The dream.

He ate mechanically, barely tasting anything. The lantern. The boy walking. The eyes that looked past him to someone else. The taller boy appearing from nowhere.

He rinsed his bowl in the sink, grabbed his backpack, and headed out.

The bike leaned against the side of the house where he'd left it last night—an old ten-speed his mom's boyfriend got in a trade with some shop. "Better than walking," he'd said, like Jason should be grateful. And he was, sort of. It worked well enough, even if it looked like hell. The paint, what was left of it, was a dark red that almost hid the rust if you squinted and pretended.

Jason threw his leg over and pushed off, coasting down the driveway onto 24th Street.

The morning was cool, mist still clinging to the grass, the air carrying that smell—the one that came in early September when summer finally broke and autumn started creeping in at the edges. Jason breathed it in deep, trying to clear his head.

He turned south on Western Avenue, pedaling hard now, the pavement rough under his tires. The town was just waking up—a few cars, some lights on in houses, the hum of the factory in the distance. He passed under the railroad trestle, the shadow cold and sudden, then turned onto 8th Street.

"Fucking bitch," he muttered.

His thighs burned as he climbed, standing on the pedals to get enough leverage. 8th Street cut straight up through the nice part of town—the part where lawns stayed trimmed and houses had fresh paint and nobody's bike looked like it had been pulled from a junk-yard. Jason kept his head down and pedaled.

At the top, he crossed Highway 44 and kept going, the houses getting bigger now, perched on the hillside like they were looking down on everyone below. Connersville High School sprawled across the ridge—brick buildings connected by walkways, the football field visible beyond, the flag already raised and snapping in the breeze.

Jason coasted into the parking lot and locked his bike at the rack near the bus drop-off. Buses were already pulling in, kids spilling out in clusters, loud and careless. He could've taken the bus. Probably would've been faster. But he hated it. Hated sitting with the other jerks who called him names, hated the smell of diesel and old vinyl seats, hated being trapped.

The bike was shitty, but it was his. Got him here on his own terms.

He slung his backpack over one shoulder and headed toward the main building.

First day. Driver's Ed first period. Maybe this year would be different.

Maybe.

Jason followed the flow of students into the main building, the halls already loud with first-day chaos—locker doors slamming, voices bouncing off cinderblock walls, the squeak of sneakers on polished floors. He checked his schedule card, already wrinkled from being folded and unfolded too many times.

Room 127 was in the basement, down a narrow staircase that felt colder and dimmer than the rest of the school, like the building itself didn't care much about what was tucked beneath. The fluorescent lights buzzed overhead, flickering just enough to make it hard to focus.

Jason pushed through the door and stopped, taking in the room. Pale yellow-green walls that had faded into the color of spoiled milk. Rows of desks crowded the center, each carved with initials and band names from kids who'd sat here years before. Along the far wall sat the simulators—squat contraptions with cracked vinyl seats, steering wheels slick with decades of palms, and plastic dashboards faded to gray. They looked like they'd been scavenged from the old high school before it moved in '69.

Driver's Ed.

Jason slid into a seat near the back—not the very back, that drew attention, but far enough to have an exit and enough space to be ignored. He dropped his backpack on the floor and stared at the simulators.

He wouldn't even have a car to drive. His mom's rusted Civic was barely holding together, and she needed it for work. His mom's boyfriend had a truck, but Jason wasn't about to ask him for anything. So what was the point? Still... maybe someday. Maybe his mom would let him borrow the car sometimes. Run errands. Drive himself places instead of relying on the bus or that shitty bike.

Maybe.

The room filled slowly—kids shuffling in, claiming seats in pairs or small groups, already talking and laughing like they'd never left for summer. Jason recognized a few faces but didn't bother trying to catch anyone's eye. He pulled his notebook from his bag and flipped it open, pretending to read over blank pages.

The dream flickered at the edges of his thoughts. The lantern. The boys. The amber moon.

He was so lost in it he almost didn't notice when someone slid into the desk beside him.

Jason glanced up.

The boy was neat—that was the first thing he noticed. Sandy blond hair combed carefully, a collared shirt buttoned just high enough to look intentional without being stiff. His posture was straight, shoulders square, like someone had taught him how to sit properly and he'd never forgotten. He set his notebook down—pristine, no bent corners, no doodles on the cover—and pulled a pen from his bag.

Everything about him was... careful. Polished. Like he'd stepped out of some catalogue Jason's mom got in the mail but never ordered from.

The boy glanced over and caught Jason staring.

"I've uh..." He cleared his throat, fumbling with his pen, clicking it nervously. "I've seen you around, but I don't know your name. Sorry. I'm Christopher."

Jason shifted. "Jason." He nodded toward the other boy. "Chris, right?"

"Christopher." The correction came quick—automatic, like he'd said it a thousand times before. Then his ears went pink. "Sorry. I just... I prefer Christopher. If that's okay."

"Sure." Jason shrugged. "Christopher."

Silence stretched between them. Christopher's face was still flushed, and he seemed to be studying his desk like it held the secrets of the universe. Jason wasn't sure if he'd offended him or if the guy was just awkward. Maybe both.

"I like your, uh... t-shirt."

Christopher's face went red the second the words left his mouth. His ears were burning. Jason could practically see him wanting to crawl under his desk.

Jason laughed—a short bark of surprise—and then immediately caught himself, the sound dying in his throat. He looked embarrassed, like he'd been caught doing something wrong.

"Sorry, I—" Jason shook his head. "That wasn't... you were being nice."

Christopher just stared at his desk, looking like he wanted to disappear.

Jason cleared his throat. "Uh, thanks. It's... it's old. Hand-me-down, I think. You know?"

Christopher nodded quickly, though something in his expression suggested maybe he didn't know. Everything about the guy screamed department store tags and back-to-school shopping with both parents. The idea of wearing someone else's old shirt probably hadn't crossed his mind before today.

But he seemed nice. A little buttoned-up, maybe. A little out of place talking to a kid in a faded Def Leppard shirt. But nice.

They sat in awkward silence, both staring forward now, neither sure what to say next.

The dream flickered at the edges of Jason's thoughts. The lantern. The boys. That moment of desperate eye contact.

He shook it off.

"So, uh..." Jason tried. "You nervous? About the driving stuff?"

Christopher exhaled, grateful for the lifeline. "A little. I mean, I've never really... my parents always drive. So."

"Yeah. Same." Jason picked at the edge of his notebook. "Well, my mom. She's got this old Civic that barely runs, but... yeah."

"My dad's got a Buick," Christopher offered, then immediately regretted it. That sounded like bragging. "I mean, it's not—I probably won't get to drive it much anyway."

"Still cool though." Jason's voice was genuine, not bitter. Just... matter-of-fact.

Another pause. But this one felt less painful. Like maybe they were figuring out how to talk to each other.

The bell rang, sharp and metallic. Mr. Barnes swept into the room, far too cheerful for 8:00 AM, clapping his hands like he was warming up a pep rally.

"Good morning, drivers! Welcome to Driver's Education! Let's make this the best semester yet!"

Groans rolled across the room. Jason caught Christopher's eye for just a second—both of them suppressing smiles at Barnes's enthusiasm.

Something passed between them. Not much. Just a flicker of shared understanding.

But it was enough.

Mr. Barnes clapped his hands together, beaming like he'd just won the lottery instead of facing a room full of skeptical teenagers at 8:00 AM.

"Welcome, welcome! I'm Mr. Barnes, and yes—before you ask—I'm also your guidance counselor, which means if any of you have a crisis, you know where to find me." He gestured broadly at the room like it was a palace instead of a basement with spoiled-milk walls. "But today, we're here to talk about the open road, freedom, and the responsibilities that come with operating a two-ton vehicle!"

Someone in the back groaned. Barnes' smile didn't falter.

"Now, I know what you're thinking. 'Mr. Barnes, when do we get to drive?' Well, patience, young grasshoppers! First, we learn the rules. Then we learn the machine. *Then—*" he paused dramatically, "—we take to the streets!"

Jason slouched lower in his seat. This was going to be a long semester.

"But first things first—roll call! Let me learn your names, and you can start getting to know your fellow drivers."

Barnes pulled out a clipboard and began reading names. Jason only half-listened, his mind drifting back to the dream. The lantern swinging in the darkness. Those eyes, desperate and pleading.

"Christopher Avery?"

"Here." Christopher's voice beside him, clear and polite.

Jason glanced over. Christopher had straightened even more, if that was possible, like being called on required perfect posture.

Barnes continued down the list. Names blurred together—Julie Davis, Ben Johnson, Susan Miller. Kids Jason recognized but didn't really know. The ones who ran in different circles, had different lives.

"Jason Reynolds?"

"Here," Jason said, barely loud enough to carry.

Barnes looked up, squinting toward the back. "Jason! Good to see you, son. Haven't seen you around the guidance office lately. Everything going well?"

Heat crawled up Jason's neck. Great. Draw attention to the poor kid who needed counseling. Perfect.

"Yeah. Fine," Jason managed.

"Good, good! Glad to hear it." Barnes moved on mercifully to the next name.

Beside him, Christopher shifted slightly, a question in the movement. Jason kept his eyes forward, jaw tight.

The rest of roll call dragged on. When it was done, Barnes launched into his overview—semester structure, grading policy, the importance of completing both classroom instruction and behind-the-wheel training. Fridays would be quiz days. Midterm and final exams. Blah blah blah.

Jason pulled out his notebook and clicked his pen, pretending to take notes. Mostly he just drew spirals in the margins and tried not to think about Barnes calling him out in front of everyone.

Or about Christopher sitting right there, hearing it.

"Now!" Barnes clapped again, making half the class jump. "Before we dive into the riveting world of traffic laws and road signs, let's talk about partnerships."

That got everyone's attention.

"You'll each be assigned a partner for the duration of this course. When we get to the driving portion, you'll share a vehicle. Individual grades, but partnership matters! Learning to work together, communicate, trust each other—these are vital skills for the road *and* for life."

He started pointing around the room, pairing people off seemingly at random. Two jocks in the front groaned when they got paired with each other instead of girls. A couple of friends squealed when they ended up together.

Jason's stomach tightened. He'd probably get stuck with some jackass who'd make his life miserable, or—

"Christopher Avery and Jason Reynolds," Barnes called out, looking down at his clipboard. "You two are already sitting together. Perfect! Stay put."

Jason's head snapped toward Christopher, who looked equally surprised but not... upset. Just startled.

"Uh," Jason said eloquently.

"Is that okay?" Christopher asked quickly, like he needed permission.

"Yeah. Sure. Fine."

"Good." Christopher offered a small smile. Nervous, but genuine.

Barnes finished assigning partners and then dove into the first lesson—basic traffic laws, right-of-way, speed limits, the kind of stuff that would definitely be on Friday's quiz. Jason tried to focus, but his awareness kept getting pulled sideways to the person next to him.

Christopher took notes. Actual notes, in neat handwriting that somehow managed to look formal even when he was just writing "STOP = complete cessation of motion." He underlined important points. Used a ruler to draw straight margins.

Who the hell brought a ruler to Driver's Ed?

Jason found it... weirdly endearing. Which was stupid. It was just notes. Neat handwriting didn't mean anything.

But he kept noticing anyway. The way Christopher tilted his head when he concentrated. The small crease between his eyebrows when Barnes said something confusing. The way he clicked his pen absently—three clicks, pause, three more clicks, like a pattern he wasn't aware of.

Jason was so busy watching Christopher's pen-clicking that he completely missed whatever Barnes had just said. Something about... blood alcohol limits? Or was that yield signs?

He leaned toward Christopher, keeping his voice low. "What'd he just say?"

Christopher glanced up from his notes, then slid his notebook slightly toward Jason so he could see.

BAC limit in Indiana: 0.10% for adults, 0.02% for minors

Jason nodded, starting to lean back, when Christopher added in a whisper: "Though I have no idea how they measure—"

"Mr. Reynolds? Mr. Avery?" Barnes called from the front. "Something you'd like to share with the class?"

Both of them froze. Christopher's face went red.

"No sir," they said in unison.

Barnes gave them a look that said *I'm watching you* but went back to his lecture about brake fluid and DUI penalties.

Jason slumped in his seat, mortified. Christopher pulled his notebook back, looking like he wanted to sink through the floor.

After a moment, Jason leaned over one more time, barely breathing the words: "Sorry."

Christopher shook his head slightly—*it's okay*—but kept his eyes firmly on Barnes for the rest of class.

"You okay?"

Jason met his eyes. Christopher looked genuinely concerned. Not mocking. Not dismissive.

Just... worried.

"Yeah," Jason said quietly. "I'm okay."

Christopher nodded and went back to his notes, but something had shifted. Some invisible wall had gotten a little thinner.

When the bell finally rang, they gathered their things in silence. At the top of the stairs, Christopher paused.

"So... see you tomorrow?"

"Yeah," Jason said. "Tomorrow."

Christopher smiled—that small, careful smile—and walked away toward Chemistry.

Jason stood there a moment longer, watching him go.

Then he shook his head, adjusted his backpack, and headed to English.

It was just one class. Just one day.

It didn't mean anything.

But the thought felt like a lie even as he thought it.

Chapter 2

Give-a-fuck-itis

Wednesday morning, Jason almost took the bus.

He stood at the corner of 24th and Western, watching it rumble toward him, and thought about how much easier it would be. No hills to climb. No burning thighs. Just sit in the back, keep his headphones on, ignore everyone.

But then he remembered the names. The shoves. The way David Keller had "accidentally" knocked his books out of his hands last year and laughed when Jason scrambled to pick them up before they got trampled.

The bus hissed to a stop. The doors opened.

Jason turned and walked back to get his bike.

Twenty minutes later, he was locking it at the rack, legs aching but his head clear. Small victories.

Inside, the hallways were louder on day two—everyone settling into routines, the nervous first-day energy replaced by something more comfortable. Jason made his way to the basement stairs, trying not to think about whether yesterday's conversation had been a fluke— whether Christopher would be distant now, polite but closed off, the way people sometimes got after accidentally being too friendly with someone they didn't really want to know.

He was early. The classroom was still mostly empty—just a couple of kids in the front row already reviewing their notes like the quiz was today instead of Friday. Jason dropped into the same seat as yesterday, near the back, and pulled out his notebook.

The dream had come back last night. Shorter this time, just fragments—the lantern swinging, the sound of footsteps on gravel, that amber moon hanging wrong in the sky. He'd woken up at 3 AM with his heart racing and couldn't fall back asleep for an hour.

He didn't know what it meant. Didn't know why his brain kept pulling him back to those images.

"Morning."

Jason looked up. Christopher stood there, books tucked under one arm, and slid into the desk beside him.

"Hey," Jason said.

Christopher pulled out his pen, clicked it once. "Sleep okay?"

"Like shit, actually. You?"

Christopher's eyes widened slightly—not shocked, just... interested. Like Jason had said something unexpectedly honest. "Yeah. I stayed up too late reading, but..." He trailed off with a self-deprecating smile. "Story of my life."

"What, like porn? Respectable." Jason kept his face completely straight.

Christopher choked on air, his face going red. "What? No! I meant—fantasy books. Dragons and—oh my god, you're messing with me."

"Little bit." Jason grinned. "Your face though. Priceless."

Christopher tried to look annoyed but couldn't quite pull it off. "You're terrible."

"Yeah, but I'm funny terrible. There's a difference."

More students filed in, filling the desks around them. Barnes arrived in his usual flurry of energy, immediately launching into the day's lesson about defensive driving techniques and accident prevention.

This time, Jason tried to actually pay attention. He took notes—not neat like Christopher's, but something. When Barnes showed a filmstrip about drunk driving that was clearly from the '70s based on the cars and fashion, Jason caught Christopher trying not to laugh at the narrator's dramatic voice-over.

Their eyes met. Christopher bit his lip, shoulders shaking with suppressed laughter. Jason had to look away before he lost it too.

After class, they walked out together again—not planned, just happening. At the top of the stairs, Christopher paused.

"What do you have next?"

"English. You?"

"Chemistry. Other end of the building."

"That sucks."

"Yeah." Christopher shifted his books. "Well... see you tomorrow, I guess."

"Yeah. See you."

Christopher walked away, and Jason watched him go again. This was becoming a pattern. A stupid pattern he needed to break before someone noticed and started asking questions he didn't have answers to.

In English, Mrs. Grant assigned them "The Love Song of J. Alfred Prufrock" and told them to read it for homework and be prepared to discuss the theme of paralysis and missed opportunities. Jason stuffed the photocopied poem into his bag and tried not to think about the line that snagged in his brain: *Do I dare disturb the universe?*

The rest of Wednesday passed in the usual blur—classes he cared about (English, Art) and classes he endured (Math, History). Lunch was spent with Scott and Allison at their usual table. Scott complained about football practice. Allison complained about the new choir director. Jason ate his cafeteria pizza and contributed the minimum required to not seem weird.

But his mind kept drifting back to Christopher laughing at the drunk driving filmstrip.

———

Thursday morning, Jason was early again.

He told himself it was just because he'd woken up before his alarm and figured why waste time sitting around the house. It had nothing to do with wanting to see Christopher's face when he walked in.

Nothing at all.

Christopher showed up five minutes before the bell, looking slightly harried—hair a little less perfect than usual, collar not quite as crisp. He dropped into his seat—their seats, Jason's brain unhelpfully supplied—with a heavy exhale.

"You okay?" Jason asked.

"Yeah. Just... morning was chaotic. My mom needed the car, so my dad had to drive me, but he was running late for work, and..." Christopher waved it off. "It's fine. I'm here."

"Barely," Jason said, but his tone was light.

"Barely counts." Christopher pulled out his notebook, then paused. "Hey, did you do the reading for English? That Prufrock poem?"

"Grant assigned you that too?" Jason asked.

"Yeah." Christopher tapped his pen against his notebook. "I read it last night but I have no idea what it's actually about. Do you?"

"Oh." Christopher looked pleased they shared a teacher even if not the period. "So did you read it?"

"Skimmed it. Why?"

"I'm trying to figure out what it's about. Like, I get the words, but I don't get what he's *saying*. You know?"

Jason thought about it. "It's about a guy who's too chickenshit to do anything. Just paralyzed by overthinking every goddamn thing. Afraid of how people will judge him."

Christopher blinked at the casual profanity but didn't flinch away from it. "That's... actually really good. Did you look up analysis or something?"

"No. It's just..." Jason shrugged. "Dude's in his own head so much he can't get out of his own way. Classic case of give-a-fuck-itis."

"Give-a-heck-itis?" Christopher said carefully, substituting the word without even thinking about it.

Jason's eyebrows shot up. "Did you just say 'heck'?"

Christopher's face went red. "What?"

"Give-a-HECK-itis." Jason was grinning now. "That's not what I said."

"I know what you said, I just—" Christopher shifted uncomfortably in his seat.

"You can't even say it, can you?"

"I can say it."

"Then say it."

Christopher's ears were burning. "Why does it matter?"

"Because it's hilarious that you can't." Jason leaned forward, that challenging grin getting wider. "Come on. Just once. Give-a-fuck-itis. The proper medical term."

"I'm not going to—"

"Why not? It's just a word."

"My parents would kill me if they heard me talk like that."

"Your parents aren't here." Jason was clearly enjoying this way too much. "Nobody's here but me and Barnes, and Barnes is too busy falling asleep at his desk to notice. One word. That's all I'm asking."

Christopher glanced at Barnes, who was indeed slumped in his chair with his eyes closed. Still, he hesitated. "I don't... I don't usually swear."

"No kidding." Jason's grin softened slightly, became less mocking and more genuinely amused. "How do you make it through a day without swearing? Especially in this place?"

"I just... find other words."

"Like 'heck.'"

"Yes. Like heck."

Jason laughed—not mean, just delighted. "Okay. Okay. I respect that. But I'm making it my personal mission this semester to get you to swear. Naturally. Without thinking about it."

"That's a terrible mission."

"Best one I've got." Jason stuck out his hand. "Tell you what. If I can get you to swear—really swear, not 'darn' or 'heck' or whatever—before the end of the semester, you buy me lunch. If you make it through without breaking, I'll buy you lunch."

Christopher stared at the offered hand. "That's not fair. You're going to try to make me swear on purpose."

"That's the whole point."

"And if I accidentally swear when you're not around?"

"Doesn't count. Has to be in front of me. Those are the rules."

Christopher considered this, looking at Jason's challenging grin, those eyes daring him to back down. There was something about the whole thing that made him want to laugh despite himself.

He shook. "Deal. But when I win, you're buying me Pizza King."

"When you lose, I'm getting the works."

Jason sat back, satisfied. "So yeah. Prufrock's got terminal give-a-fuck-itis. Should probably get that checked out."

Christopher was still smiling. "You should say that in class. Use those exact words."

"Oh yeah, Grant would love that. 'Mr. Reynolds, your literary analysis is that Prufrock has give-a-fuck-itis?' I'd get detention."

"It'd be worth it to see her face."

"You're secretly a troublemaker, aren't you?"

Christopher's ears went pink. "No. I just... I like how you explain things. You make it make sense."

The honesty in his voice made Jason's chest tighten. He deflected with humor. "What I'm hearing is you want me to corrupt you with talking shit and showing you how to tell people to fuck off."

"That's not—" Christopher realized Jason was teasing again. "You're doing it again."

"Doing what?"

"Making me feel stupid for taking you seriously."

"You're not stupid. You're just too..." Jason gestured vaguely at Christopher's whole existence. "You know. Proper."

"Proper?"

"Yeah. Like you were raised by English teachers or some shit. All buttoned up."

Christopher looked down at his literally buttoned-up collar. "I can't tell if that's an insult or not."

"It's not. Just an observation. You're wound pretty tight."

"And you're not?"

"Oh, I'm fucked up in different ways," Jason said easily. "But at least I know it."

Barnes burst through the door before Christopher could respond, but Jason caught him hiding a smile behind his hand.

"Good morning, drivers! Pop quiz!"

The entire class groaned in unison.

"I'm kidding, I'm kidding!" Barnes laughed at his own joke. "But you should see your faces! Friday, people. Friday is quiz day. Today, we're learning about vehicle maintenance and the importance of checking your fluids!"

Jason pulled out his notebook and tried to focus on Barnes explaining oil changes and tire pressure, but Christopher's words kept echoing in his head.

I like how you explain things.

Nobody said that. Not teachers, who looked at his last name and address and expected less. Not his mom, who was too tired to notice. Not his mom's boyfriend, who barely acknowledged Jason existed.

But Christopher had said it like it was obvious.

When Barnes dismissed them, Christopher lingered while packing up his stuff.

"Hey, Jason?"

"Yeah?"

"Thanks. For explaining the poem. I actually get it now."

"No problem."

"And I meant what I said. You're smart. You should... I don't know. Let people know that."

Before Jason could respond, Christopher was gone, disappearing into the hallway rush with his perfect posture and his neat notebook and his absolute certainty that Jason was worth something.

Jason sat there a moment longer, staring at nothing.

You're smart.

The words felt like something fragile he needed to protect. Something he couldn't let himself examine too closely or it might break.

Or worse—it might turn into something he wanted too much.

———

Thursday afternoon blurred into evening. Jason did his homework at the kitchen table while his mom heated up leftovers. She asked how school was going. He said fine. She asked if he'd made any new friends. He said maybe, then changed the subject by asking if she needed help with anything.

She didn't, but she looked pleased he'd offered.

That night, lying in bed, staring at the ceiling while the house creaked and settled around him, Jason thought about Christopher's laugh during the filmstrip. About the way he'd rushed in Thursday morning, slightly disheveled, more real somehow. About *you're smart* said with such casual conviction.

He thought about how, when they sat together in that basement classroom, everything felt... easier. Lighter. Like maybe he didn't have to work so hard to be invisible.

Which was dangerous. Getting comfortable was dangerous. Starting to look forward to first period was dangerous.

Starting to notice the exact shade of Christopher's eyes—somewhere between gray and blue, like lake water on an overcast day—was definitely fucking dangerous.

Jason rolled over, pulled the pillow over his head, and tried to stop thinking.

It didn't work.

Friday morning, he told himself, would be just another day. Just Driver's Ed and a quiz and going through the motions.

But some part of him—the part he was trying really hard to ignore —knew he was lying to himself.

Because Friday morning meant seeing Christopher again.

And that thought made his stomach flip in a way that had nothing to do with nerves about the quiz.

Chapter 3

Scantrons

Jason knew it was going to be a weird day the moment he woke up.

Not bad-weird. Just... off. Like the air pressure had changed overnight and his body was still trying to adjust. He lay there for a minute, staring at the ceiling, trying to identify what felt different.

Then he realized: he was looking forward to first period.

Looking forward to Driver's Ed. To Barnes and his too-loud enthusiasm and that basement classroom's fucking gross walls.

To Christopher.

"Shit," Jason muttered, throwing off the sheets.

This was starting to feel fucked up.

He went through his morning routine on autopilot—shower, cheap cologne, store-brand toothpaste, not giving a shit about his hair. Pulled open his drawer to discover he had no underwear. Fuck. He grabbed a pair from the hamper, gave them a sniff, shrugged, then turned them inside out. Problem solved.

Clean-enough jeans from the floor. The least-faded t-shirt he owned—black, plain, no logo. Worn Nikes with the split at the toe.

In the kitchen, he opened the fridge. No milk. Which meant no cereal. He remembered his mom saying payday was Friday. Guess that meant making do one more day.

He dug through the cabinet until he found it—the last Pop-Tart, forgotten in the back, the foil wrapper crumpled. Breakfast of champions.

His mom had already left for work, her coffee mug still sitting in the sink with lipstick on the rim.

Jason ate the Pop-Tart standing by the counter, staring at nothing in particular. The dream. Christopher. The quiz they'd have to take together in an hour.

He shook his head, grabbed his backpack, and headed out.

———

The bike ride to school felt faster than usual, like his body knew where it wanted to be and was trying to get there before his brain could talk him out of it. By the time he locked up at the rack, his heart was hammering—from the hills, he told himself. Just from the hills.

He made it to the basement classroom with five minutes to spare. Christopher was already there, notebook open, reviewing what looked like traffic signs and their meanings. He glanced up when Jason dropped into the seat beside him.

"Hey. Ready for this?"

"Quiz?" Jason shrugged. "Guess so."

"I'm terrible at standardized tests," Christopher admitted, clicking his pen nervously. "I always second-guess everything."

"You'll be fine. You take better notes than anyone I've ever seen."

"That doesn't mean I remember it all."

"Then we'll figure it out together."

Christopher looked at him, something shifting in his expression—surprise, maybe, or gratitude. "Yeah. Okay."

Barnes swept in right as the bell rang, carrying a stack of papers and wearing a grin that suggested he was enjoying this way too much.

"Good morning, drivers! It's Friday, which means—"

"Quiz," the class chorused in resigned unison.

"Exactly! Now, don't panic. This is just to see what you've

retained from our first week. Twenty questions, choose-and-loose, you've got twenty minutes." He started passing out Scantron sheets and question packets. "And remember—you're working with your partners. No notes allowed! Talk it through, come to consensus, but you each need to fill out your own answer sheet. Individual bubbles, people!"

Jason took his materials and glanced at the first question:

---

1. In Indiana, what is the maximum speed limit on rural inter-state highways unless otherwise posted?

He was pretty sure it was 65, but Barnes had rattled off a lot of numbers on Tuesday and they all kind of blurred together.

"What do you think?" Christopher whispered, leaning closer. "65?"

"Yeah, I think so."

"Okay. Let's go with that."

They worked through the quiz like that—Jason reading the questions aloud quietly, both of them trying to remember what Barnes had said, debating the trickier ones. Question seven stumped them both at first

---

7. When parking uphill with a curb, which way do you turn your wheels?

Jason reasoned through it aloud.

"Away from the curb, right? So if the car rolls, it goes into the curb instead of into traffic?"

"That makes sense. Yeah."

Question twelve was about blood alcohol content and legal limits. Jason answered without hesitation, and Christopher just nodded, bubbling in the same answer.

By question fifteen, they'd hit a rhythm. Christopher's ability to remember specific details combined with Jason's logic meant they were moving faster than most of the class. Some partners were arguing quietly. Others looked completely lost.

Jason and Christopher just... worked.

They finished with a few minutes to spare. Christopher carefully reviewed each answer on his Scantron, making sure all the bubbles were filled in completely and no stray marks existed. Jason just flipped his quiz over and leaned back, watching him.

"You're really thorough," Jason observed.

Christopher looked up, self-conscious. "I know. It's probably excessive."

"I didn't say it was bad."

"You think I'm neurotic."

"I think you care about getting things right. That's not the same as neurotic."

Christopher held his gaze for a beat, something unreadable passing across his face. Then he smiled—small, almost shy. "Thanks."

The moment stretched just slightly too long. Jason felt it, that pull again, the one that made his stomach flip and his brain scramble for solid ground.

He looked away first.

"Time!" Barnes called, even though most people were still frantically bubbling. "Pencils down, pass your materials forward."

Groans rippled through the classroom. Christopher and Jason handed in their quizzes, and Barnes collected them with his usual enthusiasm.

"Excellent work, everyone! I'll have these graded by Monday. Now, let's talk about what we're covering next week—vehicle inspections and the anatomy of a car!"

The rest of class was Barnes showing diagrams of engines and explaining the difference between brake and transmission fluid. Jason tried to pay attention, but his mind kept drifting sideways to the person next to him.

To the way Christopher had looked at him when he'd said *we'll figure it out together*.

To the way their hands had almost touched when they were both reaching for the question packet at the same time, and how Christopher had pulled back quickly, like he'd been shocked.

To the weird, growing certainty that something was happening between them that Jason didn't have words for yet.

When the bell rang, they walked out together—routine now, familiar. At the top of the stairs, Christopher paused.

"That wasn't too bad," Christopher said. "The quiz, I mean."

"Yeah. We make a pretty good team."

"We do." Christopher shifted his books. "So, uh... have a good weekend."

"Yeah. You too."

An awkward pause. Christopher seemed on the verge of adding something, then thought better of it. "See you Monday."

"Yeah. Monday."

Christopher walked away toward Chemistry, and Jason watched him go.

Something about the way Christopher had hesitated made Jason think maybe he'd wanted to say more. Wanted to suggest hanging out, maybe. But hadn't.

Which was fine. They barely knew each other.

Except it didn't feel fine. It felt like a missed opportunity for something Jason couldn't quite name.

He shook his head and headed to English.

———

By lunch, Jason's head was buzzing with thoughts he didn't want to examine too closely. Mrs. Grant had spent all of second period dissecting Prufrock, and every line felt like it was aimed directly at him.

Do I dare disturb the universe?

Yeah, that was *the* fucking question.

He grabbed his tray from the cafeteria line—pizza that looked like it had been made sometime last week, reheated until the cheese turned into plastic—and headed into the main lunchroom.

The noise hit him first, the usual chaos of voices and trays clattering. He scanned the crowd, looking for Scott and Allison, when his eyes caught on a table near the wall.

Christopher sat three rows over with a couple of other kids Jason vaguely recognized but couldn't name. He was listening more than talking, nodding politely while someone told a story. His lunch was neat—sandwich cut in half, apple sliced, everything arranged just so.

Jason's feet slowed without him meaning to. He watched Christopher laugh at something, that same careful smile from this morning.

"Stalk much?"

Jason jerked his head around. Allison stood right behind him in line, eyebrow raised, holding her own tray.

"What?"

"You planning to stand in the middle of the lunchroom watching that table all day, or are you gonna move?"

"I'm going." Jason started walking again, weaving through tables toward where Scott was already sitting by the windows, already eating something he must have brought from home. Jason dropped into his usual seat across from him, and Allison slid in beside Jason.

"Dude, finally," Scott said around a mouthful of what appeared to be last night's dinner. "You won't believe what happened at practice yesterday. Coach made us run suicides for like twenty minutes because Henderson fucked up the play."

"That sucks," Jason offered, not really listening. His eyes drifted sideways again, back toward Christopher's table.

Allison caught him. Of course she did. She always caught everything.

"Who are you looking at?" she asked, voice casual but pointed.

"Nobody." Jason shoved a forkful of salad into his mouth to avoid elaborating.

"Bullshit." Allison leaned back in her chair, arms crossed, studying him. "You've been staring at that table for like five minutes."

"Have not."

"Have too." She turned to look, scanning the tables. "Let's see... is

26

it Jenny Morrison? No, you'd actually talk to her if you liked her. Maybe... oh." Her eyes landed on Christopher's table, then swung back to Jason with a knowing look. "Interesting."

Jason's face went hot. "What's interesting?"

"Nothing." But Allison was smiling now, that smile that meant she'd figured something out and was enjoying watching him squirm.

Scott was oblivious, still ranting about football. "And then Coach was like, 'You think Friday's gonna be easier?' and I'm like, no sir, but—"

"Who's the kid with the neat hair?" Allison interrupted, still looking at Christopher's table. "Three rows over, blue shirt."

Jason wanted to die. "I don't know what you're talking about."

"Uh huh." Allison's grin widened. "You know him?"

"We're in Driver's Ed together." Jason stared hard at his pizza, willing his face to stop burning.

"That's it? Driver's Ed?"

"We're partners. For the class."

"Oh, you're partners." Allison drew out the word like it meant something else entirely.

"Shut up."

"I didn't say anything." But she was laughing now, quiet and knowing.

Scott finally noticed something was happening. "What'd I miss?"

"Nothing," Jason said quickly.

"Jason's got a—" Allison started.

"Don't," Jason cut her off, voice sharper than he meant. "Seriously. Don't."

Allison's expression softened, the teasing edge dropping away. "Okay. I won't." She reached over and stole one of his fries. "But for what it's worth? He keeps looking over here too."

Jason's head snapped up. "What?"

"Your Driver's Ed partner. He's looked over at this table like three times since you sat down."

"Bullshit."

"I'm serious." Allison popped the fry in her mouth. "Check for yourself if you don't believe me."

Jason absolutely was not going to turn around and check. That would be obvious. That would be pathetic. That would be—

He turned around.

Christopher was looking right at him.

Their eyes met for half a second before they both looked away at exactly the same time, equally startled.

Jason turned back to find Allison grinning at him like the cat that ate the canary.

"Told you," she said.

"Fuck off," Jason muttered, but there was no heat in it.

Scott had already gone back to his meatloaf sandwich or whatever the hell it was, completely unaware, as usual. Allison just smiled and changed the subject, launching into some story about choir practice, but she caught Jason's eye once more and winked.

Jason spent the rest of lunch very carefully not looking at Christopher's table.

But he felt the weight of those glances anyway, like a current running under his skin.

———

After Art—his last class of the day—Jason was shoving charcoal-stained papers into his backpack when he heard the final bell ring. Friday afternoon, everyone exploding out of classrooms, voices echoing off lockers, the weekend stretching ahead like an exhale.

He took his time getting to the bike rack. No rush. Nothing waiting for him at home except a silent house and leftover casserole.

He was crouched by his bike, fighting with the rusty chain lock, when he heard the voice behind him.

"Hey."

He turned. Christopher stood there, backpack slung over one shoulder, looking slightly uncertain like he wasn't sure if stopping to talk was okay.

"Hey," Jason said back.

"Heading home?"

"Yeah. You?"

"My mom's picking me up." Christopher glanced toward the parent pickup lane, then back. "Any cool plans this weekend?"

Jason snorted. "No. Boring. You?"

"Me too." Christopher shifted his weight. "I've gotta mow the lawn. Start getting all the leaves up. I'll be happy when it's winter."

"Really?" Jason blinked. "I haven't mowed our lawn in forever."

"Why not?"

"It's like a postage stamp. Barely big enough to bother with." Jason kicked at his bike tire. "Where do you live?"

"We're out by the golf course." Christopher made a face. "My dad makes me mow the lawn every weekend in summer. And I have to shovel our whole driveway when it snows. It..."

"Sucks ass?"

"Uh, yeah." Christopher laughed nervously, clearing never having heard the expression before. "I.. I guess so." Looking towards the pickup area to change the subject, he turned back to Jason's gaze. "What about you? Where do you live?"

"Up on 24th. Shitty little rental. But at least I don't have to mow much."

"Trade you," Christopher said, only half-joking.

A car horn honked. Christopher glanced over and winced. "That's my mom. I should—"

"Yeah. Go."

Christopher hesitated, like he wanted to say something else. "So... see you Monday?"

"Yeah. Monday."

Christopher smiled—that small, careful smile—and jogged toward the waiting car. Jason watched him climb in, watched the car pull away, giving him a little wave, then looked down at his shitty rusted bike. Jason surprised himself by waving back. Where did *that* come from?

Out by the golf course.

He could find that.

If he wanted to.

————

29

The rest of Friday passed in a blur. By the time he biked home, his legs were rubber and his head was full of static.

He microwaved leftover spaghetti for dinner hoping it tasted better than the casserole, did the dishes because his mom had asked him to that morning, then retreated to his room and pulled out the Prufrock poem for English.

> *Do I dare*
> *Disturb the universe?*

Yeah. That was the question still, wasn't it?

He fell asleep around eleven with the light still on and the poem on his chest.

————

The dream came differently this time.

More vivid. More detailed. Like his subconscious had decided he needed to pay closer attention.

He stood at the widow's peak railing again, hands gripping weathered wood, splinters catching his palms. The moon hung low and amber, almost full but not quite, casting everything in a strange golden light that felt wrong but beautiful.

Below, the boy emerged from the smaller farmhouse, nightshirt pale against the darkness, lantern swinging in his hand. The flame danced but never went out.

Jason—or whoever he was in the dream—watched the boy walk up the road. Bare feet on gravel. Steady, certain, like he'd made this journey countless times.

The boy stopped at the base of the house. Looked up.

Their eyes met—dark, desperate, full of longing so intense it made Jason's chest ache.

The gaze held. Held impossibly long. The boy's face was still blurred, features soft and indistinct like looking through fogged glass, but the emotion was crystal clear.

Then, like before, Jason felt the presence beside him before he saw it.

He turned.

The second boy stood there—taller, broader through the shoulders, wearing a similar nightshirt. But this time, instead of just a silhouette, Jason could actually see his face.

Sandy hair catching moonlight. A straight nose, strong jaw. Eyes that were somewhere between blue and gray. Posture perfect even in sleep, even here.

The recognition hit like a fist to the sternum.

Christopher.

Not exactly—the features weren't quite right, the age was different, the clothes were from another century. But the essence of him, the way he held himself, the careful control even here in this dream-memory-whatever it was.

It looked like Christopher.

The boy's lips moved, speaking words Jason couldn't hear. His expression was gentle, sad, full of the same desperate longing the lantern boy had shown.

Jason tried to speak, to ask who they were, what this meant, why he kept coming back here—

———

Jason jerked awake, gasping, his whole body convulsing like he'd been shocked. His t-shirt was soaked with sweat. The alarm clock read 3:47 AM.

The dream clung to him, refusing to fade like most dreams did. The image of that second boy's face was seared into his brain—the way the moonlight had caught in his hair, the sad smile, the careful way he'd moved.

Christopher.

His brain had looked at that dream boy and seen Christopher Avery from Driver's Ed.

"Fuck," Jason whispered. "Fuck, fuck, fuck."

He threw off the covers and stumbled to the bathroom, splashed cold water on his face until his breathing slowed. Looked at himself in the mirror—eyes too wide, hair sticking up, looking half-wild.

What the hell was wrong with him?

It was just a dream. Dreams were random. Your brain took pieces of your day and scrambled them up with old memories and fears and whatever else was floating around in there. It didn't mean anything that he'd superimposed Christopher's face onto some imaginary ghost boy from a hundred years ago.

It didn't mean anything.

But when he went back to bed, he couldn't fall asleep. He just lay there, staring at the ceiling, thinking about Christopher saying *see you Monday* with that hesitation, like maybe he'd wanted to say more.

Thinking about *out by the golf course.*

Thinking about how maybe tomorrow—this morning, really, as soon as the sun came up—he could go for a bike ride. Just to get some air. Just to explore. Christopher would be mowing the lawn, right? Maybe he'd see him. Maybe they'd talk. Maybe—

When his alarm went off at 8:30 AM, Jason was already awake.

And he'd already decided.

He was going for that ride.

Chapter 4

Stalker White Trash

Jason pedaled west on 24th Street, the morning sun already warm on his shoulders despite the September cool still clinging to the shadows. At Western Avenue he turned left, heading south past the factories that never quite stopped humming, even on weekends. The smell of Roots Manufacturing hung in the air —oil and hot metal and something chemical that probably wasn't great to breathe but everyone did anyway because what choice did you have?

He cut through the back way up the hill, his thighs burning as the road climbed, ultimately making his way over to Country Club Road. The golf course sprawled ahead, all manicured greens and white buildings that looked like they belonged in a movie about old money and quiet corruption. Just beyond that, the "Richie Rich" section—the neighborhoods where Christopher lived.

Jason slowed as he approached, suddenly aware of how he must look. Shitty rusted bike. Faded t-shirt. Hair sticking up because he'd barely bothered to comb it. He didn't belong out here and everyone who saw him would know it.

Just look like I'm taking a normal Saturday ride, he told himself.

No big deal. No stalker white trash kid on a shitty ass bike here. Just a typical bike rider out for a nice little jaunt.

The lie felt hollow even as he thought it.

What the hell was he even doing?

He'd told himself he was just going for a ride. Getting some air. Exploring. All perfectly reasonable bullshit excuses that didn't explain why he'd checked how he looked in the mirror three times before leaving, or why he'd changed his shirt twice, or why his stomach felt like he'd swallowed a live wire.

He was riding out here because Christopher Avery had mentioned, in that careful, polite way of his, that he lived "out by the golf course." That was it. That was all Jason knew. Not an address. Not even a street name. Just "out by the golf course" in the vague direction of people who had money and lawns that stayed green all summer and cars that didn't sound like they were dying every time you turned the key.

He'd never spent any time over here. Wasn't sure which road to try first. The neighborhoods all looked the same—perfect homes, perfect driveways, perfect lives.

So yeah. Totally normal Saturday activity. Ride around rich neighborhoods hoping to accidentally run into the kid from Driver's Ed who'd laughed nervously at "sucks ass" like he'd never heard the expression before.

Jesus Christ, he was pathetic.

The thing was—and this was the part that kept gnawing at him, the part he couldn't quite shove down into whatever mental box he usually crammed uncomfortable thoughts into—he *wanted* to see Christopher. Not in that "hey, maybe we'll hang out" way he'd felt about Scott or Allison back in middle school before they'd drifted into their own orbits. This was different. This was the kind of wanting that sat in his chest like a stone and wouldn't dissolve, the kind that made him replay their awkward conversations over and over, analyzing every word, every pause, every tiny shift in Christopher's expression.

The way Christopher had clicked his pen nervously on Tuesday. The way his ears had gone red when Jason made that porn joke. The way he'd straightened his notebook exactly parallel to the edge of his desk, like if everything was lined up just right, the world would be okay.

Christopher wouldn't know what that factory smell was. Christopher probably drove past those places with his windows rolled up, AC on, some NPR station playing softly while his dad explained the stock market or whatever the hell people talked about in Buicks.

And there it was. The edge that kept him from fully... what? Admitting he wanted to be Christopher's friend? That wasn't quite right either.

His brain skittered away from the real question like a stone skipping across water, never quite sinking deep enough to get at the truth underneath.

Why Christopher? Why was he thinking about him this much? Why did the idea of maybe seeing him today make Jason's pulse kick up like he'd just sprinted the length of 8th Street?

And that dream. Fuck, that dream.

Last night it had come back—longer this time, clearer. The same lantern boy walking up the dark country road between those two farmhouses, bare feet on gravel, moving like he'd made that walk a hundred times before. He never understood how he didn't get his feet all cut up. And that same goddamn amber moon hanging low and wrong in the sky. The same desperate eye contact when the boy looked up from the base of the widow's peak, like he wanted something.

But this time, when Jason had turned to find the second boy standing beside him on that high platform, he could actually see his face, even if it was like looking through a cloud. Just for a second. Just enough.

Sandy hair catching moonlight. Straight posture even in sleep. That careful, measured way of holding himself.

And his brain—his stupid, traitorous, absolutely fucked-up brain— had looked at that face and thought: *Christopher.*

Jason had jerked awake gasping, heart hammering, the image seared into his retinas like he'd stared too long at the sun.

Which made no goddamn sense. The dream boys were from like a hundred years ago, wearing those weird nightshirt things people only wore in old-timey movies. They were his subconscious working through some bullshit, not actual people. And they definitely weren't Christopher Avery from Driver's Ed who probably ironed his underwear and had never said "fuck" in his entire pristine life.

But there it was. His brain making connections he didn't want to examine too closely.

Jason gripped the handlebars tighter and pedaled harder, like he could outrun his own thoughts.

He knew what it looked like. He knew what those questions meant—the wanting, the constant awareness of Christopher in his peripheral vision, the need to see him outside of that fluorescent-lit basement classroom where they sat side by side and pretended to care about proper following distance and three-point turns.

He knew, and he couldn't let himself go there. Not yet. Maybe not ever.

Because what if he was right? What if this weird pull, this magnetic thing that made his stomach flip when Christopher smiled or his thoughts scatter when their hands brushed reaching for the same piece of paper—what if it meant what he thought it might mean?

Then he was fucked. Completely and utterly fucked.

Boys didn't like boys. Not in Connersville, Not in Indiana. Not in 1989. Not in any world Jason knew.

Sure, there were rumors. Whispers about certain teachers, certain kids who dressed wrong or talked wrong or looked at people the wrong way. Jason had heard the words—*faggot, queer, cocksucker*—hurled like grenades in locker rooms and hallways, designed to explode and leave nothing standing.

He'd heard them directed at him once or twice, back in middle school when he was weirder, happier, before he learned to keep his head down and his mouth shut and his thoughts locked so far inside they couldn't escape even if they wanted to.

So no. He couldn't go there. Couldn't follow that thread to wherever it led because he already knew: it led nowhere good.

Better to just... ride. Clear his head. Maybe accidentally run into Christopher mowing the lawn and have something normal to say like "hey, small world" or "nice neighborhood" or literally anything that didn't sound like he'd spent the last twelve hours thinking about him nonstop like some kind of obsessed weirdo.

Country Club Road stretched west, practically a straight line. To his right, the developments sprawled—neat rows of homes nestled amongst the trees, their streets branching north toward the west end of the golf course, toward the ninth tee.

Jason slowed, coasting now, scanning driveways and yards. Looking for what? A sandy-haired kid mowing the lawn? Christopher washing a car? Playing basketball in a driveway? Did rich kids even do that shit themselves or did they have people for it?

Jason had no fucking clue what he was looking for. Just... Christopher. Somewhere. Anywhere.

He turned down one street, then another, weaving through the neighborhoods to his right. Checked every yard, every driveway, every window. Nothing. Just empty lawns and closed garages and the occasional dog walker giving him suspicious looks like *what's this kid doing here.*

After an hour of riding in circles through the developments, getting nowhere, seeing no one who even remotely resembled Christopher, Jason finally admitted what he'd known all along: this was stupid.

Christopher could be anywhere. Could be inside watching TV. Could be at the actual country club doing whatever people did at country clubs. Could be in Richmond watching a movie or Cincinnati buying his perfect-fitting clothes. Could be literally anywhere except conveniently outside in his yard waiting for Jason to ride by like some pathetic stalker.

"Fuck it," Jason muttered, turning his bike back toward Country Club Road.

He felt stupid. Felt foolish for even thinking he might find Christopher like this. Felt embarrassed that he'd wanted to badly enough to waste his whole morning riding around like an idiot.

Why did he even care? What was he hoping would happen? That they'd run into each other and suddenly become best friends? That Christopher would invite him inside and they'd... what? Play Nintendo? Watch movies? Sit around and talk about nothing?

Jason didn't even know what he wanted. Just that he wanted *something*, and the not-knowing made him feel even more pathetic than the looking.

He pedaled harder, jaw tight, trying to outrun the disappointment sitting heavy in his gut.

If he wasn't going to find Christopher, he might as well actually explore. Get further out of town. See what was past all these perfect lawns and perfect lives. Stop thinking about neat handwriting and careful smiles and the way someone made him actually like sitting next to them in class.

Jason kept riding, not really paying attention anymore, just moving, just trying to stop thinking. Definitely not allowing his mind to fantasize about..

"Goddamnit!" He was pissed at himself now, telling his own fucking brain to shut the hell up. He stood on the pedals and hammered down, burning the anger into speed.

Past the golf course and the neighborhoods, the houses grew fewer and farther between. The developments fell away behind him. The road stretched on, flanked by woods now, occasional farmhouses sitting back from the road. Then even those disappeared. Corn on both sides, tall and rustling in the breeze that carried the smell of earth and growing things. The morning sun slanted across everything, turning the whole landscape gold.

Jason wasn't thinking about where he was going. Wasn't thinking about Christopher or the dream or the stupid bike ride that had turned into a stupid waste of time. He was just riding, following the curve of Country Club Road as it wound west into farmland, his mind blank, his chest still tight with disappointment he didn't want to name.

Which is why he almost missed them.

He'd rounded a curve, legs burning now from the distance, when something made him slow. Made him look up from the pavement to the landscape around him.

And there they were.

Two farmhouses, facing each other across the road like mirror images of different lives.

Jason's foot hit the ground so hard he nearly fell off his bike.

One sat up on a hillside to his right—white paint peeling, shutters hanging crooked, but still somehow grand. Two stories with a widow's peak jutting up from the center, its iron railing rusted and falling down in sections, windows dark and watching. The porch sagged, and the yard had gone wild, but you could see the bones of what it used to be. Probably beautiful once. Probably the kind of place where people threw parties and felt important.

The other farmhouse sat lower, closer to the road on his left. Smaller, more modest. Just a plain two-story box with a porch and a couple of outbuildings behind it. One looked like it might've been a barn once, before time and weather had their way with it. The roof had caved in on one side, and the whole structure leaned like it was drunk.

Jason stopped completely now, both feet on the ground, straddling his bike. He stared.

He knew these houses.

Not *knew* knew—he'd never been here before in his life. But something about them felt familiar in a way that made his skin prickle and his breath catch.

The dream.

The lantern boy had walked this road. From that smaller farmhouse up there to the one on the hill. Jason could see it in his mind's eye, superimposed over the daylight scene in front of him: darkness, moonlight, the swing of a lantern, bare feet on gravel.

"Holy shit," he whispered.

He'd dreamed about actual places. Not made-up dreamscape bullshit his brain invented while he slept, but *real* places that existed in the world and sat right here on some nameless country road west of town.

His heart kicked up, thudding hard against his ribs. This was... what? Coincidence? Some kind of déjà vu? Had he been here before and forgotten? Seen these houses from a car window once and his subconscious filed them away?

But no. He'd remember. You didn't forget a widow's peak like that, tall and strange and watching.

Jason let his bike fall against the roadside gravel and walked closer to the hillside farmhouse. The driveway was overgrown, choked with weeds and saplings trying to reclaim what used to be clear. A chain hung across the entrance with a rusted NO TRESPASSING sign swinging from it, the letters faded almost to nothing.

He ducked under the chain.

The grass was knee-high, still wet with dew that soaked through his jeans as he climbed toward the house. Crickets and grasshoppers exploded away from his steps. The air smelled like decay and old wood and something else—something that made him think of time itself, if time had a smell.

Up close, the house was even more wrecked. The porch steps were rotted through in places, some boards missing entirely. Windows were broken, glass scattered across the porch like jagged teeth. The front door hung open a crack, darkness beyond.

Jason stopped at the base of the porch steps and looked up.

The widow's peak loomed above him, the windows on the second floor were mostly intact but filthy, reflecting the morning sun back in blind squares of gold.

In his dream, he'd stood up there. Looked down at this exact spot where he was standing now. Watched the lantern boy approach.

"This is insane," Jason muttered.

But his hands were shaking, and his pulse hadn't slowed, and some part of him—the part that read too much and thought too much and noticed things other people missed—knew this wasn't coincidence.

Something about these houses mattered. Something about the dream mattered.

Something about *him* being here mattered.

He backed away slowly, unwilling to turn his back on the house like it might do something if he wasn't watching. Only when he reached the road again did he allow himself to look away.

The smaller farmhouse across the way was even more decrepit. The porch roof had collapsed entirely, and vines had grown up over most of the first floor. Behind it, that leaning barn looked one strong wind away from total collapse.

Jason retrieved his bike and stood there, straddling it, looking from one house to the other.

In his dream, two boys had met in secret. One from each house. The lantern lighting the way.

Who were they? When had they lived here? Why was he dreaming about them?

And why the hell had the second boy's face looked like Christopher?

"Fuck," Jason said aloud, just to hear his own voice in the quiet morning. "Fuck, fuck, fuck."

He had no answers. Just more questions piling up like a car crash in his head.

He should leave. Go home. Forget about this. Forget about Christopher and the dream and these creepy abandoned houses that made him feel like he was standing on the edge of something he didn't understand.

But he didn't move.

He stayed there, bike between his legs, staring at the house, trying to make sense of anything.

Christopher. That's who he'd been looking for. Christopher he'd spent all morning trying to find. And instead he'd found... this. Whatever the hell this was.

The disappointment from earlier felt distant now, replaced by something else. Something that felt like fear and fascination twisted together until he couldn't tell them apart.

Finally, after what felt like hours but was probably only minutes, he forced himself to turn around and pedal back toward town.

He didn't find Christopher. He'd completely forgotten that was supposed to be the reason he came out here.

But he'd found something else instead.

Something that felt like it might be more important than he wanted it to be.

By the time Jason made it home, the sun was high and his shirt was stuck to his back with sweat. He dropped his bike against the side of the house and went inside, grabbed a glass of water from the kitchen, and drained it standing at the sink.

His mom was at work. The house was silent except for the hum of the refrigerator and the distant sound of someone's lawnmower down the street.

Jason went to his room, closed the door, and sat on the edge of his bed, staring at nothing.

The farmhouses were real.

The dream had shown him real places.

Which meant... what, exactly? That he was psychic? That he'd somehow seen these places before without remembering? That his subconscious had cobbled together random images that happened to match reality?

Or that something else was going on. Something he didn't have words for yet.

He pulled out his notebook—the one he kept hidden under his mattress, filled with half-finished thoughts and song lyrics and sketches of things he couldn't get out of his head. Flipped to a blank page.

Drew the widow's peak from memory. The way it jutted up from the roofline, tall and watching. The shittier farmhouse across the road. The barn leaning.

Then, before he could stop himself, he drew the lantern boy. Bare feet, nightshirt, the lamp swinging in his hand. Face blurred because he still couldn't see it clearly even in memory.

And beside him, on that roof, the second boy.

Jason's hand hesitated over the page.

Then he drew sandy hair. Straight posture. That careful way of standing like everything had to be just right.

He drew Christopher.

Or the boy who looked like Christopher. The boy from a hundred years ago who couldn't possibly be Christopher but somehow was anyway, at least in Jason's fucked-up dream logic.

Jason stared at the sketches, his chest tight.

"What the hell is happening?" he whispered.

The page didn't answer. The house stayed silent. The dream stayed locked in his head, replaying on an endless loop.

He needed to tell someone. Needed to make sense of this before he lost his mind completely.

But who? His mom would think he was crazy. Scott would laugh. Allison would try to psychoanalyze him.

Christopher, though...

Christopher had listened when Jason explained give-a-fuck-itis. Had taken him seriously about Prufrock when everyone else just zoned out. Had looked at him like what he said mattered.

Maybe Christopher wouldn't think he was insane.

Maybe.

Jason closed the notebook and shoved it back under his mattress.

Monday, he decided. Monday he'd tell Christopher about the farmhouses. About the dream. About all of it.

And if Christopher thought he was crazy, well... at least he'd know.

At least he wouldn't be carrying this alone anymore.

Chapter 5

You Believe in Ghosts?

Jason woke up before his alarm, staring at the ceiling in the gray pre-dawn light, his stomach twisted in knots. He'd spent all of Sunday replaying Saturday in his head—the failed search for Christopher, the discovery of the farmhouses, the drawing he'd made that he couldn't stop looking at even though it freaked him the fuck out.

He had to tell Christopher. Had to tell someone. And Christopher was the only person who might not think he'd lost his mind.

Maybe.

The bike ride to school felt longer than usual, his legs heavy, his brain spinning through a dozen different ways to bring it up. *Hey, so I dreamed about you as a ghost from a hundred years ago.* Yeah, that'd go over great. *So I was stalking your neighborhood on Saturday and found these creepy houses.* Even better.

By the time he locked his bike and headed down to the basement classroom, his chest was tight and his palms were sweating.

Christopher was already there, of course. Neat as always, notebook open, reviewing something. He looked up when Jason dropped into the seat beside him, and his whole face lit up in that small, careful smile.

"Hey. Good weekend?"

Jason's brain blanked. "Uh. Yeah. You?"

"Pretty boring. Mowed the lawn. Watched some TV." Christopher clicked his pen. "Did you end up doing anything?"

Just rode around looking for you like a creep, then found the houses from my recurring dream where you're a ghost.

"Went for a bike ride," Jason said instead. "Out west."

"Oh yeah? Where?"

Jason opened his mouth, then closed it. Not here. Not now. Not in a classroom full of people with Barnes about to barrel in any second.

"Just... around," he said lamely.

Christopher gave him a curious look but didn't push. "Cool."

Barnes swept in right on cue, already talking before the bell even rang. "Good morning, drivers! Hope everyone had a restful weekend because we're diving deep into vehicle systems today! Steering, suspension, brakes—all the fun stuff that keeps you from wrapping your car around a tree!"

Someone in the back groaned. Christopher bit back a laugh, shoulders shaking. Jason tried to focus on Barnes, on the diagrams being drawn on the chalkboard, on literally anything except the fact that Christopher was sitting right there and Jason had no idea how to say what he needed to say.

The rest of class blurred. When the bell rang, they walked out together like always, climbed the stairs like always, paused at the top like always.

"So, uh—" Christopher started.

"Hey, can I—" Jason said at the same time.

They both stopped, laughed awkwardly.

"You first," Christopher said.

Jason's throat went tight. "I was just... do you have plans after school sometime this week?"

Christopher's eyebrows went up. "Like, to hang out?"

"Yeah. Maybe. If you want."

"Yeah, definitely." Christopher shifted his books. "When?"

"I don't know. Wednesday?"

"Wednesday works. My parents won't care." Christopher pulled a pen from his pocket, grabbed Jason's hand without asking, and scribbled a phone number on his palm. "Call me. We can figure it out."

Jason stared at the numbers on his skin, his brain catching on the casual way Christopher had just grabbed his hand, like it was nothing. Like it didn't make Jason's pulse kick up.

"Okay," Jason managed. "Cool."

"Cool." Christopher smiled again, then headed toward Chemistry.

Jason stood there, looking at the phone number written on his hand, feeling the ghost of Christopher's touch still buzzing across his skin.

Wednesday. He'd tell him Wednesday.

———

The rest of Monday and all of Tuesday passed in a fog. Jason kept the phone number on his hand, retracing it with pen every time it started to fade. He didn't call. Wasn't sure what he'd say. *Hey, wanna hear about my fucked-up dreams?* didn't seem like great phone conversation.

By Wednesday morning, his nerves were shot. He'd barely slept, the dream coming back again—different this time, worse. The usual sequence: the lantern boy walking up the road, the desperate eye contact, turning to find the second boy beside him on the widow's peak. Sandy hair catching that amber moonlight.

But this time, the boy turned. Looked directly at Jason. Not through him or past him, but *at* him, those eyes locking onto his like they could see straight through to whatever Jason kept buried deep inside. The boy's expression shifted—sad, longing, desperate—and he started moving closer, reaching out with one hand—

Jason had jerked awake gasping at 4 AM, his heart hammering so hard he thought it might crack a rib. The image burned behind his eyelids even when he squeezed them shut. He couldn't fall back asleep after that.

In Driver's Ed, Barnes was going on about tire rotation and tread depth, his voice a monotonous drone. Jason sat beside Christopher, trying to work up the courage to say something, anything.

Christopher glanced at him after a few minutes. "You didn't call."

Jason blinked. "What?"

"I gave you my number. Monday. You didn't call." Christopher's tone wasn't accusatory, just... observant. Maybe a little disappointed.

"Yeah. I... sorry. I didn't know what to say over the phone."

"You could've just said hi."

"I'm not really a phone person."

Christopher nodded, like that made sense, but Jason caught something in his expression—hurt, maybe, or confusion. Like he'd thought Jason didn't want to talk to him after all.

"I wanted to," Jason said quickly. "Call, I mean. I just... I needed to tell you something face-to-face. Something weird."

Christopher's expression shifted. "How weird?"

"Like... pretty fucking weird."

A pause. Christopher set down his pen. "Okay?"

"You believe in ghosts?"

Whatever Christopher had been expecting, it wasn't that. His eyes widened. "Uh... what?"

"Ghosts. Like, do you think they're real? Or just bullshit people make up?"

Christopher looked genuinely thrown. "I... I don't know. Why?"

Jason chewed his lip, weighing whether to keep going. Fuck it. In for a penny. "What about dreams? Like, recurring dreams. You think they mean anything?"

"Are you okay?" Christopher's voice had shifted from confused to concerned. "Did something happen?"

"No. Maybe. I don't know." Jason ran his hand through his hair. "Forget it. It's stupid."

"It's not stupid if it's bothering you."

"Mr. Reynolds? Mr. Avery?" Barnes called from the front. "Something you'd like to share with the class?"

"No sir," they said in unison.

Barnes gave them a look that said *I'm watching you* but went back to his lecture about proper tire inflation.

Jason slumped in his seat, regretting bringing it up. But Christopher leaned closer, dropping his voice to barely a whisper.

"After class. Tell me."

Jason met his eyes. Christopher looked serious, intent. Not mocking. Not dismissive.

Just... curious.

"Yeah. Okay."

———

They ended up sitting on the steps outside the music building, tucked away where most people didn't bother going between classes. Christopher had Chemistry second period, but he waved it off like missing the start didn't matter.

"So," Christopher said. "Ghosts and dreams. What's going on?"

Jason stared at his hands, trying to figure out where to start. "This is going to sound insane."

"Try me."

"I've been having this dream. Same one, over and over. Started a couple weeks ago, before school even started."

"What kind of dream?"

"There's these two old farmhouses. Out in the country, facing each other across a road. And there's this kid—like, our age—wearing old-fashioned clothes. A nightshirt, you know? And he's carrying a lantern, walking from one house to the other in the middle of the night."

Christopher listened without interrupting, his expression unreadable.

"I'm watching from this widow's peak on the bigger farmhouse. And the kid looks up at me, and it's like..." Jason struggled for words. "Like he's trying to tell me something. Desperate, you know? And then I turn and there's another kid standing next to me, and—"

"And what?"

Jason's throat went tight. He couldn't say *he looks like you*. Not yet. Not when he didn't understand it himself.

"And then I wake up," he finished lamely.

"That's intense," Christopher said quietly. "But dreams are just... you know. Your brain processing stuff."

"Yeah. That's what I thought too." Jason took a breath. "Except Saturday, I went for a bike ride. Out west, past the country club. And I found them."

Christopher's head snapped toward him. "Found what?"

"The farmhouses. From the dream. They're real. Abandoned, falling apart, but real. Exactly the same as in the dream—the widow's peak, the smaller house across the road, everything."

"Holy shit," Christopher breathed.

Jason grinned despite himself. "Did you just—? Oh man, your ears must be on fire from that one."

Christopher's face went red. "I didn't—I mean—" He looked both embarrassed and weirdly pleased with himself, like he'd done something mildly rebellious. "It just came out."

"Nah, it was perfect. Very natural." Jason was still grinning. "You're learning."

"Shut up," Christopher muttered, but he was smiling too.

"Yeah."

"You're serious."

"Dead serious."

Christopher sat back against the brick wall, processing. "So you dreamed about places you'd never seen before, and then found them?"

"Yup."

"That's..." Christopher trailed off. "That's either a really weird coincidence or—"

"Or I'm losing my goddamn mind?"

"I was going to say 'or something else is going on.'" Christopher looked at him directly. "I don't think you're crazy."

"You don't?"

"No. I mean, it's bizarre as hell, but you don't seem crazy. You seem... I don't know. Freaked out. Which makes sense."

The simple validation made Jason's chest tight. "Yeah. Freaked out pretty much covers it."

Christopher clicked his pen a few times, looking like he wanted to say something but wasn't sure if he should.

"What?" Jason asked.

"Nothing. Just..." Christopher trailed off.

"Just what?"

"I don't know if I should ask."

"Ask what?"

Christopher bit his lip, then: "Why tell me? I mean—not that I'm not glad you did, I just... you didn't have to."

Jason looked at him for a long beat, then shrugged. "Because most people are full of shit. They pretend to listen but they're just waiting for their turn to talk, you know? But you actually give a fuck about what people say. Like with that Prufrock thing—you didn't just blow it off, you actually wanted to understand it." He kicked at the ground. "Plus I figured you wouldn't immediately think I was batshit crazy. Or at least, if you did, you'd be polite enough not to say it to my face."

Christopher's face flushed, a slow warmth spreading across his cheeks. "I don't think you're crazy."

"Well, that's good to know."

"I think this is..." Christopher struggled for words. "I think it's really cool that you trusted me with it."

"Yeah, well. Don't make it weird."

Christopher laughed. "So these farmhouses. Where are they exactly?"

"Country Club Road, if you keep going west past the golf course. Maybe three, four miles out. Just sitting there in the middle of nowhere."

"And you went inside?"

"Climbed up to the house, looked around. Didn't go in—looked like the porch would collapse if I breathed on it wrong."

Christopher was quiet for a moment, then: "I want to see them."

Jason blinked. "What?"

"The farmhouses. I want to see them. Can you show me?"

"You want to go to some creepy abandoned houses because I had a weird dream about them?"

"Yeah." Christopher said it like it was obvious. "This is the most interesting thing anyone's told me in forever. Of course I want to see them."

Jason stared at him. Most people would've backed away slowly.

Would've made excuses and found reasons to be somewhere else. But Christopher was leaning forward, eyes bright with genuine curiosity.

"You're kind of weird, you know that?" Jason said.

"Says the guy who dreams about ghost boys with lanterns."

"Fair point." Jason couldn't help smiling. "Okay. Yeah. We can go check them out. This weekend maybe?"

"Saturday?"

"Saturday works."

Christopher's whole face lit up in a way that made Jason's stomach flip. "Cool. It's a date."

The word hung in the air between them. *Date.* Christopher's eyes widened slightly, like he'd just heard what he said. "I mean—not a date-date. Just... you know. Plans. An appointment. A scheduled—"

"Christopher."

"Yeah?"

"Shut up. I know what you meant."

Christopher laughed, embarrassed but relieved. "Okay. Good."

The warning bell rang. They both stood, brushing off their jeans.

"Thanks," Jason said. "For not thinking I'm insane."

"I didn't say you're not insane. Just that you're not crazy." Christopher grinned. "There's a difference."

"Oh, fuck off," Jason said, but he was smiling.

Christopher opened his mouth—Jason saw it, the reflexive urge to say it right back—then caught himself, face going red.

"Oh my god." Jason was delighted. "You were about to tell me to fuck off."

"I was not."

"You absolutely were. I saw it on your face."

"It doesn't count if I don't actually say it."

"The bet's still on. And I'm making progress."

Chapter 6

Admitting Defeat

J ason knew it was going to be a weird day the moment he woke up.

Not bad-weird. Just... off. Like the air pressure had changed overnight and his body was still trying to adjust. He lay there for a minute, staring at the ceiling, trying to identify what felt different.

Then he realized: he was looking forward to today. To seeing Christopher. To showing him the farmhouses and finding out if any of this was real or if he'd just lost his mind completely.

"Shit," Jason muttered, throwing off the sheets.

This was starting to feel fucked up.

He went through his morning routine on autopilot—shower, cheap cologne, store-brand toothpaste, not giving a shit about his hair. Pulled open his drawer to discover he had no underwear. Fuck. He grabbed a pair from the hamper, gave them a sniff, shrugged, then turned them inside out. Problem solved.

Clean-enough jeans from the floor. Then he stopped.

His usual black t-shirt sat on top of the drawer. Safe. Familiar. The kind of thing that made him invisible, that let him blend into backgrounds and avoid questions.

His hand moved past it.

There, shoved in the back, was the dark green one. He'd forgotten he even had it—his mom must've bought it last year thinking he'd actually wear color. He pulled it out, held it up, grimaced at his reflection in the mirror above his dresser.

Color made him visible. Made his body visible—the shoulders that were too narrow, the chest that was too flat, all the ways he didn't quite measure up to the other guys at school who seemed to fill out their shirts without even trying.

He put it on anyway.

The fabric felt different against his skin. Not bad, just... noticeable. Like he was admitting something by wearing it.

But admitting what?

That he cared how he looked today? That he wanted Christopher to... what? Notice him? Think he looked nice?

"Fuck," Jason muttered again, tugging at the hem.

He turned back to the dresser, opened the top drawer where he kept the comb he never used. Picked it up. Set it down. Picked it up again.

This was insane. He didn't comb his hair. He ran his fingers through it in the shower and called it good. That's what he did. That's who he was.

Except apparently today he was someone who combed his fucking hair.

Jason dragged the comb through the tangles, wincing when it caught. His reflection stared back—dark hair actually lying flat for once, green shirt that made his eyes look different somehow. Less defensive. More... open.

He looked like someone trying.

The realization made his stomach twist. Because why was he trying? Why did it matter what Christopher thought of how he looked? They were just hanging out. Just friends checking out some creepy old houses because Jason had weird dreams.

Friends.

Right.

Jason set the comb down and stared at himself in the mirror.

When had this happened? When had Christopher Avery gone from the too-polite kid in Driver's Ed to someone Jason thought about constantly? Someone who made him change his shirt twice and comb his hair like he was going on a—

No.

Jason slammed that thought down before it could finish forming. Because that way led to questions he wasn't ready to answer. Questions about why his stomach flipped when Christopher smiled. Why he'd spent hours last weekend riding around rich neighborhoods hoping to accidentally run into him. Why the idea of spending today together made him feel electric and terrified in equal measure.

Back in his room, he grabbed his backpack—water bottle, the notebook with his sketches, a flashlight. His hand reached for the cheap cologne on his dresser before his brain caught up, dabbing it on his neck. He caught himself wondering if Christopher would notice.

He headed for the kitchen before he could spiral any further.

———

His mom was already up when he came out, coffee in hand, wearing her weekend clothes: faded jeans and one of those oversized sweatshirts that had seen better days. She glanced up when he walked in.

Then did a double-take.

Her eyebrows shot up. She set down her coffee mug slowly, deliberately, like she needed both hands free to process what she was seeing.

"Well," she said, drawing out the word. "Look at you."

Jason felt his face heat. "What?"

"Green looks good on you, honey. Really brings out your eyes." She was smiling now, that soft mom-smile that meant she was genuinely pleased. "And did you—" She gestured at his head. "Did you actually comb your hair?"

"It's not a big deal."

"It's a very big deal. You haven't combed your hair voluntarily since..." She paused, thinking. "Actually, I don't think I've ever seen you comb your hair voluntarily."

"Jesus, Mom—"

"I'm serious. This is a momentous occasion. I should mark it on the calendar." She was teasing now, but gently. "So who is she?"

"There's no—" He stopped, regrouped. "I'm not trying to impress anyone. I'm just hanging out with a friend."

"A friend." His mom picked up her coffee, took a sip, eyes never leaving his face. "Well, I hope you have fun. Where are you going?"

"Just riding around. Exploring old houses and stuff."

"Sounds nice. What's her name?"

Jason hesitated, just a fraction of a second. "Christopher. From Driver's Ed."

The pause that followed was barely noticeable. But Jason caught it —the slight widening of her eyes, the way her smile froze for just a moment before recovering. Her hand tightened almost imperceptibly around her coffee mug.

"Christopher," she repeated carefully. "Well. That's... that's nice, honey."

The air had shifted. Not hostile, not angry. Just... different. Careful. Like she was trying to process something and not quite succeeding at hiding it.

Jason's stomach twisted. "I should go. Don't want to be late."

"Of course. Have fun. Be safe." Her voice was normal again, but Jason could feel the weight of things unsaid pressing down on the kitchen. "Call if you'll be late for dinner."

"Yeah. Okay."

He grabbed a Pop-Tart and his backpack and got the hell out before she could ask anything else. Before she could give him that look again—the one that said she was connecting dots she hadn't wanted to connect.

————

The ride to Christopher's house felt endless.

Jason had mapped the route in his head a dozen times—down 24th to Western, south past the factories, up the hill through the nice neighborhoods, hang a right on Dorsett. Simple. Maybe twenty-five minutes if he pushed it.

But his brain wouldn't shut up.

Why do you care so much?

The thought kept circling back, relentless. Why did it matter what Christopher thought of him? Why had he spent twenty minutes this morning staring at shirts like it was a life-or-death decision? Why did the idea of spending the day together make him feel like he'd swallowed lightning?

Jason pedaled harder, trying to outrun the questions.

A horn blared.

Jason jerked his handlebars right, his front tire missing the truck's bumper by inches. The driver yelled something Jason couldn't hear over the rush of adrenaline, then roared past.

"Fuck," Jason gasped, both feet on the ground now, straddling his bike. His hands were shaking.

He'd almost gotten hit. Had been so lost in his head thinking about Christopher—about why Christopher mattered so much—that he'd blown right through an intersection without looking.

Brilliant. Get yourself killed before you even make it there.

Jason forced himself to breathe, to focus. The road. The route. Nothing else.

He made it up 8th Street without incident, his thighs burning as the road climbed.

At the crest of the hill, he coasted down toward Country Club Road, letting gravity do the work. Past the nice houses with their perfect lawns and fresh paint. Past the lives that looked nothing like his.

And promptly hit the pothole.

The one he knew about. The one he'd been avoiding for weeks, on your way towards the golf course. The one that was impossible to miss if you were paying attention.

But he wasn't paying attention.

His front tire dropped into the crater, the impact jolting through the frame, and he racked himself hard—balls slamming into the crossbar so hard he saw stars. Pain exploded white-hot through his pelvis, radiating into his stomach, and for a second he couldn't breathe.

"MOTHERFUCKER!" The word tore out of him as he somehow kept the bike upright, coasting to a stop on the shoulder. He slid off carefully, legs shaky, everything between them screaming in protest.

He stood there bent over his handlebars, breathing hard, waiting for the nausea to pass and the pain to subside from oh-god-I'm-dying to just regular awful.

This was Christopher's fault. All of it. The distraction, the near-miss with the truck, the goddamn pothole that he knew about and somehow forgot existed because his brain was too busy trying to figure out why one person could make him feel so completely off-balance.

"Get it together," Jason muttered to himself.

He walked the bike for a minute until the pain faded to a dull ache, then climbed back on and pedaled slowly the rest of the way.

———

Christopher's house appeared exactly as he'd described it: white with navy blue shutters, bigger than Jason's place but not ostentatious. Just... solid. Comfortable. The kind of house that looked like actual families lived there, not just people trying to survive until the next paycheck.

Christopher was already outside, sitting on the porch steps with his own backpack. He stood when Jason rolled up, and his whole face lit up in a way that made Jason's stomach do that stupid flipping thing again.

"You came," Christopher said.

"Yeah. Why wouldn't I?"

"I don't know. Thought maybe you'd think it was dumb. The whole ghost thing."

"It's definitely dumb," Jason said, grinning despite himself. "But I'm here anyway."

Christopher laughed, then his expression shifted—suddenly nervous. "So, uh... my parents."

"What about them?"

"They kind of... they said they wanted to meet you. Before we go." Christopher looked pained, like he was about to ask Jason to do something terrible. "I tried to get out of it, but they were pretty insistent."

"Oh." Jason's stomach dropped. "Do we have to?"

"I think we kind of have to. They're already watching from the window." Christopher grimaced. "I'm sorry. It'll be quick. I promise."

"It's fine." It wasn't fine. "Let's just get it over with."

Christopher led him toward the house, both of them walking like they were heading to detention.

———

"It'll be quick" turned out to be a lie.

Jason followed Christopher through the front door into a living room that looked like something from a magazine—not fancy, just put-together in a way that spoke of people who had time to arrange throw pillows and actually dust. Family photos lined the mantle. A bookshelf stretched along one wall, packed with actual books people had actually read.

Diane and Mark Avery emerged from the kitchen together, and Jason's first thought was that they looked exactly like parents were supposed to look. Not too old, not too young. Comfortable with each other in that way people got after years together. Diane had the same sandy hair as Christopher, pulled back in a ponytail. Mark wore glasses and a weekend polo shirt.

"Mom, Dad," Christopher said, and Jason heard the nervousness underneath the formal tone. "This is Jason. Jason, these are my parents."

"Hi," Jason managed, suddenly aware of how he must look. Faded jeans. Rusted bike outside. The green shirt that had seemed like a good idea this morning but now just made him feel conspicuous.

"Jason!" Diane's smile was genuine, warm. "It's so nice to finally meet you. Christopher's mentioned you."

He has? Jason glanced at Christopher, whose ears had gone red.

"Just that we're partners in Driver's Ed," Christopher said quickly.

"And that we were going to check out some old houses today. For... architecture."

Jason almost choked. Architecture. Right.

"That sounds fascinating," Mark said, and Jason couldn't tell if he was being genuine or polite. "Where are these houses?"

"Out west," Christopher said. "Just some old farmhouses Jason found."

"And you're interested in old buildings?" Diane asked Jason directly.

"Uh..." Jason scrambled for an answer that wouldn't sound completely insane. "Yeah. Kind of. They're just... interesting. You know. History and stuff."

Christopher shot him a look that clearly said *history and stuff?*

"Well, I think it's wonderful you boys are exploring and learning," Diane said. "Just please be careful. Those old structures can be dangerous."

"We will," they said in unison, then glanced at each other.

Mark was watching them with an expression Jason couldn't quite read. Not suspicious, exactly. Just... observant. Like he was cataloging the way they stood slightly too close, the way Christopher kept fidgeting with his backpack strap, the way Jason couldn't quite meet anyone's eyes directly.

"How long have you two been friends?" Mark asked.

"Just since school started," Christopher said. "But we, uh... we get along really well."

"That's great. Christopher doesn't usually..." Diane paused, choosing her words carefully. "He's selective about who he spends time with. So if you've made the cut, you must be pretty special."

Jason felt his face heat. "I don't know about special."

"I do," Christopher said quietly, then immediately looked like he regretted it.

The silence that followed lasted maybe three seconds but felt like an hour. Diane and Mark exchanged a glance—quick, meaningful, the kind of wordless communication people developed after years of marriage.

"Well," Mark said finally, pulling out his wallet. "You boys should have some spending money. In case you want to grab lunch some-where." He handed Christopher a twenty.

"Thanks, Dad. We probably won't—"

"Take it anyway. You never know." Mark's expression softened. "Have fun. Be safe. And Jason?"

"Yes sir?"

"You're welcome here anytime. Seriously. Don't be a stranger."

The genuine warmth in his voice made Jason's throat tight. He thought about his own father—gone for nearly a decade now, for reasons Jason still didn't fully understand. Thought about how different his life might have been with a dad who said things like "you're welcome here anytime" and meant it.

"Thank you," Jason managed.

Christopher was already moving toward the door, clearly eager to escape before his parents could ask anything else. Jason followed, but caught Diane's smile as they left—knowing, gentle, like she understood something Jason and Christopher hadn't figured out themselves yet.

———

They didn't talk until they turned onto Country Club Road.

The ride from Christopher's house had been quick—down Dorsett, a few turns, maybe five minutes total. But they'd been silent the whole way, like they'd both agreed without discussing it to wait until they were safely out of parent territory before saying anything real.

Now, as they headed west past the last few houses, Christopher finally broke the silence.

"Sorry about that. My parents can be... intense."

"They were nice."

"They were interrogating you."

"That wasn't interrogating. That was just... parent stuff." Jason glanced over. "They seem cool."

"They are. They're not like other parents. They actually pay atten-tion, you know? Like, they notice things."

"What kind of things?"

Christopher's ears went red again. "Just... things. Forget it."

They rode past the last few houses, into the stretch where Country Club Road opened up into farmland. Corn on both sides, tall enough now that you could barely see past the first few rows. The only sounds were their tires on pavement and the rustle of stalks in the breeze.

"Your dad seems cool," Jason said. "Like, actually cool. Not trying-too-hard cool."

"He is. He's..." Christopher trailed off. "He's a good dad. Really good."

Something in his voice made Jason look over. Christopher was focused on the road ahead, jaw tight.

"You're lucky," Jason said quietly.

"I know."

"My dad's been gone since I was like seven. I barely remember him."

Christopher glanced over, surprised. "Gone like...?"

"Gone like left and never came back. My mom doesn't really talk about it. I know it wasn't good, whatever happened. But the details are fuzzy."

Christopher's whole expression changed—not just surprised, but genuinely upset. Angry, even. "That's fucked up."

Jason blinked, staring at him. Not just because Christopher had sworn, but because he actually meant it. Like Jason's shitty situation with his dad genuinely bothered him.

"That's really fucked up. How do you just leave your kid? How do you—" He stopped, shaking his head. "I'm sorry. I know it's not my business, but that makes me so angry."

Jason's chest felt tight. "You just said fuck. Twice."

"I know. Because it is. It's—" Christopher stopped. "Wait. Am I close to losing the bet?"

"One more time and you owe me lunch money."

"Good. Because your dad is a fucking asshole for leaving."

Jason laughed—surprised, genuine, a little breathless. "There it is. You owe me."

"Worth it," Christopher said firmly.

61

They rode in silence for a moment, but it felt different now. Warmer. Like something had shifted between them.

"Thanks," Jason said quietly.

"For what?"

"For giving a shit. Most people just..." He shrugged. "Nobody really cares, you know?"

"I care," Christopher said simply.

———

They rode in silence for another minute. Then Christopher said: "For what it's worth, I think you turned out pretty okay. You know. Despite the abandonment issues and terrible fashion sense."

Jason laughed—surprised, genuine. "Excuse me? Terrible fashion sense?"

"Jason, you wear the same black t-shirt every day. It's like you're in mourning for your own personality."

"Oh fuck off. At least I don't look like I'm about to sell someone a golf club membership."

"These are normal clothes!"

"Normal boring clothes."

"Says the guy who owns exactly two colors: black and slightly darker black."

"I'm wearing green right now!"

"I know!" Christopher's grin was wide, delighted. "I noticed! It's very brave. Very avant-garde. Next week are you going to try blue?"

"You're an asshole."

"I'm learning from the best."

Jason couldn't stop smiling. This—this easy back-and-forth, the teasing that didn't have an edge, the way Christopher had gotten comfortable enough to actually joke around—this was what he'd been craving without knowing it.

"Okay, speaking of terrible," Jason said. "Tell me your most embarrassing moment. And it better be good."

"Why would I tell you that?"

"Because we're friends and that's what friends do. They share humiliating stories so they have blackmail material on each other."

"That's a terrible definition of friendship."

"It's the only one I've got. Come on. Most embarrassing moment. Go."

Christopher was quiet for a moment, pedaling. Then: "Fourth grade. Music class. Mrs. Henderson made us all sing 'America the Beautiful' for some assembly thing."

"Okay..."

"I was super nervous. Like, almost-throwing-up nervous. And right in the middle, during the part about purple mountains' majesty or whatever—"

"Oh no."

"—I farted. Loud. In front of the entire school."

Jason nearly fell off his bike laughing. "You did not."

"I did. And it was completely silent in that moment, you know? Like everyone had stopped singing just in time for me to rip ass in front of three hundred people."

"Oh my god."

"The principal stopped the assembly. Mrs. Henderson looked like she wanted to die. I wanted to die. Pretty sure I actually did die and this is hell."

"That's incredible. That's the best thing I've ever heard."

"Your turn," Christopher said. "Most embarrassing moment."

Jason thought about it. "Seventh grade. I had a crush on this girl— Amy Martinez. Thought I was being real smooth, you know? Left a note in her locker asking if she wanted to go to the movies."

"And?"

"And I signed it from 'Your Secret Admirer' because I thought that was romantic. Except I'd been using the same pen in math class earlier, and I'd written my name on my homework. The ink was still wet when I folded the note."

"No."

"So it transferred. My name was printed backwards on the inside of the note. She opened it, saw 'Your Secret Admirer' and then immediately saw my name printed in reverse like I was the world's dumbest detective."

Christopher was laughing now too. "What did she say?"

"Nothing. Absolutely nothing. Just looked at me in the hallway the next day with this expression like I was a puppy who'd peed on the carpet. Total pity."

"That's actually worse than farting in front of the school."

"Right? At least your thing was involuntary. I actively did that to myself."

They were both still laughing as the farmhouses came into view around the curve.

And then, like someone had flipped a switch, the laughter died.

———

The mood shifted so abruptly it felt physical—like riding from sunlight into shadow, except the sun was still bright overhead. The air felt thicker here. Heavier. Like the space around the farmhouses was holding its breath.

Jason's hands tightened on his handlebars. Beside him, Christopher had gone quiet, his earlier ease evaporating into something warier.

"That's them?" Christopher asked, his voice barely above a whisper.

"Yeah."

The farmhouses looked exactly as Jason remembered—maybe worse in the full light of day, everything exposed. He watched Christopher take it in, saw his face change as the wrongness of the place settled over him.

"It's..." Christopher trailed off, searching for words.

"Yeah," Jason said.

They'd stopped at the edge of the road without discussing it, both straddling their bikes, neither quite ready to move closer.

"We were just laughing," Christopher said quietly. "Like, thirty seconds ago we were laughing about farting and now I feel like I'm looking at a graveyard."

"I know."

"Does it always feel like this?"

Jason thought about his first visit—the way the air had felt wrong even then, even in daylight, even before he knew about the dreams. "Yeah. Pretty much."

Christopher took a breath. "Okay. Well. We came all this way. Might as well look around."

They left their bikes by the road. Jason led the way under the chain, Christopher close behind.

"This is so illegal," Christopher murmured, glancing back at the road like he expected a cop to materialize.

"You worried about getting arrested?"

"Little bit."

"We'll be fine. Come on."

They made their way up toward the house.

"Can we get inside?" Christopher asked.

"Porch steps are rotted. Look." Jason pointed. Several boards were missing entirely, others cracked and splintering.

"What about that tower thing at the top?"

"The widow's peak?"

"Is that what it's called?"

"Yeah. It's like a lookout. Ship captains' wives used to watch for their husbands coming home." Jason shrugged. "Read it somewhere."

Christopher glanced around at the cornfields and woods. "Not a lot of ocean out here."

"Okay, smartass. I didn't say it made sense. Just that's what it's called."

Christopher was still staring up at it. "Can we get up there?"

"Would have to go through the house. And I'm not risking falling through the floor."

Christopher nodded. "In your dream, you were up there."

"Yeah."

"Looking down at the other boy."

Jason's throat went tight. "Yeah."

They walked around the house, peering through broken windows into darkness. Everything inside was wrecked—furniture overturned, wallpaper peeling off, debris scattered everywhere.

"It's wrecked inside," Christopher said, cupping his hands against a window to see better. "Like, completely trashed. Furniture everywhere, wallpaper peeling off... it's kind of sad, actually."

"Sad?"

"Yeah. Someone lived here once. Probably loved this place. Sat up there watching for someone to come home, looked at the stars, thought they'd be here forever." Christopher pulled back from the window. "And now it's just... falling apart. Forgotten."

Jason looked at him, surprised by the melancholy in his voice. "You okay?"

"Yeah. It's just..." Christopher gestured vaguely at the house. "Everything ends, you know? Even the things you think will last forever."

"Jesus, Christopher." The words came out sharper than Jason intended, defensive. "You want to talk about your feelings or you want to check out the other house?"

Christopher flinched slightly, his expression closing off. "Sorry. Sometimes I get weird."

Jason felt immediately guilty. Christopher had just shared something real—something vulnerable—and he'd thrown it back in his face with sarcasm. That's what he always did. Push people away before they could get too close.

"Wait," Jason said. "I'm sorry. That was... I shouldn't have said that."

Christopher looked at him, surprised. "It's okay—"

"No, it's not." Jason ran his hand through his hair, frustrated with himself. "I'm glad you can talk to me about stuff like that. Really. I just... I don't always know how to respond, you know? I'm not good at the feelings stuff."

"You don't have to be good at it."

"But I want to be. For you." Jason met his eyes. "What you said about the house? About things ending? That wasn't weird. That was real. And I like when you're real with me."

Christopher's expression softened. "Yeah?"

"Yeah." Jason managed a small smile. "Come on. Let's check out the other house."

They walked toward the smaller farmhouse, and Jason felt something shift between them—something warmer, more solid. Like they'd just figured out how to be honest with each other.

———

The smaller farmhouse was worse—structurally unsound, the porch roof completely collapsed, vines everywhere. They circled it once, found a broken window they could probably climb through, but the drop inside looked dangerous.

"I don't think we should," Christopher said.

"Agreed."

They headed for the barn instead.

The structure leaned so badly Jason was surprised it was still standing. The roof had caved in on one side, sunlight pouring through the gap to illuminate the interior in shafts of dusty gold. Other sections were cast in deep shadow.

They stopped at the entrance—or what used to be an entrance before the doors rotted away.

"Look." Christopher pointed.

A loft, or what remained of one, clung to the far wall. Below it, debris everywhere—old tools, broken equipment, things Jason couldn't identify covered in decades of dirt and rust.

"Your dream," Christopher said. "The boys. They came here."

"Yeah."

But nothing moved. No ghosts, no visions, nothing but dust floating in the sunlight.

Christopher stood there, staring into the shadows. "Can I ask you something?"

Jason looked over. "Yeah?"

Christopher opened his mouth, then closed it. Shook his head. "Never mind. It's dumb."

"What is?"

"Nothing. Forget it." Christopher turned away from the barn. "Come on. Let's check the woods out back."

Exiting through a gap in the back wall, and into the woods that flanked the property, the temperature dropped immediately under the canopy. The air smelled green—moss and leaves and damp earth. Their footsteps were muffled on the carpet of old leaves.

They walked without talking, moving deeper into the trees. The mood had shifted again, but different this time. Less ominous, more... peaceful. Like the woods didn't care about anything except being woods.

"Hey," Christopher said after a few minutes. "Listen."

Jason stopped. In the distance, faint but distinct: a low rumble. Rhythmic. Getting closer.

"Train," Jason said.

"Where?"

They kept walking, following the sound. The woods thinned ahead, opening into another cornfield. And beyond that, cutting across the landscape in a straight line: railroad tracks.

The train appeared around a bend—a long freight train, nothing passenger about it. Just car after car of containers, the whole thing moving with that heavy, inexorable momentum that freight trains had. The wheels squealed occasionally as metal hit metal, and the whole thing rumbled low enough that Jason felt it in his chest.

But no whistle. No dramatic horn blast. Just the steady thunder of machinery doing what it was built to do.

"That's the same line that goes over the trestle," Christopher said. "By St. Gabriel. We've driven under it like a million times."

"Yeah. Guess this is where it leads. West toward Indianapolis, probably."

They watched the train pass, car after car, hypnotic in its sameness. Finally the last car disappeared around another bend, the sound fading, and the world felt strangely quiet in its wake.

"Come on," Christopher said. "We should head back before your ghost boys show up and—"

He stopped.

Jason turned. "What?"

Christopher was staring at the cornfield on the far side of the tracks. His face had gone pale.

"Christopher?"

"Did you see..." Christopher took a step forward. "There was someone. Two people. Right at the edge of the field."

Jason's heart kicked up. "Where?"

"They went into the corn. I saw them— they were just..." He was already moving, walking faster now, toward the tracks.

Jason followed, scanning the cornfield. The stalks rustled in the breeze, but he didn't see any movement that looked human.

"Christopher, I don't—"

"There!" Christopher pointed.

And Jason saw them.

Two boys, maybe their age, running through the corn. Not in nightshirts. Not carrying lanterns. Just... boys. Wearing what looked like normal clothes from another time—suspenders, loose shirts, something that could've been from the 1890s or 1920s or whenever the hell those farmhouses had been occupied.

They were laughing. Chasing each other. One of them—shorter, dark hair—looked back over his shoulder, grinning, and nearly tripped. The taller one caught up, grabbed his arm, and they both stumbled into the corn, disappearing from view.

But Jason could still hear them. Laughter. The rustle of stalks. Footsteps.

He and Christopher broke into a run without discussing it.

They reached the tracks, scrambled across, pushed into the corn. The stalks were taller than them, blocking out the sky, turning the world into a maze of green and gold. The sound of the boys was ahead —always ahead, always just out of reach.

Jason circled back, Christopher right behind him, both of them breathing hard now. The corn opened into a small clearing near the tracks—

And there they were.

The boys had stopped. They were climbing up onto the railroad tracks, balancing on the rails, arms out for balance. Playing some kind of game. The shorter one jumped to a tie, then back to the rail. The taller one laughed and did the same.

They looked so normal. So alive. So much like Jason and Christopher that for a second, Jason wondered if they were seeing some kind of mirror, some weird reflection.

Then the boys took off running down the tracks, still laughing, still playing.

And vanished.

Not faded. Not slowly dissolved. Just... gone. One second they were there, the next the tracks were empty.

Jason and Christopher stood frozen at the edge of the corn, staring.

Christopher made a sound—something between a gasp and a laugh or a sob.

"Holy fucking shit," he whispered.

Jason couldn't speak. Couldn't move. His heart was hammering so hard he thought it might crack a rib.

They stood there for a long moment, both breathing hard, Christopher's hand still gripping Jason's arm.

Then Jason started laughing.

Christopher looked at him like he'd lost his mind. "What? That was terrifying and you're laughing?"

"I know," Jason gasped, trying to catch his breath. "I know it was. But you've said 'fuck' like a million times today. I've created a monster."

Christopher blinked. "I have?"

"You absolutely have. Started with my dad being a 'fucking asshole,' and you've been on a roll ever since." Jason was grinning despite everything. "The bet's over. I already won. You owe me lunch money."

"Are you serious right now? We just saw actual ghosts and you're thinking about lunch money?"

"Hey, I'm just appreciating my handiwork. But you know what?" Jason's grin widened. "New bet. If you can go the rest of the day without saying it, I'll buy you lunch instead."

"That's not fair. You already corrupted me."

"Exactly. That's what makes it fun."

Christopher stared at him for a moment, then started laughing too —breathless, slightly hysterical. "You're terrible. You're actually the worst person I've ever met."

"And yet here you are. Swearing like a sailor."

"It's your fault. You're a bad influence." But Christopher was smiling now, the terror starting to fade into something else. Something lighter.

They started walking back toward the barn, and Christopher—still giddy with adrenaline—threw his arm around Jason's shoulders.

The contact was casual, friendly. The kind of thing guys did all the time.

Except it didn't feel casual.

Jason became hyper-aware of Christopher's arm across his shoulders, the warmth of him pressed against his side, the way they were walking in perfect sync. Christopher seemed to realize it at the same moment—his steps faltered slightly, but he didn't pull away.

They walked like that for maybe ten seconds. Ten seconds that felt electric and terrifying and perfect all at once.

Then Christopher pulled back, clearing his throat, his face flushed. "So, uh... should we head back?"

"Yeah," Jason said, his own voice rough. "Yeah, we should."

But neither of them moved right away.

———

The ride back was different.

They couldn't stop talking now—interrupting each other, finishing each other's sentences, theories tumbling out faster than they could organize them. But underneath the ghost talk, something else was happening.

"So what do we do next?" Christopher was saying. "Library? Historical society?"

"And we need to find out who lived there. When they—"

"Hey Christopher?"

"Yeah?"

"Say fuck again."

Christopher nearly wobbled on his bike. "What?"

"I want to hear you say it again. It's hilarious watching you try to be all rebellious." Jason was grinning. "Come on. Just once more."

"I'm not saying it just because you want me to."

"Please? It'll make my day."

"No."

"Pretty please?"

Christopher, without looking over, stuck his middle finger up in Jason's direction.

Jason burst out laughing—genuine, delighted laughter that echoed across the empty road. "Oh my god. Did you just flip me off?"

"Yes." Christopher was trying not to smile and failing.

"That's amazing. You're like a whole new person. Next you'll be getting tattoos and joining a motorcycle gang."

"Shut up."

"Seriously though, that was pretty good. But you gotta buy me dinner first if you're gonna do that."

The words were out before Jason could stop them.

Christopher's head whipped around so fast he nearly swerved. His face had gone bright red. "What?"

Jason felt his own face burning. "I—nothing. Forget I said that."

"No, what did you—"

"It was a joke. Bad joke. Moving on." Jason pedaled harder, trying to get ahead, trying to escape his own stupidity.

But he could hear Christopher laughing behind him.

———

By the time they pulled onto Dorsett Drive, the sun had shifted lower in the sky. Christopher's parents' car was in the driveway.

They came to a stop in front of the house, both slightly out of breath, both still riding the high of what they'd seen.

"So," Christopher said. "That happened."

"Yeah."

"We saw ghosts."

"We really did."

They stood there, straddling their bikes, grinning at each other like idiots.

The front door opened. Diane stepped out onto the porch.

"There you are! We were starting to worry. Did you boys have fun?"

"Yeah," Christopher called back. "Really fun. Can Jason stay for a bit? We were going to—"

"Actually," Mark appeared behind Diane, "we were thinking of heading up to Richmond for an early dinner. There's that Italian place your mom's been wanting to try. Jason, would you like to join us?"

Jason's first instinct was to say no. To make excuses. To get out of there before he had to navigate a meal with Christopher's parents where they'd notice things and ask questions and see too much.

But Christopher was looking at him with this hopeful expression, and the idea of going home to his empty house and leftover casserole versus spending more time with Christopher—

"I should call my mom," Jason said.

"Of course!" Diane gestured inside. "Phone's in the kitchen."

His mom answered on the second ring. Jason explained quickly—Christopher's parents wanted to take him to dinner in Richmond, was that okay?

There was a pause. Longer than there should have been.

"That sounds wonderful, honey," she said finally. Her voice was normal, carefully normal. "Have a great time. Just be home by nine."

"Okay. Thanks, Mom."

"Jason?"

"Yeah?"

Another pause. "I'm glad you're making friends."

The way she emphasized "friends" made Jason's stomach twist. Like she knew. Like she'd figured out something he hadn't even figured out himself yet.

"Yeah," he said. "Me too."

When he hung up, he stood there for a moment, staring at the phone.

His mom was putting pieces together. Drawing conclusions.

Maybe wrong ones. Maybe right ones. He wasn't sure which scared him more.

———

When he came back out, Christopher was waiting in the hallway. "So?"

"She said yes."

"Good." Christopher's smile was wide now, unguarded. "Come on, you can clean up in my room. We've got a few minutes."

Jason followed him upstairs.

Christopher's room was exactly what Jason had expected: organized, neat, posters of bands carefully arranged on the walls, a desk with an actual computer, bookshelves lined with fantasy novels. Everything in its place.

"Bathroom's through there," Christopher said, pointing. "Towels in the cabinet if you want to wash your face or whatever."

Jason splashed cold water on his face, ran wet hands through his hair, gave up trying to make it look less wild. When he came back out, Christopher was pulling a clean polo over his head.

They stood there in the small bedroom, suddenly alone, suddenly aware of the quiet.

The ghost-hunting adrenaline was fading, leaving behind something else. Something that had been building all day—all week, really—but was only now impossible to ignore.

"So," Christopher said.

"So," Jason echoed.

"That was..." Christopher trailed off. "I mean, we saw actual ghosts."

"Yeah."

"And they looked like us."

"Yeah."

"That's insane."

"Pretty much."

Silence. Christopher was fidgeting with the hem of his shirt, not quite meeting Jason's eyes.

"Back at the barn," Jason said quietly. "When you said if you could ask me something and then said it was dumb..."

Christopher looked caught, but lowered his head and inhaled courage.

"It wasn't dumb. I just... I chickened out."

Jason's heart kicked up. "What did you want to ask?"

Christopher took another breath. Let it out. "What would you do if... if some person tried to kiss you?"

"Some person?" Jason stepped closer. "What kind of person?"

"Just... I don't know. Anyone. Some... someone."

"Christopher." Jason's voice was gentle but insistent. "What kind of person?"

Christopher's face was flushed. "Does it matter?"

"Yeah. It kind of does."

"Why?"

"Because 'some person' could mean anyone. Could mean a girl. Could mean..." Jason paused, his heart hammering. This was it. The moment everything became real. "...a guy. Could mean—"

"A guy," Christopher said quickly, barely above a whisper. Then louder, like he needed to commit to it: "A... uh... guy. I meant... what would you do if some guy tried to kiss you?"

The word hung in the air between them. Guy. Not person. Not someone. Guy.

Jason's mouth had gone dry. Every nerve in his body was screaming at him to run, to deflect, to crack a joke and change the subject.

But Christopher was looking at him with this expression—hopeful and terrified in equal measure—and Jason realized this was it. The moment.

"Depends," Jason said, his voice rough. "Who's the guy?"

"Just... hypothetically. Some guy. Any guy."

"Christopher."

"Yeah?"

"Stop being hypothetical."

"I don't..." Christopher swallowed hard. "I don't know how."

Jason stepped closer. Close enough that he could see the exact shade of Christopher's eyes—somewhere between gray and blue, like lake water on an overcast day. Close enough that he could count the breaths between them.

His heart was pounding so hard he could hear it in his ears. This was terrifying. This was insane. This was everything he'd been trying not to think about for weeks.

"You want to know what I'd do?" Jason asked quietly.

"Yes."

"If some guy tried to kiss me?"

"Yes."

"I'd probably kiss him back," Jason said. "If it was the right guy."

Christopher's eyes widened. "You... what?"

"I'd kiss him back. Because I've been thinking about it for weeks and it's driving me crazy." The words were tumbling out now, too fast to stop. "And I know that's probably fucked up and I should keep it to myself but you asked and I can't... I can't keep pretending I'm not thinking about it."

"You think about kissing..." Christopher trailed off.

"You," Jason finished. "I think about kissing you. Constantly. It's actually kind of a problem. I'm failing at paying attention in class because I'm too busy thinking about your stupid perfect face."

Christopher made a sound that was half-laugh, half-something else entirely. "My face isn't perfect."

"It really is. It's annoying how perfect it is."

"Jason—"

"Yeah?"

"Can I... can we..." Christopher took a shaky breath. "Can I kiss you? For real this time. Not hypothetically."

Jason's throat had gone tight. "Yeah. Yeah, you can."

Christopher moved slowly—painfully slowly—like he was afraid Jason might change his mind. His hand came up to Jason's face, fingers barely touching his jaw. His eyes searched Jason's one more time, looking for permission, for confirmation, for anything that said this was okay.

Jason stayed perfectly still, barely breathing.

Christopher leaned in.

"BOYS?" Diane's voice from downstairs, cheerful and completely oblivious. "We're ready when you are!"

They sprang apart like they'd been electrocuted.

"COMING!" Christopher yelled back, his voice cracking halfway through.

They stood there, both breathing hard, both staring at each other in mutual frustration and disbelief.

"I'm going to kill her," Christopher said.

Jason laughed—breathless, slightly hysterical. "Rain check?"

"Definitely. Absolutely. The second we get back." Christopher looked at him seriously. "I mean it."

"I know."

"I really wanted to kiss you just then."

"I know. Me too."

"Really?"

Jason nodded, knowingly committing to something he'd been avoiding for weeks.

"This is probably going to be the longest dinner of my entire life."

"Same."

Christopher grinned despite himself. "Come on. Before they come up here."

———

They headed downstairs, trying to look normal and failing spectacularly. Diane and Mark were waiting by the door, keys in hand.

If they noticed the boys' flushed faces or the way they couldn't quite look at each other directly, they didn't say anything.

But Jason caught Mark and Diane exchanging another one of those glances—the kind that said *we'll talk about this later.*

The drive to Richmond took thirty minutes. Jason sat in the back seat next to Christopher, hyper-aware of every inch of space between them. Their thighs weren't quite touching. Their hands weren't quite touching. But the almost-touch felt electric.

Diane made conversation from the front seat, asking about the old houses, about school, about Driver's Ed. Christopher answered in his polite, composed way, giving nothing away.

Jason tried to focus on the conversation, but his brain kept replaying the moment in Christopher's room. The way Christopher had looked at him. The way he'd asked—not hypothetically, not indirectly, but for real: *Can I kiss you?*

And Jason had said yes.

Under the cover of his dad's story about some client, Christopher's hand found Jason's on the seat between them. Just fingers touching fingers. Nothing anyone could see from the front seat.

But Jason felt it everywhere.

———

By the time they pulled into the restaurant parking lot, Jason's heart had mostly calmed down. Mostly.

The Italian place was nice—not fancy, but nicer than anywhere Jason usually ate. Cloth napkins. Actual menus instead of laminated plastic. A waiter who asked if they wanted sparkling or still water like that was a normal question people got asked.

They ordered. The food came. Jason tried to pay attention to the conversation, to be a good guest, to not stare at Christopher across the table.

He failed at that last one repeatedly.

"So Jason," Diane said, halfway through her chicken parmesan, "what do your parents do?"

"My mom works at the bank. The First Financial downtown."

"And your father?"

Jason felt Christopher tense beside him.

"He's not around," Jason said simply. "Hasn't been for a while."

"I'm sorry to hear that," Diane said, and she sounded like she meant it. "That must be difficult."

Jason shrugged. "You get used to it."

Mark changed the subject smoothly, asking about Jason's classes, his interests. Easier territory. Jason relaxed incrementally.

The dinner passed in a pleasant blur. The food was good. Christopher's parents were easy to talk to once Jason got past his initial nervousness. And every time Jason glanced at Christopher, he found him already looking back.

———

By the time they made it back to the house, the sun had set. Jason's mom would be expecting him home soon.

"I should probably go," Jason said, standing on the driveway beside his bike.

"Yeah." Christopher looked like he wanted to say more but couldn't with his parents twenty feet away on the porch.

"Thanks for today. For believing me. For..." Jason trailed off. "For everything."

"Thank you for showing me. For trusting me." Christopher's voice dropped lower. "And for... earlier. What we talked about."

"Rain check still on?"

"Definitely."

They stood there, neither wanting to be the first to leave.

Finally Jason climbed on his bike. "See you Monday?"

"Monday."

Jason pedaled away, glancing back once to see Christopher still standing in the driveway, watching him go.

———

The ride home felt both too long and too short. His brain wouldn't shut up—replaying the ghosts, the almost-kiss, the way Christopher had said *I want to kiss you* like it was the bravest thing he'd ever admitted.

His mom was waiting when he got home, sitting at the kitchen table with her usual cup of tea.

"How was it?" she asked.

"Good. Really good."

She studied his face. "You look happy."

"Yeah. I guess I am."

"This Christopher must be pretty special."

Jason felt his face heat. "He's just a friend, Mom."

"I know, honey." She smiled. "But you're allowed to have special friends. People who make you happy. That's good. That's important."

Jason nodded, not trusting himself to say more.

"Go on," she said. "Get some sleep. You look exhausted."

He was. But it was the good kind of exhausted—the kind that came from living a day so full it couldn't possibly fit in your head all at once.

Jason went to his room, pulled out his notebook, and stared at the sketches he'd made before. The lantern boy. The taller boy with the sandy hair.

Then he flipped to a new page and started writing everything he could remember. Every detail. The clothes the boys had worn. The way they'd moved. The sound of their laughter.

The way the taller one's hair had caught the light, exactly like Christopher's.

He wrote until his hand cramped, until the words started blurring together. Then he closed the notebook, shoved it under his mattress, and lay back on his bed.

Tomorrow was Sunday. Then Monday. Then Driver's Ed first period, sitting next to Christopher in that basement classroom with the spoiled-milk walls.

Maybe he'd call him tomorrow. He didn't know if he could wait.

And maybe—if he was brave enough—he'd actually talk to Christopher about what came next.

About the ghosts they'd seen.

About the almost-kiss they'd shared.

About what it meant that Jason couldn't stop thinking about him.

Jason closed his eyes and let himself smile in the darkness.

Tomorrow couldn't come fast enough.

Chapter 7

Troubled

Sunday felt like the longest day of Jason's life.

He woke up late—almost noon—his body finally catching up on sleep his brain had been too wired to take the night before. The house was quiet. His mom had left a note on the kitchen counter: *Went to the store. Be back around 2. Love you.*

Jason made himself a sandwich, ate it standing at the counter, and tried not to think about Christopher.

Which was impossible.

Because every time he closed his eyes, he was back in that bedroom. Christopher's hand on his face. The way he'd leaned in. The heat between them that had felt like it might actually set the air on fire.

Can I kiss you?

Yeah. Yeah, you can.

And then his mom's voice from downstairs, cheerful and oblivious, shattering the moment.

Jason groaned and pressed his palms against his eyes.

He should call. Christopher had given him his number on Monday—had written it right on Jason's palm like it was nothing.

Jason had memorized it within an hour and retraced it with pen every time it started to fade.

But what would he say? *Hey, so about almost kissing you yesterday? Still thinking about your stupid perfect face? Want to finish what we started?*

His stomach twisted.

This was insane. He'd never felt like this about anyone. Not Amy Martinez in seventh grade with her perfect smile and her devastating pity. Not the random girls he'd thought maybe he was supposed to like because that's what guys did.

Christopher was different.

Christopher made him feel like he'd swallowed lightning. Like every nerve ending in his body had been turned up to maximum volume. Like he was standing on the edge of something huge and terrifying and he couldn't tell if he wanted to jump or run.

Jason grabbed the phone. Stared at it. Put it back.

Grabbed it again.

This was stupid. They were friends. Friends called each other. It didn't have to mean anything. He could just... check in. See if Christopher was okay. Ask if he wanted to start researching the farmhouses.

Yeah. That was normal. That was fine.

Jason dialed before he could talk himself out of it.

The phone rang once. Twice. Three times.

"Hello?" Christopher's voice, slightly breathless like he'd run to answer.

Jason's mouth went dry. "Hey. It's me. Jason."

"I know." Christopher sounded... pleased? Relieved? "I was hoping you'd call."

"Yeah?"

"Yeah. I've been thinking about yesterday. All of it. The farmhouses, the ghosts, and..." He trailed off.

"And?"

"And everything else," Christopher finished quietly.

Jason's heart was doing that thing again where it tried to escape his chest. "Me too."

Silence stretched between them, but it wasn't uncomfortable. It was loaded. Electric.

"So," Christopher said finally. "What do we do now?"

"About the ghosts or about...?"

"Both, I guess."

Jason leaned against the kitchen counter, phone cord stretching. "Uh..the library. We should hit the library tomorrow after school. Look up anything about those farmhouses, you think?"

"Good idea. My mom can probably drive us if you want. Or we could ride our bikes."

"Bikes are fine. I don't want..." Jason struggled for words. "I don't want to have to explain what we're researching. Your parents already think we're weird."

"They don't think we're weird."

"Christopher. Your dad watched us the entire time at dinner like he was trying to solve a puzzle."

"That's just how he looks at people."

"No, that's how he looks at his son sitting next to a guy who can't stop staring at him."

The words were out before Jason could stop them.

Silence.

"You were staring at me?" Christopher asked quietly.

"I—" Jason's face burned. "Maybe. I don't know. Shut up."

Christopher laughed, soft and surprised. "Good. Because I was staring at you too."

Jason's chest felt too tight. "This is weird, right? This whole thing. It's completely insane."

"Probably."

"But you don't... you're not freaked out?"

"About the ghosts or about us?"

"Both."

"The ghosts are terrifying," Christopher said. "But also kind of amazing? Like, we saw actual ghosts, Jason. Dead people from a hundred years ago just... playing on railroad tracks like it was nothing. That's incredible."

"And the other thing?"

Another pause. Then: "I'm scared. But not freaked out. Not... I don't want to stop. Whatever we are doing."

Jason closed his eyes. "Me neither."

"So we'll just... figure it out."

"Together."

"Yeah," Christopher said, and Jason could hear the smile in his voice. "Together."

They talked for another twenty minutes—about the farmhouses, about what records they might find, about whether they should go back out there at night when the dreams always took place. By the time Jason heard his mom's car in the driveway, his face hurt from smiling.

"I should go," Jason said. "My mom just got home."

"Okay. See you tomorrow?"

"Yeah. First period."

"I'll be there."

Jason hung up and stood there for a moment, staring at the phone, a smile still on his face.

His mom came in carrying grocery bags. She took one look at him and caught his smile.

"You look happy."

Jason felt his face heat slightly. "Just... thinking about stuff."

"Good stuff, I hope."

"Yeah."

She set the bags on the counter. "You deserve to be happy."

You deserve to be happy. That was a weird thing to say. Jason helped her unpack the groceries, trying not to think about how much his mom was noticing. How much she was putting together. How many questions she wasn't asking yet but probably would eventually.

But for now, she just let him be.

And Jason was grateful for that.

————

Monday morning came too fast and too slow at the same time.

Jason woke up before his alarm, his stomach doing flips. He went through his morning routine on autopilot—shower, cheap cologne, the same black t-shirt he always wore because the green one was in the wash and he wasn't ready to commit to color as a permanent thing.

When he came into the kitchen, his mom wasn't there.

Her boyfriend—Rick—stood at the counter pouring coffee, still in his work clothes from the night shift. He glanced up when Jason walked in.

"Morning," Rick muttered.

"Where's my mom?"

"Left early. Some important meeting at work or something." He shrugged, clearly not particularly interested. "Said she'd be home regular time."

Jason grabbed a Pop-Tart from the cabinet. A meeting. That was unusual. His mom never had meetings—she was a teller, not management. She counted money and processed transactions and came home tired.

But he shrugged it off. Probably nothing.

"You heading to school?" Rick asked.

"Yeah."

"Good. Stay out of trouble."

It wasn't said with concern. More like a statement of fact. Stay out of trouble so I don't have to deal with you. Jason had gotten used to Rick's brand of disinterest over the years. At least he wasn't actively hostile.

Jason grabbed his backpack and headed out.

The bike ride to school felt different. Like the world had shifted slightly overnight and Jason was still trying to find his balance. Everything looked the same—the factories, the hill, the nice houses—but somehow it felt like anything could happen.

Or maybe that was just him.

He locked his bike at the rack and headed inside, down to the basement classroom. His heart was hammering by the time he reached the door.

Christopher was already there.

He looked up when Jason walked in, and his whole face lit up in that way that made Jason's stomach flip. But there was something else there too—nervousness, maybe. Or anticipation.

Jason slid into the seat beside him. "Hey."

"Hey." Christopher's voice was quieter than usual. "How was the rest of your weekend?"

"Long. Boring. Thought about stuff too much."

"Me too."

They sat there, suddenly awkward in a way they hadn't been since that first week. Like acknowledging what was happening between them had made everything simultaneously easier and harder.

"So," Jason said. "Library after school?"

"Yeah. Definitely." Christopher clicked his pen. "I've been thinking about what we should look for. Property deeds, obviously. But also old census records, death certificates, newspaper archives..."

"You've been planning."

"I couldn't sleep." Christopher's ears went red. "I kept thinking about them. The ghost boys. Who they were. Why you're dreaming about them. Why they're showing themselves to us."

"And?"

"And I don't have any answers. But I think we'll find them."

Barnes swept into the room right as the bell rang, already talking. "Good morning, drivers! Hope everyone had a restful weekend because we're diving into parallel parking today! Yes, I can hear your groans, but trust me—this is a crucial skill that will serve you well for the rest of your driving lives!"

Jason tried to focus on Barnes explaining the angles and distances, the importance of using your mirrors, the way you had to turn the wheel at just the right moment. But his attention kept drifting sideways to Christopher.

To the way Christopher's tongue stuck out slightly when he concentrated on taking notes. The way his handwriting stayed neat even when he was rushing. The way his knee bumped Jason's under the desk and neither of them moved away.

It was distracting as hell.

"Mr. Reynolds?" Barnes called from the front. "Care to explain the proper technique for parallel parking?"

Jason blinked. "Uh..."

Christopher's hand moved under the desk, his finger poking Jason's leg. Getting his attention, pointing to a line in his notebook with his other hand: *Turn signal. Check mirrors. Reverse at 45 degrees.*

The touch on his leg sent a jolt through Jason's system. He became hyper-aware of exactly where Christopher's finger was, the heat of it through his jeans, the casual intimacy of the gesture.

"Turn signal," Jason said aloud, his voice slightly rough. "Check your mirrors. Reverse at a forty-five degree angle until your car is aligned with the space."

Barnes looked pleased. "Excellent! See, this is why partnerships work, people. You help each other learn."

Christopher pulled his hand back from the notebook but his finger stayed on Jason's leg for another few seconds before sliding away.

Jason immediately crossed his legs, shifting in his seat. Because that touch had done things to him that were absolutely not appropriate for a classroom, and if Christopher accidentally moved his hand any higher, they were both going to have a problem.

Christopher glanced at him, a small smile playing at the corner of his mouth like he knew exactly what he'd done.

Barnes continued with his lecture. "Now, tomorrow we'll be using the simulators—getting you all comfortable with the controls and basic maneuvers. And then next week, the exciting part! We start actual behind-the-wheel training. You and your partner will take turns, of course. One drives while the other observes. Real cars, real roads, real experience!"

A few students perked up at that. Jason tried to focus on what Barnes was saying, but his brain was still stuck on Christopher's finger on his leg and the way his entire body had reacted to such a simple touch.

This was getting dangerous.

The rest of class dragged. When the bell finally rang, they walked out together like always, climbed the stairs like always, paused at the top like always.

Except nothing felt like always anymore.

"Library," Christopher said. "Right after last period?"

"Yeah. I'll meet you at the bike racks."

"Okay." Christopher shifted his books. "Jason?"

"Yeah?"

"Thanks. For calling yesterday. I was worried you might... I don't know. Change your mind about everything."

"I'm not changing my mind."

"Good." Christopher smiled—that small, careful smile that was starting to loosen around the edges when he was with Jason. "See you later."

He walked away toward Chemistry, and Jason watched him go.

This was becoming a habit. A dangerous one. But he couldn't seem to stop.

———

The rest of Monday passed in a blur of classes Jason barely paid attention to. In English, Mrs. Grant lectured about Sylvia Plath and the confessional poets, talking about vulnerability and truth in art. Jason took notes but his mind was elsewhere—on ghost boys and abandoned farmhouses and Christopher's hand on his leg.

At lunch, Allison cornered him immediately.

"Okay, spill."

Jason looked up from his cafeteria Sloppy Joe. "Spill what?"

"Whatever happened this weekend that's got you looking like that."

"Like what?"

"Like you either won the lottery or got hit by a truck. I can't tell which." She sat down across from him, studying his face. "Did something happen with Chris-whats-his-face? The one from Barnes' class?"

Jason's stomach dropped. "What? No. We just... hung out. Looked at some old houses."

"Uh huh." Allison stole one of his fries. "And that's why you look like someone who just discovered electricity? Because you looked at old houses?"

"We found some cool stuff, okay? Historical stuff. It's interesting."

"You hate history."

"I don't hate history. I just think it's boring when teachers talk about it. But actual history—like, old buildings and stuff—that's different."

Allison raised an eyebrow but didn't push. "Fine. Keep your secrets. But Jason?"

"Yeah?"

"Whatever this is—whoever this is—I'm happy for you. You seem... lighter. Less angry at the world."

Jason didn't know what to say to that. So he just shrugged and took another bite of his Sloppy Joe.

Scott showed up a few minutes later, complaining about football practice, and the conversation shifted to safer territory. But Jason caught Allison watching him a few times, that knowing look on her face that said she'd figured something out but was waiting for him to confirm it.

He wasn't ready for that conversation yet.

Maybe he'd never be ready.

———

By the time last period ended, Jason was practically vibrating with anticipation. He grabbed his stuff and headed straight for the bike racks.

Christopher was already there, backpack on, looking slightly nervous.

"Ready?" Jason asked.

"Yeah. Let's go."

The Connersville Public Library sat on Grand Avenue, just down from the railroad tracks. It had been built in the early '80s—dark brick and modern glass that seemed almost too nice for this side of town. The kind of building that said someone had cared about making it welcoming, making it matter.

They locked their bikes out front and headed inside.

The smell hit Jason immediately—that distinctive library smell of old paper and dust and the world. Christopher took a visible breath, his shoulders relaxing slightly. He loved this smell, Jason realized. Loved being here among the books and the quiet and the knowledge.

Jason had his own secret relationship with libraries. Most people didn't know he liked hiding back in the shelves, exploring books no one else bothered with. Finding stories in forgotten corners. But he'd never told anyone that. It felt too vulnerable somehow. Too revealing.

Today, though, they weren't here for stories.

They were here to find ghosts.

Behind the front desk, a woman in her fifties looked up and smiled.

"Can I help you boys find something?"

Christopher stepped forward, suddenly all polite composure. "Yes, ma'am. We're doing research on local history. Specifically old farmhouses west of town on Country Club Road. We were wondering if you had property records or historical documents we could look at?"

The librarian's expression brightened. "Oh, how wonderful! We don't get many young people interested in local history. Let me show you our archives section."

She led them to a back corner of the library where older materials were kept. Filing cabinets lined the walls. Shelves held bound volumes of old newspapers. A microfiche machine sat in the corner, looking like something from another era.

"Property records are here," she indicated one cabinet. "Organized by location and date. Newspapers are on microfiche—these are the Reader's Guides that will help you search by date or topic. And we have some old maps here that might help you locate specific properties."

"Thank you," Christopher said. "This is perfect."

"Of course. Let me know if you need anything else." She paused at the door. "What's your research for, if you don't mind me asking? School project?"

"Something like that," Jason said.

She nodded and left them to it.

As soon as she was gone, Christopher turned to Jason, eyes bright. "Okay. Where do we start?"

"Property records. Find out who owned those farmhouses."

They pulled open the filing cabinets, searching through dusty folders until they found what they were looking for: property deeds for the section of Country Club Road where the farmhouses sat.

The larger house—the one with the widow's peak—had been built in 1887 by a family named Thorne. William and Margaret Thorne. The deed listed them as owning forty acres of farmland.

The smaller house across the road was built the same year by the Hartley family. Robert and Elizabeth Hartley. Twenty acres.

"Neighbors," Christopher said quietly. "They were neighbors."

"Look at this." Jason pointed to a note at the bottom of the Thorne deed. "There's a son listed. William Thorne Jr. Born 1873."

Christopher was already pulling out the Hartley file. "And the Hartleys had a son too. Daniel. Born 1874."

Their eyes met.

"Same age," Jason said. "They would've been the same age."

"Do you think...?"

"I don't know. But it fits, doesn't it? Two boys. Same age. Living across the road from each other."

Christopher pulled out his notebook and started writing down names, dates, everything they could find. "We need to find out what happened to them. If they're in the census records, death certificates, anything."

They spent the next hour digging through files. The 1890 census showed both families still living on their properties. William Thorne Jr. would've been seventeen. Daniel Hartley was sixteen.

But the 1900 census told a different story.

The Thorne property was listed as abandoned. The Hartley farm showed Daniel Hartley as the owner—his parents had passed, and he'd inherited the property.

"Something happened to the Thornes," Christopher said. "Between 1890 and 1900. The family left or... something."

"Check death records."

They found them in a separate cabinet—handwritten ledgers from the county clerk's office, copied and bound for the archives.

And there it was.

December 16, 1890. One name.

William Thorne Jr., age 17. Cause of death: Blunt trauma to body and head. Train accident.

Jason stared at the entry, his chest tight.

"He was hit by a train," Christopher whispered.

"The railroad tracks. Where we saw them playing."

"Oh my god."

They kept reading. The notes were sparse—just the basics. William Thorne Jr. had been killed by a train near Hanna Creek. Body discovered December 16, 1890. Death ruled accidental.

But Daniel Hartley's name wasn't there.

Jason flipped through more pages. "Where's Daniel?"

Christopher was already pulling another volume. "If he inherited the farm in 1900..."

They found it in a different section. Death records from 1930.

Daniel Hartley, age 56. Died of natural causes at his home on Country Club Road. Never married. No surviving family. Property transferred to the county.

"He lived alone," Jason said quietly. "His whole life. Never married. Never had kids. Just... lived in that farmhouse by himself for forty years."

"After William died," Christopher added, his voice barely above a whisper.

They sat there in silence, the weight of it settling over them.

"We need to find newspaper articles," Christopher said finally. "There had to be something written about it. A boy getting killed by a train—that would've been news."

They moved to the microfiche machine. It took them another thirty minutes of searching through the old Connersville News-Examiner before they found it.

December 18, 1890. Front page.

TRAGEDY STRIKES LOCAL FAMILY

Young Man Killed in Railroad Accident

The community mourns the loss of William Thorne Jr., 17, who was struck and killed by a freight train near Hanna Creek on the evening of December 15. The accident occurred while William and his companion, Daniel Hartley, 16, were on the tracks together.

According to witness accounts, both young men were on the railroad line when the westbound freight approached. William apparently saw the train and heard the steam whistle, but his foot became caught in a wooden tie where ballast had eroded and fallen away. Despite his frantic efforts to free himself, he was unable to escape in time.

Young Mr. Hartley witnessed the entire tragedy but was unable to reach his friend before the locomotive struck. The engineer, Mr. Thomas Crawford, reported seeing a lantern light on the tracks ahead but stated he had just opened the throttle coming out of town and was traveling at too great a speed to stop the train in time.

Mr. Hartley, who witnessed his companion's death, was said to be in a state of shock and is being cared for by his family. Sheriff's deputies are questioning why the two young men were on the tracks at such a late hour, though no wrongdoing is suspected.

William was known as a quiet, thoughtful young man. The Thorne family is devastated by this tragic loss. A funeral service will be held at the Methodist Church on December 20.

Jason and Christopher read the article in silence.

"Daniel was there," Christopher said finally, his voice cracking. "He watched it happen."

"William's foot was stuck. Daniel saw him trying to get free."

"And couldn't save him."

Jason stared at the screen, at those words. *His companion, Daniel Hartley.* "The lantern. William had a lantern. Just like in the dreams."

"And the sheriff questioned why they were out there late at night." Christopher's eyes met Jason's. "Together. Alone. On the railroad tracks."

The implication hung in the air between them.

"Daniel lived alone," Jason said quietly. "For forty years. Never married. Never moved away from that farmhouse."

"He couldn't," Christopher whispered. "How could he? He watched William die. Right there on those tracks. And then had to live with it every single day, looking out his window at the place where it happened."

"The article says his foot was caught. That he saw the train coming. Heard the whistle."

"William knew he was going to die." Christopher's voice broke slightly. "And Daniel had to watch and couldn't do anything to stop it."

They sat there, the microfiche machine humming between them, the weight of a tragedy from 1890 pressing down on them like it had just happened yesterday.

"We should go back," Jason said finally. "To the farmhouses. At night this time. When I always dream about them. Maybe... maybe we'll see more. Learn more."

"That's insane."

"Probably."

"We could get in serious trouble. Trespassing at night, messing around abandoned buildings..."

"I know."

Christopher looked at him for a long moment. Then: "When?"

"Friday night?"

"Okay."

"You sure?"

"No. But I'm doing it anyway." Christopher's voice was steady despite everything. "Someone's gotta keep you from doing something stupid."

"I do plenty of stupid things without supervision, thanks."

"Exactly. Which is why I'm coming with you."

They copied down everything they could find, took notes on the newspaper articles, and packed up their stuff. By the time they left the library, the sun was starting to set, casting long shadows across Grand Avenue.

They rode their bikes back toward Christopher's neighborhood in comfortable silence. At the corner of Country Club Road and Dorsett, they stopped.

"So," Christopher said. "Friday night. What time?"

"Late. Like, midnight? When everyone's asleep?"

"How do we meet up without our parents finding out?"

Jason thought about it. "I can sneak out easy. My mom's bedroom is on the other side of the house. You?"

"Maybe. My parents go to bed around eleven. If I wait an hour..." He trailed off. "This is insane. We're planning to sneak out in the middle of the night to visit haunted farmhouses."

"You can back out if you want."

"I'm not backing out." Christopher said it firmly. "I just wanted to acknowledge how completely insane this is."

"Acknowledged."

They stood there, neither quite ready to say goodbye.

"I should go," Christopher said finally. "Dinner's probably ready."

"Yeah. Me too."

"Jason?"

"Yeah?"

"Today was good. The research, I mean. We actually found stuff. Real information about them."

"William and Daniel."

"Yeah. William and Daniel." Christopher's expression was haunted. "Daniel watched him die. Can you imagine? Being right there, seeing your friend trapped, hearing him scream, watching the train coming and not being able to do anything?"

"And then living with that for forty years."

"In the house across from where it happened. Never marrying. Never leaving. Just... existing. Alone."

"What do you think that means?"

Christopher looked at him—really looked. At the way the fading sunlight caught in Jason's dark hair. At the intensity in his eyes. At the expression on his face that was thoughtful and sad and determined all at once.

"I think it means he couldn't forget," Christopher said quietly. "I think it means William was more than just a friend. And losing him that way—watching it happen—destroyed something in Daniel that never healed."

The words hung in the air between them.

"The article said the sheriff questioned why they were out there," Jason said. "Late at night. Together. Alone."

"Back then," Christopher added. "When two guys being alone together at night would've meant... something."

"Yeah."

They stood in silence, both understanding what they couldn't quite say aloud.

"I'll see you tomorrow," Christopher said finally.

"Yeah. Tomorrow."

Jason watched him ride away, then turned his bike toward home.

———

When he got home, Jason's mom was making dinner—actual dinner, not leftovers or cereal. Spaghetti with sauce from a jar, but still. The effort was there.

"How was school?" she asked as he walked in.

"Good. Went to the library after."

"The library?" She raised an eyebrow. "Voluntarily?"

"Had to research something. For that project I mentioned."

"With Christopher?"

"Yeah."

She stirred the sauce, not looking at him. "He seems like a nice boy. His parents too, taking you to dinner."

"They are."

"You're spending a lot of time with him."

Jason's guard went up. "We're working on a project together. That's kind of how it works."

"I know, honey. I'm just..." She trailed off. "I'm glad you have a good friend. Someone who makes you happy."

"Why do you keep saying that? That he makes me happy?"

"Because you smile more now. You seem lighter. Less..." She struggled for the word. "Less alone."

Jason didn't know what to say to that. So he just grabbed plates from the cabinet and started setting the table.

They ate dinner in comfortable silence. His mom asked about his classes. He asked about her day at the bank.

"Actually," she said, setting down her fork. "Something interesting happened today. That meeting I had this morning?"

"Yeah?"

"A branch in Indianapolis needs a new bank manager. And they asked if I'd be interested in the position."

Jason's stomach dropped. "Indianapolis?"

"It's just preliminary. They're talking to several people. Nothing's decided yet." She was trying to sound casual, but Jason could hear the excitement underneath. "It would be a big step up. Better pay. Better opportunities."

"But that's like... an hour away."

"About that, yeah."

"So we'd have to move."

"If it happens, yes. But Jason, it's not definite. It's just something they're considering me for. I probably won't even get it."

But she wanted it. Jason could see it in her face. The hope. The possibility of something better than counting money at a small-town bank for the rest of her life.

"When would you know?" he asked.

"A few weeks. Maybe a month. They're still figuring things out." She reached across the table, squeezed his hand. "But if it happens—if we have to move—it won't be until summer. You'd finish the school year here."

Summer. That gave him... what, eight months? Nine?

Eight months with Christopher before everything fell apart.

"That's great, Mom," Jason managed. "Really. You should go for it."

"You sure you're okay with it?"

"Yeah. It's fine. It's just... a lot to think about."

"I know, honey. But nothing's decided yet. Let's not worry about it until we have to."

After dinner, he retreated to his room, pulled out his notebook, and wrote down everything they'd learned at the library.

William Thorne Jr. - born 1873, died December 15, 1890 (17) - Struck by train

Daniel Hartley - born 1874, died 1930 (56) - He found William's body

Daniel lived in the farmhouse for 40 years after William died - "William had seemed troubled in recent weeks"

He stared at that last line.

Troubled. What did that mean? Depressed? Scared? Hiding something?

Had William walked onto those tracks on purpose? Or had it really been an accident?

And Daniel—living across the road from where his friend died, alone for forty years, growing old while carrying that memory.

Jason flipped to a blank page and started sketching. The widow's peak. The barn. The railroad tracks. The two boys running through the corn, alive and happy and together.

And then, without meaning to, he drew Christopher. Just his face. That careful expression he wore most of the time, the one that was starting to crack around the edges when they were alone.

Jason stared at the drawing for a long time.

Then he thought about his mom's news. Indianapolis. A new job. Moving away.

He'd just found Christopher. Just figured out what this feeling was. Just admitted—barely—that he wanted something he'd never let himself want before.

And in eight months, it might all be over.

Jason closed the notebook and shoved it under his mattress.

Friday. They'd go back Friday night.

And maybe—if they were lucky—William and Daniel would show them what they needed to see.

Before time ran out.

Chapter 8

Racist Homophobic Bigots

Tuesday Morning, Jason woke up thinking about Daniel Hartley.

Forty years. Forty years living alone in that farmhouse, looking out at the railroad tracks where William had died. Never marrying. Never moving on. Just... existing.

Jason tried to imagine it. Waking up every day and seeing the place where your friend—or whatever William had been—had gotten his foot caught. Where you'd watched him struggle. Heard him scream. Seen the train coming and been powerless to stop it.

How did you live with that?

How did you keep going?

Jason rolled out of bed and went through his morning routine on autopilot. Black t-shirt. Jeans. The usual armor. But his mind was still stuck on Daniel.

Daniel never married.

That line from the death certificate kept circling back. In 1890, in small-town Indiana, everyone got married. That's just what you did. You found someone, settled down, had kids, carried on the family name.

Unless you couldn't.

Unless the person you wanted to marry was someone you weren't allowed to want.

Jason grabbed his backpack and headed downstairs.

His mom was already gone—another early morning, probably more meetings about that Indianapolis job. Rick was at the kitchen table with coffee and the newspaper, barely acknowledging Jason's existence.

Fine by him.

Jason grabbed a Pop-Tart, his mainstay lately, and headed out.

The ride to school felt longer than usual. His brain wouldn't shut up about William and Daniel, about the lantern and the railroad tracks, about Daniel living alone for forty years with nothing but memories and ghosts.

By the time he made it to Driver's Ed, Christopher was already there, looking like he hadn't slept much either.

"Hey," Jason said, sliding into the seat beside him.

"Hey." Christopher's voice was quiet. "I kept thinking about them. All night."

"Me too."

"Daniel watched him die."

"I know."

They sat there in silence until Barnes swept in, all enthusiasm and energy despite the early hour—a living example of jazz-hands personified.

"Good morning, drivers! Today's the day—we're hitting the simulators! Now, I know they don't look like much, but these babies will teach you the fundamentals of vehicle control before we put you behind the wheel of an actual car. Safety first, people!"

The class groaned collectively, but Jason found himself almost grateful for the distraction. Anything to stop thinking about trapped feet and steam whistles and forty years of loneliness.

Barnes divided them into groups. Jason and Christopher ended up at simulator number three—a setup that looked like it had been built sometime in the '70s and never updated. Cracked vinyl seats. A steering wheel that wobbled slightly. A screen showing a grainy road simulation.

"Okay, partners," Barnes called out. "One of you drives, one observes. Switch every ten minutes. The goal is to get comfortable with steering, acceleration, braking. Nice and easy. Let's begin!"

Christopher gestured to the driver's seat. "You first?"

"Sure."

Jason climbed in, adjusted the seat, gripped the steering wheel. The simulator rumbled to life, the screen showing a straight road stretching ahead.

It was ridiculous. It was clearly fake. But somehow it still made his heart race a little.

Christopher leaned over his shoulder, close enough that Jason could smell his shampoo—something clean and expensive that probably came in a bottle that didn't say "2-in-1" on it.

"Okay, so just... accelerate slowly," Christopher said. "And try to stay in your lane."

Jason pressed the gas pedal. The simulator lurched forward on screen. He gripped the wheel tighter, overcorrecting when the road curved.

"Easy," Christopher said, his voice right by Jason's ear. "Small movements. You're doing fine."

The road curved again. Jason adjusted, still oversteering but getting better.

"Good," Christopher encouraged. "See? You've got it."

Jason became aware of how close Christopher was. How his hand had come to rest on the back of Jason's seat. How if Jason turned his head even slightly, their faces would be inches apart.

Focus. Just focus on the fake road.

But it was hard to focus when every nerve in his body was screaming awareness of Christopher's proximity. When he could feel Christopher's breath on his neck. When his brain kept supplying helpful images of what might happen if he just turned his head, if he just—

The simulator car on screen crashed into a fence.

"Oops," Jason said.

Barnes appeared beside them. "Everything alright here, Mr. Reynolds?"

"Yeah, just... getting used to the controls."

"Take your time. Remember—smooth inputs. Small corrections." He moved on to the next simulator.

Christopher was trying not to laugh. "You okay there?"

"Shut up," Jason muttered.

"I didn't say anything."

"You're thinking it loudly."

They switched places. Christopher slid into the driver's seat with his usual careful precision, adjusted everything just so, gripped the wheel at ten and two like Barnes had demonstrated.

The simulator started. Christopher drove perfectly—smooth acceleration, gentle turns, staying exactly in the center of his lane.

Of course he did.

Jason leaned against the side of the simulator, watching. "Show-off."

"I'm just following instructions."

"You're making the rest of us look bad."

"That's not my fault."

A curve appeared on screen. Christopher navigated it flawlessly.

"Seriously, have you done this before?" Jason asked.

"No. I'm just paying attention."

"That's not a thing normal people can do, you know. Be perfect at everything."

Christopher's hands tightened slightly on the wheel. "I'm not perfect."

"Could've fooled me."

"Jason." Christopher's voice had gone quiet. "I crashed my bike into a mailbox two weeks ago because I was distracted thinking about you. I almost failed a math test because I couldn't stop replaying our conversation about Prufrock. I've said 'fuck' more times in the past week than in my entire life combined." He navigated another curve. "I'm not perfect. I'm a disaster. I'm just good at hiding it."

Jason stared at him. "You were thinking about me when you crashed your bike?"

"That's what you got from that?"

"I mean, the fuck thing is impressive too, but—"

"Mr. Avery! Mr. Reynolds!" Barnes called from across the room. "Less talking, more driving!"

Christopher's ears went red, but Jason caught the smile he was trying to hide.

They spent the rest of class taking turns on the simulator. By the end, Jason could navigate the fake roads without crashing, and Christopher had loosened up enough to actually make a mistake or two.

Progress.

When the bell rang, they walked out together. At the top of the stairs, Christopher started to head toward Chemistry, but Jason caught his arm.

"Hey. You want to... I mean, do you want to have lunch with me? And my friends?"

Christopher blinked. "Really?"

"Yeah. I mean, if you want. No pressure. But Scott and Allison are pretty cool. Well, Scott's oblivious to everything, but Allison's cool. She'll probably interrogate you, but—"

"I'd like that," Christopher interrupted.

A thought occurred to Jason. "Unless... do you usually sit with people? I don't want to mess up your lunch plans or anything."

Christopher's expression flickered—something vulnerable passing across his face. "Not really. I mean, there are some kids I know from my classes, but we're not... we don't really hang out. I usually just sit wherever there's space."

Jason's chest felt tight. Christopher had been eating lunch alone. Or with people who weren't really friends. Just going through the motions.

"Well, now you've got a place," Jason said firmly. "If you want it."

Christopher smiled—that small, genuine smile that made Jason's stomach flip. "I want it."

"Okay. Cool. I'll meet you at the cafeteria?"

"Yeah. Okay."

They stood there for a moment, both smiling like idiots.

"See you at lunch," Christopher said.

"Yeah. Lunch."

Jason watched him walk away, feeling lighter than he had all morning.

———

By the time lunch rolled around, Jason's stomach was doing flips.

This was stupid. It was just lunch. Christopher meeting his friends. No big deal.

Except it felt like a big deal.

He grabbed his tray—Sloppy Joe again, the cafeteria apparently committed to its greatest hits—and made his way to his usual table. Scott was already there, inhaling what looked like yesterday's meatloaf. Allison sat across from him, picking at a salad.

"Hey," Jason said, sliding in.

"Hey yourself," Allison said, then her eyes went past him. "Oh. We have company."

Jason turned. Christopher stood a few feet away, tray in hand, looking uncertain.

"This is Christopher," Jason said. "Christopher, this is Allison and Scott."

"Hi," Christopher said, his voice going into that polite mode he used with adults.

"Sit, sit!" Allison gestured to the seat next to Jason. "We've heard so much about you."

Jason kicked her under the table.

"Ow! What? We have."

Christopher sat down carefully, setting his tray—which was considerably healthier than Jason's—on the table. "It's nice to meet you both."

Scott looked up from his meatloaf. "You're the Driver's Ed guy, right?"

"Yeah. We're partners."

"Cool. Jason's terrible at driving."

"I'm not terrible—"

"You said you crashed into a fence. In a simulator."

"That was one time!"

Christopher was smiling now, some of the tension leaving his shoulders. "He's getting better."

"See?" Jason said. "Christopher thinks I'm getting better."

"Christopher's being nice," Allison said, studying Christopher with unconcealed interest. "So. What do you think of our Jason here?"

Christopher's ears went slightly pink. "He's... he's great. Really smart. Funny."

"Funny-looking or funny ha-ha?"

"Allison," Jason warned.

"I'm just asking! So, Christopher. What do your parents do?"

"My dad's an accountant. My mom's a part-time librarian at the junior high."

"That's nice. And you live over by the golf course?"

"Yeah. On Dorsett."

"Fancy." Allison's tone wasn't mean, just observational. "And you and Jason are working on a project together?"

"Local history. Old farmhouses."

"Sounds boring."

"It's actually really interesting," Christopher said, and there was genuine enthusiasm in his voice. "We found these records about two boys who lived there in the 1890s, and—"

He stopped, glancing at Jason.

"And it's cool to see how people lived back then," Jason finished. "Different time, you know?"

Allison's eyes narrowed slightly, like she knew there was more to that story, but she didn't push. "Well, I'm glad Jason has someone to nerd out about history with. God knows I'm not doing it."

Scott had gone back to his meatloaf, completely uninterested in the conversation. But Allison kept watching them—the way they sat slightly too close, the way they kept glancing at each other, the way Christopher relaxed incrementally as lunch went on.

By the time the bell rang, Christopher was actually laughing at one of Scott's terrible football stories, and Jason felt something loosen in his chest.

"That was nice," Christopher said as they walked out together. "Your friends are nice."

106

"Allison likes you. She would've eviscerated you if she didn't."

"That was her liking me?"

"Trust me. You got off easy."

They reached the fork where Christopher had to go to his next class and Jason to Art.

"Thanks," Christopher said. "For inviting me."

"Yeah. Anytime."

They stood there for a beat too long, neither wanting to leave.

"See you tomorrow," Christopher said finally.

"Yeah. Tomorrow."

———

Wednesday passed in a similar pattern—simulators in Driver's Ed, lunch with Christopher and the others, Allison watching them with increasing interest.

Thursday brought more of the same. Barnes was relentlessly cheerful about parallel parking techniques. Christopher had settled into Jason's lunch table like he'd always been there. Scott remained oblivious to everything. Allison's knowing looks intensified.

Thursday at lunch, Jason was halfway through his Salisbury steak when Allison suddenly stood up.

"Jason, can I talk to you for a minute?"

He looked up, mouth full. "Uh, now?"

"Yeah. It's kind of important." She glanced at Christopher and Scott. "Sorry guys. It's about... my parents. They're fighting again and I need advice."

Christopher's expression shifted to concern. "Oh. I'm sorry, Allison."

"It's fine. Just... family stuff." She looked at Jason pointedly. "Can we go?"

Jason set down his food. "I uh... guess so?"

Christopher caught his eye, giving him a supportive look that said *good luck*. Scott didn't even notice, still focused on his lunch.

Allison led Jason out of the cafeteria, through the hallways, past the gym, until they reached the theatre building. She pulled open a side door and headed backstage, weaving through the dark wings until they reached one of the small dressing rooms.

"In here," she said, flicking on the light.

Jason followed, confused. They'd done this before—used the dressing rooms when they needed to talk privately. The theatre teacher never minded as long as they didn't mess with the costumes.

Allison closed the door behind them.

"So what's going on with your parents?" Jason asked, dropping into one of the chairs.

"That story is bullshit."

Jason blinked. "What?"

"I mean, yeah, they're fighting. But when haven't they been?" Allison leaned against the counter, arms crossed. "That's not why I brought you here."

"Then what the hell, Allison?"

She took a breath. "I need to tell you about my uncle. My mom's little brother."

"What about him?"

"Shut up and listen."

Jason made a zipping gesture across his lips.

"I never got to meet him," Allison said quietly. "Want to know why?"

Jason shook his head.

"Because he's gay. And no one in the family would have anything to do with him. My grandfather threatened to kill him if he came around. At least that's what my mom told me."

Jason felt his stomach drop. "Jesus. Why?"

"Because my grandad is a white racist homophobic bigot." Allison's voice was flat. "He's still my grandad, but I got so pissed when I found out."

"How did you find out?"

Allison's expression shifted—softer now, sadder. "Because he died."

"Jesus, Allison. I'm so sorry."

"Yeah."

"What happened?"

"I don't know much. But I guess he got sick."

"And he died? How old was he?"

"Twenty-eight, I think."

"Twenty-eight? Goddamn."

Allison nodded. "But that's not what I wanted to talk to you about."

"What then?"

"I only learned about him—not because he died—but because his boyfriend came over to give my mom some of his stuff."

Jason heard the words but froze. Boyfriend. Allison looked right at him, and a shitload was spoken without a word being said.

"Wh...whh..." Jason stuttered. "Whaaaat stuff?" He felt like he was swimming through molasses.

"I guess he had some photos. And even some drawings my mom made when they were little." Allison's voice had gone quiet. "Devastated her, seeing them. Said she should've reached out to him. Was too scared after her dad did what he did. But then he was gone. And she never got to say goodbye."

Jason's heart fell out of his chest. Allison had never spoken like this before. He looked over at the wall clock and realized they were going to be late for next class.

Fuck that.

Jason stared at the floor. What did this have to do with him? He knew. But he didn't want to say.

"Jason?" Allison said quietly. "I know I'm being a bitch and sticking my nose in your shit. But I love you, and I don't want you to go through something like that."

They locked eyes. Before he could deny or divert, she calmly laid out her case.

The way he looked at Christopher. The way Christopher looked at him. The smiles. The touches. The laughter. All of it wonderful—the best she'd ever seen Jason. But did he see it himself?

Nothing he could deny.

"I can't," Jason said finally.

"Why not?"

"Jesus fucking Christ, Allison! Look around here! This ain't New

109

York or fucking San Francisco! I'd be murdered! Literally! The fucking farmers of America would beat the shit out of me, and no telling what they'd do to Christopher!"

Something snapped inside him. The pent-up worries and fears and anxieties about not only what he felt but what he thought others would think—all of it erupted like an earthquake, suddenly jolting everything in him.

Allison stood still. He felt guilty after he snapped, quickly starting to apologize, but she stopped him.

"Jason, I know that. You know that. Christopher may know that. But it's nobody's goddamn business other than your own. And—"

"And apparently yours," Jason said, a little too strong.

Allison felt the sting but let it slide.

Jason saw her eyes and felt the sharpness of guilt again. "I'm sorry, Allison. I'm fucking stupid. This... I can't even think about this shit. And..."

"Jason, please don't run away from it. I don't want you to end up like my uncle."

Ouch. Quiet.

"I didn't mean it that way," Allison said quickly.

"How did you mean it then?"

"Listen, I'm trying to be on your side. I just—goddamnit, Jason! I fucking love you and want you to be able to fucking love whomever the fuck you want, if you'd only quit being so goddamned stubborn and cut the shit!" Her voice rose. "Christopher looks like he'd marry you the moment you asked him, and you're too fucking worried about the shit-kickers in their stupid fucking blue jackets to see it!"

She was pissed now. It took Jason back. She never got angry with him. Not like this.

"Listen, Jason." She calmed a bit. "I don't care who you love. Or kiss. Or fuck. Stick it in any hole for all I care!"

Jason couldn't help but laugh, coming out of the heated exchange a bit.

"But be honest with yourself. And him. I just... I want you two to be happy. If that's what you want. And who you are."

This caused Jason to do something he'd never done before—at least not in front of any friends.

He broke down.

And Allison came up and held onto him. Not her normal self.

He cried out all the worries and the anger and hurt. The abandonment. The hatred people gave him for being poor, for not having a dad, for being into weird things rather than sports or girls or whatever. He cried it all out. And neither spoke a word.

"I feel so fucking lonely," he cried.

Allison just held him.

"And I worry that if someone finds out..."

She just listened.

"...they'll hurt us."

It was heartbreaking for her, but she demanded of herself to stay strong. For him.

His sobs became sniffs, and then he pulled away, severely embarrassed at being so vulnerable to another person—naked as much as if he didn't have a stitch on.

"It's okay, Jason," Allison said. "It really is."

"Allison," he said through crumpled hair, tears streaking his cheeks, his black shirt messed more than his normal uniform. "I'm scared."

"I know you are. But as long as you say it, you control it. It doesn't control you."

"I c-can't."

"Jason, yes you can."

"No. I can't."

"Jason," she was pushing now, "how many times have you shown me how to just say whatever the fuck comes to your mind, and whatever happens, happens? The 'Jason-Who-Gives-A-Fuck Plan,' huh?"

He tried to smile while wiping his face dry.

"Jason?"

He sniffled and looked at her.

"What?"

"C'mon."

"I'm not saying it, Allison." He began to return to his normal self.

"I'm not letting you leave."

"I'm NOT saying it, goddamnit." But he was starting to smile.

She gave him "the look."

"Nope! You can't make me!" He began to laugh.

"Jason?" She sounded like a schoolmarm.

"Fine! I'm gay. Happy?"

He spat it at her, and then stopped. So did she. Although her smile grew exponentially with her heart.

Had he just said it? Aloud? He hadn't even said it inside—always dancing around the word. But now he'd said *it*.

"I'm happy for you, Jason. I really, really am."

But he was still pondering what he'd just done. It was a simple, stupid phrase. Something that didn't mean shit. But he knew he'd remember it the rest of his life. Something so simple, yet so profound.

"You okay in there?" She knocked lightly on his head, causing him to jump.

He got quiet, then smiled a little.

"No. I'm not. I'm fucking freaking out. But I will be."

She nodded.

"You've GOT to keep this to yourself, Allison. I swear if—"

"Like I'm going to print it on the headlines of the Cohiscan? Jesus, give me some credit!" She snarked.

"Seriously. I don't want anything to happen to Christopher."

"You're in love."

She said it. And it stopped him in his tracks. Full stop. Period. The End. Done.

"You're in love. You know why?"

He could only stare at her.

"Because you're worried about him. You haven't said one word about yourself."

He hadn't, had he? She was right. He was so worried that if word got out, people would hurt Christopher, and he lov...

My god. Do I love him? Like... *love* love?

"I think you should skip the rest of the day," Allison said. "It's been one hell of a lunch."

He almost didn't hear but recovered. "I can't. I've got... uh..."

"Plans with a certain blonde cutie pie?"

He actually blushed and looked to the ground, bashful even. Jesus! What was he? One of the fucking seven dwarves now?

"Right. Go. Get out of here. My work here is done." She acted like she was an imperial sage elder.

Jason paused and looked serious. "Allison, I'm sorry about your uncle."

Her eyes went back to the harsh reality she'd had when she was talking about him earlier. "Thanks," she said softly.

"I uh... hope your mom... uh... well, I hope she..."

"She misses him," Allison finished, saving him from scrambling to conjure words that couldn't come.

There was nothing else to say.

"Now go."

Jason grabbed his books and turned.

"Oh, Jason?"

"Yeah?"

"Tell him."

He looked puzzled.

She rolled her eyes. "You 'mos are so dumb sometimes."

He flipped her off. They were good friends.

"Tell him what you feel."

He bit back a smile, knowing how difficult that would be.

But her eyes held firm, and he saw no reason to answer.

———

Jason skipped the rest of the day.

He couldn't face sitting in History or Art or any other class pretending everything was normal when his entire world had just shifted on its axis.

I'm gay.

He'd said it out loud. To another person. And she hadn't run screaming. Hadn't looked at him with disgust. Hadn't told him he was going to hell.

She'd held him while he cried. And then told him he was in love.

Jason rode his bike with no destination in mind, just pedaling through Connersville's streets, past the factories and the nice houses and the empty lots where nothing grew but weeds.

You're in love.

Was he? He thought about Christopher. About the way his stomach flipped when Christopher smiled. About how he couldn't stop thinking about him. About how the idea of Christopher getting hurt made Jason want to burn the whole world down.

Yeah. He was in love.

Fuck.

By the time Jason made it home, it was almost dinner time. His mom's car wasn't in the driveway yet. Good. He could decompress before having to put on a normal face.

He went to his room, pulled out his notebook, and stared at the blank page.

Then he started writing.

Things I know:

- I'm gay

- I'm in love with Christopher Avery

- Allison knows and she's okay with it

- Tomorrow night we're going to the farmhouses

- I need to tell him

Jason stared at that last line.

Tell him. Easy for Allison to say. What if he was wrong? What if Christopher didn't feel the same way? What if saying it out loud ruined everything?

But what if it didn't?

What if Christopher felt the same way?

What if tomorrow night, after they saw whatever William and Daniel wanted to show them, Jason found the courage to be honest?

He closed the notebook and shoved it under his mattress.

Tomorrow. Tomorrow night everything would change.

One way or another.

———

Friday morning arrived with Jason's stomach in knots.

Tonight. Tonight they were doing this.

And not just the farmhouses. Tonight, maybe, he'd tell Christopher the truth.

Barnes swept into class with his usual enthusiasm—a human exclamation point in khakis and a polo shirt, probably the only person on earth who could make Driver's Ed feel like a Broadway production.

"Good morning, drivers! Pop quiz time! Don't panic—if you've been paying attention, you'll do great!"

The class groaned as Barnes passed out the quiz sheets. Twenty questions, multiple choice, covering everything from parallel parking to right-of-way rules.

Jason and Christopher worked through it quickly, occasionally catching each other's eyes. When they finished, Barnes collected the papers and launched into his announcement.

"Excellent work, everyone! Now, I have exciting news. Starting Monday, we begin actual behind-the-wheel training! Real cars, real roads, real driving!"

A ripple of excitement went through the class.

"However," Barnes continued, "we only have two vehicles and limited time, so we'll be running on a rotation. Half the class will drive Monday and Wednesday, the other half Tuesday and Thursday. While some pairs are driving, the rest will continue simulator practice and classroom work."

He pulled out a schedule. "Mr. Reynolds and Mr. Avery, you're in the Monday-Wednesday group. Your first session is Monday at 8 AM sharp. Come prepared!"

Jason and Christopher exchanged glances. Monday. Their first real drive.

The rest of class was more simulator work, but Jason could barely focus. His mind kept jumping ahead to tonight. To midnight. To the farmhouses.

To telling Christopher the truth.

When the bell rang, they walked out together.

"Tonight," Christopher said quietly as they climbed the stairs.

"Yeah."

"You still want to do this?"

"Yeah. You?"

"Yeah. I'm terrified, but yeah."

They reached the top. Jason glanced around, making sure no one was close enough to hear.

"Let's meet Country Club parking lot. Midnight. We'll ride out together."

Christopher's relief was visible. "Okay. Midnight."

"Bring your camera. And a flashlight. And maybe—"

"I know. I've got everything ready."

They stood there, neither wanting to leave.

"See you at lunch?" Christopher asked.

"Yeah. Lunch."

———

Which was quieter than usual. Christopher picked at his food, nervous energy radiating off him. Scott was oblivious as always, but Allison kept shooting Jason meaningful looks—supportive ones, encouraging ones.

Finally, as they were cleaning up their trays, Allison caught Jason's arm.

"Whatever you're doing tonight," she said quietly, "be safe."

Jason blinked. "What?"

"You and Christopher. You're both wound tight as springs. You're doing something tonight. It's obvious. I don't know what, but... be safe. Okay?"

"We're just—"

"I don't need details. Just... be careful. Both of you."

After she walked away, Christopher leaned close. "Does she know?"

"About the farmhouses? No."

"About... us?"

Jason's heart kicked up. There was an "us" now. At least in Christopher's mind.

"She knows," Jason said quietly. "About me. But she won't say anything."

Christopher's eyes widened. "You told her?"

"She figured it out. Yesterday. And then she... she made me admit it. To myself."

"And?"

"And she's okay with it. More than okay."

Christopher's expression was unreadable. "Jason, uh... we should..."

"Talk? Yeah," Jason interrupted. "Yeah, we should."

Christopher looked scared, but Jason reassured him it would be okay.

"Let's focus on tonight, okay? We'll talk after. Promise."

Christopher only nodded reluctantly. This was scarier than the ghosts.

———

The rest of Friday passed in a blur. Classes Jason barely paid attention to, teachers whose voices turned into background noise.

Finally—finally—last period ended.

Jason met Christopher at the bike racks.

"Tonight," Christopher said.

"Yeah."

"Make sure you pack everything?"

"I will."

Christopher shifted his backpack. "Jason, I—"

"Tonight," Jason said. "Whatever you want to say, we can talk about it tonight."

Christopher nodded. "Okay. Tonight."

"I should go. Dinner with my mom."

"Yeah. Me too."

They stood there, both scared, both determined.

"Midnight," Jason said.

"Midnight."

Jason watched him ride away, then turned his bike toward home.

A few more hours.

Then everything would change.

———

Dinner that night was quiet. His mom had made chili and cornbread—one of the few things she actually cooked from scratch—and they ate while the TV played in the background.

"You okay, honey?" she asked halfway through. "You've barely touched your food."

"Yeah. Just... long week."

"How's school going?"

"Fine. Good. We're starting real driving."

"That's exciting." She smiled. "My boy, learning to drive. Next thing I know, you'll be borrowing the car."

Jason tried to smile back. "Maybe."

"And how's Christopher? You two seem to be getting close."

"He's good. He's been eating lunch with me and my friends."

"That's wonderful. I'm glad you're making good friends."

The way she emphasized "friends" made Jason's stomach twist, but he just nodded and stared at his bowl.

After dinner, Jason retreated to his room and tried to act normal. Did some homework. Listened to music. Sketched in his notebook.

At nine, he heard his mom go to her room. By nine-thirty, her light was off.

Jason lay in bed, fully clothed under the covers, staring at the ceiling. Waiting.

His backpack sat by the window, ready to go. He'd oiled his bike chain so it wouldn't squeak. Mapped out the quietest route through the house.

The clock on his nightstand ticked away the minutes.

10:00.

10:30.

11:00.

At 11:15, Jason couldn't wait anymore.

He slid out of bed, grabbed his backpack, and crept to the window. Opened it slowly—so slowly—listening for any sound from his mom's room.

Nothing.

He climbed out, dropping onto the grass below with barely a sound. Retrieved his bike from where he'd left it leaning against the house.

The street was empty. Dark. The whole town asleep.

Jason threw his leg over his bike and started pedaling.

The moon was almost full—hanging low and amber, just like in his dreams. The air smelled like autumn and earth and something else. Something electric.

Jason pedaled faster.

Past the last few houses and there, in the parking lot of the country club, was another bike.

Christopher.

Jason's heart kicked up as he rode closer. Christopher stepped out from behind a tree, backpack on, camera around his neck.

"You came," Christopher said.

"Of course I came."

They stood there for a moment, both breathing hard, both scared, both determined.

"Ready?" Jason asked.

Christopher looked west, toward where the farmhouses waited. Looked at the amber moon hanging wrong in the sky. Looked at Jason.

"Yeah," he said. "Let's find out what they want to show us."

They mounted their bikes and started riding.

Together.

West toward the farmhouses. West toward William and Daniel.

West toward whatever truth was waiting for them in the dark.

Chapter 9

Deadly Train

The ride out to the farmhouses felt longer at night.

Jason and Christopher pedaled side by side on Country Club Road, their bikes creating twin shadows in the amber moonlight. The autumn chill had finally overtaken the last vestiges of summer heat, and a slight fog was beginning to form along the ground —thin wisps at first, then thicker patches that seemed to roll and shift like something alive.

It made everything look like a horror film. The kind Jason had watched late at night when his mom was asleep, the kind that made you check under your bed before turning off the lights.

"You okay?" Jason called over.

"Yeah. You?"

"Terrified."

Christopher laughed nervously. "Good. Me too."

They rode in silence for another few minutes. The only sounds were their tires on pavement, their breathing, the occasional rustle of corn. No cars. No houses. Just the two of them and the road and that amber moon hanging low and wrong in the sky, casting everything in a sickly golden light that made the fog glow.

Jason kept glancing at Christopher. At the way the moonlight caught in his hair. At his careful posture even on a bike at midnight. At the determination in the set of his shoulders.

I'm in love with him.

The thought was still new enough to make Jason's chest tight. He'd said it to Allison. Written it in his notebook. But saying it to Christopher—actually saying the words out loud to the person they were about—that was different.

That was terrifying.

"There," Christopher said, pointing ahead.

The farmhouses emerged around the curve.

But at night, with the fog rolling across the ground and that weird moon overhead, everything felt different. More present. More real.

More wrong.

They slowed to a stop at the end of the driveway to the big house, both feet on the ground, both staring.

"It looks..." Christopher trailed off.

"Yeah."

"Like it's watching us."

"Yeah."

The widow's peak loomed above them, its windows dark and empty. But Jason couldn't shake the feeling that something was looking back. That the house itself was aware of them standing there.

"Should we leave our bikes here or bring them closer?" Christopher asked.

"Here's fine. If we need to leave fast, we don't want them too far away."

"Good point."

They leaned their bikes against a tree just off the road, hidden from view if any cars came by. Not that anyone was likely to drive past at midnight, but still. Better safe than sorry.

Jason pulled out his flashlight. Christopher did the same, the beams cutting through the darkness and hitting the fog, making everything glow and swirl. It was beautiful and eerie all at once.

"Where do we start?" Christopher asked.

Jason thought about his dreams. About standing on the widow's peak, looking down at the road. About watching the lantern boy walk up from the smaller farmhouse.

"The widow's peak," he said. "That's where I always am in the dreams. Looking down. That's where we need to be."

"How do we get up there?"

"I don't know. But let's find out."

They ducked under the rusted chain and started up the overgrown driveway. The grass was wet with dew and fog, soaking through their shoes immediately. The air smelled like decay and old wood and earth —that same smell from before, but heavier now. More oppressive.

Their flashlight beams swept through the fog, creating crazy patterns of light and shadow. Every step felt precarious, like the ground might give way beneath them.

They circled around to the back of the house, looking for a way up. The back door hung open, revealing darkness beyond, but Jason wasn't about to go inside. Not with the floors likely rotted through.

"Look," Christopher said, his flashlight beam landing on something metal.

A fire escape. Or what looked like one—old-style metal framework bolted to the back of the house, leading up to the second floor and beyond. Rusty. Ancient. Probably installed decades ago and never maintained.

"You think it'll hold?" Christopher asked.

"Only one way to find out."

Jason grabbed the lowest rung and pulled. The metal groaned but held. He put his weight on it, testing. More groaning. A creak that made his stomach drop. But it didn't give way.

"Okay," he said. "We go slow. One at a time. If it starts to collapse, we bail immediately."

"Deal."

Jason started climbing. Each step brought a protest from the metal— creaks, groans, the occasional shower of rust flakes. But it held. Christopher followed behind, both of them moving carefully, deliberately.

They made it to the second landing. Jason paused, breathing hard, his hands shaking slightly from adrenaline.

"You okay?" he asked Christopher.

"Scared shitless. But okay."

"Same."

They kept climbing. Up to where the fire escape met the roofline. Jason stopped, studying the situation. The metal framework ended here, but the roof extended another few feet to where the widow's peak jutted up.

"We have to get onto the roof," he said.

"Is that safe?"

"Probably not."

"Great."

Jason handed his flashlight to Christopher. "Hold these. I'm going to test it."

He reached out, pressing his palms against the roof. Applied pressure. The wood groaned but didn't give. He pushed harder, using his full weight.

"It's holding," he said. "I think we can make it if we crawl. Distribute our weight."

"This is insane."

"You want to go back?"

Christopher looked at the widow's peak, then back at Jason. "No. Let's do it."

They pocketed their flashlights—they'd need both hands for this. The moonlight would have to be enough.

Jason went first, pulling himself onto the roof and immediately dropping to his belly. The shingles were rough under his hands, some loose, some missing entirely. He could feel the structure sag slightly under his weight.

"Slow," he called back to Christopher. "Stay on your belly. Crawl."

Christopher followed, and Jason's heart was in his throat the entire time. If Christopher fell, if the roof gave way—

But it held.

They crawled side by side toward the widow's peak, inches at a time. When they reached it, Jason grabbed the iron railing and pulled himself up. Reached back for Christopher, grabbing his arm, then his back, pulling him up onto the platform.

The closeness wasn't lost on either of them. Jason's hand on Christopher's back. Christopher's hand gripping Jason's arm. Their faces inches apart as they steadied each other.

"We made it," Christopher breathed.

"Yeah."

They stood carefully, both holding the rusted iron railing, trying not to shift too much for fear of the roof collapsing beneath them. But once they were stable, once they could look around—

"Oh," Christopher said softly.

The view was incredible.

From up here, they could see everything. The road stretching east and west. The cornfields rolling away in every direction. The woods dark against the lighter fields. And far to the east, barely visible through the fog, the lights of Connersville proper.

"You can see the city," Christopher said, pointing. "It's so small from here."

"Look up," Jason said.

Christopher tilted his head back. The stars were everywhere— thousands of them, millions maybe, more than Jason had ever seen. The amber moon hung low but above it, the sky was clear and infinite.

"It's beautiful," Christopher whispered.

"Yeah."

The wind picked up slightly, cutting through their clothes. Neither of them had thought to bring warm jackets. Jason regretted it immediately, feeling Christopher shiver beside him.

But part of him—a bigger part than he wanted to admit—was secretly glad for the cold. Because it gave him an excuse.

He put his arm around Christopher's back, pulling him close.

"Body heat," Jason said. "We need to share body heat."

"Right. Body heat."

But they both knew it was more than that.

They stood there, huddled together against the cold, looking out at the landscape below. The fog continued to roll across the ground, thicker now, creating an otherworldly effect. Everything felt peaceful up here. Quiet. Safe.

Except for the pounding of their hearts as they held onto each other and the rusted railing.

"Where did you see him?" Christopher asked after a few minutes. "In your dreams. The boy with the lantern."

Jason looked down, trying to overlay his memory onto the scene before them. The road was dark. The smaller farmhouse barely visible through the fog. But he remembered the path.

"There," he pointed toward the smaller farmhouse. "He'd come out of that house and walk up this road with his lantern. And I'd be standing here watching him."

They both focused on that spot, staring into the darkness. Waiting.

Nothing. Just the cricket sounds gradually making their way up from below. Just the fog flickering across the ground. Just the wind and their breathing.

Jason felt Christopher start to shiver more violently. Without thinking, he pulled him closer, wrapping his arm more firmly around his back.

"Better?" Jason asked.

"Yeah. Thanks."

Christopher noticed it then—the shift in Jason. The lack of snarkiness. No sarcasm. No deflection. Just genuine concern. Politeness, even. Vulnerability.

It felt like he was getting to see a side of Jason people rarely got to see, if ever.

Minutes passed in silence. The cold seeped deeper. Jason rubbed Christopher's arm, trying to generate warmth.

"Jason?" Christopher said quietly.

"Yeah?"

"You said we'd talk tonight. About... everything."

Jason's chest tightened. "Yeah. We should."

"Allison knows. You said she figured it out."

"Yeah."

"What exactly did she figure out?"

Jason took a breath. The cold air burned his lungs. Or maybe that was fear.

"That I'm..." He stopped. Started again. "That I'm gay."

The words hung in the air between them.

Christopher didn't pull away. Didn't stiffen. Just stayed close, warm against Jason's side.

"And she's okay with it?" Christopher asked.

"More than okay. She supports me. She... she told me about her uncle. Her mom's little brother. He was gay. And her grandfather threatened to kill him. So he stayed away. And then he died. At twenty-eight. And her mom never got to say goodbye."

"That's horrible."

"Yeah. But Allison... she made me admit it. To her. To myself."

He paused, feeling Christopher's eyes burn a hole in him, listening to his own voice quake a little thinking about it.

"And she told me I deserve to be happy. Didn't want me to end up like him. Even if it's scary. Even if it's dangerous."

Christopher was quiet for a long moment. Then: "I knew."

Jason turned to look at him. "What?"

"I knew. About you. I mean, I thought I knew. I hoped I knew." Christopher's voice was soft. "Because I've known about myself since seventh grade. And I've been hiding ever since. Pretending. Being who everyone expects me to be. But with you... I don't have to pretend."

"You're...?"

"Gay. Yeah. I'm gay."

Jason felt something crack open in his chest. Relief. Joy. Terror. All of it at once.

"We're both so fucked," Jason said, and laughed—breathless, half-hysterical.

Christopher laughed too. "Yeah. We really are."

They stood there, holding each other against the cold, both trying to process what they'd just admitted.

"There's more," Christopher said after a moment. "Something else. I can feel it. Something you're not saying."

Jason's stomach flipped. "It's stupid."

"Tell me anyway."

"It's too soon. We barely know each other. It's only been a few weeks and I don't want to scare you off or make you think I'm crazy or—"

"Jason." Christopher pulled back enough to look at him directly. "Just say it."

Jason took a shaky breath. Looked out at the fog-covered landscape because he couldn't look at Christopher's face while saying this.

"I'm in love with you," he said quietly. "I know that sounds insane. I know it's too fast. But I can't stop thinking about you. And the idea of you getting hurt makes me want to burn the whole world down. And when you're not around, I feel like something's missing. And I'm terrified because every time I've ever known anyone to fall in love, it never ends well. It always ends in pain or loss or someone leaving. And I can't... I don't know how to do this. But I'm in love with you anyway."

Silence.

Jason couldn't look at him. Couldn't bear to see rejection or pity or worse—nothing.

"Jason," Christopher said finally.

"It's okay if you don't—"

"Jason, look at me."

Jason forced himself to turn. Christopher's face was soft in the moonlight. His eyes bright. His expression open in a way Jason had never seen before.

"I've dreamed about this," Christopher said. "About someone loving me. Actually loving me. Not the person I pretend to be, but the real me. The one I keep hidden." His hands came up to cup Jason's face. "I've dreamed about it. But I never thought it would actually happen."

"Christopher—"

Christopher leaned in and kissed him.

Not a peck. Not a brief press of lips like they'd both imagined a hundred times but never dared to do. This was real. This was long and deep and transformative. His hands cupped Jason's face, holding him like something precious. Jason's hands gripped Christopher's back, pulling him closer, needing him closer.

The wind picked up around them, colder now, cutting through

their clothes. The fog rolled thicker below. The stars wheeled over-head. And none of it mattered because Christopher was kissing him like he was the only real thing in the entire world.

When Christopher finally pulled back to catch his breath, his eyes were wet.

"I love you too," he whispered. "Jason, I love you too."

Jason's throat was too tight to speak. He just pulled Christopher close again, burying his face against his shoulder, holding on like Christopher might disappear if he let go.

They stood there, wrapped around each other, both crying a little, both laughing a little, both terrified and exhilarated and more alive than either of them had ever felt.

That's when Jason noticed it.

Movement over Christopher's shoulder. Something bluish-grey, translucent, slowly materializing.

His eyes went wide. His body went rigid.

Christopher felt the change immediately. "What? What is it?"

He started to turn, and Jason grabbed him tighter—not to stop him, but to hold onto him.

There, standing at the edge of the widow's peak not five feet from them, was the ghost boy.

The taller one. The one with sandy hair that caught the moon-light. William.

He was looking down at the road. Didn't seem to notice them at all. His expression was focused, intent, waiting for something.

Jason and Christopher froze, barely breathing, holding onto each other.

William's mouth moved—saying something—but there was no sound. Just the wind. Just their breathing. It was like watching a silent movie play out.

Christopher's grip on Jason's arm tightened. Together, they followed William's gaze down to the smaller farmhouse.

The door opened.

A light appeared—warm, yellow, flickering. A lantern.

Daniel emerged, wearing his nightshirt, carrying the lantern. He slowly walked down the road and into the drive before he looked up toward the widow's peak. His mouth moved in the lantern light—whispering something—and William's mouth moved in response.

Even though Jason and Christopher couldn't hear the words, the emotion was clear. Longing. Love. Desperate need.

Then William turned.

And vanished.

He reappeared instantly down below, beside Daniel. Both boys translucent in the moonlight, both silent, both smiling at each other like they held the whole world in that moment.

They began walking. Down the road and toward the old barn by the smaller farmhouse.

"Come on," Jason said, already moving.

They scrambled back across the roof on their bellies. Jason went first, practically sliding down to the fire escape, not caring about the noise anymore. Christopher followed, both of them taking the metal ladder as fast as they dared, not slowing until their feet hit the ground.

Then they ran.

Through the fog, their flashlights bouncing crazily, both trying to catch up to the ghosts who had already disappeared into the barn.

The barn loomed ahead, darker than the darkness around it. That same lean, that same gap in the roof. But there was light inside now—that warm yellow glow from the lantern, spilling out through the cracks in the walls.

Jason and Christopher slowed as they approached, both breathing hard, both trying to be quiet.

They crept to the entrance and peered inside.

William and Daniel stood in the center of the barn. Daniel held the lantern, its flame steady despite the breeze coming through the roof. They were talking—Jason could see their mouths moving—but still no sound reached him.

Then William took the lantern from Daniel and set it on the ground. Stepped closer. Put his hands on Daniel's face and kissed him.

This kiss was different from the one Jason and Christopher had just shared. It had the same intensity, the same love. But there was something desperate in it. Something final.

When they pulled apart, William was smiling. But there was sadness there. Resignation.

He said something. Daniel shook his head, vehement, and said something back. An argument. Or a plea.

William touched Daniel's face one more time. Then he picked up the lantern and walked toward the barn entrance.

Toward Jason and Christopher.

"Hide," Jason hissed, pulling Christopher behind a broken piece of equipment.

William walked right past them. So close Jason could have reached out and touched him. But William didn't see them. Didn't react to their presence at all.

He walked out of the barn and headed toward the tracks.

Daniel stood frozen in the center of the barn, watching him go. His expression was anguished. Desperate. Like he wanted to follow but couldn't make himself move.

Then he did move. Running after William, his mouth open— calling out, though still Jason couldn't hear the words. But he could see the panic in Daniel's face.

"Come on," Jason said, following.

They ran through the fog, through the woods, stumbling over roots and rocks. By the time they reached the clearing by the railroad tracks, William was already there, standing on the rails, the lantern at his feet.

Waiting.

Daniel came out of the woods and stopped at the edge of the tracks. He said something. William shook his head.

A sound in the distance. Low. Rumbling. Growing louder.

A train.

"No," Christopher whispered. "Oh god, no."

Jason was equally struck by how vivid everything was and the realization they could *hear the train*. How was this possible?

The steam whistle blew. Long and mournful, echoing across the empty fields. William's head snapped toward the sound, toward the train coming around the bend.

But he didn't move off the tracks.

Instead, William looked down. Deliberately. At his feet. At the railroad tie beneath him.

He adjusted his position. Carefully. Testing the tie, finding the spot where the ballast had eroded away.

Then he placed his foot there. Wedged it in. Pushed down.

"Oh god," Jason breathed. "He's doing it on purpose."

William tried to pull his foot free—yanking at it, his face showing something like panic. But Jason could see it. The way he didn't pull quite hard enough. The way his movements looked frantic but weren't fully committed.

He was making it look like an accident.

The train was closer now, the rumble turning into a roar, the headlamp cutting through the fog like a blade. The steam whistle blew again and again.

Daniel ran onto the tracks. Grabbed William's arms, pulling, trying to free him. His mouth was open, screaming—Jason could see it even if he couldn't hear it. His whole body convulsing with the effort.

But William's foot stayed stuck.

Because William wanted it to stay stuck.

Daniel grabbed William's face, kissed him hard and fast and desperate, knowing this was the last time, then tried once more to pull him free.

Nothing.

The train bore down on them, massive and unstoppable, the whistle screaming, the fog swirling in its wake.

Daniel fell back, off the tracks, into the gravel.

William looked at him. Their eyes met across that small distance.

And William stopped struggling. Just stood there. Waiting.

Then the train hit.

Christopher screamed and fell to the ground.

Jason couldn't move, couldn't breathe, couldn't look away.

The train passed through William like he wasn't there. Because he wasn't there. This had happened a hundred years ago. This was memory, not present. This was the past playing out on an endless loop.

When the train was gone—just vanished into the fog like it had never existed—William was gone too.

Daniel lay in the gravel beside the tracks, curled into a ball, sobbing. Silent sobbing. The kind that shook his whole body but made no sound.

The lantern still burned where William had left it. The only light in the darkness.

Then everything began to fade. Daniel. The lantern. The tracks themselves seemed to blur and lose solidity.

And Jason and Christopher were alone in a cornfield at midnight, staring at empty railroad tracks under an amber moon.

———

Neither of them spoke for a long time.

Christopher was shaking. Jason realized he was too. His whole body trembling, teeth chattering, and not from the cold.

Christopher made a sound—half sob, half gasp—and rose to his knees in the gravel.

Jason dropped beside him immediately, wrapping his arms around him as Christopher buried his face against Jason's shoulder.

"He knew," Christopher choked out. "Did you see? He knew the train was coming. He stood there. On the tracks. Waiting for it."

Jason had seen. William positioning himself carefully. Testing the tie where his foot would go. Making sure.

"And his foot," Christopher continued, his voice breaking. "When he... when he tried to pull free... he wasn't trying hard enough. He could have... if he'd really wanted to..."

"He didn't want to," Jason whispered. "He wanted to die."

"But Daniel came. Daniel tried to save him and William just... he just let it happen. He made Daniel watch."

They were both crying now—ugly, gasping sobs that hurt Jason's chest and made it hard to breathe.

"Why?" Christopher asked. "Why would he do that? Why would he make Daniel see that?"

"Because..." Jason's voice cracked. "Because he couldn't... he couldn't handle being..."

"Being..." Christopher finished. "Being gay? Loving Daniel? Living in a world that would never let them be together?"

"He..." Jason couldn't finish the sentence.

"He killed himself!" Christopher yelled. "He stood on those tracks and he let that train hit him because dying was easier than living with who he was."

The words hung in the fog-thick air.

"Jesus! I can't believe Daniel had to watch," Jason said. "He fucking tried to save him. Had to live with that for forty fucking years."

"Alone," Christopher added. "He lived alone. He fucking was... alone."

They clung to each other, both shaking, both crying, both trying to process what they'd just witnessed.

"I can't..." Christopher gasped. "I can't stop seeing it. His face when the train... when it..."

"I know. I know."

"And Daniel screaming. Even though we couldn't hear it, we could see it. We could see him screaming."

Jason held Christopher tighter. "It's okay. It's okay."

"It's not okay!" Christopher pulled back, his face wet, his eyes wild. "It's not okay! William loved him and it killed him! Loving Daniel killed him!"

The implication hung between them.

"No," Jason said firmly, cupping Christopher's face. "No. That was... that was a hundred years ago. Things are different now."

"Are they?" Christopher's voice was desperate. "Are they really? Because it fucking feels the same. It's so *fucked up!*"

"But we're not..." Jason struggled to find the words. "We're not giving up. We're not... we're not doing what William did."

"How do you know?"

"Because we're not alone. We have each other. And we have Allison. And... And we're going to be careful. We're going to be smart."

"But what if we fuck up?" Christopher was crying harder now.

"What if someone finds out? What if the everyone won't let us... what if we can't..."

"We can," Jason said, even though he wasn't sure. Even though fear was eating him alive. "We have to. Because the alternative is... the alternative is... We're going to be okay, Christopher. We just are."

Christopher nodded, swallowing hard and calming down a little. "It's got to be better. Right? It has to be better than back then. Right?"

"Yeah. It is. It has to be."

But they both heard the uncertainty in Jason's voice.

They sat there in the gravel beside the tracks, holding each other, crying for William and Daniel and for themselves. For the impossibility of loving someone the world said you couldn't love. For the fear that came with it. For the knowledge that even admitting it out loud could get you killed.

"I'm scared," Christopher whispered. "Jason, I'm so scared."

"Me too."

"But I meant what I said. Up on the widow's peak. I love you."

"I love you too."

They held each other as the fog continued to roll, as the horror of what they'd witnessed slowly settled into something they could carry.

"No one knows," Christopher said after a long while. "No one knows what really happened to them. The newspaper said it was an accident. That his foot got caught."

"But we know."

"Yeah. We know."

"William killed himself because he couldn't live with being gay. And Daniel spent forty years grieving alone."

"It's the saddest thing I've ever heard."

"Yeah. It is."

They stood up slowly, helping each other, both unsteady. Their clothes were damp from the dew and fog. Christopher's jeans were torn at his knees. Jason's shirt had dark streaks from the roof shingles. Their faces were blotchy from crying. They looked at each other—really looked—and saw their shared trauma reflected back.

"We're the only ones who know the truth," Jason said.

"Yeah."

"About William and Daniel. About what really happened."

"And about us," Christopher added quietly.

"Allison sorta' knows."

"She does?"

"I didn't say anything but she knows."

Christopher looked torn, but grabbed Jason's hand and held tight.

They walked back down the road towards the bigger house, moving slowly, neither wanting to let go of the other. When they reached their bikes, they stood there, close enough to touch.

"It's still dangerous," Christopher said. "Just because I love you."

"Yeah."

"But we're doing it anyway. Fuck everyone else."

"Yeah. Fuck them," Jason smiled a little, seeing how worked up Christopher had gotten, and how his raw, true to life emotion was spilling over from his carefully controlled persona most people saw.

Christopher leaned in and kissed him—soft, gentle, still tasting of tears. "I love you."

"I love you too."

"We're going to be okay. Right?"

Jason wanted to say yes. Wanted to promise that everything would work out, that they'd be safe, that their story would have a happier ending than William and Daniel's.

But he couldn't lie. Not after what they'd just seen.

"I don't know," he said honestly. "But we're going to try."

Christopher nodded. "I guess that has to be enough."

They climbed on their bikes and started riding back toward town. Side by side, like they'd come. But everything was different now.

They'd confessed their love. They'd kissed. They'd witnessed a tragedy from a hundred years ago that felt like a warning, a mirror, a prophecy they were desperately trying not to fulfill.

They rode in silence, both lost in their own thoughts, both still shaking slightly from the trauma of what they'd seen. The amber moon was lower now, the fog still thick in patches, the world absolutely silent except for the sound of their tires on pavement and their breathing.

Jason kept glancing over at Christopher. Making sure he was okay. Making sure he was still there.

Something had shifted in him. Watching William die—watching Daniel fail to save him—had awakened something protective in Jason. Something fierce. Christopher was his now. His to protect. His to keep safe. And Jason would be damned if he'd let the world do to Christopher what it had done to William.

By the time they reached Dorsett Drive, it was 2:30 in the morning. The moon had moved across the sky but was still visible, still that wrong amber color. The streets were empty. The houses dark.

They stopped at the corner where Christopher's street branched off.

"I should..." Christopher gestured toward his house.

"Yeah."

But neither moved.

Jason looked at Christopher—really looked. At the tear tracks still visible on his face. At the way his hands were shaking slightly. At the exhaustion and trauma and love all mixed together in his expression.

"Come here," Jason said.

Christopher stepped closer. Jason pulled him into a hug—tight, protective, like he could shield Christopher from everything that had happened tonight just by holding him close enough.

"You need to get some sleep," Jason said quietly.

"So do you."

"I will. But you first. I need to know you're okay."

"I'm okay. We're okay."

Jason pulled back just enough to see Christopher's face. "I love you. You know that, right? I really mean it. Not just... not just because we said it tonight. I mean it."

Christopher's expression softened. "I know. I love you too."

"Tonight changed things."

"Yeah. It did."

"We're going to be okay," Jason said, and he was surprised by how certain his voice sounded. "I don't know how yet, but we are. I promise."

136

Christopher stared at him, something shifting in his expression. Warmth. Gratitude. Love.

"You're different right now," Christopher said softly.

"What do you mean?"

"Protective. Like... like you'd fight anyone who tried to hurt me."

"I would."

Christopher smiled—small but genuine. "No one's ever... I've never had anyone feel that way about me before."

"Well, you do now."

Christopher leaned in and kissed him—one more time, soft and sweet. "Thank you."

"For what?"

"For loving me. For not running away after what we saw. For being... you."

Jason's chest felt tight. "Get some sleep. Okay? And call me tomorrow. Or I'll call you. Just... let me know you're okay."

"I will. I promise."

"Good."

They stood there a moment longer, neither wanting to leave. Finally, Christopher pulled away.

"Goodnight, Jason."

"Goodnight."

Jason watched Christopher ride down his street toward his house. Watched him get off his bike, walk it quietly up to the garage, glance back once, and wave. He waved back.

Only when Christopher had disappeared inside did he turn his bike toward home.

The ride back was lonely. The streets felt emptier without Christopher beside him. The fog seemed thicker. The amber moon more ominous.

But Jason felt something he hadn't felt in a long time.

Purpose.

He had someone to protect now. Someone who loved him back. Someone worth fighting for.

And if the world tried to take that away—if it tried to do to them what it had done to William and Daniel—Jason would fight back.

He wouldn't give up.
Not like William had.

———

When Jason climbed back through his bedroom window, the house was still silent. His mom still asleep. Rick still passed out on the couch —Jason could hear him snoring.

He stripped to his underwear, messed up his bed to make it look slept in, and collapsed onto it.

He was exhausted. But every time he closed his eyes, he saw William on those tracks. Saw his foot stuck. Saw the train coming. Saw Daniel screaming.

Jason pulled out his notebook with shaking hands and started writing.

> *What I learned tonight:*
> *- William and Daniel were together*
> *- William killed himself on purpose*
> *- He made Daniel watch*
> *- Daniel spent 40 years alone*
> *- I told Christopher I love him*
> *- He loves me back*
> *- We kissed on the widow's peak*
> *- We watched William die*
> *- We cried together*
> *- We're the only ones who know the truth*
> *- I'm terrified*
> *- But I'm not giving up*
> *- We're __not__ going to end up like them*
> *- We can't*
> *- I need to protect him*
> *- I __will__ protect him*

He stared at those last two lines for a long time, then added one more:

- Please God, don't let us end up like them

Jason closed the notebook and shoved it under his mattress.

He was exhausted. Every time he closed his eyes, he saw William on those tracks—probably would for a long time.

But underneath the trauma, underneath the fear, was something else. Determination. He'd said the words, and Christopher had said them back. They'd kissed on the widow's peak while ghosts moved below them. They'd promised to be careful, to be smart, to fight for what they had.

Tomorrow he'd call Christopher. They'd talk it through, process what they'd seen, remind each other that 1989 wasn't 1890. Monday, they'd sit side by side in Driver's Ed like always, pretending to be just friends while knowing they were so much more. It would be hard. Dangerous. It would require them to hide and lie and be constantly careful.

But it would be worth it.

Jason finally let himself sleep, the memory of Christopher's kiss still warm on his lips, the words *I love you too* echoing in his mind. And underneath it all, a quiet promise—to himself, to Christopher, to the ghost of a boy who'd made a different choice a hundred years ago.

He wouldn't give up. No matter what.

Chapter 10

Ghostly Family Trees

C hristopher couldn't sleep.

He lay in his bed, staring at the ceiling, watching the first hints of dawn creep through his blinds. His body was exhausted—bone-deep, aching tired—but his brain wouldn't shut up.

The ghosts. The train. William's foot stuck in that tie—*deliberately* stuck. The look on Daniel's face as he watched the person he loved die. Screaming silently. Trying to save him and failing.

How had Daniel lived with that? Forty years of waking up every morning knowing he couldn't save William. Knowing William had chosen death over a life with him. What had Daniel told the sheriff? His family? What lies had he constructed to hide the truth?

Christopher didn't know if he could have done it. Carried that secret alone for forty years. Never telling anyone what really happened. Never being able to grieve properly because grief would require explaining why it hurt so much, why losing a *friend* felt like losing everything.

He rolled over, pulling the covers up to his chin. His mind kept circling back to the barn. To William and Daniel arguing—he'd seen their mouths moving, seen the desperation in Daniel's expression.

What had they been fighting about? Why had William fled? And why hadn't Daniel immediately followed?

Something didn't make sense.

Christopher couldn't help it. He kept imagining if it had been him and Jason instead of those two. He would have stopped him, wouldn't he? Would have told him they'd figure something out. That dying wasn't the answer.

But what *was* the answer?

This was 1989, not 1890. A hundred years of progress. Things were different now.

Except... were they?

Christopher thought about Connersville. About the way people talked. About the slurs he'd heard thrown around in the hallways at school. About the way even the word "gay" was used as an insult, as something shameful, as something wrong.

What solution would he and Jason have had in 1890? Run away? Where would they go? How would they live? Two teenage boys with no money, no education, no way to support themselves. They'd have been found and dragged back. Or worse.

Maybe William had looked at all the options and realized there weren't any. Maybe dying had seemed like the only way out.

Christopher's chest tightened. No. He and Jason weren't going to end up like that. They couldn't.

His thoughts drifted to Jason. To what had happened on the widow's peak just before everything went wrong.

I'm in love with you.

Had Jason really said that? Had Christopher really said it back?

I love you too.

His heart sank into the warmth of his covers. Jason was his boyfriend. An honest-to-god, real boyfriend. The boy he'd been crushing on since the first day of Driver's Ed was his.

And the way Jason had changed after witnessing William's death —the protectiveness, the fierce determination. Jason holding him while he cried. Jason promising to keep him safe. Jason being strong for both of them when Christopher was falling apart.

That pseudo "don't give a shit" attitude Jason displayed for everyone else was a facade. Christopher had seen who he truly was. Although he suspected Jason wouldn't reveal that vulnerable side in public. Maybe ever. Maybe only with Christopher.

That thought made him feel special. And terrified. And overwhelmed with love.

He spent another hour tossing and turning before giving up on sleep. If he couldn't rest, he might as well wake up properly.

The shower helped. Hot water beating down on his shoulders, washing away some of the grit and fog-smell and fear. He stood under the spray until it started to run cold, then got out and dressed carefully. Saturday clothes—jeans, a plain blue t-shirt. His hair combed neatly even though no one would see him except his parents.

Habit.

Downstairs, his dad was already up, reading the paper at the kitchen table with his coffee.

"Morning," Christopher said.

"Morning." His dad looked up, studied him. "You're up early for a Saturday."

"Couldn't sleep."

"Hmm." His dad went back to the paper, then said, casually: "Did you leave your bike outside last night?"

Christopher's stomach dropped. "What?"

"Your bike. It was outside this morning. I could have sworn I saw it in the garage when I locked up last night."

Christopher's mind raced. He was terrible at lying. Always had been. Couldn't bluff in poker to save a dollar. When faced with a situation where he didn't want to tell the truth, he usually did the only thing he could: kept quiet.

"Huh," he said noncommittally, pouring himself orange juice.

His dad watched him over the top of the paper. "Everything okay?"

"Yeah. Fine."

"You sure?"

"Yeah, Dad. I'm sure."

His father studied him a moment longer, then went back to his reading. But Christopher could feel the question hanging in the air.

His dad was more curious than anything, not angry. But Christopher realized that even if he was being careful, this sneaking-out business was going to screw him eventually.

He needed to be smarter. They both did.

Christopher ate breakfast mechanically—cereal, toast, more orange juice. His mom came down around eight, bright and cheerful as always. She kissed his dad's cheek, ruffled Christopher's hair (which he immediately tried to fix), and started making herself coffee.

"Big plans today?" she asked.

"Not really. Thought I might go back to the library."

"Again?" But she sounded pleased, not suspicious. "You and Jason must really be into this project."

"Yeah. It's... it's interesting."

More interesting than you know, he thought.

It was still only 8:30. Too early to call Jason, Christopher figured. Jason, the "bad boy who was really a sweetheart," didn't seem the type to get up early unless he had to. Especially since they'd been out until nearly 3 AM.

Christopher figured Jason would sleep until noon.

He couldn't have been more wrong.

Jason had tossed and turned for what felt like hours, sleep evading him completely. Every time he closed his eyes, he saw William on those tracks. Saw Daniel screaming. Saw the train passing through like William was already a ghost.

Finally, beyond exhausted, he must have drifted off because suddenly he was back in the dream.

The same dream he'd been having for weeks. Standing on the widow's peak, looking down at the dark road. The amber moon overhead. The fog rolling across the ground.

Below, the door to the smaller farmhouse opened. Daniel emerged with his lantern, the flame steady despite the breeze. He began walking up the road, just like always.

Jason watched, his dream-self unable to move, unable to call out.

Daniel reached the base of the house. Looked up.

But this time—

This time, beside Jason on the widow's peak, William didn't just stand there looking down at Daniel.

This time, William turned and looked directly at Jason.

Their eyes met. Held.

William's mouth moved. Speaking words Jason couldn't hear. But the look in his eyes was clear: *Help him. Don't let him end up like me.*

Jason tried to respond, tried to say something, but no sound came out.

William's image flickered. Started to fade.

Help him.

Jason woke with a start, gasping, his heart hammering. The red LEDs on his alarm clock showed he'd only been asleep fifteen minutes.

Fifteen minutes. That was all. But it had felt like hours.

Had William seen him? Like, really *seen* him? Not just looked in his direction but actually seen him, acknowledged him, tried to communicate with him?

Jason sat up, running his hands through his hair. He needed to pee. Needed to move. Needed to do something other than lie there replaying that moment over and over.

He walked down the hallway toward the bathroom, the early morning light just starting to filter through the living room windows and nearly bumped into Rick coming out from his mom's bedroom. He had been passed out on the couch earlier—Jason had heard him snoring when he came in.

Rick stopped, looked at Jason, grunted, and moved on.

Jason quickly shut himself in the bathroom, peed, washed his hands and face. Stared at himself in the mirror. He looked like hell: dark circles under his eyes, face pale and drawn, like he'd aged a year overnight.

Back in his room, he couldn't just lie there. He pulled out his notebook and a flashlight, re-reading what he'd written just a few hours earlier.

I need to protect him. I will protect him.

He felt so strongly about it. But now, in the harsh light of morning (well, the harsh light of his flashlight), he wondered how he would actually protect Christopher.

There was no question he would. But he was a dork. A loser. A white trash kid who didn't have money and no knowledge of how to fight or do... well... anything useful. What was *he* able to do? Bitch at someone? Call them a dumb fuck if they so much as gave his boyfriend any shit?

God, he was a loser.

Still, something in his belly tightened with determination. He would protect Christopher the way he would want to be protected. He wouldn't abandon him.

Like...

Like he had been.

Jason never wallowed in self-pity. That was bullshit. Shit happened in life. Get over it. Move on.

But he also never let out what hurt him most. And he wasn't about to start now.

Fuck his dad. Fuck him for leaving. Fuck him for walking out without even saying goodbye, without a single fucking explanation. Fuck him for making Jason and his mom literally scratch to keep a roof over their heads and food on the table while he was off somewhere living his life like they didn't exist. Fuck the kids at school who called him "Salvation Army" and laughed at his thrift store jeans. Fuck the nice neighborhoods where people like Christopher lived, where dads stuck around and moms didn't have to count quarters for groceries. Fuck all of it.

But he wasn't going to cry about it. He just wasn't.

Yet he did. Quietly. Face pressed into his pillow so no one would hear.

He was going to protect Christopher, goddamnit. Just like he'd wanted someone to protect him.

It just was going to be that way.

By 9:30, Jason couldn't wait anymore. He picked up the phone and dialed Christopher's number.

It rang twice before someone picked up.

"Hello?" A woman's voice. Christopher's mom.

"Hi, um, is Christopher there? This is Jason. From school."

"Oh! Jason, hello! Yes, just a moment."

He heard her call for Christopher, heard footsteps, heard the phone being passed over.

"Hello?" Christopher's voice, slightly breathless.

"Hey. It's me."

"Jason." Christopher's voice immediately softened. "Are you okay? I've been thinking about you all morning."

"Yeah. I'm... I'm okay. You?"

"Couldn't sleep. Can't stop thinking about last night."

"Yeah. Me too." Jason lowered his voice even though his mom was at work and Rick was passed out again. "Listen, I was thinking... do you want to go back to the library? See if we can find anything else about William and Daniel?"

"Yes." Christopher's response was immediate. "I've been thinking the same thing. Something about last night doesn't make sense."

"The barn. Right? Their argument?"

"Yeah. And why Daniel didn't immediately follow him. What were they fighting about?"

"We need to know more." Jason paused. "Can you meet me there? Like, around noon?"

"Yeah. I'll be there."

"Okay. See you then."

"Jason?"

"Yeah?"

"I'm glad you called."

"Me too."

After they hung up, Jason felt lighter. Just hearing Christopher's voice had helped. Knowing they were on the same page, that Christopher was okay, that they'd see each other soon.

He showered, dressed in his usual uniform of jeans and a black t-shirt, and tried to eat something. His mom had left before he woke up —early shift at the bank—but there was cereal in the cabinet and milk in the fridge.

By the time he headed out on his bike, he felt almost human again.

Christopher hung up the phone and turned to find his mother watching him from the kitchen doorway.

"That was Jason," he said unnecessarily.

"I gathered." She smiled. "You two are going back to the library?"

"Yeah. We want to... we're trying to find out more about those boys who lived at the farmhouse. For the project."

Christopher's mom set down her coffee cup. "You know, I could help. The head librarian there—Carolyn Patterson—she and I work together sometimes. She helps out with the junior high library. I could call ahead, let her know you're coming. Maybe she could pull some resources?"

Christopher felt panic rising. This was supposed to be quiet research. Under the radar. How did you tell your mom what you'd seen without being classified as a number-one weirdo?

"We can handle it," he said quickly. "It's no big deal. Just curiosity. Part of a school project about local history."

But his mom was already reaching for the phone. "It won't take a minute. Carolyn loves this kind of thing. And they have a staff member—Margaret—who's an amateur genealogist. She might be able to help track down family connections."

"Mom, really, we—"

But she was already dialing. Christopher watched in growing horror as his mom chatted pleasantly with Carolyn, explaining what Christopher had told her. The librarian apparently got excited, said she had some old resources they could look at, suggested getting Margaret involved.

"What are the names?" his mom asked, phone tucked against her shoulder.

Christopher felt overwhelmed. How was he going to tell Jason that this had taken on a life of its own? Weren't they just talking about being discreet and staying under the radar? Now half the library staff and his mother knew.

Well, at least they only knew about the ghost boys. Not about... the other thing.

"Christopher?" His mom was waiting. "The names?"

"William Thorne Junior," Christopher said reluctantly. "And Daniel Hartley."

His mom repeated them into the phone, then listened, nodded, thanked Carolyn, and hung up.

"All set! Margaret will start pulling records before you get there. This is going to be wonderful research for your project!"

Christopher tried to smile. Tried not to look like his carefully controlled world was spiraling out of control.

"Thanks, Mom."

"Of course, honey. When are you heading over?"

"Around noon. Jason's meeting me there."

"I'll drive you. I want to pop in and say hello to Carolyn anyway."

Christopher's stomach sank but he nodded. There was no getting out of this now.

Jason arrived at the library first. He locked his bike at the rack and stood there, waiting, anxiety building in his chest.

He'd kissed Christopher last night. Multiple times. They'd confessed their love on a widow's peak in the middle of the night while fog rolled around them like something out of a gothic novel.

And now they were meeting in broad daylight in a public place and Jason had no idea how to act.

Were they different now? Did Christopher expect him to be different? Should he—

A car pulled into the parking lot.

Christopher's mom's car.

Christopher got out of the passenger side, looking distressed. He spotted Jason and immediately hurried over.

"I tried to call you back but you'd already left," Christopher said in a rush. "My mom called ahead and they're doing research for us and she insisted on driving me here because she wanted to make sure we got connected with the right people and I'm sorry, I didn't know how to—"

"Breathe," Jason said, putting a hand on Christopher's arm before remembering where they were and quickly pulling back. "It's okay. We're just doing a school project, right? That's what you told her?"

"Yeah, but—"

"Then we're fine. Let's just... let's see what they found. It might actually help."

Christopher looked at him, something settling in his expression. "You're not mad?"

"No. I'm not mad." Jason wanted so badly to kiss him. To pull him close and tell him everything would be okay. But they were standing on Grand Avenue in broad daylight with Christopher's mom thirty feet away.

Later. They'd figure it out later.

Christopher seemed to understand. Their eyes met, held just a beat too long, communicated everything they couldn't say aloud.

"Come on," Christopher said. "Let's get this over with."

Inside, Jason was introduced to Carolyn Patterson, the head librarian, who greeted him like they were old friends. She was in her fifties, with steel-gray hair pulled back in a neat bun and reading glasses on a chain around her neck.

"You must be Jason! Christopher's told us so much about your project. This is wonderful—young people interested in local history. We don't get enough of that."

Christopher's mom stood beside Carolyn, beaming. Jason could feel her studying him—not unkindly, just... observantly. Like she was trying to figure something out.

"Come on," Carolyn said. "Margaret's already pulled some materials. She's very excited to help."

They were led to a side table near the archives where a plump middle-aged woman who looked exactly like a librarian sat surrounded by papers and old ledgers. She looked up as they approached and smiled warmly.

"You must be the young researchers! Carolyn says you're researching the Thorne and Hartley families?"

Christopher's mom gave Margaret a quick hug. They obviously knew each other from Diane's job at the junior high library.

"Yes," Christopher said. "We're just curious about the boys who lived there. William Thorne Junior and Daniel Hartley."

"Well, you picked an interesting pair," Margaret said, gesturing for them to sit. "I've already found quite a bit."

She pulled out documents they'd already seen at the library—census records, death certificates. But then she pointed out things they hadn't noticed.

"See here?" She indicated William's death record. "His father's name was William Thorne Senior. He was quite prominent in town—ran for mayor in 1888. Lost, but still. He was well-known."

She pulled out another document. "And here—the family came from Philadelphia. William Senior worked for the Baltimore & Ohio Railroad. He took a promotion and moved the family to Connersville shortly after the Civil War."

Jason and Christopher leaned in, fascinated despite themselves.

"William had an older brother who died young," Margaret continued. "That made William Junior the eldest surviving son." She traced her finger along the census records. "Given his father's position with the railroad and their prominence in the community, the family would have expected him to follow that path—railroad career, maybe take over the farmland, eventually settle nearby with a family of his own." She looked up. "Until he died in that accident. Must have devastated them."

"What happened to them?" Christopher asked. "After William died?"

"Well, his younger sister was all that remained. Sarah Thorne. She was about eighteen when William died."

Christopher's mom, who had been standing back letting Margaret work, suddenly stepped forward. "Can you look into her? Sarah?"

"Of course."

Margaret pulled out more documents, cross-referencing records. "Let's see... Sarah Thorne married in 1892, two years after her brother's death. Her husband was..." She traced her finger down the page.

"Thomas Avery. He moved from Hamilton, Ohio. Helped set up a dry goods store over by the depot on Conwell Street."

Christopher's mom leaned over Margaret's shoulder. "Avery? That's my husband's family name."

"Really?" Margaret's eyes lit up. "Well then, let me see..."

She pulled out more documents, started constructing a family tree on a blank piece of paper. Jason and Christopher watched in growing shock as she traced the line from Sarah Thorne and Thomas Avery down through the generations.

"Yes, look here. They had three children. The eldest son—Thomas Junior—he would have been your husband's grandfather, or great-grandfather perhaps?"

Christopher's mom was staring at the documents. "Mark barely knows anything about this. His grandparents died when he was young, and his father never liked talking about the past." She shook her head slowly. "There was a farm, I think. Somewhere outside of town. But something happened—some kind of family tragedy—and after that, they just... stopped talking about it."

She turned to Christopher, and her expression was a mix of wonder and something else. Something heavier.

"Christopher, this means William Thorne was your great-great-great-uncle."

The words hung in the air.

Jason's jaw dropped. He literally could not close his mouth. Could not breathe.

Christopher had gone white. "What?"

"William Thorne. The boy who died in 1890. He was your blood relative."

Jason stood like a codfish—mouth wide open, unable to process what he was hearing.

Christopher just stared at the family tree Margaret had drawn, at the line connecting William Thorne's sister Sarah to the Avery family, down through the generations, ending at his name.

William was his family.

The boy they'd watched die on the railroad tracks. The boy who'd killed himself because he couldn't live with being gay. The boy who'd

151

loved Daniel so much and been so desperate he'd chosen death over a life without him.

That was Christopher's great-great-great-uncle.

"Boys?" Christopher's mom was looking at them with concern. "Are you alright? I thought you'd find this fascinating. Christopher, this is part of your family history!"

Christopher couldn't speak. Neither could Jason.

"We never knew," Christopher's mom continued, excitement building. "I need to tell your father about this. His family—our family—owned those farmhouses. And that boy, William, he was..." She trailed off, studying their faces. "What's wrong? You both look like you've seen a ghost."

Jason made a strangled sound that might have been a laugh if it wasn't so close to a sob.

Christopher found his voice. "We're fine. It's just... it's a lot to process."

"I suppose it is," his mom said, though she still looked puzzled by their reaction. "History coming alive like this. It's quite something."

Margaret pulled a few more documents, continued building out the family tree. She found connections to Christopher's grandparents, started mapping out the full Avery line. Jason and Christopher sat there in stunned silence, trying to act normal while their entire understanding of the situation shifted.

William wasn't just some random ghost boy from a hundred years ago.

He was Christopher's family.

And he'd killed himself rather than live with being gay.

And now Christopher—his great-great-great-nephew—was in the exact same situation. In love with another boy. Terrified of being discovered. Desperate to find a way to make it work.

History wasn't just repeating itself.

It was fucking rhyming.

After what felt like hours but was probably only thirty minutes, Margaret declared she'd found enough for them to have a solid foundation for their "school project." She'd need more time to fill in all the details, but she could continue researching if they wanted.

"That would be wonderful," Christopher's mom said. "Thank you so much, Margaret."

Outside, standing by the car, Christopher suddenly turned to his mom. "Can Jason spend the night tonight? We could work on the project together."

Jason's eyes went wide, but Christopher didn't look at him—didn't give him a chance to refuse.

"That's a wonderful idea," his mom said, smiling. "But only if Jason's mother approves."

Jason felt his heart start to pound. Spend the night. At Christopher's house. With Christopher.

"She's at work," Jason said. "At the bank. Just a couple blocks away."

"Can we go ask her?" Christopher pressed. "Please?"

"Well, I don't want to interrupt her at work..."

"It'll be fine," Jason said quickly. "The bank closed at 2:30 on Saturdays so we have just enough time to get there."

Christopher's mom looked between them, something shifting in her expression that Jason couldn't quite read. "Alright. Let's go ask."

Jason's mom was busy finishing up with a customer when they arrived. She looked rushed, but then she saw Jason standing with a woman she recognized but didn't know and—she assumed—Christopher. The boy Jason had mentioned.

This must be his mother, judging by the resemblance.

But why were they all here? Had something happened?

Her manager nodded for her to close up her drawer, noticing her son there. She gave a "one moment" finger gesture, finished filing her last items, and locked everything away.

"Hey, Mom," Jason said before she could even reach them.

"This is—" he started.

Christopher's mom stepped forward, extending her hand. "Hi, I'm Diane Avery. Christopher's mother. It's so nice to finally meet you."

Jason's mom shook her hand, feeling suddenly underdressed even though she was in her work clothes. Diane wasn't dressed especially lavishly, but she had that effortless put-together quality that made Jason's mom feel... less than. But Diane's smile was warm, her hand-shake firm but not aggressive, and there was no hint of judgment in her eyes.

"I'm Sarah Reynolds. It's nice to meet you too. Jason's mentioned Christopher."

"This is my son," Diane said, gesturing. "Christopher, but I assume you've met already?"

"No, Jason's mentioned him, but this is the first." Jason's mom turned to Christopher with a genuine smile. "Nice to meet you, Christopher. I assume it's not Chris?"

"Please," Christopher said simply, appreciating her taking the time to ask. He extended his hand politely.

Diane beamed. "He's always been Christopher ever since reading Winnie the Pooh years ago."

Christopher's face went red. Jason loved it—imagining his boyfriend correcting people when he was seven so he could be like Christopher Robin.

"That's adorable," Jason's mom said, and she meant it.

Jason was beaming without realizing it. Both mothers noticed and exchanged a glance that spoke volumes.

"Anyway," Diane continued, "Christopher and Jason have asked if Jason could spend the night at our home tonight, and I've agreed. But obviously I wanted to make sure you were in agreement as well. I know we've never met and—"

Jason's mom smiled at her son. A smile that made him want to sink through the floor because he knew what she was thinking.

"Of course," she said. "I don't think I can remember a time he's ever spent the night with a friend."

"Come to think of it," Diane said, "I don't think I can either. These two seem to be fast friends."

The mothers chatted for a few more minutes—pleasantries about school, about Driver's Ed, an invitation for Sarah to come to dinner sometime. Jason stood there trying not to squirm under his mother's knowing looks.

Finally, Sarah had to finish her closing duties. The bank was about to lock the doors.

"Jason, be good tonight. And make sure you're home tomorrow before dark. It's a school night."

"I'll make sure he is," Diane promised.

They agreed on logistics—Jason would ride his bike home to pack a few things, and Diane and Christopher would pick up some snacks and drinks for the boys, giving Jason time to get ready.

As they left the bank, Jason felt a mixture of excitement and terror.

Christopher had only known he lived off 24th Street. Had never been to his house. And compared to Christopher's, his was...

Well. Poor.

And he was embarrassed.

Jason rode his bike faster than necessary, legs burning as he pedaled hard. He had maybe twenty minutes before Christopher and his mom arrived.

Twenty minutes to make his house look less like what it was.

He slammed through the front door, dropped his bike in the yard, and ran to his room. He didn't have any luggage, so he dumped out his school backpack and started grabbing things. Toothbrush. Another pair of socks. Clean underwear—thank god his mom had done laundry yesterday. Another t-shirt.

He paused, holding his usual black shirt. Then he remembered— the green one. Christopher had said he liked him in it. Jason threw the black one back in the drawer and stuffed the green one into his bag.

He stood there, feeling like he should bring something else but not knowing what. His eyes swept his sparse room—the NASA posters taped to the fake wood paneling, his made bed (meaning he'd pulled the comforter up and fluffed the pillow), his dresser painted red, white, and blue but faded and scratched.

Then he made a decision that scared him.

He reached under his mattress and pulled out his notebook. The one where he wrote everything. His thoughts, his fears, his sketches, everything he kept hidden from the world.

He had no idea why. Or what he was going to do with it. But he stuffed it into his backpack before he could chicken out.

A knock at the door made him jump.

Shit. They were here already.

Jason rushed to the door, intending to just step outside—he hadn't picked up the house, hadn't prepared anything, was afraid of what Christopher would think—

"Can I use your bathroom?" Christopher asked before Jason could even say hello. "I've needed to pee since we left the library."

Oh jesus. It wasn't like he could say no. *Piss yourself, but you're not coming in because I'm afraid you'll judge my house.*

The house wasn't a disaster. It was actually pretty tidy. Lower class, sure, but clean. His mom made things nice in her own way.

Jason opened the door wider and let Christopher in.

Christopher took it all in without comment. The old Zenith TV on a stand that looked like it was from the '70s, rabbit ears meaning they didn't have cable. The sofa—one of those brown and beige prints with mushrooms and birds on the cushions, worn but fluffed. A green La-Z-Boy recliner with cracking vinyl arms but otherwise cared for.

The kitchen was a mishmash of painted mushrooms and Tupperware from the Brady Bunch era, offset with an old toaster oven and a loaf of generic white bread on the counter—not Wonder Bread like Christopher always had. Their table had mismatched chairs, with a lazy Susan in the middle full of plastic salt and pepper shakers, an instant coffee jar, napkins from fast food places, and a shot glass full of toothpicks.

"The bathroom's down here," Jason said, leading him.

Christopher stopped when he saw Jason's bedroom. "Is this your room?"

Jason felt suddenly, intensely vulnerable. Prepared to be judged, even though he knew Christopher wasn't like that. But Christopher had shown him his room. Why not the other way around?

"Uh... yeah."

"Can I look?"

"It's not much. It's just—"

"It's wonderful," Christopher said, and Jason couldn't tell if he was being kind or if he really meant it.

Christopher stepped inside, taking it all in. Jason watched him look—at the NASA posters, the sparse furniture, the smallness of it compared to his own room. Waited for judgment that didn't come.

At least the place was tidy. At least his dirty underwear wasn't strewn across the floor for Christopher to see.

Christopher's eyes landed on the model car sitting on its box in the corner. Halfway assembled, pieces scattered around it.

"I got that in eighth grade," Jason said before Christopher could ask. "Started putting it together but never finished. One day, maybe?"

"Your bed looks so cozy," Christopher said, then blushed, realizing how it sounded. Like he wanted to try sleeping in it. With Jason.

Jason smiled, catching his embarrassment. "Maybe you'll find out one day?" He wiggled his eyebrows, causing exactly the reaction he wanted.

Christopher used the bathroom, and when he came out, he was smiling. "Thanks for showing me around."

"It's not much. Not as nice as your—"

"Stop it." Christopher's voice was firm but gentle. "It's nice, Jason. And I feel at home here already. Okay?"

Jason normally would have gotten defensive. Would have made some sarcastic comment to deflect. But with Christopher, he simply felt what he said. Nodded. Smiled.

Then quickly stole a kiss before they left.

It felt naughty. Exciting. Kissing his boyfriend in his own house, where no one could see—

Except Christopher's mom.

She was sitting in the car outside, radio on, watching the front door. Lost in the song, humming along, not thinking about anything in particular except that it was nice to see her son making a friend.

Then she saw Christopher being kissed by Jason through the front window.

At first, she didn't process it. The image didn't compute. Her son and his friend standing in the living room, and then—

A kiss.

Quick, but unmistakable.

Diane's breath caught. Her hand went to her chest, not from shock but from the sudden weight of understanding.

Her heart sank a little. Not because she was offended or in denial or had any moral objection to her son kissing another boy. But because she immediately understood what this meant.

The danger.

In a small town like Connersville, in 1989, this could get them hurt. Badly.

She had no time to process further. Christopher emerged through the front door, followed by Jason—his *friend*, she caught herself thinking. What did you call him now? Boyfriend? Was that just for girls? Did boys have another term?

There was no time to think.

She turned her smile back on. "Got everything?" she asked as the boys opened the car door and climbed in.

"Yes, ma'am," Jason said. He was incredibly polite, even though he looked like he could tumble with any bully and win. Smaller than Christopher, hair with a life of its own, clothes a little too big like he was trying to hide in them.

But then she noticed something she hadn't seen before—or hadn't let herself see. How incredibly caring Jason was with her son. Opening the car door for Christopher and closing it before getting in the back. Always asking Christopher what he thought, what he wanted, if things were okay with him. When she'd asked earlier if they wanted anything, Jason had deferred to Christopher immediately: *Whatever he wants would be great.*

Boys didn't normally speak like this. Behave this way. But Jason—now that she was looking with new eyes—was caring for Christopher. They were caring for each other.

She'd need to have a quiet discussion with her husband tonight. After the boys went to bed.

There was so much she'd learned in just a few hours today.

And she suspected there was more to come.

Chapter 11

Spoons

The drive to Christopher's house felt longer than it actually was.

Jason sat in the back seat of the Averys' car, his backpack on his lap, watching the neighborhoods change after they climbed the hill away from downtown. The houses got bigger. The lawns more manicured. The cars in driveways newer, shinier.

His stomach twisted tighter with each block.

Christopher kept glancing back at him from the front passenger seat, catching his eye, offering small smiles. Jason tried to smile back, but his face felt frozen.

When they pulled into their driveway, Jason's heart was hammering. He'd been here before, sure. But that was different. That was a quick stop, grab Christopher, head out for adventure. This was... staying. Overnight. In this house with its two-car garage and its perfectly trimmed hedges and its white siding that actually looked clean.

"We're here!" Diane said brightly, putting the car in park.

Christopher was out first, opening Jason's door before Jason could even unbuckle his seatbelt. Their eyes met. Christopher's expression was gentle, understanding.

"Come on," Christopher said quietly. "You've been here before."

Easy for you to say, Jason thought, but he climbed out and followed Christopher up the walkway.

Mark was in the garage, organizing something on his workbench. He looked up when he heard them, smiled, and came out wiping his hands on a rag.

"Jason! Good to see you again. You boys have a good time at the library?"

"Yes, sir," Jason said, falling back on politeness because he didn't know what else to do.

"Found out some interesting family history," Diane added, coming around the car. "I'll tell you about it over dinner. Boys, why don't you go get settled? Jason, make yourself at home."

Jason nodded, following Christopher through the garage into the house.

Inside was exactly like before—clean, organized, comfortable. The kind of house where everything had a place and stayed in that place. Where the carpet didn't have stains and the furniture matched and the kitchen counters weren't cluttered with fast food napkins and old mail.

Christopher led him upstairs. Jason had been in Christopher's room before—they'd almost kissed here just last week before his mom called them down. But this felt different. This time he was staying. Sleeping here.

With Christopher.

"You can put your stuff anywhere," Christopher said, setting his own bag down by his desk. "I cleared out a drawer if you want to put clothes in it, or you can just leave everything in your backpack. Whatever's easier."

Jason stood in the doorway, backpack in hand, feeling like an intruder.

Christopher's room was still perfectly organized. Bed made with precision. Desk neat. Books alphabetized. Everything in its place.

Jason thought about his own room—his stuff was hand-me-downs or junk he found and made work. The contrast hit him all over again.

"Jason?"

He looked up. Christopher was watching him with concern.

160

"You okay?"

"Yeah. Your room is so much nicer than..." He trailed off, unable to finish.

Christopher studied him for a moment, then made a decision. He crossed to the door and closed it gently.

"Sit down," Christopher said, gesturing to the bed.

"I'm fine, really—"

"Jason. Sit."

There was something in Christopher's voice—not commanding, but certain. Jason found himself moving to the bed and sitting on the edge. Christopher sat beside him, close enough that their shoulders touched.

"I know this is weird," Christopher said quietly. "My house compared to yours. And I want you to know... I get it. I understand we live in different types of homes."

Jason's jaw tightened. "It's fine. I don't care about—"

"Let me finish. Please." Christopher's voice was gentle. "I'm lucky. I know I'm lucky. I have parents like I do, and stuff like I do, and a nice house. But the stuff and the nice home and the clothes... they really don't mean much to me. What matters is..." He paused, searching for words. "It's the love I feel from my folks. That's what makes this feel like home, not the furniture or whatever."

Jason felt something crack in his chest. Christopher's words were kind, meant to reassure. But they landed like stones in water, rippling outward to touch something Jason usually kept locked away.

Love from his folks.

Plural.

Christopher seemed to realize it at the same moment. His eyes widened slightly, and he bit his lip. "Jason, I didn't mean—I wasn't trying to—"

"It's fine."

"No, it's not. I just... I remember you mentioning your dad wasn't around, and I shouldn't have—"

"I said it's fine."

They sat in silence for a moment. Jason could feel Christopher looking at him, could feel the weight of unasked questions.

Then Christopher did something unexpected. He shifted on the bed, turning to face Jason more directly, and spoke very softly.

"You don't have to tell me. But... if you wanted to... I'd like to know. About your dad. About what happened."

Jason's throat went tight. "There's nothing to tell."

"Okay."

"He left. That's it. End of story."

"Okay."

"I was eight. He just... left. Didn't say goodbye. Didn't leave a note. Just packed his shit and disappeared one day while I was at school."

Jason hadn't meant to say that much. The words just came out, bitter and sharp.

Christopher didn't say anything. Just waited.

And somehow, in that silence, Jason kept talking.

"Mom came home from work and found all his stuff gone. His clothes, his tools, that stupid bowling trophy he was so proud of. Everything. Like he'd never existed." Jason's hands were clenched in his lap, knuckles white. "She tried calling around. His work said he'd quit that morning. His friends said they hadn't seen him. Nobody knew where he went."

"Did you ever find out why?"

"No. We never heard from him again. No phone calls. No letters. Nothing." Jason's voice cracked slightly. "Mom filed for divorce after a year. Had to do it in the newspaper because we couldn't find him to serve papers. It was..." He couldn't finish the sentence.

"Humiliating," Christopher supplied gently.

"Yeah."

"And you were just... left wondering."

"Every fucking day." Jason's eyes were burning now. "I kept thinking I'd done something wrong. That if I'd been better, or different, or less of a pain in the ass, maybe he would've stayed. Mom said it wasn't my fault, but how could it not be? He didn't even say goodbye to me."

"Jason—"

"I used to watch for him. For years. Every time a car that looked

162

like his drove by, I'd think maybe it was him coming back. Maybe he'd explain. Maybe he'd apologize. Maybe he'd..." Jason's voice broke completely. "Maybe he'd want me."

The tears came without permission. Hot and angry and full of grief he'd been carrying for eight years without really acknowledging it. He'd never told anyone this. Not his mom—she had enough to deal with. Not Scott or Allison—they wouldn't understand. Not anyone.

But Christopher was there, and Christopher was safe, and somehow Jason couldn't stop the words from tumbling out.

"I hate him. I hate him so fucking much for leaving. For making Mom struggle. For making me feel like I wasn't good enough. For making me wonder every single fucking day what I did wrong." Jason was crying openly now, ugly gasping sobs. "But I also miss him. And I hate that I miss him because he doesn't deserve shit from me. He doesn't deserve anything. But I can't stop wanting him to come back and tell me why. Just... fucking why."

Christopher wrapped his arms around Jason and pulled him close. Jason buried his face against Christopher's shoulder and let himself fall apart in a way he hadn't since he was eight years old and realized his dad was really, truly gone.

Christopher didn't say anything. Didn't offer platitudes about how it would be okay or how his dad was the one missing out. Just held him and let him cry and rubbed small circles on his back.

They stayed like that for a long time. Long enough for Jason's sobs to quiet into hitching breaths. Long enough for the shame to creep in— shame at crying, at being weak, at dumping all this on Christopher.

"Sorry," Jason finally managed, pulling back and wiping at his face. "That was... fuck. Sorry."

"Don't apologize."

"I'm a mess."

"You're human." Christopher reached up and gently wiped a tear from Jason's cheek. "Thank you for telling me. I know that wasn't easy."

"I never told anyone before. Not like that."

"I'm honored you told me."

Jason laughed—wet and shaky but genuine. "Honored? Jesus, Christopher."

"I am." Christopher's expression was serious. "You trusted me with something important. That means everything to me."

Before Jason could respond, Diane's voice echoed up the stairs.

"Boys! Come down here for a minute! We need to figure out dinner!"

The interruption was perhaps welcomed. Jason automatically stood and headed for the bathroom without asking—needing to wash his face, make himself presentable. Christopher didn't have to show him where it was or give permission. Jason had forgotten his fear and anxiety about being a guest.

He felt at home.

And Christopher noticed, watching Jason disappear into the bathroom like he'd lived here his whole life. Watched him emerge a few minutes later with his face washed, hair finger-combed, eyes a little red but otherwise composed.

"Ready?" Christopher asked.

"Yeah. Let's see what's for dinner."

———

Downstairs, Diane and Mark were in the kitchen having what sounded like a playful debate.

"I'm just saying, we could grill," Mark was saying. "One of the last nice nights before it gets too cold."

"It's already getting cold at night," Diane countered. "And by the time we get the grill going and everything cooked, it'll be almost dark."

"So we eat in the dark. That's romantic."

"You're impossible."

Christopher cleared his throat from the doorway. "What are we doing?"

"Well," Diane said, turning to them with a smile, "we could pick up Pizza King and bring it home. Or we could all go out to eat somewhere. Or your father wants to freeze us all by grilling in September."

"It's not that cold," Mark protested.

"Pizza King sounds good," Jason offered quietly.

"Pizza King it is," Mark said decisively. "I can drive over and pick it up."

"Can I come too?" Christopher asked. "I mean, obviously, but I can help order or whatever."

"And Jason will come too, right?" Diane said, though it wasn't really a question. "Why not make it everyone?"

Twenty minutes later, they were all sliding into a booth at Pizza King, the familiar smell of baking pizza and the sound of video games from the corner filling the small restaurant. Christopher grabbed the menu and the booth phone, dialing the number for the counter even though they were literally fifteen feet away.

"Hi, yeah, we want a large pepperoni pizza and a pitcher of Coke. Four glasses." He paused, listening. "Twenty minutes? Thanks." He hung up and grinned at Jason. "See? Easy."

"Very impressive," Jason said, unable to stop smiling.

Mark was studying the dessert menu. "You know what sounds good? Those chocolate chip cookies they make. Jason, you want one?"

Jason felt his face flush. He did want one—they were huge and warm and cost a dollar fifty, which was more than he should spend when he barely had any money left. But he wanted to buy Christopher one. Wanted to do something nice for him.

"I could... I mean, I can get one for Christopher if—"

"That sounds great," Mark interrupted smoothly. "Let me order a couple. Actually, make it four—one for each of us. My treat. Jason, keep your money."

The casual way Mark waved off Jason's attempt to pay didn't feel patronizing. Didn't make Jason feel poor or out of place. It felt like... like Mark was his dad too. Just a little. Like he cared about him.

Jason felt his throat tighten again but managed to nod. "Thanks, Mr. Avery."

"Please, call me Mark."

Diane was watching the exchange with soft eyes. Watching the way Jason had wanted to buy something for Christopher even though he clearly couldn't afford it. Watching the way her husband had

165

handled it with grace. Watching the way Christopher leaned against Jason as he laughed at one of Mark's terrible dad jokes.

"What do you call a fake noodle?" Mark asked, grinning.

Christopher groaned. "Dad, no—"

"An impasta!"

Jason burst out laughing despite himself. Christopher covered his face with his hands, shaking his head, but he was laughing too. And as he laughed, his hand naturally came to rest on Jason's arm.

Diane saw it. Saw the way they gravitated toward each other. Saw Christopher touch Jason's back when Jason leaned across the table to grab a napkin. Saw Jason hold Christopher's shoulder when Christopher nearly knocked over his Coke.

Small things. Easy to miss if you weren't looking.

But she was looking now. And she couldn't remember the last time she'd seen her son this happy. This relaxed. This... himself.

And Jason—who she didn't know well, but could read in the way his shoulders had slowly dropped from around his ears, the way his smile came easier as the meal went on, the way he looked at her son like Christopher was the best thing he'd ever seen—Jason seemed just as happy.

She caught Mark's eye across the table. Saw that he'd noticed some of it too, though he didn't yet understand what it meant.

The pizza arrived steaming hot. They ate and talked about normal things—school starting, Driver's Ed, the Homecoming football game in a week.

"Oh, Mark," Diane said suddenly, remembering. "I need to tell you what we found at the library today. Margaret—you know Margaret, the genealogist?—she was helping the boys research those farmhouses for their project."

"And?" Mark looked interested.

"William Thorne's sister, Sarah, married a man named Thomas Avery in 1892."

Mark's fork stopped halfway to his mouth. "Avery?"

"Your great-great-grandmother. William Thorne was your great-great-great-uncle."

"Holy shit!" Mark set down his fork. "You're serious?"

Both boys giggled—hearing Christopher's dad actually swear was unexpectedly funny. Diane shot Mark a look and redirected the conversation.

"Margaret traced the whole line. Christopher, you're directly descended from Sarah Thorne."

Christopher and Jason exchanged a glance but stayed quiet.

"That's incredible," Mark said, processing. He looked at Christopher. "So that farmhouse—the one with the widow's peak—that belonged to your ancestors."

"Yeah. Apparently."

Mark sat back, shaking his head in wonder. "My father—your grandfather—he passed away when you were only six, Christopher. He never talked much about his family. I always wanted to ask him more, but..." He shrugged. "He kept things close. I remember once, when I was about your age, I asked him about where his parents grew up. He just said 'on a farm somewhere' and changed the subject. Looking back, I think there was something painful there he didn't want to talk about."

"The accident," Diane said quietly. "William's death."

"An accident?" Mark looked between them. "What happened?"

Christopher and Jason exchanged a glance.

"He was struck by a train," Christopher said quietly. "In 1890. He was only seventeen. We found a newspaper article about it when we were researching."

Mark's expression shifted. "Jesus. That's... that's terrible." He was quiet for a moment. "That kind of tragedy... families don't always recover from it." He looked thoughtful. "I wonder who owns that land now? Might be interesting to look into. See if it stayed in the family somehow."

Jason tried not to reveal how significant all this was to him. But sitting in this booth with Christopher's family, eating pizza and laughing at bad jokes and being included in the family conversation like he mattered—it was everything he'd never had.

He had his mom, of course. And Rick, technically, though Rick barely acknowledged Jason existed most of the time. But not like this.

Not a family that talked and laughed and cared about each other openly.

For a few hours, he could pretend this was his family too.

———

Back at the house, full of pizza and cookies, Christopher led Jason upstairs again. This time Jason didn't hesitate at the doorway. Just walked in and dropped onto the floor, propping his back against Christopher's bed.

Christopher turned on the radio—K96 out of Richmond, playing something by The Cure—and turned the volume low. Then he sat cross-legged on the floor across from Jason.

"So," Christopher said. "William being my great-great-great-uncle."

"Yeah."

"That's... I don't even know what that is."

"Intense?"

"Intense," Christopher agreed. "I mean, we watched him die. And now I find out he's family. That I'm literally descended from his sister. That the reason my family doesn't talk about the past is probably because of what he did."

"Because he was gay and killed himself."

"Yeah." Christopher's voice went quiet. "Do you think... do you think that's our future? Is that what happens to people like... *us?*"

"No." Jason's response was immediate and fierce. "No, Christopher. We're not ending up like them."

"But what if—"

"We're not." Jason leaned forward. "I won't let that happen. Whatever it takes."

"How can you be so sure?"

"Because I'm not giving up. And neither are you."

They sat in silence for a moment, the weight of history pressing down on them.

"Can I show you something?" Jason asked suddenly.

"Of course."

Jason pulled his backpack over and unzipped it, withdrawing the battered notebook from where he'd hidden it under his clothes. He handed it to Christopher.

"What is this?"

"My notebook. Where I... where I write things. Draw things. It's private, but..." Jason swallowed hard. "I want you to see it."

Christopher took it reverently, like it was something precious. He opened to the first page and started reading.

Jason watched his face as Christopher read. Watched his expressions shift—surprise, sadness, understanding, love. Christopher turned pages slowly, reading Jason's observations about Driver's Ed, his sketches of the farmhouses, his notes about William and Daniel.

Then Christopher stopped. His eyes went wide.

"Jason..."

"What?"

Christopher turned the notebook around so Jason could see.

It was the drawing. The one Jason had done weeks ago, sitting in his room late at night, unable to stop thinking about the boy from Driver's Ed. Christopher's face rendered in careful pencil strokes. His careful smile. His neat hair. The way he held his shoulders.

Jason had completely forgotten about it.

"Oh. Uh. That's—"

"That's me," Christopher said softly. "You drew me."

"Yeah. Sorry, I—"

"Why are you apologizing? This is incredible." Christopher stared at the drawing. "I didn't know you could draw like this."

"It's not that good—"

"Jason. This is really good. Like, really good. You should be taking art classes. You should be pursuing this." Christopher looked up at him. "How did I not know you could do this?"

"I don't really tell people."

"Why not?"

Jason shrugged. "What's the point? It's not like I can do anything with it. Can't afford art school. Can't afford supplies half the time. It's just... something I do."

"It's not just something you do. It's talent." Christopher turned back to the notebook, flipping through more pages. Stopped on another entry—recent, from just last night.

Jason's stomach dropped as he realized what Christopher was reading.

I need to protect him. I will protect him.

Christopher looked up, his eyes bright. "You really meant this."

"Of course I meant it."

"No one's ever..." Christopher's voice caught. "No one's ever wanted to protect me before. I'm always the one taking care of other people, making sure everyone else is okay. But you... you actually care about keeping me safe."

"Of course I do. Christopher, I love you."

Christopher set the notebook aside carefully and leaned forward, closing the distance between them. His hand came up to cup Jason's face, gentle and certain.

"I love you too."

Christopher leaned in to kiss him. Jason's eyes started to close, his heart hammering, everything narrowing down to this moment, this boy, this feeling—

The door opened.

They jerked apart, Christopher scrambling back to his spot, Jason's hands automatically going to the notebook like he'd been showing Christopher something innocent the whole time.

Mark stood in the doorway, his hand still on the knob.

"Oh! Sorry, didn't mean to interrupt. Just wanted to check in before bed." His eyes moved between them, taking in their positions on the floor, the sudden movement, the guilty expressions. "Everything okay in here?"

"Yeah, Dad. Fine. We're just... looking at notes. For the project."

"Right. The project." Mark's voice was carefully neutral. "Well, don't stay up too late. Jason, do you need anything? Extra blanket, different pillow?"

"No, sir. I'm good."

"Okay. Well. Goodnight, boys. What are your plans for the morning? Breakfast around eight?"

"Sure, Dad. That's fine."

"Sounds good," Jason managed.

Mark closed the door softly.

Jason and Christopher stared at each other in the sudden silence.

"Oh my god," Christopher whispered, his face white. "He saw. He definitely saw."

"We don't know that—"

"Jason, we practically jumped apart when he opened the door. We were leaning toward each other. He *saw*."

Jason felt nervous laughter bubbling up despite himself. Christopher looked terrified, and here he was wanting to laugh because what else could you do with that kind of energy?

"Listen," Jason said, trying to get control of himself. "Christopher. I'm sure he didn't see anything. Seriously."

"What if he did?"

"Then... we deal, I guess. But I don't think he did. Honest."

"Honest?"

"Yeah." Jason hoped his voice sounded more confident than he felt. "He seemed normal, right? Just checking in before bed."

Christopher didn't look convinced, but he nodded slowly. "Okay. Maybe you're right."

"We should probably get ready for bed anyway. It's late."

"Yeah. Okay."

Christopher stood and went to his dresser, opening the bottom drawer. "I think I have some pajamas in here somewhere. Under my winter clothes..."

"I don't really wear them," Jason said.

"Oh." Christopher stopped searching and looked at him. "Me neither, actually. But I thought..."

They both looked at each other, the implication hanging in the air. Sleeping in just their underwear felt too forward. Too intimate. But also... more honest?

"Fuck it," Jason said finally, making a decision. "It's just underwear. What's the big deal?" He started unbuttoning his jeans.

Christopher tried to follow suit, tried to act normal, no big deal. But he couldn't help watching as Jason pushed his jeans down and stepped out of them. Couldn't help noticing the way his t-shirt rode up slightly, revealing a strip of pale skin above his briefs.

Jason caught him looking and grinned. "See something you like?"

Christopher's face went red. But then something shifted in his expression—courage, maybe, or just the realization that Jason was his boyfriend and he was allowed to look.

"Yes," Christopher said, meeting Jason's eyes. "I do. And I want to see more, please."

It was Jason's turn to go red. He hadn't expected that. Hadn't expected Christopher to be so... direct.

"Spin for me," Christopher added, making a little twirling motion with his finger.

"Oh my god, you did not just—"

"Spin," Christopher repeated, grinning now.

Jason laughed despite his embarrassment and did a slow turn, feeling ridiculous and exposed and oddly thrilled all at once.

"Your turn," Jason said when he was facing Christopher again. "Drop 'em."

Christopher's eyes went wide. "What?"

"You heard me. Fair's fair."

For a moment Jason thought Christopher would back down. But then Christopher's hands went to his waist and he pushed his jeans down slowly, making a little show of it, stepping out of them with exaggerated care.

Jason's face went hot. "Oh my god."

"What?" Christopher was trying not to laugh. "You told me to."

"I didn't think you actually would."

"Well, I did." Christopher pulled his shirt over his head, standing there in just his blue-colored briefs, and did his own slow spin. "Satisfied?"

Jason couldn't speak. Could barely breathe. Christopher was beautiful. All lean lines and pale skin and that careful posture even when he was standing there in his underwear showing off for his boyfriend.

"Jason?" Christopher's voice was softer now, uncertain. "Are you okay?"

"Yeah. I'm..." Jason swallowed hard. "You're beautiful. You know that?"

Christopher's face went red again, but he was smiling. "So are you."

They stood there for a moment, looking at each other, the air between them electric.

"We should probably..." Christopher gestured toward the bed.

"Yeah. Definitely."

They climbed into bed—Christopher against the wall, Jason on the outside edge. Christopher reached over and turned off the lamp, plunging the room into darkness broken only by the faint glow of streetlights through the curtains.

"Goodnight," Christopher whispered.

"Goodnight."

They lay there for a moment, looking at the ceiling. Jason was hyperaware of Christopher beside him. Could hear him breathing. Could feel the warmth of his body six inches away.

Then Christopher shifted, rolling over practically on top of Jason, and kissed him.

Not the quick, interrupted kiss from earlier. This was real. Deep. Christopher's hands cupped Jason's face, Jason's hands found Christopher's waist, and they kissed like they'd been waiting their whole lives for this moment.

They stayed that way for what felt like forever, exploring each other, quiet kissing and a little groping, feeling each other under the comforter. Jason's hands mapped the planes of Christopher's back, the curve of his hip. Christopher's fingers tangled in Jason's hair, traced the line of his jaw.

Both of them were breathing hard. Both of them were aroused. Both of them were terrified and exhilarated in equal measure.

Finally Christopher pulled back, gasping for air.

"That was..." Christopher whispered.

"Wonderful," Jason finished.

"But maybe we should... stop there. Before..."

"Before it gets..."

"Before I can't stop."

Jason understood. He felt it too—the pull toward something more, something they weren't ready for yet. Not tonight. Not like this.

"One more," Jason said softly.

Christopher leaned down and kissed him again—sweet and gentle and full of love.

"Goodnight," Christopher whispered against his lips.

"Goodnight."

Christopher rolled onto his side, his back facing Jason. For a moment they lay separate, and Jason felt the loss of contact like a physical ache.

Then, instinctively, Jason rolled onto his side and scooted close, wrapping his arm around Christopher's waist, pulling him back against his chest.

Christopher pressed back into his body and pulled Jason's arm tighter around him, feeling protected and loved.

Which he was.

They both drifted off to sleep like that—two boys holding each other in the dark, safe for at least one night from a world that would never understand.

———

Downstairs, Mark found Diane in their bedroom, already changed into her nightgown, sitting on the edge of the bed.

"So," Mark said, closing the door. "That was interesting."

"What was?"

"I just walked in on the boys. They were sitting on the floor, and when I opened the door they jumped apart like I'd caught them doing something."

Diane looked up at him. "Did you catch them doing something?"

"I don't know. Maybe? They were sitting really close together, leaning toward each other. And they jumped apart so fast." He sat down beside her. "Diane, I think... I think they were about to kiss."

She was quiet for a moment, then made a decision.

"This afternoon, when I drove them to Jason's house to get his things. I was waiting in the car and I looked up and saw them through the living room window." She took a breath. "They were kissing."

Mark's eyes went wide. "What?"

"It was quick. Just a peck. But it was definitely a kiss."

"Are you sure?"

"Mark. I'm sure."

He processed this information. Opened his mouth. Closed it. Opened it again.

"So our son is..."

"Gay. Yes. I think so."

Mark stood up, ran his hand through his hair, sat back down. "Okay. Okay. I need a minute."

Diane waited, watching her husband process.

"When I walked in just now," Mark said slowly, "they were sitting close together. Really close. And they jumped apart so fast. I thought maybe I was seeing something that wasn't there. But you're saying..."

"They're together. Christopher and Jason. As more than friends."

"Jesus." Mark stood up again, pacing. "Has he told you? Has he come out?"

"No. He doesn't know I know."

"Do we talk to him about it?"

"I don't know."

They sat in silence for a moment.

"I always wondered," Diane said softly. "Didn't you?"

"Yeah. Yeah, I guess I did." Mark sat back down. "Remember when he was nine and insisted on being Prince Eric for Halloween because he had a crush on him?"

Diane laughed quietly. "Or when he was twelve and couldn't stop talking about that boy from summer camp. What was his name?"

"Trevor. He talked about Trevor for months."

"I thought maybe I was reading too much into it. But..." Diane shook her head. "I think we both knew. We just didn't say it out loud."

"So we're okay with this?" Mark asked. "I mean, we're okay with our son being gay?"

"Are you okay with it?"

Mark thought about it. Really thought about it. Christopher was his son. His only child. He loved him more than anything in the world.

"Yeah," he said finally. "Yeah, I'm okay with it. I mean, it's not what I expected, but... he's still Christopher. He's still our son. And if Jason makes him happy—and it seems like he does—then I'm okay with it."

"Good." Diane squeezed his hand. "Because I'm okay with it too."

They sat together, processing this new reality.

"But I'm worried," Diane said after a moment. "Mark, this isn't San Francisco. If people find out..."

"They could get hurt."

"They could get killed."

"Oh, I don't think *that* could happen, honey. I mean—"

"I don't know." Diane's voice was firm. "You've heard what people say around here about..." She couldn't finish the sentence.

The words hung heavy in the air.

"What do we do?" Mark asked.

"I don't know. Do we talk to them? Make sure they're being careful?"

"How do we do that without making them think we're spying on them or disapproving?"

"I don't know."

More silence.

"What about Jason's mom?" Mark asked. "Do you think she knows?"

"I don't know. When I met her at the bank today, she looked at the boys a certain way. Like she suspected something."

"Should we talk to her?"

"And say what? 'Hi, we think our sons are dating, do you want to coordinate parenting strategies?'"

Mark laughed despite himself. "When you put it like that..."

"We'd mortify Christopher. And Jason."

"But we can't just ignore it."

"No. We can't."

They sat with that for a moment.

"There's something else," Mark said quietly. "Something we need to think about."

"What?"

"AIDS. Diane, we've seen it on the news. We know it's spreading. We know gay men are getting it. If Christopher is sexually active—"

"He's sixteen, Mark. I don't think he's—"

"But what if he is? What if he and Jason are... you know. Doing things. How do we talk to him about safe sex when we don't even know what safe sex means for two boys?"

Diane closed her eyes. "I hadn't even thought about that."

"I haven't had the sex talk with him yet. I kept putting it off because he seemed so young still, and he wasn't interested in girls, and I figured I had time. But now..."

"Now everything's different."

"Yeah."

They were quiet again, both overwhelmed by the sudden weight of questions they didn't have answers to.

"Do we separate them?" Diane asked. "Make Jason sleep on the couch?"

"And have Christopher know we don't trust him?"

"But if they're in the same bed—"

"Diane, what do you want me to do? Walk in there and say 'I think you two are going to have sex and I'm not ready for that, so Jason, you need to sleep on the sofa?' That would definitely start the conversation, but I don't think it would go well."

Despite everything, Diane smiled. "No. Probably not."

"Christopher is a good kid," Mark said. "And every inclination I have tells me Jason is too. Sure, they might... fool around. I mean, come on, Diane. I know I did when I was their age."

"Really? With whom?"

"That's not the point—"

"No, I want to know. Who were you fooling around with at sixteen?"

"Diane. Focus." But Mark was blushing. "The point is, boys fool around. But I don't think they'll actually... you know. Have sex. Not yet. They're probably too scared of their own shadows."

"You're probably right." Diane sighed. "Besides, I trust them. And the minute we walk in and start laying down rules about sleeping arrangements, we might as well have the conversation then and there. Because they'll know we suspect."

"Or know," Mark added.

"Or know," Diane agreed.

They sat together, holding hands, trying to figure out how to parent a situation neither of them had ever imagined dealing with.

"So what do we do?" Mark asked finally.

"We... give them space. We watch. We wait for Christopher to come to us when he's ready."

"And if he doesn't come to us?"

"Then we'll figure it out. But pushing him before he's ready will just make him close down. You know how he is."

"Yeah."

"But we need to educate ourselves," Diane said firmly. "About AIDS, about safe sex for gay men, about... all of it. Because when he does come to us—or when we have to talk to him—we need to know what we're talking about."

"Agreed."

"And we protect them. However we can. Even if they don't know we're doing it."

"Okay."

They sat there a while longer, processing. Worrying. Hoping they were making the right decisions.

"I love him so much," she said quietly. "Our boy. Our sweet, careful, kind little boy."

"Me too. But he's not little anymore, Diane."

"I just want him to be happy. And safe."

"I know. Me too."

Upstairs, Jason slept fitfully, the dream pulling him back to the widow's peak, back to William's desperate message: *Help him. Don't let him end up like me.*

And Christopher snuggled up to Jason, who was still holding him, feeling warm and protected and loved in a way he'd never felt before.

Safe, for at least one night, in his boyfriend's arms.

Chapter 12

Daniel's Voice

Jason awoke to warmth.

Not the usual morning cold of his bedroom, the thin blanket barely keeping out the September chill. This was different. This was body heat. Another person pressed against him, breathing slowly, still asleep.

Christopher.

Jason's arm was wrapped around Christopher's waist, holding him close. Christopher's back was pressed against Jason's chest, their legs tangled together under the comforter. Christopher's hair—slightly messed from sleep—tickled Jason's nose.

For a moment, Jason just lay there, not moving, barely breathing, trying to memorize exactly how this felt.

He'd never woken up with someone before. Never held someone through the night. Never felt this particular combination of contentment and arousal and tenderness all mixed together.

Christopher stirred slightly, making a small sound, and pressed back against Jason more firmly.

Jason's body responded immediately. He went still, mortified, hoping Christopher wouldn't notice—

"Morning," Christopher mumbled, voice thick with sleep.

"Morning."

"You're poking me."

Jason's face went hot. "I—sorry, I can't—it's just morning and—"

Christopher laughed softly. "I know. Me too." He shifted slightly, and yeah, Jason could feel that Christopher was in the same state. "It's biology. Don't apologize."

"This is so embarrassing."

"Why? It's natural." Christopher rolled over to face him, their faces inches apart in the dim morning light filtering through the curtains. "Besides, I think it's kind of... nice."

"Nice?"

"Yeah. Means you're attracted to me."

"I thought that was pretty obvious already."

Christopher smiled—that careful, genuine smile that made Jason's chest ache. "Still. Nice to have confirmation."

They lay there looking at each other, neither quite sure what to do next. The world outside Christopher's bedroom didn't exist yet. It was just them, tangled together under the covers, safe and warm and together.

"I don't want to get up," Jason said quietly.

"Me neither."

"Can we just stay here forever?"

"I wish." Christopher reached up and brushed Jason's hair back from his forehead. "But my parents are probably awake. We should probably..."

"Yeah. Probably."

Neither of them moved.

"Jason?"

"Yeah?"

"Last night was... it was perfect."

Jason felt his throat tighten. "Yeah. It was."

"I love you."

"I love you too."

Their kiss—slow and sweet was unhurried; morning breath be damned. This was theirs. This moment. This feeling.

Eventually, reluctantly, they untangled themselves and got up.

Christopher lent Jason a sweatshirt—his CHS one with a red Spartan on the front, faded from washing. He pulled it on and immediately wanted to keep it forever because it smelled like Christopher.

Downstairs, they found Diane already in the kitchen, making pancakes. Mark sat at the table with his coffee and the Palladium Item Sunday edition.

"Morning, boys!" Diane's voice was bright. Maybe too bright. "Did you sleep well?"

"Yeah, Mom. Fine."

"Jason? Comfortable enough? I worried that bed might be too small for both of you."

Jason's face heated. "No, ma'am. It was fine. Really comfortable."

Mark lowered his paper and smiled at them over the top. "Good. Good. Pancakes sound good?"

"Yeah, Dad."

"Great. I'll help your mother." Mark stood and joined Diane at the stove, and they worked together with easy familiarity—him flipping pancakes, her preparing the plates, both moving around each other like they'd done this a thousand times.

Jason watched them and felt something twist in his chest. This is what a family looked like. Two people who loved each other, taking care of their kid, making Sunday breakfast like it was the most natural thing in the world.

"Jason?" Diane was looking at him. "Orange juice okay?"

"Yes, ma'am. Thank you."

They sat down to eat. The pancakes were perfect—fluffy and warm with butter melting into all the little holes. Jason ate mechanically, aware of Christopher beside him, aware of Mark and Diane across the table watching them with expressions he couldn't quite read.

"So," Mark said, setting down his fork. "Aren't you both getting behind the wheel soon? Have you actually been out in the car yet?"

"I think we're supposed to get in the car tomorrow," Christopher said. "Just staying in the parking lot first, I think."

"Nervous?"

"I'm okay," Christopher replied confidently.

"How about you, Jason?"

"Terrified," Jason said, making everyone laugh.

Mark grinned. "Don't worry. Mr. Barnes is a good teacher. I actually went to school with him, you know. He was... 'enthusiastic' back then, too. Lots of kids thought he was..." Mark paused, something shifting in his expression. "Well. A handful."

"What, Dad?"

Mark was quiet for a moment, his smile fading. "Just that... back then, a lot of kids thought he was gay. Or... I hate to admit it, but they called him a—" He stopped himself, the word dying on his lips. "Well. They weren't kind. I never did, but it made me cringe now thinking about it."

The table went silent. Diane was watching her husband carefully.

"I think I'll call him this week," Mark said suddenly, looking down at his coffee. "Been forever since we spoke. We were friendly back then, but... He didn't deserve that."

Mark looked up, as if suddenly realizing what he'd just said - what he'd just revealed about his feelings on the subject. His eyes darted to the boys, then to Diane.

Diane caught it immediately. She reached over and squeezed Mark's hand, her expression soft. "I think that's really important, honey. People need to know they're valued. That they matter. No matter who they are."

The emphasis on those last words hung in the air.

Jason and Christopher sat very still, both staring at their plates.

"More pancakes, anyone?" Diane asked brightly, breaking the moment.

Diane was smiling at them—at Jason and Christopher sitting close together, at the way Christopher's shoulder kept bumping against Jason's. Her expression was soft. Almost wistful.

"You know what?" Diane said suddenly. "I want to take a picture. Of you boys. Just... to remember."

"Mom—" Christopher started.

"Please? Just one. You both look so nice this morning."

"We're in sweatpants," Christopher protested.

"I don't care. Come on, humor me."

She was already standing, pulling the disposable camera from the junk drawer where they kept everything—stray batteries, rubber bands, mystery keys, half-used birthday candles. Mark was smiling too, like this was expected behavior.

"Stand by the window. The light's good there."

Christopher groaned but stood, pulling Jason with him. They positioned themselves by the dining room window, morning sun streaming in.

"Closer together," Diane instructed. "Like you're actually like each other."

Christopher moved closer until their shoulders touched. Jason tried to smile naturally, aware of how awkward he probably looked.

"Perfect. Don't move."

The camera flashed. Then flashed again.

"Mom, you said one picture."

"I'm taking backups. You never know." But her eyes were bright, and Jason realized she was trying not to cry.

What was happening?

"Okay, okay," Diane said, lowering the camera. "Thank you. Now finish your breakfast before it gets cold."

They sat back down. Jason caught Christopher's eye, and Christopher gave a small shrug that said *I have no idea what that was about either.*

———

After breakfast, they went back upstairs. Christopher closed the door behind them and immediately turned to Jason.

"Oh god, you don't think Dad actually saw something last night?"

Jason thought about it. "I don't think so. But your parents were definitely acting weird."

"Really weird."

"Did you hear what your dad said at breakfast?" Jason asked quietly. "About Mr. Barnes?"

Christopher sat on the edge of the bed. "Yeah. I mean... everyone kind of knows. But nobody ever just says it like that."

"No kidding." Jason leaned against the dresser. "And the way he said it—like he felt bad about what happened back then?"

"He basically just told us he's okay with it. Right? That's what that was?"

"I think so." Jason's voice was uncertain. "And your mom after —'No matter who they are.' She was looking right at us."

Christopher's stomach flipped. "So... do they know?"

"I don't know. Maybe?" Jason shifted uncomfortably. "But if they do, it doesn't seem to matter. They seem... okay with it?"

They looked at each other, both feeling the strangeness of it but not quite able to believe what it might mean.

"We should probably get ready," Christopher said eventually. "My dad said he'd drive you home around eleven."

"Yeah. Okay."

They started gathering Jason's things before he went to the bathroom to shower—happy he was using Christopher's shampoo, his soap, everything smelling like him. When he came back, towel wrapped around his waist, Christopher was changing into clean clothes.

Jason stopped in the doorway, suddenly uncertain. Should he change in front of Christopher? They'd slept together last night, but that was different. This was... broad daylight. Deliberate.

Christopher caught him hesitating and smiled. "You can change in here. I don't mind."

"You sure?"

"Jason. We've seen each other in our underwear. It's fine."

Right. Okay. Jason dropped his towel and pulled on his briefs, hyperaware of Christopher in his peripheral vision. When he looked up, Christopher was definitely watching.

"See something you like?" Jason asked, echoing last night's teasing.

"Yes," Christopher said simply. "I do."

Jason's face went hot, but he grinned. "Good."

They finished getting ready in comfortable silence. But as Jason pulled his shirt over his head, something shifted. Tomorrow was Monday. Tomorrow was school.

"Christopher?"

"Yeah?"

"About tomorrow. At school." Jason sat on the bed, and Christopher joined him. "We have to... we have to be careful. You know that, right?"

"I know."

"I mean really careful. We can't..." Jason struggled for words. "We can't act like we do here. We have to play it straight."

"I know, Jason."

"And I need you to understand—just because we're doing that, just because I can't touch you or kiss you or hold your hand or anything—it doesn't mean I don't love you. Okay? It doesn't mean that."

Christopher's expression softened. "I know."

"It's going to be hard. Really hard. I'm going to want to..." Jason's jaw tightened. "I'm going to want to keep my hands on you all the time. Make sure you're okay. Make sure nobody's bothering you."

"Jason—"

"And if anyone gives you any shit—any shit at all—you tell me. Immediately. I don't care if it's in the middle of class or lunch or whatever. You tell me."

"You're being very protective."

"Yeah. I am." Jason looked at him directly. "Because you're mine. And I take care of what's mine."

The possessiveness in his voice surprised even himself. But Christopher didn't look put off. He looked... pleased. Almost awed.

"I'm yours," Christopher repeated softly.

"Yeah. You are."

"And you're mine."

"Yeah. Yeah, I am."

The kiss was harder than they'd meant it to be, both of them trying to pack everything they felt into one moment before they had to pretend to be "just friends" in public.

When they pulled apart, both breathing hard, Christopher rested his forehead against Jason's.

"This is going to suck," Christopher whispered.

"Yeah. It really is."

A knock on the door made them jerk apart.

"Boys?" Mark's voice. "Ready to head out?"

"Yeah, Dad. Just finishing up."

Jason grabbed his backpack, made sure he had everything. Christopher walked him to the door, both of them suddenly awkward again.

In the car, Mark said, "Hey Jason, you should come back next weekend. We could all go see a movie or something. Haven't done that in a while."

Christopher's face lit up. "Really, Dad?"

"Sure. If Jason wants to."

Jason was dumbfounded. Mark seemed like he was trying to concoct ways for the two of them to spend time together. "Uh, yeah. That sounds great. Thank you, Mr. Avery."

"Mark," he corrected gently. "And it's no trouble. We'd love to have you."

In the back seat, Christopher sat beside Jason, their knees touching where Mark couldn't see. Jason glanced at Christopher, who looked thrilled he didn't have to come up with an excuse to see him again.

Mark knew exactly what he was doing. He wanted them to know he was okay with them spending time together. That he approved. That he supported them. All without being pushy or making them uncomfortable by acknowledging what he suspected.

When they pulled up to Jason's house, Mark looked at it with interest. The small one-story rental. The patchy lawn. The old Zenith visible through the living room window.

"Nice neighborhood," Mark said, and he sounded genuine. "Quiet."

"Yeah. It's okay."

"Christopher, why don't you help Jason carry his stuff in? I'll wait here."

They climbed out. Christopher followed Jason to the front door. Mark's request was deliberate—another subtle way of giving them time together, letting them have a proper goodbye away from his eyes.

Inside, Jason's mom looked up from the couch where she was reading a McCall's magazine. Her face lit up when she saw the boys.

"Christopher! How lovely to see you again!"

"Hi, Mrs. Reynolds. Sorry to barge in. We just need to grab something for class."

"Of course, of course. Will you stay for dinner later? I was thinking of making spaghetti again."

"Oh, my dad's waiting outside. But thank you. Maybe another time?"

"Anytime, honey. You're always welcome here."

They escaped to Jason's room. The excuse about getting something for class was flimsy, but Jason's mom seemed to buy it. The door was barely closed before they were kissing again—desperate, hungry, trying to get enough to last them through tomorrow.

"I can't believe we have to wait all day to do this again," Christopher gasped between kisses.

"I know."

"When can I see you? Really see you? Not at school."

"I don't know. We'll figure it out."

They made a show of rustling through Jason's closet, talking loudly about "finding the notebook" while actually just stealing a few more kisses, a few more touches.

Finally, reluctantly, they had to stop. Had to go back out. Had to say goodbye.

At the car, Mark was humming along to a song on the radio and tapping his finger on the steering wheel while his son hugged Jason quickly—a friend hug, nothing suspicious—and climbed into the passenger seat.

Jason watched them drive away, feeling the loss like a physical ache in his chest.

This was going to be impossible.

———

Sunday afternoon dragged.

Jason's mom made dinner—meatloaf, mashed potatoes, green beans from a can instead of the planned spaghetti after all. Rick showed up around five, grabbed a plate, and settled in front of the

187

TV. Jason sat with them out of obligation, but his mind was elsewhere.

He missed Christopher. Missed him with an intensity that was almost embarrassing. They'd only been apart a few hours and Jason felt like he'd lost a limb.

His mom noticed. Of course she noticed.

"You're quiet tonight," she said as they did dishes together. "Everything okay?"

"Yeah. Fine."

"How was staying at Christopher's?"

"Good. His parents are really nice."

"They seem like good people." She handed him a plate to dry. "You two are getting pretty close, huh?"

Jason's hands stilled on the dish towel. "We're friends, mom."

"I didn't say you weren't."

But her tone suggested she was thinking something more. Jason didn't look at her. Just kept drying dishes and putting them away, trying not to reveal anything.

Later, Jason tried to watch TV with his mom and Rick. Some movie about cops. Rick made occasional comments, his mom laughed at the appropriate times, and Jason just sat there feeling like he was watching from underwater.

Around nine, he gave up and went to his room.

He pulled out his notebook—the one he'd shown Christopher last night. Flipped through the pages. The drawing of Christopher. The notes about the farmhouses. The protective declaration he'd written Friday night.

He turned to a fresh page and started sketching without really thinking about it. Just letting his hand move, letting something inside him work itself out through the pencil.

When he finally stopped and looked at what he'd drawn, his breath caught.

Two boys. One standing on a widow's peak, the other on the ground below. A lantern between them. The taller boy reaching out toward something—or someone—just out of frame.

He'd drawn the ghost boys.

Jason stared at the sketch, something cold settling in his stomach. He hadn't meant to draw them. Hadn't been thinking about them at all. But there they were, rendered in careful detail, the expressions on their faces almost clear enough to read.

Almost.

He closed the notebook and shoved it under his mattress. Turned off the light. Lay in bed staring at the ceiling.

Tomorrow was Monday. Tomorrow was school. Tomorrow he had to pretend Christopher was just his friend from school.

Tomorrow he had to keep his hands to himself and his love hidden and act like the best thing that had ever happened to him was nothing special.

Tomorrow was going to be hell.

———

Christopher lay in his own bed, in his own room, and everything felt wrong.

The bed was too big. Too empty. He'd gotten used to Jason beside him in just one night, and now the absence felt like a hole in his chest.

He'd tried to read. Tried to do homework. Tried to do anything to keep his mind occupied. But everything led back to Jason.

The way he'd looked this morning, still half-asleep and rumpled. The way he'd held Christopher last night, protective and tender. The way he'd kissed Christopher goodbye in his room, like he was trying to memorize the taste of him.

Christopher had never felt this way about anyone. Never knew you could miss someone so much it physically hurt.

His clock read 11:47 PM. Jason was probably asleep by now. He wished he could call him, just to hear his voice. But that would be weird. Clingy. And his parents might hear.

He rolled over, trying to get comfortable, trying to will himself to sleep.

It took a long time.

When sleep finally came, it brought dreams.

———

Christopher stood on a dark country road, fog rolling across the ground. The amber moon hung low and swollen in the sky, casting everything in strange gold light.

He knew this place. The farmhouses. But something was different this time.

He wasn't watching from above. He was down here. On the road. Standing right where—

The door of the smaller farmhouse opened.

Daniel stepped out, wearing his nightshirt, carrying the lantern. He looked up at the bigger farmhouse, at the widow's peak, and his expression was full of longing.

Christopher followed Daniel's gaze and saw Jason—no, William—standing up there looking down at them.

No. That wasn't right. Jason was William. He understood that now in the logic of dreams.

And Christopher was...

He looked down at himself. At the white nightshirt he was wearing. At the lantern in his hand.

He was Daniel.

William lifted his hand—a small wave. A signal.

Christopher—Daniel—started walking up the road. His bare feet knew every stone, every rut. He'd made this walk hundreds of times. Christopher could only think of how it didn't hurt, walking without shoes.

At the base of the widow's peak house, he stopped and looked up.

Their eyes met. The longing between them was so intense it made Christopher's chest ache. This was love. Real, desperate, impossible love.

Then William vanished from the peak.

Christopher knew what happened next. William would appear beside him. They would walk to the barn together.

But this time Christopher could move, couldn't he? This time he could follow along.

William materialized beside him, just like always, translucent in

190

the moonlight. He smiled at Daniel—at Christopher—and took his hand.

They walked together toward the barn behind the smaller farm-house. But the barn wasn't leaning and half-collapsed like Christopher had seen it in reality. This was the barn as it had been in 1890—newly built, solid, a real working structure standing strong and upright.

Inside, the lantern light flickered across sturdy equipment and fresh wood. William set the lantern down on a workbench. Turned to face Daniel.

Christopher could hear them now. Could hear actual words instead of silent mouth movements.

"I need to tell you something," William said. His voice was young, scared, determined.

"What is it?" Daniel's voice—Christopher's voice—sounded worried.

"I can't do this anymore."

Christopher felt Daniel's heart drop. Felt the sudden stab of pain, the confusion.

"What do you mean?"

"This. Us. Hiding. Sneaking around. Living in fear that someone will find out." William's hands were shaking. "It's killing me, Daniel. Every day I wake up and I'm terrified that today will be the day my father discovers the truth. That today will be the day I destroy our families."

"So what are you saying?" Daniel's voice was breaking. "Are you... are you ending us?"

"I'm setting you free." William's eyes were bright with tears. "I won't be a burden to you anymore."

The words hung in the air.

Christopher felt Daniel's confusion. The hurt. The interpretation that William was breaking up with him. Ending their relationship because it was too hard, too dangerous.

"William, please—" Daniel reached for him.

"I'm sorry. I love you so much. But I can't..." William pulled away. "I have to go."

"William, wait—"

But William was already moving, walking out of the barn, grabbing the lantern, darkness closing in except for that one point of light.

Daniel stood frozen, his mind trying to process what had just happened. The boy he loved had just broken up with him. Had just said he was a burden. Had just walked away.

Christopher wanted to scream at Daniel to move, to follow, to understand—

But he was Daniel. He could only feel what Daniel felt. The shock. The heartbreak. The paralysis.

Then, slowly, Daniel's mind started working through the words.

I'm setting you free. I won't be a burden anymore.

Not "I don't want to be with you." Not "I don't love you."

I won't be a burden anymore.

Because he wouldn't be there to be a burden.

Because he was going to—

"No!" Daniel gasped, understanding flooding through him. "No, no, no—"

He ran from the barn, heart hammering, desperate. Ran toward the railroad tracks, following the light of the lantern bouncing ahead of him. That same lantern that had illuminated their path to each other countless times in the dark was now guiding Daniel to witness the greatest tragedy of his life.

Christopher ran with him, felt every step, every surge of terror, every prayer that they'd be in time.

Through the woods. Through the fog. The sound of the train whistle in the distance.

They burst into the clearing by the tracks.

William stood there, one foot wedged in the railroad tie where the ballast had eroded away. His face calm. Resigned. Ready.

"William!" Daniel screamed—Christopher screamed—voice raw with desperation.

William looked at him. Looked at them. And smiled sadly.

"I love you," William said. "This way you'll be free."

"No! Please!" Daniel ran to him, grabbed his arms, tried to pull him away. But William's foot stayed stuck. William acted like he was helping, pulling against Daniel's grip, but Christopher could see the truth—he was struggling to get Daniel to leave. To live. To be safe.

The train was coming. Closer. Louder. The whistle screaming.

Daniel kissed him. Hard and desperate and full of everything he'd never get to say. William kissed back, tears streaming down both their faces.

Then Daniel tried one more time to free William's foot. Pulled with all his strength.

William pushed against him, desperate for Daniel to let go, to save himself.

Nothing.

The train bore down on them, massive and unstoppable.

William shoved Daniel away from the tracks with all the strength he had left.

Daniel fell backward into the gravel, the lantern rolling alongside.

Their eyes met one last time.

I love you.

The train arrived.

Christopher felt Daniel's scream tear through his throat. Felt Daniel's world shatter. Felt all of his grief condense into one moment of absolute devastation.

But Christopher also felt something else. Something Daniel couldn't feel in that moment.

Christopher knew what came after.

Knew Daniel would live alone for forty more years, never loving anyone else.

Knew William's family would collapse under the weight of their loss and shame.

Knew Sarah would marry Thomas Avery and have children who would have children who would have children, down through generations, carrying the tragedy in their blood.

Knew Christopher himself existed because of this moment.

Knew it had all been preventable.

If William had just told Daniel what he was planning. If Daniel had understood sooner. If they'd run away together. If they'd fought instead of giving up. If William hadn't believed that dying was the only way to protect the person he loved.

The grief was unbearable. The waste of it. The preventable, senseless, tragic waste.

But beneath that grief, Christopher felt something else rising.

Terror.

Because Jason had the same protective instincts William had. The same self-loathing. The same belief that he wasn't good enough. The same willingness to sacrifice himself for the people he loved.

Jason, who'd been abandoned by his father and never forgave himself for it.

Jason, who thought he was "white trash" and didn't deserve nice things.

Jason, who'd written *I will protect him* in his notebook like a promise or a threat.

Jason, who might decide the best way to protect Christopher was to "set him free."

Not by dying—Christopher didn't think Jason would do that. But by leaving. By pushing Christopher away. By convincing himself that Christopher would be better off without him.

The train was gone. Daniel was alone in the gravel, sobbing silently, his world ended. The lantern lay on its side, flame extinguished, as dark as Daniel's future.

And Christopher knew—felt with absolute certainty—that if he and Jason didn't find a way to navigate this, didn't find a way to fight for what they had—

History would repeat itself.

Maybe not in the same way. Maybe not with a train and a railroad track. But in the same spirit. In the same tragic, preventable, heartbreaking way.

———

Christopher woke up sobbing.

His face was wet with tears. His pillow damp. His whole body shaking with grief that wasn't entirely his own.

The dream clung to him like cobwebs. Daniel's emotions. William's face. The kiss. The train. The waste of it all.

And underneath everything, the terror that Jason might choose to leave him rather than fight for them.

Christopher looked at his clock: 3:17 AM.

Jason was probably asleep in his own bed, a few miles away, having no idea what Christopher had just witnessed.

Christopher pulled his covers up to his chin and stared at the ceiling, trying to calm his breathing.

He couldn't stop crying. Couldn't stop feeling Daniel's grief mixed with his own fear.

Tomorrow he'd see Jason at school. Tomorrow they'd have to pretend to be just friends. Tomorrow they'd start the hard work of hiding what they were to each other.

And Christopher would have to watch Jason carefully. Would have to make sure he wasn't pulling away. Wouldn't convince himself that Christopher would be better off without him.

Because Christopher had just lived through forty years of Daniel's loneliness in the space of one dream, and he'd rather die than let that happen to Jason.

Or to himself.

Outside his window, the moon hung low and amber in the sky.

Almost full, but not quite.

Just like in the dream.

Chapter 13

Coming Out

Christopher woke to his alarm, his eyes crusted and swollen from crying hours earlier.

Living that dream—Daniel's grief, William's death, that terrible moment of understanding—he had cried until he couldn't anymore. When he finally fell back asleep, it was fitful and broken.

Now, morning light filtered through his curtains, and Christopher felt hollowed out. Exhausted. But beneath the exhaustion was a certainty that wouldn't go away.

He had to tell Jason.

He dragged himself through his morning routine—shower, clothes, attempting to make his hair look less like he'd been through trauma. Looking in the mirror, he looked almost normal. Polished, as always.

But something was off. He could see it even if no one else would.

Downstairs, his mom had already left for work. His dad was finishing coffee, reading the paper at the kitchen table.

"Morning," Mark said, looking up. "You okay? Rough night?"

"Didn't sleep well."

"First day back after a fun weekend. Happens." Mark folded the paper. "You're getting in the car this morning, right? Actually driving?"

"Yeah. I think so."

"That's great! I'll need to take you out this week so you can practice. Get some real road time in." Mark grabbed his keys. "Hey, Jason's welcome to come practice with us too, if he'd like. I'm sure his mom would appreciate it."

Christopher's head snapped up. His dad was... offering to take Jason driving? Trying to include him?

"Uh... thanks, Dad. I'll ask him."

"Good. Now come on, I'll drive you to school."

In the car, Mark kept the conversation light—asking about next weekend's plans, about how Christopher and Jason had become such fast friends, how much he'd enjoyed having Jason over.

"He's a good kid," Mark said as they pulled into the CHS parking lot. "I like him."

There it was again. That deliberate emphasis. That knowing tone.

"Yeah," Christopher managed. "He's really great."

"See you tonight, kiddo. Have a good day."

Christopher climbed out, his mind spinning. His dad definitely knew something. Or suspected. And seemed... happy about it?

———

Jason woke up and realized immediately something was different.

He'd dreamed about Christopher—nothing supernatural, just normal dreams of lying next to him, holding him, kissing him. The warmth of being next to him. Their time together over the weekend.

It was the first time in what seemed forever that he hadn't dreamed about the ghost boys. Which was weird. But maybe... maybe dreams about Christopher were more important than ghost dreams.

Maybe those were the dreams that actually mattered.

Maybe since they now figured out who the ghosts were, he didn't need to dream about them anymore.

He got ready quickly, his mind already focused on seeing Christopher first period. They were gonna' be in the car this morning to actually drive, which was cool but also sort of scary. But mostly he was just thinking about Christopher. About how long yesterday had felt

197

without him. About how much he missed him even though they'd only been apart since the afternoon.

The bike ride to school felt longer than usual. Jason kept replaying Saturday night—waking up with Christopher in his arms, the breakfast with his parents, that moment in Christopher's room when they'd almost kissed before his dad walked in.

How were they supposed to go back to pretending after that?

It's just like before, Jason told himself. *You had feelings before and managed not to show it. This is the same thing.*

Except it wasn't. Before, the feelings were uncertain, unspoken, terrifying. Now they were real and acknowledged and returned.

Now hiding felt impossible.

Jason thought about CHS's no-PDA rule. Most teachers looked the other way when couples held hands or stole quick kisses. But Mr. Delaney was the exception. The history teacher who everyone agreed must have actually lived back when history was being made—ancient, perpetually grumpy, constantly patrolling the hallways near his classroom with a stack of detention slips at the ready. He'd write up any couple he caught being affectionate, treating teenage romance like a personal insult.

But even if every teacher was lenient, even if PDA was encouraged—Jason and Christopher couldn't do any of it.

Because they were two boys. And that changed everything. It fucking sucked.

———

Christopher got to class early, taking his usual seat near the back. Jason arrived a few minutes later, and their eyes met across the room.

Jason looked... tired wasn't quite right. He'd clearly slept better than Christopher. But there was something in his expression—longing, maybe. Need.

Christopher felt it echo in his own chest.

Jason slid into the desk beside him. "Hey."

"Hey."

Jason studied Christopher's face, and Christopher saw the exact

198

moment Jason noticed something was wrong. No one else would see it —Christopher looked put-together as always. But Jason knew. They had some sort of chemistry that way.

"You okay?" Jason asked quietly.

"Rough night. I'll tell you later."

The bell rang, and Mr. Barnes burst through the door right on cue, his usual enthusiasm cranked to maximum.

"Good morning, drivers! Hope everyone's ready because today we're taking this show on the road! Well, not the road exactly—the parking lot. Baby steps, people, baby steps!" He was already pulling out his roster, his keys jangling. "Now, before we head out, let me explain the setup. Half of you will stay here with Ms. Anderson—"

A woman in her thirties wearing a CHS Physical Education shirt waved from the back of the room.

"—who has graciously volunteered to supervise you on the simulators while I take the other half outside. You'll each get about ten minutes behind the wheel today. Just the basics—starting, stopping, steering, not hitting anything. Sound good?"

Nervous laughter rippled through the classroom.

"Alright, let me call out today's lucky drivers. Johnson and Miller, Davis and Chen, Reynolds and Avery..." He continued down the list. "Everyone I called, grab your partner and follow me. The rest of you, Ms. Anderson will get you set up here."

They filed out, Christopher and Jason trailing behind the others. As soon as they had a moment of relative privacy in the stairwell, Christopher leaned close.

"I had the dream again. But this time I was Daniel. I saw everything from his perspective. I heard them in the barn—"

"Avery! Reynolds! Let's keep moving, boys!"

They jerked apart, hurrying to catch up with the group.

"Since you two are the last ones here," Mr. Barnes called as they emerged into the parking lot, "you'll be first in the car. Go ahead and get in—Christopher, you up front, Jason, hang in the back there— while I address everyone else."

Christopher climbed into the driver's seat. Jason slid in behind him. Through the windshield, they could see Mr. Barnes gathering the other students on the sidewalk.

"I need to tell you the rest," Christopher said urgently, turning in his seat to look at Jason. "William told Daniel he was setting him free. That he wouldn't be a burden anymore. And Daniel thought—he thought William was breaking up with him. But then he realized William was going to—"

"Kill himself."

"Yeah. And I'm worried that you might—not that, I don't think you'd do that—but that you might feel like you're not... well, good enough or something stupid. And that with all the worries about us being caught, you might decide it's easier to just... let go. To leave. To leave... me."

Jason reached forward immediately, squeezing Christopher's shoulder. "Hey. Look at me."

Christopher turned again, eyes bright with unshed tears.

"I'm not going anywhere, Christopher. Yeah, I can see how you might feel that way after the dream. And I worry about being good enough for you, sometimes."

"Stop that, Jason! You're just as good. Better!"

Jason's chest tightened. Students were just outside, but here they were nearly in tears. He inhaled, accepting Christopher's fear even though he didn't quite feel worthy of the love behind it. "But I want you. I love you. I'm not leaving."

Christopher felt something loosen in his chest. Maybe he was overthinking this. Maybe Jason didn't feel that way. Maybe this wasn't exactly what Daniel was trying to tell him.

"Okay," Christopher whispered. "Okay. I'm sorry."

"Don't be, babe. I'm here."

Jason squeezed his shoulder one more time, then quickly pulled his hand back as the passenger door opened.

Mr. Barnes climbed in, his cheerful demeanor firmly in place. "Alright, gentlemen! Ready to learn how to operate a motor vehicle without causing property damage or bodily harm?"

Jason worried Barnes had seen him touching Christopher's shoulder. But Barnes gave no indication, just launched into his instructions about mirrors and seat positions and where to put your hands on the wheel.

But he had noticed. Added it to the other moments he'd witnessed between these two boys. The way they looked at each other. The way they moved in each other's orbit.

He saw it because he'd lived it. Twenty-five years ago, in these same hallways, trying to hide who he was while dying inside from the effort.

"Okay, Christopher," Mr. Barnes said. "Let's start the engine."

———

By lunch, Jason felt like he'd been holding his breath all morning.

The driving had been fine—Christopher was a natural, careful and precise. Jason's turn had been shakier, but Barnes had been patient and encouraging. And then they'd separated for their different classes, and Jason had been counting down the minutes until lunch.

Until he could see Christopher again.

The periods after driving felt like they'd been separated for months instead of hours. Jason found his usual table in the cafeteria, spotting Scott already there. Then Allison appeared, tweaking his side and making him jump.

"What's gotten into you, Mr. Crabby Pants?" She was already pulling him into the lunch line.

Jason was scanning the cafeteria for Christopher. Where was he? He should be here by now—

Then Christopher came almost running in, slightly out of breath. He headed straight for his boyfriend like a magnet, and for a moment Jason thought he was going to hug him right there in front of everyone.

Christopher caught himself at the last second, stopping short and quickly fixing his hair to cover his near-miss.

"English exam," Christopher gasped. "Finished early but Mrs. Grant made us all stay until the last person turned theirs in. Bell rang two minutes ago. I sprinted here."

Allison grabbed Christopher and pulled him in front of her in line. "Well then, you're first. Jason, you're behind me."

They got their food and sat down. Jason and Christopher fell into their usual rhythm—talking about classes, about homework, about nothing important. But something was different. Allison could feel it. The way they looked at each other. The way Christopher leaned slightly toward Jason when he talked. The way Jason's whole body oriented toward Christopher like a sunflower following light.

Scott launched into a story about football practice, something about forcing a fumble from the quarterback. Christopher looked genuinely interested, nodding in all the right places, and both Allison and Jason knew he had absolutely no clue what Scott was talking about.

Allison caught Jason's eye, giving him a significant look. *Well?*

Jason looked away quickly.

"Did I ever tell you the story," Allison said loudly, "about my best friend from band camp in junior high? Everyone thought he was gay, but—"

Jason's eyes bulged. Scott wasn't paying attention, still walking Christopher through his imaginary play-by-play on the table. But he looked up when he heard the word "gay."

Jason gritted his teeth and smiled at Allison. "No. I don't think you've *ever* told us *that* story." His eyes said: *What the fuck are you doing?*

She beamed back. "It's a good one."

"I didn't know you were in band camp," Christopher interjected quickly, his voice tight. "What was it like?"

"Oh yeah, there's *lots* you don't know about me." Allison's smile widened. "But I bet there's *lots* I don't know about *you* either. Right?"

"Oh, I'm pretty simple," Jason said through clenched teeth. "I think you know all that's interesting."

"Really?" She turned to Christopher and Scott, who looked annoyed because he was just getting to the best part of his football story. "What about you, Christopher? Have any fun stories about yourself we don't know?"

Christopher looked like he might throw up. Jason kicked Allison's leg under the table while simultaneously giving Christopher a *she's just being a bitch* look.

"Uh, I'm kinda... normal, I guess. Boring."

Allison kicked Jason back, playfully. "Really? You look like an interesting guy. I bet you probably could tell some fun stories, right?"

"Uh..."

"We climbed up to the top of that old farmhouse on Saturday," Jason interjected, trying to save Christopher from further embarrassment. He'd bitch-slap Allison later. Well, not literally—she'd kick his ass. But still, what the fuck was she trying to pull?

Allison's eyes shot up, momentarily forgetting her fishing expedition. "Really? And you didn't fall through the roof?"

Christopher found his voice, annoying Scott who was just "getting to the good part" of his story. "Oh my god, it was so scary. We laid on our stomachs and crawled up the last bit."

"You? And him?" Allison pointed at Jason. "Had to crawl? Jesus! I'd be fucking scared shitless."

"But the view was amazing," Christopher added, warming to the safer topic. "It was so... so quiet. Just the wind. And you can see Connersville off in the distance to the east. The lights are actually pretty from way up there."

"Wait. You did this at night?"

Jason blushed and looked down. "Well... yeah. We sorta had to do it after everyone was asleep."

"Hold on, hold on." Allison was leaning forward now. "You both snuck out of your houses?"

They nodded guiltily.

"So you could climb a haunted farmhouse to the roof?"

More nods.

"Which you could've fallen through?"

They just looked at her.

Scott was staring at everyone like they'd lost their goddamn minds.

"Wow!" Allison clapped her hands together, causing the tables around them to wonder what was up. "That takes balls! I just sneak out to buy ciggies, but this haunted house shit? That's... that's kinda fucked up!"

Christopher didn't know if she was praising or admonishing them.

Jason knew her well enough to recognize she was impressed. He'd never been a "bad ass" to her despite what people thought. Allison had always seen him as her vulnerable friend.

"But Christopher's right," Jason said. "It was pretty fucking cool to look out at night."

"I bet. I can't even..." Allison got quieter, leaning in. "Wait. Did you see any... ghosts?"

Christopher shot Jason a look that betrayed their defenses.

Allison's eyes went wide. "No. Fucking. Way." She mouthed the words.

Jason just stared.

"I want details."

Jason nodded subtly toward Scott and around them. *Not here.*

"Oh." She corrected herself immediately, slapping Jason's arm playfully. "You're fucking with me!"

Scott rolled his eyes. Jason exhaled with relief.

Lunch had been a fucking roller coaster.

Scott picked back up with his football story. Christopher tried to look engaged while keeping his ears perked for whatever Jason and Allison were planning to throw at him next.

Allison's eyes lit up. She made a show of setting down her fork and sliding her cafeteria tray away in disgust. "This shit is... well, shit!"

She turned to Christopher, as if suddenly remembering something. "Didn't you say you were gonna help me with that Calculus problem I had?"

Her eyes commanded him to go along with it.

Christopher looked up, caught her gaze, almost asked "What Calculus problem?" but suddenly read her message. He turned to Jason, who side-eyed Allison with an *I dunno* shrug but kept quiet.

"Uh... oh... uh, yeah. That... uh... problem. Yeah."

Allison stood. "We've still got twenty minutes left. Just enough time before I have to turn in my homework."

Jason looked at her, then at Christopher who was rising along with her like an actor who hadn't been given the script. Then he understood.

He stood. "I'm coming too. Lunch sucks." He looked at Scott apologetically. "Sorry, man. Next time."

The three nodded to Scott, who still hadn't finished his story. He was almost at the best part.

———

Allison pulled Jason and Christopher into the backstage dressing room —the same place she'd brought Jason last week.

Christopher was nervous and uncertain and completely unaware that he was clinging to Jason as if for protection. This immensely amused Allison.

"So, you two," she said, crossing her arms. "Spill it!"

Christopher panicked, but Jason reached over and patted his arm. Christopher realized he'd been clinging and let go quickly.

Allison was grinning. "The jig is up."

"Fine," Jason said. "But you've gotta SWEAR not to say a word!"

She crossed her fingers over her heart, then mimed locking her lips and throwing away the key.

Christopher's head whipped to Jason. Was he really going to—?

"We're boyfriends."

He did.

Allison's smile turned up to eleven. She clapped her hands together like dinner had been served. "I knew it! I knew it! I'm so happy for you guys!"

Jason couldn't help but smile, even as his heart tried to escape his chest.

Now Christopher thought everyone had lost their goddamn minds.

"It's okay, Christopher." Allison walked toward him. He didn't realize he was backing up like she was an attacker until Jason put his arm around him and held him close.

"It's okay, babe."

"Babe?" both Allison and Christopher said simultaneously, making Jason self-conscious.

"Well," Jason said defensively to Allison, "he's my boyfriend!"

Turning to Christopher, who was now properly distracted from just being outed: "I'm sorry, babe. She... well, she knew. Sorta."

"Sorta," Allison confirmed.

"I mean, she's..." Jason struggled.

"Cool with it," Allison interrupted. "I actually am so happy for you both!"

Christopher felt like he was happy and angry and worried and confused all at once. He sat down in a plastic chair by the makeup counter.

"I'm sorry, Christopher," Allison said, her cocky demeanor suddenly maternal. "I... I really just wanted you two to feel like you had an ally, you know?"

He could only shake his head. Jason knelt beside him, rubbing his back.

"Babe? Are you okay?"

Christopher could only hear the word "babe." He looked at Jason, who looked genuinely worried. Then at Allison, standing there with unexpected kindness in her eyes.

This wasn't how he'd planned to come out to anyone. He hadn't even really come out—it just happened. This was so surreal. And he was worried people would hurt him. But Jason didn't seem worried. Allison seemed supportive. He was just getting to know her, but maybe he could trust her. Maybe...

"Babe?" The word came out of Christopher's mouth to no one in particular.

Jason grinned. Allison breathed again.

Christopher turned to Jason. His face relaxed. "Yeah. I guess I like hearing it."

The cold room suddenly warmed.

"Listen, Christopher, this is all my fault. I get these ideas in my head and you know me—I can't go without fucking up something!" Allison tried to lighten the mood.

"I accept your apology, but..." Christopher got quiet before turning to both of them. "Can you give me at least a heads-up next time before everyone goes complete batshit crazy?" He grinned.

Jason fell back off his knees onto the floor. He needed this laugh.

Allison bit her lip and ran over, enveloping Christopher in a big hug. "Okay, next time I'll just yell out that I'm off my meds!"

Everyone laughed.

"Seriously though, guys. I'm really happy for you. You're right for each other."

They blushed. Jason realized how much he wanted to go back and hold Christopher, but something held him back as he sat on the floor.

Allison noticed. "Jesus, Jason—get off your ass and hug your boyfriend, why don't you? What are you? A heathen?"

He smiled and got up, grabbing Christopher from behind and slinging his arms around him. This felt wonderful.

Christopher's fears, his anxiety, the whirlwind that had been the last fifty minutes—it all vanished once he felt Jason's arms around him. Holding tight. Warm. Loving.

Both looked up at Allison, who was beaming. "You two look so happy together."

They blushed collectively but looked down.

The bell rang. Jason instinctively pulled his arms away. "Time to get back to pretending."

Christopher's eyes dropped. Allison noticed immediately.

"Listen, uh, guys... Your secret is safe with me. And I'm sorry."

"You already apologized," Christopher said.

"No, I mean... I'm sorry you both need to keep it secret. It fucking sucks. But I get it."

They didn't respond. What was there to say?

"But you're welcome to be yourselves with me, at least. I know that's worth jack shit, but I support you both. Okay?"

They nodded. It was a nice gesture.

"And listen," she looked at Jason. "If anyone gives you any shit, so help me, I'll tear off their dicks and make them eat it."

Christopher winced at the thought. Jason giggled—he knew where her heart was.

"Maybe we could double date sometime?" Allison suggested.

Jason rolled his eyes. "Yeah, right!"

"Why not?"

"Uh, obvious, party of two!"

Christopher giggled but understood.

"Oh, fuck them and the horse they rode in on. We can go bowling or to the movies or—"

"Bowling. Now there's a gay-friendly date night!" Jason snickered at his own sarcasm.

The word hung in the air.

Gay.

Up until now, everyone had spoken about "it" without naming "it." Now it was here. And it felt... taboo but powerful. Empowering.

Both Christopher and Jason felt it. Allison noticed.

"That's right," Jason said suddenly, like he needed to say it. "I'm gay, Allison."

"So am I," Christopher added. "Gay." He tacked it on just to be sure.

They moved closer together, Christopher placing his arm around his boyfriend. The pair looked like they dared anyone to contest it.

Allison folded her arms and stood back, admiring their spunk. "No," she finally said, causing them to tense with concern. "You're fabulous!"

She snapped her fingers.

"You're such a bitch," Jason laughed.

Christopher looked wide-eyed, but Allison quickly responded: "No, I'm *the* bitch, thank you very much!"

Christopher allowed himself to laugh. His boyfriend and their friend—she was something else.

"C'mon, boy toys. We gotta get to class!"

———

David Barnes sat in his small office, eating a sandwich and grading quizzes when his phone rang.

"This is David Barnes."

"David? It's Mark Avery."

David froze, sandwich halfway to his mouth. Mark Avery. From high school. They'd been friendly back then—not close, but friendly. Mark had been one of the few who hadn't participated in the whispers and names.

But they hadn't really talked since high school. Sure, they'd run into each other over the years—pleasantries at the grocery store, a wave across a parking lot—but they hadn't really talked. Had to be twenty, twenty-five years.

"Mark. Wow. It's been a long time."

"I know. Too long." Mark's voice was warm. "My son's in your class. Christopher Avery."

"Oh! Yeah, Christopher's a great kid. Doing really well."

"That's good to hear. Listen, David…" Mark paused. "I know this is out of the blue, but recently I've been talking with my son and… well…"

"Is Christopher okay?"

"Oh yes, he's doing quite well, actually. Now that he's found a friend."

Mark had said it like a slip. Like he'd revealed more than he meant to.

"Jason Reynolds," David said. "Yes, they seem to have really joined at the hip. Jason's a nice kid. They seem to do well together in class."

"Yeah, he was over this weekend. And we were chatting about when I was in high school. And, well…" Mark got quiet. "One thing led to another. And I think they're trying to figure things out, if you know what I mean."

David's breath caught. He knew exactly what Mark meant.

"And I just remember how kids were back when we were their age," Mark continued, stammering slightly. "And, well… I felt really bad about all the grief everyone gave you. I should've said more back then. I would like to make it up to you. Especially now that I'm trying to be there for my son."

David felt his throat close. "That's… Mark, that's really kind of you to say."

"I mean it. But listen, I would legitimately like to catch up. Not just talk about my son. I'm sure there are plenty of stories all around. Would you want to come over for dinner? This Thursday?"

"I…" David was thrown. "I don't want to impose—"

Michael Manosca

"You're not imposing. I'd love to hear your stories, if you'd like to share. Diane—my wife—would love to meet you too."

David felt his carefully constructed armor crack just a little. "Uh, sure. That would be fun."

"Perfect. Six o'clock? I'll give you the address." Mark rattled it off, and David scribbled it down.

"Sounds good."

There was a pause. David was about to hang up when Mark spoke again—quickly, casually, like an afterthought:

"Oh, and David? If there's someone you'd like to bring along, we'd love to have him."

David's breath stopped.

Him.

Not "them" or "someone" or "a friend." *Him.*

Mark knew. Or suspected. And was letting David know—gently, carefully—that it was okay. That whoever David wanted to bring would be welcome.

"I... thank you, Mark. I'll let you know."

"Great. Looking forward to it. See you Thursday."

The line went dead.

David sat there, phone still pressed to his ear, his sandwich forgotten.

Mark Avery had just apologized for high school. Had invited him to dinner. Had made it clear that David's partner—Jim, whom David had never mentioned, never talked about openly at school—would be welcome in his home.

After all these years.

David set down the phone and pressed his hands over his face. He wasn't going to cry. He was forty-two years old, for god's sake. But his eyes were burning.

When was the last time someone had made him feel this seen? This accepted?

He pulled himself together and went back to grading quizzes. But his hands were shaking slightly.

Christopher and Jason. He'd been watching them for weeks now. Had deliberately paired them as partners because he recognized some-

210

thing in them—the careful distance, the stolen glances, the way they orbited each other even as they tried to resist.

He saw it because he'd lived it. Twenty-five years ago, in these same hallways, trying to hide himself.

And now Mark Avery—whose son was living the same struggle—was reaching out. Creating a safe space. Opening a door.

David needed to talk to Jim., of course. Needed to figure out if bringing him was brave or reckless.

Needed to figure out how to help those two boys without exposing them—or himself—to danger.

Thursday was going to be very interesting indeed.

———

After school, Jason waited by the bike rack, pretending to check his tire while scanning for Christopher.

He spotted him coming out of the main building. Christopher's eyes found Jason immediately, and he altered his path.

"Hey," Christopher said, a bit too loudly for show. "Can you... do you have a minute?"

They were overdoing their pretending a bit. Jason played along. "Yeah, sure."

They walked his bike toward the edge of the parking lot, away from buses and crowds. Found a spot near the fence where no one was paying attention.

"You okay?" Jason asked. "After lunch? After Allison?"

"I don't know. It's still hitting me." Christopher looked dazed. "We came out. We actually came out to someone."

"I know."

"And she was... she was okay with it. More than okay."

"She was happy for us."

"Yeah." Christopher's voice was wondering. "She was."

They stood there, and Jason felt the ache of wanting to touch him.

"I want to kiss you so badly it hurts," Jason said quietly.

Christopher's breath hitched. "Me too."

"We can't."

"I know."

"Can I call you tonight? After dinner? I want to talk. About every-thing. The dream. Allison. All of it."

"Yeah. Please."

Jason forced himself to step back. "I should go."

"Yeah. Okay."

They stood there a moment longer.

"Jason?"

"Yeah?"

"Thank you. For being brave for me. For telling Allison. I don't think I could have done it without you."

"We did it together."

Christopher smiled—small and genuine. "Call me later?"

"I will. I promise."

———

Dinner at the Avery house was quiet—Christopher and his parents, eating the chicken and rice Diane had made.

"So," Mark said. "I called David today. You know, like I mentioned yesterday at breakfast?"

Christopher looked up. "Oh yeah? How'd it go?"

"Really well. He's coming for dinner Thursday night."

Christopher set down his fork carefully, trying to look casual. "That's nice."

"And I was thinking—Jason should come too. Make it a real dinner party. What do you think?"

Christopher's stomach flipped. "Jason? Yeah, I mean... sure. I'll ask him."

"Great!" Mark went back to his chicken like he hadn't just set Christopher's entire world spinning. Diane gave both of them a look and changed the subject.

After dinner, Christopher escaped to his room and immediately called Jason.

Jason picked up on the second ring. "Hey."

"Okay, so Thursday. Mr. Barnes is definitely coming. And my dad wants you there."

"I figured. Your dad mentioned it yesterday, right?"

"Yeah, but it's actually happening. Jason, do you think they know?"

"They have to. This is too deliberate."

"Should we say something before Thursday?"

"Like what? 'Hi Mom, pass the butter, by the way I'm gay and my partner in Mr. Barnes's class is my boyfriend'?"

Jason laughed. "When you put it like that..."

They talked for over an hour—about Allison, about saying the word "gay" out loud, about how it felt both terrifying and powerful. About the dream Christopher had and what it meant. About Thursday and what might happen.

When they finally hung up, Christopher lay in bed trying to process everything.

But before he could get too deep in his thoughts, he heard voices downstairs. His parents talking in the living room. He crept to his door and opened it slightly.

"...really think bringing David into this is a good idea?" his mom was saying.

"I think it's exactly what we need to do," his dad replied. "Show Christopher that we're not just okay with it—we support it. And having David there, someone who's lived through this, who understands..."

"You're right. I just hope we're not pushing too hard."

"We're not pushing. We're opening a door. Christopher will walk through it when he's ready."

Christopher closed his door softly, his heart pounding.

They definitely knew.

And they were okay with it.

More than okay—they were trying to help.

———

Jason hung up the phone and wandered into the living room where his mom and Rick were watching TV.

"Mom?"

She looked up. "Yeah, honey?"

"Mr. Avery invited me to a dinner he's having Thursday. Can I go? I know it's a school night, but—"

"Christopher's dad?"

"Yeah. He's having Mr. Barnes over for dinner and since he's our teacher, he thought we'd like to join. I guess they know each other or something."

"You and Christopher?"

"Yeah."

She glanced at Rick, who wasn't paying attention, and shrugged. "Sure, that sounds fine." But then she paused, a thought crossing her face. Jason knew that look.

She got up from the sofa and pulled out the phone book. She could've asked Jason for the number, but something told her he'd be embarrassed if he knew what she was about to do.

Finding the Averys' listing, she dialed.

"Hello?" Christopher's voice.

"Hi Christopher, this is Jason's mom. Is your father home?"

Jason's jaw dropped. What was she doing? Calling to verify he'd actually been invited? Didn't she trust him?

He stood close enough to eavesdrop, not even trying to hide it.

"Hi, it's Sarah Reynolds," his mom said. "Sorry for the late call. Listen, Jason tells me you've invited him to dinner Thursday?"

Jason's heart sank. She was checking up on him. She didn't believe—

"I think it's a great idea," his mom continued. "But since it's a school night and I need to be in Indianapolis early Friday, I'm wondering if you'd object to Jason staying over? That way I wouldn't worry about him riding his bike home late."

Jason's jaw dropped further.

"You will? Oh, I'm sure he'll be thrilled. I'll tell him. Yes, that'd be fine. Oh, I'd love to have you both over as well. We'll plan it sometime soon. Yes, soon. Okay, thanks Mark. Goodnight."

She hung up and turned to find Jason staring at her.

"Mr. Avery agreed it would be better if you stayed with Christopher Thursday. That way you don't have to head home late. I've got meetings in Indianapolis Friday morning, and you can just ride to school with Christopher."

Was he living in a dream? Had his mom just... arranged an overnight for him?

He nearly ran and hugged her. But he played it cool, forgetting to ask about her meetings or what they meant. He assumed it was about her job, but he was too consumed with Thursday to think clearly.

"Is that okay, honey?"

She was looking at him funny. He realized he hadn't said a word.

"Oh, uh, yeah. That works." He tried to sound nonchalant.

Inside, he was high-fiving and jumping for joy.

She knew though. She could tell. The twinkle in his eye. The way his mind had gone elsewhere while she explained. She'd just waited for him to realize she'd spoken.

And she knew. Finally knew for certain.

Her son was in love with Christopher.

Maybe he'd tell her one day. When he was ready.

Chapter 14

Jim

Wednesday night, David sat at the kitchen table staring at the home address Mark had given him, a glass of wine half-empty beside him.

Jim came up behind him, reading over his shoulder. "You're over-thinking this."

"I know."

"It's just dinner."

"With my student and, I'm pretty sure, his boyfriend. And his parents who apparently know and are trying to help." David rubbed his face. "What if bringing you makes it worse? What if—"

"David." Jim pulled out the chair beside him and sat, reaching for David's hand. "What are you really worried about?"

"That people will talk. That Christopher and Jason will be exposed because of us. That I'll lose my job. That—" He stopped, took a breath. "That we'll make it harder for them instead of easier."

Jim was quiet for a moment, his thumb tracing circles on David's hand. Then, in that gentle way he had: "How long, love? How long do we keep hiding? Keep pretending we're something we're not?" He squeezed David's hand. "If we can't show those boys that it's possible— that two men can love each other and build a life—then who will? And

216

if people want to ostracize us for just existing in this town you grew up in, this place I've come to love as much as you do, then where would we go? Where would be different enough to actually matter?"

David looked at him. "Nowhere."

"Exactly. Nowhere." Jim's voice was soft but certain. "So maybe it's time we stop acting like loving each other is something to apologize for."

"I'm not ready to march in a pride parade."

Jim laughed, warm and easy. "God, neither am I. But having dinner with a family who invited us—*both* of us, knowing what we are—that's not a parade, honey. That's just being ourselves."

David took a long sip of wine. "What if the boys freak out?"

"What if they don't?" Jim leaned forward. "What if they need to see it? That two guys can be happy together? Really happy?"

"We are happy."

"I know we are. But do they?" Jim smiled. "Let's show them."

David nodded slowly. "Okay. But we keep it normal. No need to show up making announcements."

"Agreed."

"But no hiding either. At least not from this family."

"Exactly. We'll just be ourselves." Jim grinned. "And we're pretty damn good at that, aren't we?"

David smiled despite his nerves. "Yeah. We really are."

Jim stood, then paused at the doorway. "Oh, and David?"

"Yeah?"

"Tomorrow night? You won't be at school. So no need to come in with all that manic teacher energy, okay?"

David bristled. "I don't do that."

Jim actually laughed out loud.

"Well. Okay, maybe I do a little, but—"

"Be yourself," Jim said softly, coming back to cup David's face. "The man I fell in love with. Not the performance. Just you. For me. For yourself. For those boys."

Thursday morning, David Barnes did something unusual.

After another round of students behind the wheel—Christopher and Jason in the classroom on simulators this time—he waited until the bell rang, then made a decision that was probably against his better judgment.

As students filed out, he approached Ms. Anderson. "Could you do me a favor? Have the office call Christopher Avery and Jason Reynolds down just before lunch?"

"Sure thing. Everything okay?"

"Everything's fine. I just need to speak with them about... something."

He spent the rest of the morning second-guessing himself, eating lunch at his desk while waiting for them to arrive.

Jason was walking toward the cafeteria when he heard his name over the intercom.

"Jason Reynolds and Christopher Avery, please report to Mr. Barnes's office."

Students around him immediately started razzing him. "Ooooh, getting detention?" "What'd you do?" "Barnes is gonna talk you to death!"

Jason's stomach dropped. He changed direction, heading toward the guidance office, his mind racing. Had someone seen something? Said something? Were they in trouble?

Christopher arrived moments later, looking absolutely terrified. They stood in front of the secretary's desk, exchanging panicked looks that said everything words couldn't.

David emerged from his office, his usual enthusiasm dialed up. "Boys! Come on in! Ms. Patterson, hold my calls please."

He ushered them into his office and closed the door. His lunch bag sat on the corner of his desk. The boys noticed how lonely it must be, eating at your desk with no one to talk to.

They sat in the chairs angled in front while David settled into his own, something shifting in his demeanor. The performance dropped. He seemed more himself—relaxed, real.

He looked at both boys and sighed.

"Relax. You're not in trouble."

Christopher actually let out the breath he'd been holding. David noticed and smiled gently. Jason kept darting his eyes between Christopher and Mr. Barnes, still tense, ready to protect if needed.

"I didn't get a chance to see you before class ended, but I had a thought." David leaned forward, hands folded on his desk. "I'm giving you both a lift to your house for dinner tonight, Christopher. If that's okay?"

They blinked. That was... not what they'd expected.

"Oh." Christopher's shoulders dropped slightly. "Uh, sure. But—"

"I know, your father said six. But I thought, if you don't mind..." David's mind raced, trying to figure out how to say this without it sounding wrong. "I'd like to introduce you to someone before we all show up at your door. Someone your father invited to dinner as well. Give you a chance to meet him first, maybe chat a bit before the whole family thing."

He saw their confused looks. His heart hammered. God, was he really doing this?

"I'd like you to meet my partner."

Both boys' eyes went wide.

So it was true. *Partner.* That meant boyfriend, right?

"He's coming to dinner too, and I thought..." David was fumbling now, could hear himself rambling. "He's a wonderful person. Really interesting stories—he's a pilot, travels all over. It's rare he's home for something like this, which makes it special, and I just thought maybe if you met him first, at our place, it might be—" He caught himself. "Sorry. I'm rambling."

Jason's smile started curling at his lips without him meaning it to. He found himself nodding, like his body knew before his brain caught up. Christopher caught his smile, felt his own starting.

David saw it and stopped mid-thought, bracing for the worst. He always did on those rare occasions when he spoke of Jim out loud.

But Jason spoke up, voice warm and certain. "I'd really like that, Mr. Barnes."

Christopher looked at Jason, then at David, then back at Jason. His mind was spinning but something about Jason's confidence made him nod too. Still shy, still nervous about being outed—this was all so new. But then he realized Mr. Barnes wasn't outing them. He was outing *himself*. Sort of. And he seemed so genuine, so nervous himself.

And Christopher found himself curious. What was it like for two people like him and Jason to actually *live* together? Real life. Especially here in Connersville. He didn't even think it was possible. Wouldn't they get harassed? Wouldn't people...

But then he realized—he would've heard about it. Connersville was small. People knew everyone's business. Sure, there were whispers about Mr. Barnes. The limp wrist gestures. The knowing looks. But nobody really said anything mean. And lots of people genuinely liked him—his energy at school events, his terrible jokes that somehow made everyone laugh anyway.

"Christopher?" David asked gently, pulling him from his thoughts. "Would that be okay? I'd like your permission before I call your father to let him know."

"Oh. Yeah. Sure." Christopher realized he'd been lost in his head. "Sorry, I was just thinking."

David knew exactly what he was thinking. Had a pretty good idea anyway. He'd thought the same things at their age.

He wasn't sure this was the right move. But Jim's words from last night—about being role models, about showing these boys it was possible—they'd struck something deep.

He couldn't out himself to the whole school. That was still too dangerous, too risky. But sitting here with these two boys, watching their faces as he talked about Jim, something told him this was right.

They needed people like him and Jim. Needed to know there was life beyond the fear.

And maybe—just maybe—this would help him and Jim step a little further out of their own fear too.

"Great. I'll call your father, let him know the plan. Why don't you both come by after school?"

"Okay," Jason said easily.

Christopher just nodded, already retreating back into his anxious thoughts.

As they stood to leave, David added one more thing, and his voice carried weight now.

"Guys? What we talk about today—what you see at our home—I'd appreciate if we kept that between us and our families." He looked at them directly. "I want to be sensitive to you both, and to be honest, to Jim and myself too."

"Of course, Mr. Barnes," Christopher said quickly, understanding immediately.

"I mean it," David continued, softer now. "Obviously we're looking forward to reconnecting with your father, Christopher, meeting your mother. And Jason—" He turned. "I'm happy to share our life with your family too. I want everyone to feel comfortable. Safe."

"We get it," Jason said, and something in his voice made David believe him. "We won't say anything."

Jason understood what David was really saying. This was as much for them as it was for David and Jim.

David exhaled, not realizing he'd been holding his breath. "Great. Then I'll see you after school."

The boys left and walked slowly toward lunch, the hallway noise washing over them as they processed what had just happened.

Christopher felt like his head was spinning. Were they that obvious? Had Mr. Barnes figured them out so completely that he felt comfortable coming out to them? Did this mean they'd joined some secret club? And that felt kind of wonderful—like they weren't totally alone. But also terrifying. Because if Mr. Barnes could tell, and Christopher's parents clearly knew (or strongly suspected), and Jason's mom was acting strange, and Allison knew...

Did others know too?

Was it only a matter of time before everyone knew?

They'd spent the last few days trying so hard to just act normal. To be like they were before. But it was exhausting, like being on stage every second, having to watch every word, every gesture, fighting the constant urge to reach for each other.

Before they'd gotten together, they'd just chat casually here and there. Easy. Natural.

Now they still chatted, but underneath it all was this desperate want—to hold hands, to touch, to be alone together, to stop pretending.

Jason glanced at Christopher and saw it all over his face—the anxiety, the overthinking, the fear trying to crowd out the hope.

"Hey," Jason said quietly as they walked. "It's gonna be okay."

Christopher looked at him, and some of the tension eased. "Yeah?"

"Yeah. I promise."

Back in his office, David stepped into the outer lobby, pretending to check his mailbox. Through the window, he watched Jason and Christopher cross the courtyard toward the cafeteria, heads close together, talking in hushed tones with gestures only they understood.

He knew exactly what they were discussing. The same things he'd agonized over at their age.

Returning to his office, he closed the door, picked up the phone, and looked up Mark Avery's work number.

What the hell was he doing?

He hoped Jim would be okay with this.

The phone rang twice before Mark picked up.

"Mark Avery."

"Mark, it's David Barnes."

"David! Good to hear from you. Everything okay?"

"Everything's fine. I just wanted to run something by you about tonight..."

After school, Jason and Christopher met Mr. Barnes at his car in the faculty parking lot. The afternoon sun was warm, the parking lot mostly empty now.

"Alright, gentlemen," David said cheerfully, unlocking the doors. "Who wants to drive?"

They looked at each other, then at the car—Mr. Barnes's personal car, not the beat-up Driver's Ed mobile.

Jason hesitated. "Uh..."

"Come on, Jason." David's voice was encouraging, not pushy. "It's just a few blocks. Over toward Gray Road. Good practice."

Jason reluctantly climbed into the driver's seat, his heart already hammering. What if he screwed up and crashed Mr. Barnes's actual car?

Christopher jumped in the back without thinking and immediately leaned forward, his hand finding Jason's arm. "You can do it."

The touch was instinctive, natural. David saw it from the passenger seat and felt his heart clench with recognition. God, that was him and Jim twenty years ago.

"Relax," David said gently as Jason's knuckles went white on the steering wheel. "It's just like we practiced. You can go slow. I promise I won't let you crash, Jason."

Jason started the engine, hands shaking slightly.

They made it to David and Jim's home in about five minutes, Jason driving twenty miles per hour at most, white-knuckling the entire way.

When he finally shifted into park, David smiled. "You can breathe now."

"You did it!" Christopher said from the backseat, squeezing Jason's shoulder. Pride and relief in his voice.

Jason realized he'd been holding his breath practically the entire drive.

"We're here," David said, climbing out.

The house took their breath away. A well-kept brick ranch nestled among trees, the yard sprawling and green. The garage sat off to the side. But the landscaping—that's what really caught their attention. Autumn flowers and carefully planned greenery, leaves just beginning to collect in a small gulch at the back. The front porch wrapped around, extensive and welcoming.

It was nicer than most homes in town. Nicer even than Christopher's house.

Jason and Christopher took it all in, following David around to the side entrance that led into the kitchen.

"Jim!" David called as he opened the door. "I have, uh, a surprise!"

From somewhere inside—the front room, it sounded like—they heard a voice calling back. "You're home early, love! I thought we weren't leaving until—"

Jim appeared in the kitchen doorway and stopped mid-sentence.

He saw Jason and Christopher standing just behind David.

"Surprise?" David said meekly.

Jim took half a second to process, then his whole face lit up with genuine warmth. "Well, hello there! Welcome to our home!" He came forward, hand extended. "I'm Jim, and you must be..."

Jim was taller than David by a good six inches—lean and graceful, with a short trimmed beard just starting to grey in a way that made him look distinguished rather than old. His hair was neat, parted to the side. His eyes were striking—bright, kind, immediately welcoming. He wore a button-down oxford with sleeves rolled at the cuffs and well-fitting jeans. Barefoot, like he'd been reading comfortably on the sofa.

Which he probably had been.

Christopher just stared. Jim was striking. Not that Mr. Barnes wasn't nice-looking, but they'd seen him a thousand times. He was their teacher. But Jim—Jim was someone entirely new. Someone who looked like he belonged in magazines or on television, not in Connersville, Indiana.

Jason stepped forward first, finding his courage more easily here than anywhere else lately. He shook Jim's hand firmly. "I'm Jason Reynolds."

Something about being here, about Jim's warmth and the safety of this space, made Jason feel like he could be more himself. Like he didn't have to hide or hold back.

"And this is my boyfriend, Christopher."

There it was. Out in the open. No taking it back.

And Jason couldn't quite believe he'd had the courage to just say it like that. Natural and easy, like it was the most normal thing in the world.

Christopher's head whipped around to stare at Jason like he'd lost his mind *again*.

But Jim just smiled—warm and genuine, completely unfazed. He reached over and extended his hand to Christopher. "Welcome, Christopher. I'm so happy you and Jason could come visit."

Christopher looked at Jim's outstretched hand, then at Jason, then back at Jim. The handshake felt like it sealed something. Made it real.

Everyone knew now. And they knew that everyone knew.

"I... uh..."

"Sorry, babe," Jason stammered, suddenly realizing he'd outed Christopher without asking. "I just—"

"It's okay," Christopher managed. "I just—"

David saw what was happening—Christopher spiraling, Jason backtracking—and stepped in smoothly. He gave Jim a quick glance that said *help*, and Jim immediately understood.

"Why don't we all sit down?" David said, ushering them into the kitchen. "Can I get you boys something to drink? We have..." He opened the refrigerator. "Coke, Dr. Pepper, lemonade..."

"Two Cokes would be great," Jason said, finding his voice again.

"I'll have lemonade," Jim added, pulling up a chair at the kitchen table across from where the boys would sit.

The kitchen was stunning—practically out of a magazine. Christopher's home was nice, but this looked like a chef lived here. Everything perfectly placed, beautifully coordinated.

David brought drinks, and Jason took a sip. Christopher was staring toward the living room, what he could see of it through the doorway. It looked even more put together than the kitchen. Behind them, a hallway presumably led to bedrooms. An office maybe?

He found himself intensely curious. What had he expected two gay men's home to look like? He'd never really thought about it before. But this was...normal. Better than normal. Beautiful and warm and *lived in*.

Jim noticed Christopher looking and smiled kindly. "I can give you the nickel tour later if you'd like. Show you around."

Christopher suddenly felt like he was being intrusive and looked down, embarrassed.

Jason noticed his boyfriend retreating into himself—had been watching it happen since they arrived. Christopher, who was usually so polished and confident around new people, had gone quiet and shy.

And Jason, who was usually the reserved one, felt strangely at ease here.

Like seeing Jim and David in their home—seeing what was possible—had unlocked something in him. Made him feel like he could be his real self without apology.

So he reached over and took Christopher's hand openly, right there on the table.

"Hey," Jason said softly, making Christopher look at him. "Why so quiet, babe? You okay?"

Christopher's eyes widened slightly at the endearment used so casually in front of others. But Jim and David just smiled, and something in Christopher eased.

It was Jim who helped, his voice gentle and understanding. "I think maybe Christopher's just processing all this. Taking it in. It's a lot, isn't it? Meeting us, being here."

He looked at Christopher with such kindness that Christopher felt tears threatening. "How long have you two been together, if you don't mind me asking?"

Jason considered the question, realizing he might've pushed too hard, said too much. He squeezed Christopher's hand. "Just about a week, officially. But we've been... I mean, I noticed him the first day of class."

Christopher finally found his voice, something warming inside him as he looked at Jason. "I noticed you too. That first day."

It came out soft, tentative. Testing the waters.

David felt his heart clench. God, he remembered that feeling. That terrifying, wonderful realization that someone saw you and wanted you back.

"Really?" Jim leaned forward, authentically interested. "That sounds like how David and I met, actually."

"David?" Christopher echoed, then blinked. Oh. Mr. Barnes's first name was David. Somehow hearing it made him seem more human. Not just a teacher. A real person.

"He was on a flight I was piloting," Jim said, his eyes finding David's across the table with unmistakable affection. "I just happened to be standing up front when passengers were boarding. And David came on, and..." He smiled. "He had the most incredible eyes I'd ever seen. We looked at each other for maybe three seconds, but it felt like the whole world stopped."

Jason sat forward, riveted. "Wait, that's where you met? On an airplane?"

"That's where we met," Jim confirmed. "And the whole flight, I kept thinking about how I could talk to him. But, you know, I was flying the plane." He laughed. "Made it a little difficult."

Everyone laughed, the tension breaking like a warm wave washing over them. Jason felt Christopher's fingers tighten around his.

"So I did something that probably should've gotten me fired," Jim continued, grinning. "Right before we landed, I asked one of the flight attendants to do me a favor..."

The boys leaned in. "What?"

David took over, smiling at the memory, completely forgetting these were his students. "The attendant came up to me during deplaning and said the pilot wanted to speak with me. Asked if I could wait a moment."

"What?!" Jason's eyes were huge.

"I panicked," David admitted, laughing. "I thought, 'Oh god, what did I do wrong?' Right? I'm standing there on the jetbridge after everyone else is gone, and here comes this tall, gorgeous man in his pilot uniform walking toward me..."

"What did you do?" Christopher asked, fully engaged now, his anxiety momentarily forgotten.

"Panicked is what I did! I had no idea why the pilot wanted to talk to me. Thought maybe I'd done something to get in trouble. I felt like I was being called to the principal's office!"

"Now you know how we felt this morning!" Jason laughed, and Jim turned to David with a questioning look.

"That's part of the surprise," David explained to Jim. "After what you said last night about being role models, I thought I'd ask if they wanted to come meet you. Meet us."

Jim's expression softened. He reached across the table and squeezed David's hand, pride evident in his eyes. "I'm glad you did."

"Wait, so what happened?" Christopher interjected, unable to contain his curiosity. "When you met on the jetbridge?"

Jim picked up the story, his voice warm. "I walked up to him and immediately started rambling. Told him I'd noticed him when he boarded and couldn't stop thinking about him the whole flight. Asked if maybe he'd want to get coffee sometime." He shook his head, smiling. "I was so nervous I could barely get the words out."

"And I was so relieved I wasn't in trouble that I said yes before he even finished asking," David added.

"And the rest is history," Jim finished, gesturing around them at the house, at their life together.

Christopher looked around, really seeing it now. This wasn't just a house. It was a home. A life they'd built together despite everything.

"But why stay in Connersville?" The question came out before Christopher could stop it. "I mean—" He backtracked, worried he'd sounded rude. "Why not move somewhere bigger? You know? Not so..."

Jim and David exchanged a knowing look, the kind that came from years together.

"I did move away, initially," Jim said. "I'm from a tiny town in Wisconsin called Cashton. Smaller than here, actually. Less than a thousand people. Dairy farms, one stoplight, post office. That's about it."

"Smaller than Connersville?" Christopher asked, incredulous.

"Much smaller. Makes this place feel like a metropolis," Jim laughed. "But my family was there. That was home. Until I came out to myself and realized I needed to leave to figure out who I was. Ended up in San Diego learning to fly. And I thought I'd never come back to small-town life."

"But then you met David," Jason said, understanding.

"But then I met David," Jim agreed, his voice softening. "And I realized home isn't a place. It's a person. And I wanted to spend my life with him, so where he was became where I wanted to be."

"I have my job here," David added. "My students. And honestly, I didn't want to let fear chase me away from the only home I've ever known."

"And I can fly from anywhere," Jim said. "So we decided to make it work here."

"But isn't it hard?" Christopher's voice was quiet, vulnerable. "Don't people... I mean, aren't you worried about..."

"About people finding out?" Jim finished gently. "About being harassed? About losing friends or jobs?"

Christopher nodded, unable to speak.

"Yeah," Jim said honestly. "We worry about that. All the time, if I'm being truthful. We're careful. We have dinner up in Indianapolis usually, or sometimes Cincinnati. Richmond is as close as we'll typically go for a date. We try to avoid being too visible here in town."

"We're pretty much homebodies anyway," David added. "I'm at school, Jim travels for work a lot. Most people don't see us together often enough to wonder."

"So you're still hiding," Jason said, and there was no judgment in his voice. Just understanding. Just recognition of their shared situation.

"Yeah," David admitted. "We are. Maybe not as much as we used to. But yeah."

"Funny, isn't it?" Christopher said quietly, and everyone turned to look at him. His eyes were bright, emotional. "All I want sometimes is to be seen. To be really understood. But then I'm terrified that people will..."

"Hurt you," Jim said softly. It wasn't a question.

Christopher nodded. Jason looked at him, his face full of protective love and helpless frustration because there was nothing he could do to fix this.

"It's normal, what you're feeling," Jim said, and his voice carried the weight of experience. "That push and pull between wanting to be seen and being terrified of the consequences. David and I still feel it. It never completely goes away, honestly."

"But it gets easier," David added. "Especially when you have people who understand. People like us to talk to. And you'll find others—in college, beyond. Maybe there are even others at school right now who are going through exactly what you are."

Christopher looked at Jason, a realization dawning. He'd never really considered there might be other students like them. It felt like such a waste that everyone had to hide. That you had to be so covert about simply wanting a friend who understood.

Jason spoke up, and his voice had that protective edge. "But how do you find those people if everyone's hiding? How do you help each other when you don't even know who the others are?"

"That's the hard part," Jim acknowledged. "When you're older, there are places—bars, groups, community centers in bigger cities. Places where it's safe to be yourself. Where everyone there is like you, so there's no guessing."

"Gaydar helps too," Jim added with a smile.

"Gaydar?" both boys said simultaneously.

Jim laughed. "It's like this sixth sense you develop. You can just kind of tell when someone else is gay. Nothing mean or obvious about it. You just... know."

"How does that work?" Christopher asked, leaning forward.

"Honestly? I'm not entirely sure. It's subtle. The way someone looks at others. How they carry themselves. Little things that straight people wouldn't notice but we pick up on." Jim's expression turned more serious. "It's how we protect each other. How we find our people in a world that often doesn't want us to exist."

"Like if you meet someone and want to know if they might be..." Jason started.

"You don't just walk up and ask, 'Hey, are you gay?'" Jim said, and everyone laughed.

"You'd get the shit kicked out of you," Jason said, then quickly covered his mouth. "Sorry, Mr. Barnes."

"Jason," David said warmly, "outside of school, it's okay. You can be yourself here."

"Right," Jim continued. "So instead, you're just friendly. You give them opportunities to get to know you both. You find ways to subtly let them know you're safe, that you understand. And if you're comfortable, that you're together. Once they realize what you're saying, it becomes easier for them to open up too. That's why they call it 'coming out,' you know? It's like stepping out from hiding. Maybe not to the whole world. But to people who you trust. Who will keep you safe."

"Like you," Jason said quietly, the realization settling over him like a warm blanket.

Jim smiled, reaching across the table to squeeze David's hand openly. "Yeah. Like us."

Christopher looked at Jason, still feeling that knot of fear in his chest. But it was smaller now. Looser. Like maybe—well, maybe they weren't completely alone in this.

"Jim?" Christopher's voice was barely above a whisper.

"Yes, Christopher?"

"I want to say something." He glanced at Jason, giving him a small smile. "And I want to say it myself this time. Not have Jason do it for me."

David unconsciously held his breath, recognizing that look. Jim squeezed his hand tighter, encouraging him to just be present.

Jason's eyes widened, understanding immediately. He almost wanted to tell Christopher it was okay, he could take his time, there was no pressure. But something told him to hold back. To let Christopher have this moment. So he placed his other hand over Christopher's where it rested on the table, offering silent support.

Christopher gripped Jason's hand like it was a lifeline. His eyes were bright with unshed tears, the emotion finally breaking through.

"I'm..." His voice cracked. Why was this so hard? He took a shaky breath. "I'm... g-gay."

The word came out broken but real.

Jim felt his heart soar. David let a single tear slip down his cheek, remembering what it felt like the first time he'd said it out loud. Wishing desperately he'd had someone like Jim there to hear it. Grateful beyond words that they could be here for these boys now.

But it was Jason's reaction that mattered most. His whole face transformed—from protective worry to fierce, overwhelming pride. Pride in his boyfriend's courage. In how Christopher had found his voice and used it without anyone pushing him.

Jason reached up and gently rubbed Christopher's back as Christopher wiped his eyes.

"Thank you for trusting us with that," Jim said, his voice thick with emotion. "That took real courage, Christopher. You should be proud of yourself."

"We're proud of you," David added softly.

Jason looked at Christopher with nothing but love—the fear, the protective instinct, the worry all melting into pure affection. He loved Christopher more than he had words for.

Christopher finally looked at Jason and rolled his eyes toward Jim and David, as if to say, *Your turn, genius.*

"What?" Jason asked, oblivious, still marveling at his boyfriend.

Christopher gave him an exaggerated shoulder slump and eye roll.

"Oh!" Jason realized, quickly turning to Jim and David. "Right. Uh, I'm gay too." He laughed nervously. "But I think that's kind of obvious by now, right?"

"You two are adorable together," Jim said, beaming. "Aren't they, hon?"

David was smiling more than usual, like he was witnessing the life he'd desperately wanted at their age. "I'm so happy for you both. And I want you to know—what you've shared with us stays only with us. This is your journey. You decide who gets to know and when. Okay?"

They both nodded, feeling the weight and gift of that promise.

Christopher suddenly realized the same applied to them. "And we're not going to say anything about you two. To anyone."

Jim waved them off gently. "We appreciate that. I'm less worried for myself—I'm in the air half the time anyway. But David's your teacher, so it's probably better this way. For all of us."

David nodded, grateful Jim had said it. He didn't need to be Mr. Barnes right now. Here, in his home, he could just be David. Just be Jim's partner. Maybe even a mentor to these boys, if they'd let him.

"Oh dear." David caught sight of the owl clock on the kitchen wall —tacky and out of place with their modern décor, but his grandmother's, so he kept it. "We need to get to your parents' house."

Everyone stood. "You're welcome to freshen up if you want," David told them. "Bathroom's through the living room, first door on the right."

Jason took Christopher's hand without thinking and pulled him toward the living room, both of them looking at every detail of the beautiful home.

Jim and David disappeared down the hallway to their bedroom.

When everyone reconvened at the front door, Jim grabbed his jacket and David his keys.

They walked out together to the car, and for a moment, Jason and Christopher stood holding hands in the driveway before climbing into the back seat.

As David started the engine, Jason spoke up from behind them. "Jim? David?"

"Yeah?" they answered together, making everyone smile.

"Thank you." Jason's voice was thick. "For letting us be here For being..." He struggled for words. "For uh... being you."

Jim turned in his seat to look back at them, his expression gentle. "You're welcome, Jason. Both of you." He glanced at Christopher. "You're safe with us. Anytime you need to talk, need a place to just be yourselves—our door is open. Okay?"

Both boys nodded, Christopher's eyes bright again.

"Alright," David said, pulling out of the driveway. "Let's go have dinner with your family, Christopher. This should be interesting."

Jim laughed and reached over to squeeze David's knee as they drove.

In the back seat, Jason and Christopher sat close together, taking the opportunity to hold each other's hand. Both of them thinking the same thing: maybe there was hope for a future together. It might just work.

Chapter 15

Cocoa

Diane opened the door before they even knocked, her smile warm and genuine.

"You're here! Come in, come in." She stepped aside, and the evening air followed them into the house—David and Jim first, then Christopher and Jason trailing behind. "Mark's in the kitchen finishing up. I hope everyone's hungry."

"Starving," Jim said easily, extending his hand. "You must be Diane. I'm Jim. It's wonderful to meet you."

"Wonderful to meet you too," she said warmly, shaking his hand. Then she turned to David. "And you must be David. I've heard so much about you from Mark. Welcome to our home."

"Thank you for having us," David said, and Jason noticed the slight formality creeping in, like he was putting on armor.

Mark emerged from the kitchen, wiping his hands on a dish towel. His face broke into a genuine smile when he saw David. "David! God, it's been too long." He pulled David into a warm hug— real and heartfelt—then turned to Jim and extended his hand. "And you must be David's partner. I'm Mark. It's great to finally meet you."

Jason and Christopher both froze slightly, exchanging a quick glance. Christopher's dad had just said it—*partner*—out loud, casually, like it was the most natural thing in the world.

"Jim," he said, shaking Mark's hand warmly. "Jim Wilson. And it's great to meet you too. Thanks for having me."

"Of course. We're really glad you both could make it."

Christopher was still processing his father's easy acceptance, the way he'd just acknowledged what Jim was to David without hesitation or discomfort. Jason noticed Christopher's stunned expression and squeezed his hand briefly before letting go.

They moved into the living room. Christopher and Jason gravitated toward the loveseat, settling close but not quite touching. David and Jim took the sofa. Mark and Diane found their chairs.

For a moment, no one quite knew where to start.

Mark laughed, breaking the tension. "Well, this is awkward. Let me grab drinks. What can I get everyone?"

The room exhaled as people called out preferences. Mark disappeared into the kitchen, and Diane leaned forward with practiced grace.

"So Jim," Diane said, settling into the conversation, "what do you do for work?"

"I'm a pilot with United," Jim said, his warmth filling the space naturally. "East Coast and Europe, mostly."

"Oh, how fascinating! You get to see the world."

"See a lot of airport terminals, anyway." He smiled. "Though mostly it's a lot of checklists and waiting around. The actual flying is the smallest part."

"But still, the travel must be exciting."

"It has its moments. But the real adventure is always coming home."

David glanced at Jim, something soft passing between them—so quick Christopher almost missed it, but he caught the edge of it and filed it away.

Mark returned with drinks, and they migrated to the dining room. The table was set beautifully—nothing ostentatious, just warm and welcoming. Roasted chicken, mashed potatoes still steaming, green beans with slivered almonds, rolls in a cloth-lined basket.

"This looks incredible," Jim said sincerely.

"It's nothing special, but I hope you'll enjoy it."

They served themselves family-style, dishes passing from hand to hand. Conversation started safe—weather, the drive over, how the boys were doing in class.

"They're both doing great," David offered. "Christopher's a natural behind the wheel. Very careful, very precise. Jason's getting there—just needs to trust himself more."

"That sounds about right," Jason muttered, earning smiles around the table.

Mark set down his fork and looked across at David. The shift in his expression made the room go quiet.

"You know, I've been thinking a lot lately. About high school. About those years."

David tensed. "Yeah?"

"Yeah. And I wanted to tell you again—properly this time, face to face, not just on the phone—how sorry I am. For how people treated you back then. For what they said."

"Mark, that was a long time ago—"

"No, let me finish. Please." Mark's voice was gentle but determined. "I was thinking about this kid—remember Tommy Sullivan? Year ahead of us?"

David frowned, searching his memory. "Vaguely. Basketball player?"

"That's him. Used to give you hell in the hallways. Called you names, knocked your books over on purpose. I watched it happen more than once and never said a word. Just kept walking like I didn't see anything."

"You weren't the one doing it."

"But I didn't stop it either. I was a coward." Mark shook his head. "And there were so many little things like that. The way people talked about you when you weren't around. The jokes. I never participated, but I never shut it down either. I just... let it happen."

Jim leaned forward slightly, his curiosity genuine rather than prying. "What kinds of things did they say?"

David shot Jim a look—*do we really want to go there?*—but Jim's expression was open, honestly wanting to understand this part of David's past that he'd never talked about.

"Just stupid high school crap," David said, trying to dismiss it.

"Tell me anyway," Jim said softly. "I want to know."

David was quiet, turning his water glass in slow circles on the table. Then he sighed.

"There was this group of guys—football players mostly. They'd walk behind me in the hallway and imitate how I walked. Make their voices higher, do the limp wrist thing." He paused. "One time someone put a note in my locker. It said—" He stopped himself. "Actually, it doesn't matter what it said. It was hateful. And I was terrified because I didn't know if they actually knew or if they were just guessing."

Christopher felt his stomach tighten. He glanced at Jason, who was staring hard at his plate.

"Did anyone ever ask you directly?" Jim's voice was careful.

"No. Because that would've required acknowledging it might be true. And back then, that was somehow worse than the teasing—the possibility that I might actually be..." He trailed off, the word catching in his throat.

"Gay," Jim finished gently. "You can say it, love."

David nodded. "Yeah. Gay. That was the worst thing you could possibly be. So people assumed and mocked, but never confirmed it. Because confirming it would make it real."

Mark looked stricken. "I had no idea it was that bad."

"Most people didn't. I got very good at hiding. At making jokes to deflect attention. Being likable enough that people would forget the rumors." David's smile was sad and practiced. "I've spent my whole adult life trying to make people like me enough not to care that I'm different."

"That must be exhausting," Diane said softly.

"It is." David's voice was quiet. "But it's also kept me safe."

The table fell into a weighted silence. Christopher was riveted, watching David reveal parts of himself he never showed in the classroom. Jason hadn't looked up, but his jaw was tight, his knuckles white around his fork.

Diane shifted in her seat, clearly trying to move toward something lighter. "How did you two meet?"

Jim's whole face brightened, and the heaviness lifted slightly. "Oh, now that's a good story."

He told it—the plane, the nervous wait on the jetbridge, asking the flight attendant to pass along his message. David added details Jim had forgotten, the memory softening both of them. They talked over each other occasionally, laughed at the same moments, their hands finding each other naturally on the table.

Christopher watched, fascinated. They weren't performing or proving anything. They were just... together. It was the most normal thing Christopher had ever seen. And at his own dining table with his parents.

"So you moved here for David?" Mark asked.

"I did. He had his job and his life here. I could fly from anywhere." Jim shrugged like it was the simplest decision in the world. "It wasn't even hard, honestly. Home is wherever he is."

"That's beautiful," Diane said, her voice catching.

"Though it's not always easy," Jim admitted, and something shifted in his tone. "David and I have to be careful."

"What do you mean?" Mark asked.

Jim glanced at David, then continued. "Well, you and Diane can kiss each other in the IGA, for example. No one would give it a second glance."

"Of course."

"If David and I tried that, it could cost David his job. At minimum, there'd be complaints to the school board. Accusations about him being inappropriate with students. His entire career could be destroyed for just... well, for us being ourselves."

Mark's fork clattered against his plate. "Jesus. I never thought about it like that."

"Why would you?" Jim's voice wasn't accusatory, just stating a fact. "Do you know any other gay couples?"

Mark looked at Diane, then back at Jim and David. "No," he admitted quietly. "I don't. You're the first gay couple I've actually known. And I feel ashamed of that. I'm sure there are others in town—there have to be. I just haven't noticed. Or maybe I chose not to."

"We're good at hiding," Jim said simply. "We have to be."

Diane's eyes became glassy. She looked across the table at her son, then at Jason beside him. Her heart was breaking for what they might face. For what they were already facing, even if they hadn't said the words yet.

She didn't want that for them. Didn't want them spending their lives hiding, pretending, being careful about where they were seen and who they told. They were so young. They deserved to just be happy.

But they hadn't come out. Not to her, not to Mark. And she couldn't force them, no matter how much she wanted to wrap them in protection and tell them it was okay. Even though she *knew*—god, she knew—she couldn't make them say it before they were ready.

Mark saw the pain in his wife's expression. Jim noticed it too, his eyes flicking between Diane and the boys. But it was David, who'd been growing quieter through this whole exchange, who finally spoke.

"Diane?"

She looked at him, trying to compose herself but not quite succeeding.

"I've been teaching for, what, twenty-odd years now?" David's voice was careful, measured. "And I've been afraid the entire time. Still am, if I'm completely honest."

Jim reached for his hand under the table, but David seemed lost in thought.

"I learned early on that it's easier if I make people like me. You know?" He looked at Christopher. "Ask your son. I know everyone groans at my jokes. They always have. But they accept me as the corny joke guy. They tolerate me. And that tolerance keeps me safe. But..."

He paused, something building behind his eyes that he couldn't quite hold back anymore.

"I'm gay, Diane." His voice cracked on the word. "I always have been. Knew it since before junior high. And—" He turned to Mark, and his hands were shaking now. "I was so scared that everyone would hate me. That I'd lose everything. That I'd be alone."

Jim reached for him again, and this time David gripped his hand for all its worth.

"I know some people did hate me. Some still do. But I try to look past them, and for the most part I've learned how. But it's so hard." His voice was breaking now, years of holding it together finally cracking open. "Especially when I look out at my classes and I see some student —someone I know is going through the same thing I did. Someone I recognize because I was them once. And my heart breaks."

A tear slipped down his cheek. "Because I don't know how to help them. How to save them from what I went through. Because I'm still so afraid. I'm still such a coward."

"David, no—" Jim started.

"I am, Jim." David pulled away slightly, needing to finish. "I've been terrified my entire career of being found out. Of being fired. Of being accused of terrible things just because I'm gay. Of people saying I'm going to hell because all I ever wanted was someone to love me."

His voice shattered completely. The room went cold with the weight of it.

Jim stood immediately, moving behind David's chair and wrapping his arms around him. "I'm so sorry," Jim said to the table, his own voice thick. "He's never—I've never seen him like this before. Perhaps we should—"

"Please don't go."

Everyone turned sharply.

It was Jason. His voice was raw and desperate.

In all the emotion swirling around David, they'd missed that Jason had been crying too. Tears streamed down his face. His whole body was rigid, trembling.

Something about watching David break open—seeing his teacher, this man who was always so put together, completely fall apart—had unlocked something in Jason that he'd been holding back for so long.

Seeing David's pain that mirrored his own. Knowing David had been sixteen once, scared and alone, trying to figure out how to survive in a world that hated him. And now here he was, twenty-five years later, still hurting. Still scared. Still hiding.

It wasn't fair. To David. To Jim. To Christopher. To himself.

And Jason couldn't hold it in anymore. The dam finally broke.

"Please stay, Mr. Barnes." Jason's voice was shaking, breaking. "I want you to stay. Don't leave me. Please."

David looked up through his tears, confused. "Leave you?"

"I can't—" Jason gasped for breath. "I don't want you to leave me. I can't take anyone else leaving me. Please don't go."

Christopher stood immediately, moving to Jason's side, his hand finding Jason's arm. "Babe, what's happening—"

But Jason was staring at David with wild, desperate eyes. "Please don't leave. Please. Everyone always leaves. Please."

Diane moved to Jason's other side, her hands gentle on his shoulders. "Sweetheart, it's okay. He's right here. Look—David's right here."

She looked at David, who was staring at Jason with his own tears still falling, and she saw the recognition there. David understood something the rest of them didn't yet.

Mark looked at Jim, both men frozen, uncertain.

David pulled away from Jim and moved around the table. Christopher shifted instinctively to give him space. David knelt in front of Jason's chair, looking up at Diane for permission.

She nodded—*yes, he needs you.*

Jason was sobbing now, his whole body shaking with it.

David wrapped his arms around him and pulled him close, holding tight. "I'm staying," he whispered against Jason's hair. "I'm here. I'm not leaving you. I promise."

They rocked together gently, David holding this boy who was shattering from years of holding it all together. Years of abandonment. Years of being strong when inside he was just a scared kid who wanted someone to love him, too. Years of pretending he knew what he was doing when he had no idea.

Jason had been the strong one. The protector. The one who made sure Christopher felt safe.

But hearing David describe how hard it was to just exist—how even decades later it still hurt, how the fear never really went away— Jason couldn't see hope anymore. Couldn't see a future where it got better.

And he was so tired of being strong.

"Jason," David whispered. "We love you. You're not alone."

But Jason was mumbling through his sobs, the words barely coherent. "Everyone hates me. Everyone always leaves."

Christopher dropped to his knees beside them, his heart breaking. David loosened his hold enough for Christopher to reach Jason's face, gently wiping away tears with his thumbs, brushing Jason's hair back from his eyes.

"I love you, Jason," Christopher said, his voice shaking but certain. "I'm not leaving you. I promise."

Jason looked up at him through the tears, fighting to catch his breath. "R-really?"

"I love you." Christopher's voice was fierce now, protective. "I'm not going anywhere."

Mark found Diane's hand, both of them knowing they were witnessing something they'd remember for the rest of their lives.

David stood slowly, his legs unsteady, and Jim was there immediately, wrapping his arms around him from behind. They stood like that—holding each other up. Mark and Diane did the same.

All four adults watching as Christopher held onto Jason. As Jason tried to breathe, tried to come back to himself.

After a long moment, Jason became aware of everyone looking at him. Embarrassment crashed over him like a wave. What the fuck was wrong with him? Why was he such a fucking crybaby? They were all staring. They all saw him break.

Christopher saw it happen—saw Jason's face shift, saw him starting to retreat back into his head, back behind his walls.

"Don't you dare," Christopher said loudly, firmly. "Don't you climb back into your head, asshole. You needed to let that out. You needed it. So be proud of it."

His voice was protective, fierce—taking care of Jason the way Jason always took care of him.

Jason nodded weakly, wiping his face with shaking hands.

Diane moved quickly to the kitchen and returned with a damp washcloth, handing it to Christopher to help Jason clean up.

Jim and David exchanged a glance. Maybe it was time to leave, give the family space. It had been such an intense evening, and David was already overwhelmed by his own breakdown.

But when David looked at Jason—saw those red-rimmed eyes darting between Christopher and them, terrified they'd disappear—he knew they couldn't go. Not yet.

Mark understood. "Christopher, why don't you take Jason upstairs to your bathroom? Help him get cleaned up."

"You're not leaving, are you?" Jason asked immediately, his voice small and scared, looking directly at Jim and David.

"No, Jason." Jim's voice was warm and solid. "We'll be right here when you come back down. I promise."

David nodded, meeting Jason's eyes. "We're not going anywhere."

Christopher helped Jason stand, guiding him toward the stairs with an arm around his waist.

Diane touched David's arm gently. "Would you like to use the powder room down here? Take a moment?"

"Yes. Thank you."

Jim and Mark stood awkwardly in the dining room, both wanting to say something but not knowing what.

"I can help clear the table," Jim finally offered. "Keep my hands busy."

"I'll help," Mark said quickly.

Diane tried for levity, her voice a little too bright. "Wow. Two men volunteering to clear dishes without being asked? I must have died and gone to heaven. Maybe we should have an after-dinner drink? Hot cocoa or tea?"

"Cocoa sounds perfect," Jim said. "Let me help."

Mark and Jim gathered plates and disappeared into the kitchen, leaving Diane alone with her thoughts.

About Jason and the depth of pain in that boy. About David and the courage it took to finally break open like that. About Jim and his steady, loving presence. About her own husband and how blessed she was to never have to hide their love.

She'd never really had to think about these things before. What it would be like to not be able to kiss Mark goodnight in front of her in-laws. To not keep his picture on her desk at work. To have to refer to him as a roommate or friend.

"I'm sorry for breaking down like that."

Diane looked up. David had returned, looking more composed but exhausted.

"David, please." Diane's voice was fierce. "Don't you dare apologize for being human."

"I try to be professional. I don't like losing control."

"You're not a robot." She leaned forward. "And if you'll pardon my language—it pisses me off that you have to hide who you are at school. That you can't just be yourself without constantly looking over your shoulder."

David smiled faintly. If that was Diane's version of rough language, he wondered what she'd think of the words flying around the hallways between classes.

"Still, it's embarrassing."

"David." She waited until he met her eyes. "If I were in your shoes, I don't know that I could've held it together for twenty years. I don't know that I'd have the strength."

He nodded, accepting her kindness.

"Can I ask you something?" Diane's voice went quieter.

He tensed slightly, his emotions still raw.

"I don't know how to help my son. And Jason." She paused. "I don't even know what to call him. I want to get it right."

David looked confused. "What do you mean?"

"Do I say Christopher's boyfriend? Partner? Friend? I know it might sound silly, but I want to use the right words. I want them to know I'm trying."

David exhaled slowly, his smile softening. "Diane, I think Christopher and Jason need to tell you themselves how they want to be addressed. They haven't officially come out to you yet."

She nodded, understanding but clearly disappointed.

"But," David continued gently, "I think those two need you and Mark—and Jason's parents—to let them know you love them. That you'll support them however you can. They're still figuring things out. So be patient. But Jason especially..." He glanced toward the stairs.

"Jason needs to know he's not just accepted but valued. That he matters. We all do."

"His father," Diane said quietly, leaning closer. "Jason's father isn't in the picture. I don't know the story, just that he's not there."

"I didn't realize." David processed this. "That explains some things."

"So it's really just his mother. And us, if he'll let us be there for him."

Christopher and Jason's footsteps sounded on the landing. Diane stood and moved toward them. Jason walked directly to her and hugged her without a word.

She held him tight, whispering, "You are so brave. So incredibly brave."

Jim and Mark emerged from the kitchen carrying mugs on a tray, the rich smell of cocoa filling the air.

"Who wants cocoa?" Jim announced with forced cheer. "Made with my secret ingredients!"

"And I helped!" Mark added, his enthusiasm a bit too bright but genuine.

Everyone needed this—the attempt at humor, the normalcy.

Before sitting, Jason walked over to Mark and hugged him too. Mark was startled but recovered quickly, wrapping his arms around the boy and holding him close.

When Jason released him, Mark leaned down and whispered something in his ear.

Christopher saw Jason's face go red, a small smile breaking through. "What did he say?"

Mark turned to his son with a gentle smile. "It's between us. If Jason wants to tell you later, he can. Right, buddy?"

Jason nodded, looking like he'd just received the best gift of his life.

"Everyone sit," Jim encouraged, passing out mugs. "Let's have a toast. To family."

"To friends," Mark added, raising his cocoa. "Old, new, and everyone in between."

There was a pause, and then Christopher stood. His hands were shaking slightly as he raised his mug.

"I have a toast."

Everyone looked at him.

"To those we love."

"Aww," Diane breathed, her eyes bright. David smiled warmly. Jim and Mark raised their mugs.

Jason looked at Christopher with an expression that was pure love.

Christopher started to sit, then stopped. He stood back up, and before his courage could desert him, the words tumbled out:

"And to my boyfriend, Jason. I love you."

Time seemed to stop.

Diane raised her mug first, tears streaming down her face. Jim and David lifted theirs immediately. But Mark set his mug down and crossed the room.

He took Christopher's mug from his hands and set it aside. Then he pulled his son into his arms—the kind of hug that said everything words couldn't.

"I love you, son," Mark whispered, his voice breaking. "I am so proud of you."

"Really?" Christopher's voice was small, disbelieving.

"More than you'll ever know."

Still holding Christopher, Mark turned to Jason. "I guess we can tell him now, right?"

Jason nodded, understanding.

"Tell me what?" Christopher asked.

Mark looked at Jason. "You want to share what I whispered to you?"

Jason looked around the table—at Jim and David, at Diane, at Christopher still wrapped in his father's arms.

"He said," Jason's voice was thick with emotion, "'Welcome to the family, son.'"

Chapter 16

Queer

No sooner had Diane, Mark, and the boys waved David and Jim off from the front porch—watching taillights disappear into the December darkness—than Mark turned to everyone with a weary smile.

"I'm completely exhausted. That was some night. A good night. But a *night*."

"I'm heading to bed," he announced. "Everyone else can do what they want."

Diane agreed, adding as they locked up, "It's a school night, though. No staying up late, you two."

"Don't worry, Mom. I'm ready to fall over anyway." Christopher yawned, and Jason rested his hand on the small of Christopher's back without thinking. He caught Diane's gaze and quickly pulled it away, embarrassed.

Diane's smile was gentle as she stepped toward him. "Jason, honey, it's okay. In our home, you're welcome to be who you are. Both of you."

Jason felt uncertain, the reality still not quite settling in. Tonight had been such a roller coaster—so much emotion and revelation packed into a few hours—that it still hadn't fully registered that he and

Christopher were out to Mark and Diane. And that they were okay with it. More than okay. They'd welcomed him with open arms, called him family.

Diane kissed Christopher's head goodnight, then turned to Jason with that same motherly warmth. "I suppose you get one too."

The gesture hit Jason harder than he expected. A wave of emotion —warm and aching—flooded through his chest. Even his own mom had stopped doing that when he was little, too busy or too tired or too worried about bills to remember those small moments of affection. He hadn't realized until right now how much he'd missed it.

"Thank you, Mrs. Avery."

"Honey, we're family now. Call me Diane."

Jason smiled, his throat tight with gratitude he couldn't quite articulate.

She pivoted back to her son with mock sternness. "But it's still 'Mom' for you, Mr. Christopher!" She tweaked his nose playfully, making Jason snicker and Christopher grin despite his feigned protest.

Mark and Diane disappeared down the hallway to their bedroom, the door closing softly behind them. The house settled into quiet.

Christopher immediately turned and grabbed Jason's hand, pulling him into a kiss right there in the middle of the foyer—tender and unhurried, where anyone could have seen if they'd looked.

Jason pulled back slightly, his instinct still to hide. "What if—"

"What?" Christopher's eyes were soft, understanding but encouraging. "No one's here. Mom and Dad went to bed. We're safe."

"I know, it's just..." Jason trailed off, the old fear hard to shake even here, even now.

Christopher found it endearing, this sudden shyness from someone usually so guarded and tough. "Come on," he said gently, tugging Jason's hand toward the stairs.

They climbed to Christopher's room, and once inside with the door closed, Christopher began to undress with casual ease. Jason just stood there, suddenly unsure of himself. They'd slept in the same bed once before, but that had been different—exhausted and trying not to think about what they wanted. This felt different. Intentional.

"Aren't you tired?" Christopher asked, pulling his shirt over his head.

"I'm gonna fall over, I think."

"Then get undressed. What are you waiting for?" Christopher stepped out of his jeans and sat on the edge of the bed to pull off his socks.

Jason watched his boyfriend sitting there in just his underwear, removing his last sock, and felt his body responding in ways that made clear thinking impossible. Tired or not, his hormones had other ideas. He needed a minute to calm down before he embarrassed himself.

"Where are you going?" Christopher asked as Jason turned toward the door.

"I just need to—"

But Christopher was already standing, crossing to him with that look in his eyes—playful and wanting and certain in a way that made Jason's breath catch. "Let me help you," Christopher said softly, reaching for the hem of Jason's shirt and tugging it upward.

"Christopher, I..." Jason's protest died as Christopher's fingers brushed against his skin.

"What?" Christopher whispered, leaning in close enough that Jason could feel the warmth of his breath against his ear, raising goosebumps along his neck.

"I'm getting a little—" Jason couldn't finish the sentence.

"I know," Christopher murmured, and there was a smile in his voice as he pressed a kiss just below Jason's ear, then another along his jaw. "Me too."

Jason felt his knees go weak, his carefully maintained composure dissolving. Every nerve ending seemed suddenly alive and humming. When Christopher nibbled gently at his earlobe, Jason made a sound he'd never heard himself make before—low and helpless.

"If you keep doing that, I'm gonna—" The words came out breathless, barely coherent.

"Gonna what?" Christopher's lips found the sensitive spot behind Jason's ear, his tongue tracing a slow path that sent electricity shooting down Jason's spine.

"Christopher," Jason managed, though it came out more like a plea than a protest. His head tilted back instinctively, offering more access, surrendering.

Christopher smiled against his skin. "Yeah?" He traced a path of kisses along Jason's neck, taking his time, savoring every small sound Jason made, every hitch of breath.

Jason's hands found Christopher's waist, pulling him closer until there was no space left between them. When their lips finally met, it was different than before—deeper, more urgent, everything they'd been holding back finally allowed to surface. Jason walked Christopher backward until his legs hit the bed, and they tumbled onto it without breaking apart.

Now it was Jason's turn to explore, to discover what made Christopher gasp, what made him arch into touch. He kissed along Christopher's collarbone, down his chest, feeling emboldened by every reaction, every whispered encouragement.

"Is this okay?" Jason breathed between kisses, while Christopher's fingers were tangled in his hair, holding him close like he was afraid this might not be real.

Lifting his head just enough to meet Christopher's eyes—those lake-water eyes that had haunted him since the first day of class, he whispered "I love you," and meant it with every fiber of his being.

"I love you too," Christopher whispered back. "More than I know how to say."

Jason smiled, but there was something new in his expression—a hint of mischief, of confidence, of desire finally allowed to breathe. This was all new territory for both of them, but something instinctive took over, his body knowing what his mind hadn't learned yet. Christopher closed his eyes as Jason kissed him deeply, then slowly made his way lower—lips and tongue exploring his chest before moving south, hands learning the geography of someone he loved.

When Christopher realized what Jason intended, his breath caught. Jason glanced up one more time, seeking permission, and Christopher nodded, unable to form words. They were giving themselves to each other completely, surrendering their innocence in the same moment, making this choice as one.

It was tender and awkward and perfect—everything a first time should be between two people in love.

―――――

Down the hall, Mark unbuttoned his shirt while Diane stood at the bathroom sink, removing her makeup with practiced efficiency. The bedroom was warm, the nightstand lamp casting soft light across familiar spaces.

"What a night," Mark said quietly, his voice carrying the weight of everything they'd witnessed.

"I know." Diane wiped away mascara, then paused to look at her husband's reflection in the mirror. "I didn't know what to expect when David said he was bringing Jim, but..."

"But they're wonderful," Mark finished. He pulled off his shirt and tossed it in the hamper. "Both of them. I'm so glad he felt comfortable enough to share that with us."

"Me too." Diane turned from the sink, her face freshly scrubbed. "You can see how much they love each other. The way Jim looks at David—"

"It's protective. But more than that." Mark sat on the edge of the bed to remove his shoes. "It's like watching any couple who's built something real, you know? It shouldn't surprise me, but it does. I'd just never... I'd never actually seen it before."

Diane pulled on her nightgown and climbed into bed. "I can't believe we never knew. I mean, I'd heard the rumors about David over the years, but seeing him with Jim—seeing how real their life is—"

"Makes you wonder how many others there are," Mark said, sliding in beside her. "People we know who are just hiding. Living half a life because they're too afraid of what might happen if anyone found out."

They lay quiet for a moment, the weight of that realization settling over them.

"I'm worried about Jason," Diane said softly.

Mark turned to look at her. "Jason specifically? Not Christopher?"

"Well, Christopher too. Of course. But..." She struggled to articulate it. "When Jason broke down tonight, when he was begging David and Jim not to leave—that wasn't just about tonight, Mark. Something's really hurting that boy."

"I know." Mark's voice was gentle. "I saw it too. The way he latched onto them, like they were a lifeline."

"Do you think something happened to him?" Diane turned onto her side to face her husband. "I mean, something must have happened with his father. Do you think he... hurt him, Mark?"

Mark considered it carefully. "I don't think so. I hope not. But I think he's been carrying whatever it is for too long. The more I think about it, it feels like he's trying to act like a tough guy, but he's really trying to protect himself, you know? And then realizing he's gay was just one more impossible thing piled on top of everything else."

"He needs us," Diane said quietly.

"We'll be there for him, Diane." Mark reached for her hand under the covers. "And Christopher's got him too. He's obviously smitten with that boy."

"That's what worries me a little," Diane admitted. "You know how Christopher is. He's going to want to fix everything for Jason. Make all his problems disappear."

"Our son the problem solver." Mark smiled despite his concern. "He gets that from you."

"Maybe. But you can't fix someone else's pain with good intentions and a plan. That's not how this works."

"No," Mark agreed. "It's not."

They fell into thoughtful silence, both processing the evening, both worried about the boys upstairs and the road ahead of them.

Then Diane propped herself up on one elbow. "Mark, have you had the conversation with Christopher yet? About sex?"

Mark's whole body tensed. "No. Not yet. I keep meaning to, but—"

"You need to." Diane's voice was gentle but firm. She paused, a realization dawning. "Mark, do you think they're having sex? Right now?"

"What? No." But even as he said it, doubt crept in. "No. You saw them tonight—they were completely wrung out. Emotionally exhausted. They probably fell asleep the second their heads hit the pillow."

"Maybe," Diane said, though she didn't sound convinced. She lay back down, staring at the ceiling. They were both quiet, but their minds were racing down the same path.

She'd thought about it earlier, actually—whether she should have Jason sleep in the guest room instead of with Christopher. Or on the sofa downstairs. If one of them were a girl, she wouldn't have hesitated. She would have separated them without question. But because they were both boys, she hadn't even considered it. And now, lying here in bed, she wondered if that had been naive. Just because they couldn't get pregnant didn't mean there weren't other reasons to be careful, to set boundaries. But they'd been so exhausted tonight, so emotionally devastated, that she honestly hadn't thought about it until now.

"I'll talk to Christopher," Mark finally said, breaking the silence. "Once Jason goes home. It'll be easier if it's just the two of us."

"What about Jason?"

"What about him?"

"Someone needs to talk to him too. You know that, right?"

"I know, but..." Mark hesitated. "I'm not his father, Diane. Wouldn't it be inappropriate for me to—"

"If our son and Jason are having sex—or about to be—someone needs to make sure they understand about being safe. And you're the only father figure either of them has right now."

Mark was quiet for a long moment. "His mother would kill me if she found out I was talking to her son about..." He couldn't even finish the sentence.

"About what, Mark? Sex? Bodies? How to be safe?" Diane turned to look at him in the lamplight. "Would you rather we just pretend it's not happening?"

"Well—" Mark started.

"They're sixteen-year-old boys. Boys with feelings and hormones and a bedroom door that closes. We can't just hope for the best."

"I know, but what two guys do is different from—" He gestured vaguely. "I mean, it's not the same as what we did at that age."

"Different how?" Diane asked directly.

"Well, they..." Mark's face flushed. "They do different stuff that I don't know anything about."

"What? Anal?" Diane said it plainly, matter-of-factly.

"Diane!" Mark nearly yelped, his embarrassment acute and total. The word seemed to echo in their quiet bedroom.

"What, Mark? That's what you're worried about, isn't it? That you don't know enough about gay sex to have this conversation?" She wasn't mocking him—her tone was gentle. "It's a fact of how their bodies work. We can't dance around it."

"I just..." Mark took a breath. "I don't want to say the wrong thing. Or make assumptions. Or..." He trailed off, frustrated with himself.

"Then be honest with them," Diane said. "Tell them you don't know everything, but that you care about them being safe. Buy condoms. Buy lubricant. Explain the basics about protection and consent and being careful with each other's bodies. That's all you can do."

Mark stared at the ceiling, overwhelmed. "I really have to buy condoms and..." he gulped. "Lube?"

"Yes, Mark. You do." Diane squeezed his hand. "And I know this is hard for you. I know it's embarrassing and awkward and you'd rather do literally anything else. But those boys need someone to care enough to have this conversation. And that someone is you."

He was quiet for a long moment. Then: "Fine. I'll do it. I'll talk to Christopher first, get my bearings. Then I'll talk to Jason too. But I'm doing it my way."

"Deal." Diane leaned over and kissed him softly. "Thank you, honey. I know this isn't easy. But you're being a good father. To both of them."

She reached over and clicked off the nightstand lamp, plunging the room into darkness. They lay there in the quiet, each lost in their own thoughts about the evening, about their son, about Jason, about everything that was changing in their lives.

Mark thought about how tired he was—emotionally drained from everything they'd witnessed. He couldn't imagine how exhausted the boys must be after the night they'd had.

He turned onto his side and was asleep within minutes.

Upstairs, in Christopher's room, the two boys lay tangled beneath the comforter, their breathing finally slowed, their bodies warm and sated. They'd given themselves to each other completely—awkward and tender and perfect in all the ways that matter when you're sixteen and in love and brave enough to choose each other.

They fell asleep like that, skin against skin, hearts beating in sync, forever changed.

———

Friday morning arrived with bright November sunlight.

Diane dropped the boys off at school, and Christopher and Jason climbed out of the car wearing matching grins they couldn't quite hide. They were simultaneously thrilled to be sharing this time and paranoid that someone would notice them arriving in the same car and somehow deduce their secret. Their protective instincts and overactive imaginations still ran a bit too hot.

Mr. Barnes swept into first period right as the bell rang, arms full of papers and wearing his trademark too-enthusiastic smile.

"Good morning, drivers! Pop quiz day! Who's excited?" He was met with the usual groans. "Oh come on, nobody? Not even a little bit? Well, here's something to brighten your Friday—why did the scarecrow get promoted?"

Silence. A few eye rolls.

"Because he was outstanding in his field!" Barnes grinned at his own joke while passing out Scantrons. "Get it? Outstanding? In his field? No? Tough crowd."

Christopher and Jason exchanged amused glances as they accepted their test sheets.

"This week we're covering drunk driving statistics and impaired driving laws," Barnes continued. "Twenty questions, you know the drill. Work with your partners, but fill out your own answer sheet. You've got twenty minutes. Go!"

David caught their eyes as they turned in their completed tests later and gave them a subtle wink. "Since everyone's back in the classroom today, we're taking it easy this morning. Simulator practice in teams!" He gestured to the battered driving machines lined against the wall. "Winter conditions—you need experience with snow and ice. Bundle up in your imagination, folks!"

———

At lunch, Jason made his way through the cafeteria line and spotted Christopher and Allison already deep in conversation near the hot food. They were gossiping like they'd been best friends for years rather than weeks. Allison saw Jason first and immediately leaned in to whisper something in Christopher's ear. They both burst out laughing.

"What was that?" Jason asked as he joined them, his paranoia automatically kicking in.

They turned to him with matching expressions of wide-eyed innocence. "Nothing!" they said in perfect unison before dissolving into giggles again.

"Seriously, what?"

"Geesh, Jason. Paranoid much?" Allison grabbed a corn dog from the steaming tray, still grinning.

"Don't worry, bab—" Christopher caught himself mid-word and Allison immediately threw her arms around him dramatically, making a show of it.

"Oh, I won't worry, snookums!" she cooed loudly enough to make Christopher turn bright red. Jason relaxed slightly, recognizing the performance for what it was—cover.

They made their way to their usual table where Scott was already eating. The moment Christopher sat down, Scott launched back into the story he'd been trying to finish for days. "So anyway, like I was saying about that play we ran against Richmond..."

Allison made a choking sound around her corn dog. Jason had to bite his lip hard to keep from laughing out loud. Christopher shot them both a desperate "help me" look but gamely turned his full attention to Scott with exaggerated interest. "That sounds so fascinating!"

"Right? That's what I thought too!" Scott continued, completely oblivious to the suppressed laughter happening three feet away.

Jason leaned toward Allison and muttered under his breath, "I tried telling him I don't give a shit about football, but he just kept going."

"Same," Allison whispered back. They ate in companionable silence, watching Christopher nod along to Scott's play-by-play breakdown like his life depended on it. When Christopher caught their amused stares, he mouthed "I'm getting you both back for this" before plastering on another interested smile for Scott's benefit.

Allison leaned close to Jason's ear, her voice barely audible. "You're gonna have to put out to make up for abandoning him like this, you know."

Jason felt heat flood his face. He stared down at his tray, suddenly fascinated by his slice of pizza.

Allison had been expecting his usual sarcastic comeback, maybe a well-placed "fuck off" delivered with a grin. Instead he just sat there looking embarrassed, unable to meet her eyes. And that's when the realization hit her like a freight train.

"Oh my god!" Her whisper-shriek made Jason flinch. Her eyes went wide as saucers. "You WHORE!" She punctuated it with a playful jab to his ribs that made him squirm and laugh despite his mortification.

Christopher and Scott both glanced over at the commotion. Allison waved them off innocently. "Nothing to see here, boys. Continue your riveting football discussion."

The moment they turned back, she leaned in again, her expression caught somewhere between shock and fierce pride. "Did you two actually fuck?"

Jason looked away, and his complete lack of poker face told her everything she needed to know. He couldn't bullshit the master of bullshit artistry, and they both knew it.

"You did!" Allison grabbed his arm, squeezing. "You actually did!"

"Shhhhh!" Jason was laughing now despite his embarrassment. "Shut the fuck up, Allison! People are gonna hear you!"

"You magnificent cock whore! I'm so goddamn proud of you!" Her whisper was somehow both quiet and emphatic, which only made them both laugh harder.

Christopher looked over again, more concerned this time. Jason was laughing so hard he couldn't look his boyfriend in the eye, which only made Allison's grin grow wider.

She composed herself with visible effort and announced in her normal speaking voice, "Jason was just sharing the intimate details of last night with me."

All the color drained from Christopher's face. Jason's jaw dropped as he frantically elbowed Allison. "I didn't say anything! She's full of shit!"

Christopher looked like he might actually faint, his eyes darting between them in panic.

Allison finally took pity on him. "I'm teasing. Relax. I was just making him laugh." She took another bite of corn dog, perfectly casual now as if she hadn't just given Christopher a minor heart attack.

Christopher exhaled shakily and shot them both a "what the hell is wrong with you people" look before Scott successfully recaptured his attention with another football anecdote.

"You're such a bitch, you know that?" Jason muttered to Allison.

"You keep saying that like it's news." She smirked. "Love you too, bestie."

———

After school, Diane dropped Jason off at his house. Christopher promised to call later that evening, and they made plans for Saturday —Jason would bike over in the morning and maybe they'd ride out to the farmhouses again, do some exploring. It was only as they were saying goodbye that they both realized neither of them had experienced the ghost dreams last night. Like something had shifted. Something was different now.

Jason felt himself blushing as he unlocked the front door, his mind drifting to Christopher's naked body, the things they'd done, the way it had felt to finally—

"Oh. Sorry, Rick. Didn't see you there. Thought no one was home."

He'd been so lost in thought he hadn't noticed Rick sprawled on the couch in his usual spot, beer in hand, eyes glazed and fixed on the television. Rick grunted something that might have been acknowledgment.

Jason made a quick escape to his room, closing the door firmly behind him. He dumped his overnight clothes into the hamper, tossed his textbooks onto the bed, grabbed fresh underwear from his drawer, and headed down the hall for a shower.

————

Sarah arrived home while Jason was still in the shower. She gave Rick a perfunctory kiss on the cheek as she passed—he grunted, as usual—then gathered the mail from the box outside. Mostly junk. Bills she'd have to figure out how to pay. One envelope was addressed to Jason, which was unusual. Probably something from school.

She walked toward his room to leave it for him and noticed his door standing open. Books scattered across his unmade bed, backpack dumped on the floor. The sound of running water down the hall confirmed he was showering.

She stepped into his small room to set the mail on his bed where he'd see it.

That's when she noticed the notebook.

It sat among his textbooks—black cover, the kind Jason used for his art. She felt a pang of nostalgia. He used to show her his drawings all the time when he was in junior high, so proud of what he'd created. But somewhere around freshman year he'd stopped sharing, would deflect or change the subject whenever she asked to see his work.

Curiosity got the better of her. She told herself she just wanted to see what he'd been working on, to understand why her talented son had started hiding his light. She picked up the notebook and opened it.

The first several pages were sketches. They were good—really good. Detailed pencil work, studies of hands and faces, a landscape that might have been the view from their back porch. She smiled, pride warming her chest. He really was gifted. Maybe being an artist wasn't a practical career, but the talent was undeniable.

She turned another page and the drawings stopped. Text filled the page instead—handwritten in Jason's familiar scrawl. A diary?

She should close it. She knew she should. This was private, personal. But her eyes had already caught on a name written there: *Christopher.*

Before she could make the conscious decision to read or not read, to respect his privacy or invade it, she was already absorbing the words on the page. Jason's thoughts about Christopher. How he made Jason feel. Things they'd talked about. Hopes and fears and—

"Mom?"

Sarah's head snapped up. Jason stood frozen in the doorway, wrapped in a towel, water still dripping from his hair. His face had gone completely white.

"Oh honey, I'm sorry." The words tumbled out, guilt flooding through her. "I was just—I didn't mean to—"

"What are you doing?" Jason's voice was barely a whisper. He couldn't move, couldn't breathe. His whole world had narrowed to that notebook in his mother's hands, his mind desperately trying to remember what he'd written, what she might have seen.

"I was dropping off your mail and I saw this—I thought it was your drawings. I wanted to see your art, sweetheart. I didn't realize—" She was fumbling the explanation badly, she knew, but there was no good way to admit she'd read her son's private journal.

Jason's mind raced, cataloging what he'd written in that book. The ghost dreams. His feelings about being different. His certainty that he was gay. And Christopher—god, had he written explicitly about Christopher? About what they'd done last night?

Sarah took a step toward him, reading the panic in his body language. This wasn't just teenage annoyance at a privacy violation. He looked terrified.

"Honey, I'm sorry. It's okay. I didn't see much—"

Much. What did "much" mean? How much was "much"? Jason felt his breathing become shallow and rapid, the room starting to tilt.

Sarah moved quickly, taking his arm and guiding him to sit on the edge of his bed. "Breathe, sweetheart. Just breathe. Slow breaths." She sat beside him, her hand rubbing gentle circles on his back the way she used to when he was small and had nightmares.

But Jason couldn't calm down. If she'd seen the parts about the ghosts, she'd think he was crazy. If she'd seen the parts about Christopher, she'd know he was gay. If she'd seen what he'd written last night after they—

Oh god.

Sarah held him steady, feeling him tremble beneath the damp towel. He wasn't crying or screaming. He'd gone completely still except for the harsh, irregular breathing. His hands were shaking. He looked like he might pass out.

"Jason, talk to me. What's going on? What's got you so scared?"

He couldn't do this. Not now. Not like this. He'd been planning to tell her eventually, when he was ready, when he'd found the right words. But not like this. Not because she'd found his private journal and read his most intimate thoughts without permission.

"Is it because of Christopher?"

The world stopped.

Every sound cut out. Time froze. Jason's mind went completely blank, then immediately into overdrive. She knew. She'd read enough to know. How much did she know? What exactly had she seen?

He looked up at her, still sitting there in just his wet towel, and something broke open inside him. Tears came suddenly—hot and unstoppable—the same way he'd cried the night his dad had left them. Deep, wrenching sobs that came from somewhere he couldn't control.

That's when Sarah knew for certain. Not just suspected, not just wondered. She knew. Her son was gay. He and Christopher were more than friends. All the little things she'd noticed over the past weeks—the way Jason lit up when Christopher's name came up, the careful way he talked about him, the obvious joy he'd shown getting ready for their time spent—it all clicked into place with painful clarity.

And she wasn't sure how she felt about it.

She'd known, hadn't she? On some level, she'd known for weeks. The way Jason lit up when he talked about Christopher. The way he'd combed his hair that Saturday morning, worn a colored shirt for the first time in years. The careful pause when he'd said "Christopher" instead of a girl's name, and the way she'd pretended not to notice.

But knowing and *seeing*—seeing her son sobbing because his mother had accidentally discovered his secret—those were different things. One she could tuck away, process slowly, on her own terms. The other was here, now, demanding something from her she wasn't sure she knew how to give.

But watching him break down like this, seeing the fear and shame and desperation in his shaking shoulders—she knew one thing with absolute certainty: she loved her son. Whatever else she might feel or think or worry about, that was bedrock.

"Jason, honey, it's going to be okay." She held him close, letting him cry himself out. "It's okay. I've got you."

Eventually the sobs subsided into hiccuping breaths. Sarah pulled back just enough to brush his wet hair away from his eyes.

"Why don't you get dressed, and I'll make us some dinner. Okay?"

He nodded wordlessly, not trusting his voice.

She stood and ran her fingers through his hair one more time—he really did have his father's hair, thick and dark and forever falling in his eyes. She smiled, trying to project a calm she didn't entirely feel, and closed his door behind her.

———

A few minutes later, Jason emerged from his room. His head was down, shoulders hunched, moving like someone who'd just been caught doing something terrible. Not grounded exactly—worse. That particular shame of knowing you've disappointed someone who loves you, and now everyone has to pretend everything's normal even though it's not.

"Honey, why don't you set the table?"

They sat down to sloppy joes on white bread. Sandwich buns cost more, and money was tight until payday. Jason noticed, the way he always noticed these small economies. He never said anything. He knew his mom was doing her best with what they had.

Rick wandered in and sat down without being invited, but dinner was dinner. He fixed his plate first, taking the biggest portions before anyone else had a chance. Jason waited, then made himself a sandwich. His mom poured him a glass of water.

"Grab me a beer," Rick said to no one in particular.

That was Rick's extent of dinner conversation. No "please," no "thank you," no acknowledgment of the people serving him. Just commands issued to the air.

Jason wondered, not for the first time, why his mom had such terrible taste in men. He almost smiled at the irony—he could probably give her some pointers about what to look for in a good man now. But he kept the thought to himself.

Sarah, however, seemed determined not to let the earlier incident just fade into silence. After making her own plate, she brought it up again. Jason was mid-bite when she spoke, and the meat with ketchup sauce slid out onto his plate, forgotten.

Rick wasn't paying attention, his chair turned half toward the blaring television in the living room.

"Is there something you want to tell me, Jason?" Her voice wasn't angry, but it carried a weight that made it impossible to ignore. The careful tone of someone trying to make space for a difficult conversation.

Jason stared at the mess on his plate—his hands still holding the soggy bread near his mouth, completely frozen.

Sarah took a bite of her own sandwich, chewed, swallowed. Then tried again with different words, searching for the right way to ask. "Are you and Christopher... special friends?"

The euphemism hung in the air, awkward and inadequate.

This was it, Jason realized. She was circling closer to the truth, giving him one opening after another to just admit it. There was nowhere left to hide.

He gave the smallest nod—barely a movement at all, but Sarah caught it. She'd been watching for it.

Rick was still eating and half-watching TV, oblivious to the charged conversation happening three feet away.

Sarah's mind worked through her next question. He'd at least acknowledged that much. So it was true—whatever she'd read in that notebook was real. Now she needed to understand exactly what that meant.

"So, are you... dating him?"

Rick's head whipped around so fast Jason heard his neck crack. "What the hell are you talking about? Dating?" He looked at Sarah like she'd lost her mind. "They can't date! You've got your head screwed on backwards, woman. Jason and that other kid are just a couple of boys. Jesus, sometimes you sure are dumb."

He took a long swig of his beer and reached for another helping of meat, already dismissing the whole ridiculous conversation.

But something protective flared hot in Jason's chest—sudden and fierce and impossible to contain.

"My mom isn't dumb, you fucktard!"

"Jason!" Sarah snapped, shocked by the profanity.

"What'd you call me, boy?" Rick stood up fast enough to knock his chair back slightly, his beard messy with bits of food and sauce. His face was already reddening.

"My mom isn't dumb!" Jason was on his feet too now, emboldened by anger. "You shouldn't say shit like that about her. It makes *you* look dumb!"

Rick's chair scraped loudly against the old linoleum as he took a step back. "You don't talk to me like that in this house!"

"Rick, calm down. Jason, just drop it—" Sarah was trying desperately to defuse the situation, her hands raised in a placating gesture.

But Jason held his ground, glaring at Rick with an intensity that surprised even himself.

"Hang on." Rick's eyes narrowed, flicking between Sarah and Jason. The pieces were connecting in his beer-fuzzy brain. "Is that what you were talking about? Dating?" He looked at Jason with dawning disgust. "Your boy is queer? He's a fucking faggot?"

The word hit Jason as if Rick had taken a swing. He'd heard it a thousand times at school—hurled casually in hallways and locker rooms, used as the ultimate insult, the worst thing you could call someone. Kids threw it at each other constantly without really thinking about what it meant. But this was different. This was an adult. This was Rick, his mother's boyfriend, standing in their kitchen and calling Jason that word with pure contempt dripping from every syllable.

The word had edges sharp enough to cut, and Jason felt it slice through him.

"You and that blonde fairy-ass boy you've been bringing around here?" Rick's voice was getting louder, more aggressive. "Just a couple of fudge packers? Jesus Christ, Sarah! How come you didn't tell me your boy was a fucking queer? It ain't right! Just look at him!" He pointed at Jason with disgust. "He's probably been eyeing me this whole time, trying to figure out how to get at me. Makes me fucking sick to my stomach!"

"Rick, don't you dare talk to my son that way!" Sarah was on her feet now too, pointing a finger at her boyfriend.

"He's a fucking fairy, Sarah! I should've known. Should've seen it coming. Just look at him!" Rick was yelling now, his face fully red, spittle flying. "That way he walks, that way he talks—"

"That's ENOUGH!" Sarah's voice cracked like a whip. "That is my son you're talking about, and I won't have it!"

"You're okay with this, Sarah? You're seriously okay with him being a fucking faggot? A pervert?" Rick was almost incoherent now, his face twisted with genuine revulsion. "He's probably out there molesting kids, spreading that AIDS—"

The slap came so fast that Rick didn't see it coming. Sarah's palm connected with his cheek hard enough to snap his head to the side, hard enough to leave a red mark blooming across his face.

The room went silent except for heavy breathing.

Jason jumped back so quickly his chair toppled with a crash.

Rick raised his hand instinctively, and for one terrible moment Jason thought he was going to hit his mother. But Rick caught sight of Jason's expression—protective and furious and ready to fight—and backed away instead.

Sarah had started crying, and Jason took a step toward her.

Rick was already stomping down the hallway, and they could hear him in the bedroom, yanking open drawers and throwing things around. His voice carried back to the kitchen, venomous and unrelenting:

"I ain't living with no fucking faggot in this house! And I sure as shit ain't gonna have some bitch slap me around! You're lucky I don't want to catch AIDS touching that queer bait, otherwise I'd knock you into next week, you fucking cunt!"

"GET OUT!" Sarah was screaming now, pulling away from Jason to march down the hall. "GET OUT OF MY HOUSE!"

Rick emerged from their bedroom with an armful of clothes—work shirts, construction boots, jeans. Still yelling: "I'm leaving, bitch! Your boy is sick, Sarah! SICK! You mark my words, he's gonna molest those neighborhood kids and spread AIDS to everyone! You better get yourself checked, Sarah. You've been touching him!"

"GET THE FUCK OUT!" Sarah yanked the front door open, cold November air rushing into the house.

Rick walked past her, and for one horrible second Jason thought he might actually hit her despite his earlier restraint. But he just kept walking, still spewing hatred: "You made your choice! Don't come crying to me when he ends up dead in some alley or dying in a hospital bed! That's what happens to people like him! That's what they deserve!"

Sarah slammed the door so hard the Last Supper picture hanging nearby fell off the wall and crashed to the floor, frame splintering. Jason jumped at the sound.

They both stood frozen, listening to Rick's truck engine roar to life, tires squealing as he peeled out of the driveway and disappeared down the street.

Then silence. Profound and ringing.

Sarah stood by the door, shaking. Jason could see her shoulders trembling, could see her fighting to hold herself together. Then the dam broke and she started crying—deep, wrenching sobs that seemed to come from her core.

Jason wanted to go to her. Wanted to comfort her. But his feet wouldn't move. He stood in the kitchen doorway, numb, watching his mother fall apart.

Another man walking out of their lives. Another man leaving them behind.

First his father, disappearing one night without explanation, without goodbye, without looking back. Jason had been eight. He remembered his mom crying for weeks, remembered learning to make his own breakfast because she couldn't get out of bed some mornings.

Now Rick. Good riddance to Rick, honestly—he'd been useless at best, hostile at worst. But still. Another man who'd lived in their house, who'd sat at their table, who'd become part of their routine. Gone.

And it was Jason's fault this time. Because of what he was. Because he'd had the audacity to exist, to fall in love with a boy and not hide.

He was the reason his mom was crying now. The reason she was alone again. The reason—

"Jason?" Sarah's voice was thick with tears. She'd turned to look at him, mascara streaking down her cheeks. "Come here, sweetheart."

He moved then, crossing the kitchen in three quick strides. She pulled him into her arms and held on tight, and they stood there swaying slightly, both of them crying now.

"I'm sorry, Mom."

Sarah pulled back to look at him, confused. "What? What are you sorry for?"

"For... this. For him leaving. For—"

"Stop." She cupped his face in her hands, forcing him to meet her eyes. "Jason, listen to me. Rick is an asshole. A complete asshole. I should've thrown him out a long time ago—I know that. This isn't your fault. None of this is your fault."

Jason didn't know what to say. She meant it—he could see that in her eyes. But he also knew that if he weren't gay, if he didn't love Christopher, Rick would still be here. His mom wouldn't be alone again.

Sarah seemed to read his thoughts. "Jason, I don't want a man in my life who talks to my son the way Rick just did and thinks those things. Who says those hateful, ignorant—" Her voice broke. She took a shaky breath. "You're my son. You're more important than any man will ever be. Do you understand me?"

He nodded, not trusting his voice.

She pulled him close again, and they stood like that for a long moment. Then Sarah gently disentangled herself, wiping at her mascara-stained cheeks. "Let's clean this up," she said, gesturing at the fallen picture, the broken glass scattered across the floor.

They moved mechanically through the motions—picking up shards from the floor, righting overturned chairs, sweeping up the mess. The normalcy of routine helped anchor them both. When the kitchen was clean, they sat back down at the table even though neither were hungry.

Jason stared at his plate. Rick's hateful words kept replaying in his head, but oddly, he wasn't as devastated as he'd expected to be. The initial shock had hit hard—that razor-edged slur cutting deep. But as Rick had kept going, spewing more and more vitriol, it had started to sound increasingly stupid. The hate became so obvious, so ignorant, so completely divorced from reality that it lost its power.

Rick's words said everything about himself and nothing of Jason.

If anything, Jason felt strangely empowered. Like he'd passed through fire and come out stronger on the other side. He'd stood up to Rick. Protected his mom. Refused to shrink or hide or apologize for existing.

That felt like something.

Sarah was staring at her water glass, lost in thought. She was processing too—not just Rick leaving, but everything she'd learned today. Her son was gay. He had a boyfriend. This was real, not just a phase or confusion or something that would pass with time.

And she didn't know how to feel about it.

She loved Jason—that was never in question. But this opened up a whole world of worry she'd never had to consider before. Would he be safe? Would people hurt him? Would he face this kind of hatred everywhere he went? How could she protect him from a world that saw him as less-than, as wrong, as deserving of violence?

And what about the practical things? Would he ever have a normal life—a partner, a home, a family? Or would he be forced to hide forever, to live a double-life?

The questions swirled, unanswered and overwhelming.

"Mom?"

She looked up at her son. He was watching her with those dark eyes—his father's eyes—waiting.

Jason took a breath. His voice was steady when he spoke. "I'm gay."

Sarah's teeth caught her bottom lip. She was working hard to keep her expression neutral, to process this without showing judgment or fear or disappointment. But Jason could see it—the wheels turning behind her eyes, all the implications and worries and questions she didn't know how to ask.

"I know, honey." Her voice was quiet but firm. "I know."

Jason nodded and looked back down at his plate.

And that was it.

No embrace. No reassurances that everything would be okay. No declaration of unconditional love.

But also no yelling. No rejection. No demands that he change or hide or lie about who he was.

Just: "I know."

The response hung between them—anticlimactic and insufficient and somehow exactly what Jason had both expected and feared. His mother knew. She'd process it in her own time, work through her own feelings about it. And right now, in the aftermath of Rick's explosion and departure, that would have to be enough.

They sat in silence, neither eating, both lost in their own thoughts about what came next.

Jason waited for more. For some kind of reaction beyond those two words. But his mother just sat there, staring at her plate, working through something internal he couldn't see.

The silence stretched.

Nothing more was said.

Nothing at all.

Chapter 17

Poison

The parking lot of Burkhart's Tavern was half-full when Rick's truck squealed in Friday night, gravel spitting from under the tires. He slammed the door hard enough to make the whole vehicle shake and stalked toward the entrance, still wearing his work clothes, still pissed off from two days ago.

Inside, the bar was exactly what you'd expect—dim lighting, Budweiser signs glowing red on paneled walls, the smell of stale beer and fried food, George Jones singing about cheatin' women playing from a jukebox in the corner. A handful of regulars occupied their usual spots, nursing beers and watching the Pacers game on an old TV sitting on a shelf behind the bar.

Rick slid onto a stool and caught the bartender's eye. "Bud. Bottle."

The bartender—Jerry, who'd known Rick for years—grabbed a beer from the cooler and popped the cap. "Rough week?"

"You got no fuckin' idea," Rick muttered, taking a long pull.

Three stools down, Tommy Walsh and Mike Henderson were already well into their night, probably four or five beers deep. They'd worked construction with Rick on and off for the past five years. Mike noticed Rick first and nearly knocked over his beer pointing.

"Well look who finally decided to show his face! Where the hell you been, man? You fall in a ditch or somethin'?"

"Yeah, Rick, what the fuck?" Tommy added, words slightly slurred. "You missed poker Tuesday. Danny took all my money."

Rick just grunted and took another drink.

Mike squinted at him. "You look like shit, by the way. When's the last time you shaved?"

"Fuck off, Henderson."

"Ooh, touchy." Mike laughed and scooted his stool closer, nearly falling off in the process. "Seriously though, where you been? Johnson was lookin' for you at the site yesterday."

"Had some personal days."

"Personal days?" Tommy snorted. "The hell is a personal day? You get your period or somethin'?"

That got a laugh from Mike and a couple other guys nearby.

"I said fuck off." Rick's voice had an edge now.

Mike held up his hands. "Alright, alright. Jesus. Can't a guy bust balls anymore?" He took a swig of his beer. "But for real though, you okay? You been gone for days."

"I'm fine."

"You don't look fine," Tommy observed. "You look like my ex-wife after I told her I was keepin' the truck."

More laughter. Rick didn't join in.

Jerry the bartender leaned over. "You need another one already, Rick?"

"Yeah."

Mike watched Rick drain his first beer and immediately start on the second. "Okay, what's goin' on? And don't give me that 'I'm fine' bullshit. I've known you long enough to know when somethin's up."

Rick stared at his beer for a long moment. Then: "I'm stayin' at the Heim."

Tommy's eyebrows shot up. "The motel? Why the hell—" Then it clicked. "Oh shit. Sarah kick you out?"

"She didn't kick me out. I left."

"Uh huh." Mike didn't sound convinced. "What'd you do?"

271

"I didn't do nothin'! Christ, why's everyone assume—" Rick caught himself, took a breath. "It wasn't me. It was her fuckin' kid."

Tommy leaned in, interested now. "What about him?"

"Just drop it."

"Come on, man. You're livin' in a shithole motel, you've been MIA all week, you look like you wanna punch somebody—"

"I do wanna punch somebody!"

"So then, what the fuck?" Mike asked, his drunk logic making perfect sense to him.

Rick stared at his beer, jaw working. The anger was building again, mixing with the alcohol, and suddenly he couldn't keep it in anymore.

"Kid's a fuckin' faggot, that's what."

The conversation at the bar died. Tommy and Mike both went still.

"Wait, what?" Tommy said.

"You heard me." Rick's voice was getting louder now, rage finding an outlet. "Little bastard's queer as a three-dollar bill. Been sneakin' around with some other fairy from school. And Sarah knew. Probably knew the whole goddamn time and didn't say shit to me about it."

Mike sat back, processing. "You're sayin' he's a... fag?"

"That's exactly what I'm sayin'!" Rick slammed his bottle down hard enough to make people jump. "I come home, sit down to eat dinner like a normal person, and she starts askin' him about his 'special friend'. And I'm thinkin', okay, what the hell is a special friend? Then that little shit admits it right there at the table—says he's a fag, proud as you please!"

"Jesus," Tommy muttered.

"And Sarah just sits there!" Rick was on a roll now, his voice carrying across the bar. "Doesn't even try to knock some sense into him. Doesn't tell him it's wrong, doesn't tell him to cut that shit out. Just sits there like it's normal! Like I'm supposed to be okay with some little cocksucker livin' under my roof, eatin' my food, probably eyein' me up while I'm tryin' to watch TV—"

"Whoa, whoa," Mike interrupted. "The kid was checkin' you out?"

"How the hell should I know? That's what they do, ain't it?" Rick grabbed his beer. "Point is, I told Sarah right then—I ain't livin' with no faggot. Man's gotta have standards. So I left. Packed my shit and got out."

Tommy was quiet for a moment. "And you've been up at the Heim since...?"

"Wednesday night. Yeah." Rick's anger was starting to mix with embarrassment now. "Just till I find a better place. But I ain't goin' back there. Not with that pervert around."

"That's rough, man," Mike said, though he sounded more interested than sympathetic. "So he's really—I mean, you're sure?"

"He said it himself! Right to his mama's face!"

"Huh." Mike took a drink. "The Reynolds kid is a fag. Who knew?"

"I didn't!" Rick exploded. "Nobody told me! I been livin' there for months and nobody thought to mention Sarah's kid is a goddamn fuckin' deviant?"

Jerry the bartender leaned in, uncomfortable. "Rick, maybe keep your voice down a little—"

"Why? So people don't find out? Well guess what—they should know! Everyone should know there's kids like that walkin' around school, pretendin' to be normal, probably recruitin' other kids—"

"Recruitin'?" Tommy looked confused.

"That's what they do!" Rick insisted. "They get their hooks in normal kids, turn 'em queer. It's like a disease or somethin'. AIDS and all that shit."

Mike shook his head. "Man, that's... that's fucked up."

"You're tellin' me." Rick signaled Jerry for another beer. "And Sarah chose him over me. Can you believe that? I give her an ultimatum—me or the faggot—and she picks him."

"Well," Tommy said slowly, carefully, "I mean... he is her kid."

"So what? Kid needs help, not coddlin'! Needs someone to straighten him out before he ends up dead in some alley with AIDS." Rick was getting louder again. "But no, Sarah wants to pretend it's all fine. Let him keep sneakin' around with his little boyfriend—"

"Wait, who's the boyfriend?" Mike asked.

"Some blonde pretty-boy from school. Probably just as queer as him." Rick spat it out like poison. "Whole town ought to know. Ought to know their kids are goin' to school with a couple of fudge-packin'—"

"Alright, Rick, that's enough," Jerry said firmly from behind the bar. "I get you're upset but you need to watch it. I don't want to talk about that shit. It's disgusting!"

Rick glared at him but settled down slightly, muttering into his beer.

Tommy and Mike exchanged glances. They'd gotten more information than they'd bargained for.

Tommy's wife worked at Frazee elementary school. She'd want to know about this.

Mike's sister had kids at the high school. She'd definitely want to know.

The conversation eventually moved on—back to the Hoosiers versus the Boilermakers, to work complaints, to the usual bar bullshit. But the seed had been planted.

By Monday morning, half the town would know.

———

Jason sat at their usual table picking at his salisbury steak that tasted like cardboard and grease. Allison was mid-story about her weekend, something involving her mom's new boyfriend and a disastrous attempt at cooking dinner. Christopher was listening with a smile, occasionally glancing at Jason with those soft eyes that made his chest tight.

Scott had joined them late, carrying his lunch from home as usual. He'd been quieter than normal, Jason noticed. Less animated. But Scott was always a little off in his own world, so Jason didn't think much of it.

Then three sophomores Jason vaguely recognized approached their table.

The leader was a stocky kid with a buzz cut and a blue FFA jacket —Brad something, Jason thought. Farmer kid. The other two flanked him like backup singers, smirking.

"Hey," Brad said, stopping right next to Jason. "You're Jason Reynolds, right?"

Jason looked up slowly, immediately on guard. "Yeah. Why?"

"Just wanted to see what a faggot looks like up close." Brad said it casually, like he was commenting on the weather.

The table went silent. Allison's fork stopped halfway to her mouth. Christopher went white. Scott stared.

Jason felt his face go hot, but he kept his voice level. "Fuck off."

"Ooh, hostile." Brad grinned at his friends. "Guess that means it's true, huh? You and pretty boy here"—he gestured at Christopher—"playing tickle the pickle after school?"

One of Brad's friends laughed. Christopher looked like he might throw up.

Allison stood up so fast her chair scraped loudly. "Get the fuck away from our table before I kick it into Rushville."

"All I'm doing is asking questions." Brad's smile widened. "I'm just curious. Word going around is that Sarah Reynolds' kid is a queer. My cousin's friend heard his old man talking about it down at Burkhart's. Just wanted to see if it's true."

Jason's blood went cold. Rick. Of course. Rick had been running his mouth.

"Rick's a lying piece of shit," Jason said, his voice harder now.

"So you're not a fag?" Brad pressed. "Because that's not what we heard. We heard you got a thing for blondes." He looked pointedly at Christopher, who was shrinking in his seat.

"I said fuck off." Jason stood now too, ready to throw the first punch if it came to that.

"Easy, easy." Brad held up his hands in mock surrender. "Just trying to get the facts straight. Or not straight, I guess." His friends laughed on cue. "Enjoy your lunch, ladies."

They walked away, still snickering. Jason sat back down, his whole body shaking with rage.

"What the fuck was that?" Allison demanded, though she was looking at Jason for answers.

"Nothing. Just assholes being assholes."

"They called you—" Christopher started, but couldn't finish the sentence.

"I know what they called me." Jason's voice was tight.

Scott had been silent through the whole exchange. Now he spoke up, his voice uncertain. "Is it true?"

Jason's head snapped toward him. "What?"

"What they said. Are you..." Scott gestured vaguely. "You know. A fag?"

"Scott!" Allison yelled.

The question hung there. Christopher was staring at his tray. Allison looked ready to murder someone.

Jason made a split-second decision. "Yeah, Scott. I am."

Scott's eyes went wide. Then he looked at Christopher. "And you?"

Christopher nodded, barely perceptibly.

Scott pushed back from the table, grabbing his lunch. "I gotta... I have to go. Sorry." He didn't quite run, but he moved fast, weaving through tables toward the exit.

"Scott, wait—" Allison called after him, but he didn't turn around.

Jason watched him go, feeling something hollow open up in his chest. Scott had been sitting at their table since freshman year. Not a close friend exactly, but steady. Reliable. And now he was gone.

"Fuck," Jason muttered.

"He'll come around," Allison said, but she didn't sound convinced.

Christopher hadn't said anything. When Jason looked at him, he was crying—silent tears tracking down his face, shoulders shaking slightly.

"Hey." Jason reached across the table, then stopped himself, remembering where they were. "It's okay. They're just—"

"I can't." Christopher's voice was choked. "I can't do this. Everyone's staring."

Jason looked around. Christopher was right. Half the cafeteria seemed to be watching them now, whispering behind hands, pointing. Word had spread fast.

"Come on." Allison stood, gathering her tray. "Let's get out of here."

They dumped their mostly uneaten lunches and left the cafeteria under dozens of curious, hostile eyes. Christopher kept his head down the whole way.

Outside in the hallway, Christopher leaned against the wall and tried to calm his breathing. "I'm sorry. I just—that was—"

"You don't have to apologize," Jason said fiercely. "Those assholes—"

"It's going to keep happening, isn't it?" Christopher looked at him with red-rimmed eyes. "Now everyone knows."

Jason didn't have an answer for that. He hoped it would die down.

———

Over the next few days, Christopher's premonition proved true; things got worse.

Christopher walked to third period and heard "faggot" muttered from somewhere behind him in the crowded hallway. He couldn't tell who said it. The next day, a group of girls giggled when he passed them at his locker, and he was sure he heard one say "I can't believe it" before they dissolved into laughter.

In science lab, his teacher Mr. Peterson called out partner assignments. Christopher waited for his name to be paired with someone.

"And Christopher, since we're down one student today, you can work independently."

That wasn't unusual—someone was absent, the numbers didn't work out. Except Christopher could count. There were twenty-four students present. Even number. And over by the windows, he could clearly see three kids huddled around one lab station instead of the usual two.

Christopher looked up at Mr. Peterson, who seemed suddenly very interested in the textbook. "The, uh... the equipment setup works better with... well, you know how it is."

The fumbled excuse hung in the air between them.

Christopher grabbed his lab sheet and walked to an empty station by himself. It was easier this way anyway. Better to work alone than sit with people who were probably thinking he was... well. Better to just work alone.

Mr. Peterson didn't meet his eyes for the rest of the period.

Christopher worked through the lab procedure by himself, acutely aware that he was the odd one out. Literally.

After class, a senior he didn't even know bumped him hard in the shoulder. "Watch it, fag."

Christopher said nothing. Just kept walking, face burning.

———

Jason had it worse.

He'd always been good at making himself invisible, blending into crowds, not drawing attention. Now everywhere he went, people stared. Some were just curious—watching the freak show. Others were hostile.

After school, someone had written "FAGGOT" in Sharpie across his locker. He scrubbed it off with a couple of alcohol patches from the nurse's office, trying to ignore the janitor's pitying look.

The next day, David Keller—a low-key bully who usually ignored Jason—went out of his way to shoulder-check him in the hallway hard enough to knock his books out of his hands.

"Oops. Sorry, fairy." David smirked as Jason scrambled gathering scattered papers.

By Thursday, Jason couldn't bring himself to go to the cafeteria.

He stood at the entrance, saw the crowded tables, heard the noise and laughter, and imagined walking in there—every head turning, every conversation stopping, the whispers starting up again. Worse, he imagined Christopher and Allison sitting there with him, becoming targets by association. Taking heat just for sitting at the same table.

He turned around and walked out the side doors instead.

The track down by the football field was empty. Cold November wind cut across the open space, but Jason barely felt it. He walked the perimeter slowly, hands shoved in his pockets, trying not to think about Christopher and Allison eating lunch without him. Trying not to imagine them relieved he wasn't there.

Maybe they were better off without him. Maybe if he just... disappeared from their daily routine, people would forget. Would leave them alone.

The thought made his chest ache, but he kept walking.

At least out here, he wasn't a walking target. At least out here, nobody was staring.

He made it three laps before the bell rang, then headed back inside for fifth period, stomach empty, hands numb from cold.

————

At home, things were no better.

Sarah had barely spoken to him since Friday night. She made dinner—silent meals where they chewed mechanically and didn't make eye contact. She asked if he'd finished his homework. He said yes. She said good.

That was it.

No "I love you." No "we'll get through this." No acknowledgment at all of what he'd told her, what had happened with Rick, what any of it meant.

Just silence.

When Christopher called, Jason kept the conversation short. His mom was in the living room, close enough to overhear. He didn't want to talk about his feelings or what was happening at school. Didn't want her to hear him being... whatever she thought he was.

"Yeah, I'm fine," he said into the phone, voice low. "Just tired. Lots of homework."

"Are you sure? Because you sound—"

"I'm fine, Christopher. Really. I gotta go."

"Okay. I love you."

Jason glanced toward the living room. His mom's silhouette was visible through the doorway. "Yeah. Me too. Bye."

He hung up feeling like shit.

The next night, the same thing. Thursday night, Christopher called again and Jason could hear the hurt in his voice.

"Did I do something wrong?"

"No. God, no. It's not you."

"Then what? Because you weren't at lunch today—Allison and I were worried. And you're barely talking to me and I don't understand what's happening."

Jason's throat tightened. They'd noticed. Of course they'd noticed. "I just... needed some air. Went for a walk."

"For the whole lunch period?"

"Yeah."

"Jason—"

"It's complicated right now. My mom... she's still processing. I don't want to make it worse."

"Make what worse?"

"Just... everything. Can we talk about this later? Maybe this weekend?"

A pause. "Yeah. Okay. This weekend."

"I'm sorry," Jason said, and he meant it. "I just need some space to figure things out here."

"Okay." Christopher sounded small. "I understand."

After he hung up, Jason sat on his bed staring at nothing. He was protecting Christopher. That's what he told himself. The less they talked, the less associated they were, the less heat Christopher would take.

It was for the best.

It felt like dying.

———

Friday after school, Christopher came home looking utterly defeated.

Diane had been watching it happen all week—her son who usually bounded through the door with energy had been progressively slowing down, day by day. Tuesday, he was withdrawn. Wednesday, he'd barely spoken at dinner. Thursday, he'd gone straight to his room.

Now Friday, he could barely drag himself through the door, shoulders slumped, eyes red-rimmed like he'd been crying or trying very hard not to.

"Christopher?" Diane set down the dish towel and met him in the hallway. "Honey?"

"I'm fine, Mom."

But he clearly wasn't. He'd been saying that all week, and each day it became more obviously untrue.

At dinner, Mark tried to engage him in conversation. "How was your day?"

"Fine."

"Just fine?"

"Yeah. Fine."

Mark and Diane exchanged glances. They'd been patient, giving him space, hoping he'd open up on his own. But whatever was happening was getting worse, not better.

"Christopher," Diane said gently. "Talk to us. What's going on? Something's been wrong all week."

Christopher pushed food around his plate. "Nothing's going on."

"That's not true," Mark pressed. "You've been withdrawn for days. Did something happen?"

"I don't want to talk about it."

"Christopher—"

"I said I don't want to talk about it!" Christopher's voice cracked. He set down his fork, his hands shaking. "I'm sorry. I'm sorry. I just... can I be excused?"

"No," Diane said firmly but kindly. "Something is clearly wrong and we want to help. Please talk to us."

Christopher's face crumpled. "People at school are calling me a fag."

The word landed like a bomb.

Mark's jaw tightened. Diane reached across the table for Christopher's hand.

"Who?" Mark demanded. "Who's saying this?"

"I don't know. Different people. In the halls. At lunch." Christopher wiped his eyes. "Everyone's staring at me. Whispering. And I don't even know why exactly because Jason won't talk to me about what happened and—"

"Wait, slow down," Diane interrupted gently. "What happened with Jason?"

"Something at his house last weekend. His mom found his notebook and then I guess her boyfriend found out Jason is gay and there was a huge fight. But Jason's barely talking to me about it. He says his mom needs space and he can't talk on the phone much and—" Christopher's words tumbled out in a rush. "And now everyone at school seems to know and they're calling us names and I don't understand how it all happened so fast."

Mark and Diane exchanged another look, this one darker. The pieces were coming together.

"Is Jason okay?" Diane asked.

"I don't know. He says he is but he won't really talk to me." Christopher's voice broke again. "And at lunch on Monday these guys came up to our table and called us faggots right in front of everyone. Scott left and never came back. And people keep staring and teachers are treating me different and—"

"Teachers?" Mark's voice went hard. "What do you mean teachers are treating you differently?"

Christopher explained the science lab situation. The convenient "odd man out." Mr. Peterson avoiding eye contact.

Mark's face was growing redder by the second.

"Does Mr. Barnes know about this?" Diane asked. "David—does he know what's going on?"

"I don't think so," Christopher said. "I mean, he's looked at us weird a few times this week. Like he knows something's wrong. But we haven't said anything to him."

"Why not?" Mark asked. "He could help—"

"Because..." Christopher struggled for the words. "Jason said... he said if Mr. Barnes gets too involved, people might... I don't know. Wonder why he cares so much about helping us. And that might make things bad for him too. We didn't want to..."

He trailed off, not quite able to finish the thought.

Diane and Mark exchanged a look, understanding immediately what their son was trying to say. Christopher was trying to protect David, even while being harassed himself.

"Honey," Diane said gently, "that's very thoughtful of you. But David is an adult. It's his job to help students who are being bullied. You shouldn't have to protect him."

"I know, but..." Christopher's voice cracked. "Jason said we shouldn't. That it wasn't fair. And maybe he's right. Maybe if we just... keep our heads down, it'll blow over."

"It won't blow over," Mark said firmly. "Not without intervention."

"Mark," Diane said quietly, a hand on his arm. Then to Christopher: "Honey, I know this is hard. But we're going to help you, okay? Both you and Jason."

"Jason doesn't want help," Christopher said miserably. "He barely wants to talk to me."

"That's because he's dealing with a lot right now," Diane said gently. "His home situation sounds... complicated. But that doesn't mean he doesn't care about you."

Christopher nodded, not looking convinced.

After dinner, Mark went into his study and called David's home number. Jim answered on the third ring.

"Hello?"

"Jim, it's Mark Avery."

"Mark! Hey, what a nice surprise!" Jim's voice was warm, genuinely pleased. "We had such a great time last weekend. David and I were just talking about how nice it was to finally meet you both properly."

"Yeah, it was really special for us too. Diane and I are so glad you came."

"Well, thank you for having us. And for the leftovers—that casserole Diane sent home was fantastic. David's been—" Jim paused, picking up on something in Mark's tone. "Everything okay?"

"Actually, that's why I'm calling. It's about Christopher. And Jason."

The warmth in Jim's voice shifted to concern. "What happened?"

Mark gave him the quick version—the harassment at school, the rumors spreading, the teachers treating Christopher differently, Jason pulling away and barely talking to anyone.

"Jesus," Jim said quietly. "When did all this start?"

"This week, apparently. It's been escalating. And Christopher just told us tonight that he and Jason have been keeping it from David because they're worried about putting him in a difficult position."

"Shit. Okay. Hold on, let me get David."

A moment later David was on the line, his voice tense. Jim had clearly briefed him. "Mark? What's going on?"

"I don't know. That's why I'm calling." Mark explained what Christopher had told them—the harassment, the rumors, the teachers treating him differently. "Did you know any of this was happening?"

David was quiet for a moment. "No. I didn't. Students don't usually... they keep things from teachers, especially something like this. But I'll look into it. Ask around carefully."

"Christopher says Jason's barely talking to him. Something happened with Jason's mother's boyfriend—apparently the guy found out Jason is gay and there was a huge blowup. He left. And now the whole school seems to know."

"Shit," David muttered. "That explains... there have been some whispers. I overheard a couple of students talking in the halls but couldn't make out what they were saying. I thought it was just normal teenage drama."

"It's not." Mark's voice was tight. "My son is being harassed. Jason's probably getting it worse. And I need to know what you're going to do about it."

"I'll handle it," David said firmly. "Monday morning I'll pull some kids aside, ask some questions. If teachers are involved, I'll address that too. But Mark, you need to understand—I have to be careful how I approach this."

"Why? Because you're—" Mark stopped himself.

"Yeah," David said quietly. "Because of that. If I come on too strong defending two boys who everyone thinks are gay, it's going to raise questions I can't afford to answer right now."

Mark felt guilty immediately. "I'm sorry. I know that's not fair to you."

"It's fine. I get it. I'm just saying I have to be strategic." David paused. "How's Christopher holding up?"

"Not great. He's scared. Confused. Feels isolated." Mark rubbed his face. "I don't know how to help him."

"Just be there. That's all you can do. Listen when he talks. Don't minimize what he's feeling. And if it gets worse—if the harassment escalates—we'll figure out next steps."

"Okay. Thanks, David."

"Of course. I'll call you Monday after I've talked to some people."

After Mark hung up, Diane appeared in the doorway. "Well?"

"David's going to look into it. But he has to be careful."

"Because he's gay."

"Yeah."

Diane sighed. "This is so unfair. To all of them."

Upstairs, Christopher heard his parents' voices through the floor but couldn't make out the words. He lay on his bed staring at the ceiling.

He wanted to call Jason. Wanted to hear his voice, wanted to tell him what was happening, wanted Jason to tell him everything would be okay.

But Jason had asked for space. Had pulled away. And Christopher didn't want to push.

So he just lay there, alone, trying not to cry.

———

Later that night, David and Jim were in bed, the room dark except for the glow of streetlights through the curtains. They'd talked for over an hour after David hung up with Mark, going over everything, trying to figure out the best approach. Now they lay in silence, both still thinking.

"I can't stop thinking about it," Jim said quietly.

David turned his head on the pillow. "About the boys?"

"Yeah." Jim was staring at the ceiling. "It reminds me too much of Cashton." He paused. "That's how things worked when I was growing up there—some drunk asshole at a bar, rumors spreading through churches and families. Picked up speed fast. And the kids who got targeted..." He trailed off.

"What?" David prompted gently.

"They get hurt. Badly sometimes. I saw it happen. It's why I left." Jim's voice was heavy with old memories. "And Jason—the way he broke down at your place, his home situation. If his mom is not even talking to him about it—he's so vulnerable right now. Really vulnerable. Add the bullshit at school, Christopher pulling away because he's scared—"

"Christopher's not pulling away. Jason is."

"Doesn't matter. It feels the same to both of them." Jim rolled onto his side to face David. "They're just figuring out they're gay and starting to be a couple. Now everything's exploding at once. This is when kids do desperate things, David. I'm worried about them. You need to talk to Jason. Pull him aside. Check on him."

"And say what? 'Hey Jason, come to the office, you're not in trouble, I just want to know if you're thinking about killing yourself?'"

"David—"

"I'm serious. That kid already thinks everyone's going to abandon him. If I call him down to the office, he'll panic. Think I'm turning on him too."

Jim was quiet, considering. "Then find another way. But you need to reach him somehow. David, think about what it was like for you at that age—alone and terrified with no one to talk to. Would you have wanted someone to notice? Someone to actually give a damn and check on you?"

David closed his eyes. "Yeah. I would have."

"Then do for them what no one did for us." Jim reached for David's hand in the darkness. "I know you're worried about drawing attention to yourself. But these kids need help. Both of them."

"I know." David squeezed Jim's hand. "I'll figure something out. I promise."

They lay in silence for a while, both lost in thought.

"Do you think Jason's okay?" Jim asked quietly.

"I don't know," David admitted. "But I'm going to find out."

Sarah Reynolds stood at the customer service desk at First National Bank, smiling professionally at JoAnne Henderson while she processed a withdrawal. She had been banking here for twenty years. Sarah knew her kids' names, knew about her husband's heart surgery last year, knew she always requested brand new bills for birthday cards.

But this particular Saturday morning JoAnne was cold.

"Thank you," she said shortly when Sarah handed her the money, not meeting her eyes.

"Have a great day, JoAnne."

No response. Just a tight-lipped nod and a quick exit.

Sarah watched her go, confused. That was the third regular customer this week who'd been unusually distant.

During her lunch break, she went to the small staff room and found two coworkers—Linda and Margaret—sitting at the table with their lunches. They stopped talking the moment Sarah entered.

"Don't let me interrupt," Sarah said lightly, heading for the refrigerator.

"Oh, you're not," Linda said, but her tone was off.

Sarah grabbed her sandwich and turned to find both women looking at her with strange expressions.

"Everything okay?" Sarah asked.

"We were just... wondering how you're doing," Margaret said carefully. "I heard Rick moved out."

Sarah's stomach dropped. "How did you—"

"Small town." Linda shrugged. "Word gets around. You doing okay?"

"I'm fine. It was for the best."

"I'm sure it was," Margaret said in a tone that suggested she knew more than she was saying. "Must be hard though. Raising a teenage boy on your own."

"I've been doing it mostly on my own anyway," Sarah said, defensive now.

"Of course. Of course." Margaret took a bite of her salad. Then, too casually: "Have you thought about getting Jason involved in church? Youth group might be good for him. Especially now."

Sarah went very still. "What do you mean, 'especially now'?"

Margaret and Linda exchanged glances.

"Just... I heard some things," Margaret said delicately. "And I thought maybe church community, some guidance from Pastor Williams—it might help. Before things get... out of hand."

The implication was crystal clear.

Sarah felt her face flush. "What exactly did you hear?"

"It doesn't matter what I heard or where I heard it," Margaret said, her voice taking on a slightly righteous tone. "What matters is that boy needs help. Needs guidance. These things don't just go away on their own, Sarah. You have to address them."

"These things?" Sarah's voice was dangerously quiet.

Linda jumped in, trying to soften it. "We're just concerned. As friends. We want to help."

"I don't need your help." Sarah shoved her sandwich back in the refrigerator and walked out, appetite gone.

Back at the front counter, she stood there trembling with anger and humiliation, trying to compose herself before the next customer approached. Rick. That bastard had been shooting his mouth off. And now everyone knew. Or thought they knew. Or were making assumptions based on bar gossip from a drunk asshole.

She thought about Jason facing this at school. Thought about the stares he must be getting, the whispers, the harassment.

She thought about her promotion. The new job waiting in Indianapolis. Better pay, better position, better opportunities.

A fresh start.

She abruptly walked to her manager's office.

Tom Brennan looked up from his computer. "Sarah? Everything okay?"

"Tom, I need to talk to you about the Indianapolis position."

"Sure, have a seat. I've been meaning to check in about your start date. You said January, right? After the holidays?"

"That's what I wanted to talk about. Something's come up." Sarah sat, folding her hands in her lap to keep them from shaking. "My landlord called this morning. Says he has someone who wants to rent my place starting December first. Wants to know if I can be out by then."

It was a lie. A complete fabrication. But it sounded plausible.

Tom frowned. "That's sudden. Can you push back?"

"Not really. Month-to-month lease. He can do that." Sarah tried to look apologetic. "I know it's earlier than we discussed, but actually—if you could use me sooner in Indy, it might work out better. I could start after Thanksgiving. Give me the holiday to move, be ready to go by December first."

Tom considered it. "Actually, that would help me out tremendously. I've been trying to manage both offices remotely and with the Christmas season coming up..." He pulled out a calendar. "Thanksgiving is the twenty-third this year. You could move that weekend, start Monday the twenty-seventh?"

"That would be perfect."

"You're sure? That's less than two weeks away."

"I'm sure." Sarah smiled, hoping it looked genuine. "It'll be good. Fresh start. Jason's young—he'll adapt quickly."

"Alright then. I'll give Bill a call and let him know we're moving up your start date. He'll be happy—he's been waiting for this position to get filled. And honestly, it'll take a load off me too. I've been driving up there every other day trying to cover that branch, and with Christmas coming..." Tom shook his head. "Let's just say my wife will be thrilled to have me home more."

Tom extended his hand. "Welcome aboard officially, Sarah. Bill's lucky to have you. You're going to do great things up there."

Sarah shook his hand and left his office feeling both relieved and sick.

Two weeks. She had two weeks to pack up their lives and get out of this town before the gossip got worse, before people started treating Jason the way Margaret had been treating her.

He'd understand, she told herself. He'd probably want to leave anyway. Small towns had nothing to offer kids like him. Indianapolis would be better—bigger, more anonymous, more opportunities.

He'd miss his friend Christopher, sure. But he was young. Resilient. He'd make new friends.

This was for the best.

She just had to tell him.

———

Jason was in his room when his mom knocked on the door.

"Jason? Can I come in?"

"Yeah."

Sarah entered carrying two plates of reheated pizza from the fridge. She handed him one and sat on the edge of his bed.

"We need to talk."

Jason's stomach clenched. This was it—the conversation he'd been dreading. She was going to tell him she couldn't accept it, that he needed to change, that he was going to hell or therapy or both.

"Okay," he said carefully.

"I have good news." Sarah smiled, but it didn't quite reach her eyes. "I got the promotion I was telling you about. The one in Indianapolis."

Jason blinked. That wasn't what he'd expected. "Oh. That's... that's great, Mom."

"It is. Better pay, better position. And I talked to Tom today—he needs me to start sooner than we planned. So we're going to move over Thanksgiving weekend."

The world tilted.

"What?"

"I know it's sudden, but the landlord wants us out by December first anyway, so the timing actually works out perfectly. We'll spend Thanksgiving packing, move that weekend, and you'll start at your new school the Monday after."

"New school?" Jason's voice sounded distant to his own ears.

"In Indianapolis. It'll be much better than here, Jason. Better opportunities. And honestly..." Sarah's voice softened. "I think a fresh start will be good for both of us. Especially after everything with Rick."

"But that's—" Jason did the math in his head. "That's two weeks from now."

"I know. But we can do it. We've moved before, remember? When we left the apartment and moved into this house? We'll make it work."

"But school. My friends. I—" Christopher. He couldn't say Christopher's name. His mom was looking at him with this hopeful expression, like she was offering him something wonderful instead of ripping his life apart.

"I know it's last minute, but I'll call up and get your school situated. And I'm sure you'll make new friends," Sarah said. "And it's not like Connersville has been..." She paused, choosing her words carefully. "I know things have been hard for you lately. I think this will be better. A chance to start over somewhere nobody knows... anything."

There it was. The real reason. She was running. They were both running. Away from the gossip, the stares, the small-town judgment.

Away from Christopher.

"I don't want to move," Jason said, but his voice came out small. Defeated.

"I know it's a lot to process. But trust me, honey. This is going to be good for us. Better money means a better place to live, better food, better everything. And Indianapolis is a real city—there's so much more to do there than here."

Jason stared at his pizza, unable to eat. Two weeks. In two weeks he'd be gone. Away from Christopher, away from the farmhouses, away from everything.

"Can I think about it?" he asked weakly.

"There's nothing to think about," Sarah said gently. "It's happening. I already accepted the position. But I promise, Jason—you're going to like it there. New start, new opportunities. Okay? If things work out well, maybe we can buy you a little car when you get your license."

"Okay," he whispered.

Sarah kissed his forehead and left him alone.

Jason sat there for a long time, the cold pizza turning to rubber on his plate. His brain wouldn't shut up. Wouldn't stop spinning through everything.

He should call Christopher. Tell him what was happening. But what would he even say? *Hey, we're moving in two weeks because my mom can't handle everyone knowing her son's a fag?*

He thought about Monday at lunch. Those assholes calling him out in front of everyone. The way Christopher had looked—small and terrified and like he wanted to disappear. Scott getting up and never coming back.

Christopher was getting shit because of him. Because everyone knew they were together. Because Rick had gone and told the whole fucking town.

And Mr. Barnes—god, if Jason wasn't there, maybe people would leave him alone too. Wouldn't wonder why he gave a shit about helping a couple of fags. Jason was making everything worse just by existing.

Maybe leaving was better.

If he was gone, people would forget. Move on to the next thing. Christopher could go back to being normal. Safe. The good kid with the nice parents and the perfect future who wasn't getting shit at school.

Jason could take all of it with him. All the hate, all the attention. Just... gone.

Christopher would be okay.

The thought of never seeing Christopher again felt like something was ripping apart inside his chest. Made him want to punch the wall or scream or break down crying. But if it kept Christopher safe...

He couldn't tell him. Not yet. If Christopher knew, he'd try to fix it. Try to find some solution, some way to make Jason stay. And Jason couldn't handle that. Couldn't handle seeing Christopher hurt on top of everything else.

Better to just... back off. Pull away. Make it easier when he finally had to leave.

It hit him then, sudden and cold: This was what William did.

William left Daniel to protect him. Thought if he was gone, Daniel would be safe. Wouldn't get dragged down by association.

And look how that turned out.

But what the fuck else was Jason supposed to do?

The phone rang in the kitchen. Jason heard it from his room—second ring, third ring. He knew it was Christopher. He'd said he'd call tonight.

His mom's voice carried down the hall. "Jason! Phone!"

Jason's stomach clenched. He walked to the kitchen where his mom stood holding out the receiver, then went back to the living room, giving him a semblance of privacy.

"Hello?"

"Hey." Christopher's voice sounded small. Hopeful. "Can we hang out tomorrow? I was thinking maybe we could ride out to the farmhouses again, or just... I don't know. Hang out?"

Jason could hear his mom moving around in the living room. Could feel her presence even though she wasn't looking at him.

"Can't tomorrow. My mom needs help with stuff around the house."

A lie. But what was he supposed to say? The truth?

"Oh. Okay." Christopher's voice got quieter. "What about Sunday?"

"I don't know. Maybe."

Silence stretched between them. Jason could hear Christopher breathing, could hear something shifting in that breath.

"Jason, did I do something wrong?" Christopher's voice cracked slightly. "Because you've been... all week you've barely talked to me, and I don't understand what's happening, and—"

"It's not you."

"Then what? Please just talk to me. I can't—" Christopher's voice broke completely. "I can't do this. I can't handle everyone at school and you pulling away and I don't know what I did—"

Jason heard it then—Christopher crying. Trying to hold it in but failing, these small choked sounds that made Jason's chest feel like it was caving in.

"Christopher—"

"I'm sorry." Christopher was fighting to get words out between sobs. "I'm sorry, I know you said your mom needs space, I know things are hard, but I just—I miss you. And I'm scared. And I don't understand why you won't talk to me."

Jason pressed his forehead against the kitchen wall, his own eyes burning. He wanted to tell him everything. Wanted to say *I'm moving in two weeks and I don't know how to tell you and it's killing me. Wanted to say I love you and I'm sorry and I'm trying to protect you but I don't know what I'm doing.*

But his mom was right there. In the next room. Listening.

"I can't right now," Jason said, his voice barely above a whisper. "I just... I can't."

Christopher made a sound like he'd been hit. "Okay. Okay, I—" Another sob. "I'm sorry. I shouldn't have—"

"Don't apologize. Please don't—" Jason's voice cracked.

"I have to go." Christopher was crying harder now. "I'm sorry. Goodnight."

"Christopher, wait—"

But the line was already dead.

Jason stood there holding the receiver, listening to the dial tone, his whole body shaking. He could hear his mom in the living room, pretending she hadn't heard any of it.

He hung up the phone carefully, like it might shatter if he moved too fast.

Then he went back to his room and closed the door and sat on the edge of his bed with his face in his hands, trying not to make a sound as he fell apart.

He was destroying Christopher. Piece by piece. And Christopher didn't even know why.

Two weeks. He had two weeks.

Two weeks until he had to say goodbye to the only person who'd ever made him feel like he mattered.

He pulled off his shirt, kicked off his jeans, and climbed into bed. Staring at the ceiling, he tried not to think about Christopher's face when he finally found out. Tried not to think about never seeing him again.

Tried not to think.

Eventually, exhaustion dragged him under into fitful, restless sleep.

The dream came back. First time in over a week.

But this time, everything was different.

He wasn't standing on the widow's peak watching the dream. He was *in* it. Down on the tracks. And he knew—with that strange dream-certainty—that he was William.

His foot was caught between the rails. Not accidentally. He'd put it there. Wedged it in deliberately, the steel cold against his ankle, pressing into bone.

In the distance, the train whistle screamed. Getting closer.

"William! WILLIAM!"

He turned. Daniel was running toward him—but it wasn't Daniel. It was Christopher. Wearing old-fashioned clothes but with Christopher's face, Christopher's desperate eyes.

"Please! Please, your foot—get it out!" Christopher was crying, yanking at his arm, trying to pull him free.

"I can't." William's—Jason's—voice came out calm. Too calm. "It's better this way."

"No! No, please—" Christopher dropped to his knees, clawing at the rail, at Jason's trapped foot, sobbing. "I can't lose you, please—"

The train whistle shrieked again. Closer. The ground began to shake.

"You'll be safe," Jason heard himself say. "Once I'm gone, you'll be—"

But Christopher wasn't listening. He lunged forward and kissed him—desperate and terrified and heartbroken—one last moment of contact before the inevitable.

Then he pulled back, and Jason saw it clearly: Christopher thought Jason was choosing this. Choosing to leave him. Abandoning him.

Just like Jason's dad had abandoned them.

The realization struck like a knife between his ribs, cutting straight through to his heart, through every promise he'd ever made, through everything he'd sworn he'd never become. *I'm abandoning him.*

The train's lamp blinded him, a white-hot point of light bearing down. The rails vibrated violently under his trapped foot. The ground literally shook, ballast stones jumping and settling.

He tried to scream, to take it back, to tell Christopher he was sorry—

The train hit.

A massive whoosh of air—every bit of oxygen sucked from his lungs. He couldn't breathe. Couldn't scream. Could only see Christopher turning away, hands flying up instinctively to protect his face—

Jason felt his body *break*. Felt something fundamental give way. And then—

Blood.

His blood spraying across Christopher's face, his hair, his clothes. Christopher falling backward onto the gravel and dirt, covered in what Jason had become. The train's steel wheels shrieking as the engineer slammed the brakes too late, far too late.

And Jason could *feel* it—not his own pain, but Christopher's. The horror. The grief. The soul-deep wound of watching someone you love choose to leave you.

What have I done?

———

Jason jerked awake gasping, soaked with sweat.

The room was pitch black. Silent except for his own ragged breathing.

He lay there shaking, the dream still vivid behind his eyes. The feeling of Christopher's pain—so real he could still taste it, metallic and bitter.

The room felt empty. Hollow.

Like his soul.

He'd been trying to protect Christopher. Trying to keep him safe by leaving, by taking all the hate and attention away with him.

But all he was really doing was abandoning him. Hurting him in a different way. Maybe worse.

Just like his dad had done to them.

Jason curled onto his side, pulling his knees to his chest. He didn't know what to do. Didn't know how to make any of this right.

Stay, and Christopher kept getting called a fag in the hallways. Kept getting stared at and whispered about and treated like he was diseased.

Leave, and Christopher would be abandoned. Left behind. Made to feel like he wasn't worth fighting for.

Either way, Jason hurt him.

Either way, there was no good answer.

He lay there in the dark, empty room, feeling like no matter what choice he made, someone he loved was going to bleed.

Chapter 18

Convergence

Christopher lay on his bed Sunday morning staring at the ceiling, straining to hear if the phone would ring downstairs. It didn't.

Jason hadn't called back last night after Christopher had broken down crying like an idiot. Hadn't called this morning. Wasn't going to call.

Christopher knew this intellectually—knew Jason was dealing with something big at home, knew his mom was still processing everything, knew Jason was under tremendous pressure. He'd told his parents all of it just days ago—the harassment at school, Jason pulling away, feeling lost and confused.

His brain understood.

But his heart just knew Jason was pulling away. And no matter what his brain said about pressure and stress and circumstances, it still felt like Jason didn't want him anymore.

He'd barely slept. Every time he closed his eyes, he heard himself crying on the phone, heard how pathetic he'd sounded begging Jason to talk to him. God, Jason probably thought he was so needy. So weak. Maybe that's why he was pulling away—because Christopher couldn't handle the pressure, couldn't be strong enough for both of them.

A soft knock on his door. It opened before he could respond.

His mom stood there, concern written across her face. "Christopher, honey. Can we talk?"

"I'm okay, Mom."

"No, you're not." Diane came in and sat on the edge of his bed. "You've been up here all morning. You barely touched breakfast yesterday. And I can see you've been crying." She reached out and brushed his hair back. "Talk to me. Please."

Christopher's throat tightened. "I don't know what to say. Jason won't talk to me. He's pulling away and I don't understand why. I know he's got stuff going on at home, but..." His voice cracked. "What if he doesn't want to be with me anymore?"

"Oh sweetheart." Diane pulled him into a hug. "I don't think that's it at all. From everything you've told us, Jason cares about you deeply. But he's dealing with a lot—more than we probably know. Sometimes when people are hurting, they push away the people they love most."

"But why?"

"Because they're scared. Because they don't know how to ask for help. Because they think they're protecting you by keeping distance." She pulled back to look at him. "Have you tried reaching out today?"

"I can't. Not after last night. I was such a mess on the phone, I—"

"You were honest about how you felt. That's not being a mess, that's being brave." Diane squeezed his hand. "But maybe what you both need right now is some space to breathe. Some time to think."

Christopher nodded, not trusting his voice.

"Why don't you get out of the house for a bit? Go for a bike ride, clear your head. Sitting up here dwelling on it isn't helping."

"Yeah. Okay." Christopher sat up, wiping his eyes. "Maybe I will."

Diane kissed his forehead and left him alone.

Christopher changed into warmer clothes and grabbed his jacket. Downstairs, his dad was reading the paper in the dining room.

"Christopher? Where are you heading?"

"Going for a bike ride."

Mark set down his paper, studying his son. "You and Jason were supposed to hang out today, weren't you?"

"Yeah. But..." Christopher shrugged, trying to keep his voice steady. "I guess I'll just go on my own. Need to quit thinking about it so much."

Mark's expression softened. "I'm sorry, son. I know this is hard."

"It's okay. I just... I need to move. You know?"

"I understand." Mark stood and gave Christopher's shoulder a squeeze. "Don't stay out too long. Gets dark early these days."

"I won't."

Christopher grabbed his bike from the garage and started pedaling, not really sure where he was going. Just away. Just somewhere he could think.

He headed west, away from the developments, away from the few scattered houses that dotted the road past where they lived. Out into farmland where the corn stood dead and brown in the fields.

The cold air stung his face, but he welcomed it. Physical discomfort was easier than the ache in his chest.

He'd been riding for maybe twenty minutes when the farmhouses appeared around a curve—the big one perched on the hill overlooking everything, the smaller one down the road with that old barn behind it.

Their place. His and Jason's. Where they'd first seen the ghosts, where they'd held hands and talked about the future like it was something they'd have together.

Christopher let his bike fall in the grass behind the smaller farmhouse and pushed through the woods. His feet found the familiar path, through bare branches and dead undergrowth, until he emerged at the railroad tracks.

The ballast crunched under his shoes—those loose stones between the wooden ties. He sat down right there on the cold ground and pulled his knees to his chest.

Daniel had sat here. Or somewhere near here. Had watched William die. Had spent forty years alone because the person he loved had chosen to leave him.

Christopher wrapped his arms around his knees and let himself cry again. He was so tired of crying. So tired of feeling like this. So tired of not understanding.

The afternoon sun was still high, but he could see it starting its slow descent. He should probably go home soon. His parents would worry if he was gone too long.

But he couldn't bring himself to move yet.

If he sat here long enough, maybe he'd figure out how to stop loving someone who didn't seem to want to be loved anymore.

Or maybe the ghosts would come and Daniel could tell him how he survived it.

————

Jason woke with the dream still clinging to him like a second skin.

The train. The blood. Christopher's face covered in what Jason had become. That moment of realization—*I'm abandoning him*—cutting through everything he'd tried to convince himself was protection.

He lay in bed staring at the ceiling, his chest tight. Two weeks. Less than two weeks now. And he hadn't told Christopher. Hadn't called him back after last night's disaster. Hadn't done anything except make everything worse.

William had thought he was protecting Daniel. Look how that turned out.

His dad had probably thought he was doing them a favor too. Leaving them to go start his new life without the burden of a wife and kid. Probably told himself it was for the best.

Jason tried to tell himself this was different. He wasn't abandoning Christopher. He was just... pulling back. Like he was a flame that could burn Christopher if he got too close. It was supposed to help. Protect him.

Abandoning someone hurt them. He wasn't doing that.

Right?

But he knew that was bullshit. He was hurting Christopher just as much as if he'd slapped him across the face.

Jason sat up, his decision made before his conscious mind caught up.

He had to see Christopher. Now. Today. Didn't know what he'd say, didn't have a plan, didn't have answers. But he couldn't leave things the way they were.

He pulled on jeans and a hoodie, grabbed his jacket. He could hear his mom wasn't home—the house had that particular quiet that meant he was alone. She was probably at the grocery store. She always went Sunday mornings when the crowds were at church, making it easier to shop in peace.

He scribbled a quick note on the pad by the phone: *Went for a ride. Back later.*

Outside, the morning was cold and clear. His breath fogged in the air as he pulled his bike from the side of the house and started pedaling toward Christopher's.

He headed down Western, his mind racing. What would he say? How would he even start? *Sorry I've been an asshole? Sorry I made you cry? Sorry I'm leaving you in two weeks and didn't know how to tell you?*

He turned onto 8th Street and started the climb—that bastard of a curvy hillside that made his thighs burn and his lungs ache. He stood on the pedals, powering through it, his whole body focused on just getting up that goddamn hill.

His mind wasn't on the climb though. It was on Christopher. On the sound of him crying on the phone last night. On how Jason had fucked everything up so completely there might not be any way to fix it.

He was so lost in his thoughts, body on autopilot, that he didn't even notice the car coming down the hill toward him.

———

Jim spotted him first.

"David, slow down."

"What?" David eased off the gas, navigating the curve of 8th Street.

"That kid on the bike." Jim pointed. "Coming up the hill. That's Jason."

David looked and his hands tightened on the steering wheel. Jason was powering up the steep incline, head down, completely oblivious to everything around him. There was something wrong about his posture, his movement. Like he was going through the motions without really being present.

"He looks like hell," Jim said quietly. "Pull over."

David found a spot to turn around and headed back up, pulling alongside Jason near the Dale Cemetery entrance.

"Jason?" David called out his window.

Jason's head snapped up, startled. His first instinct was defensive —shoulders tensing, face closing off, ready for harassment. Then recognition hit.

Jason looked at the driver—Mr. Barnes. Then his eyes shifted to the passenger seat and surprise flickered across his face. "Jim?"

David pulled into the cemetery entrance and both men got out. Jason stopped his bike, one foot on the ground, breathing hard from the climb.

"Hey," Jim said, his voice warm. "Fancy meeting you here."

"Yeah." Jason's defenses were still up, but starting to lower. These weren't threats. These were... friends. "I was just—"

"Heading somewhere specific?" David asked gently.

"Christopher's house. I need to..." Jason trailed off, not sure how to finish.

Jim and David exchanged a glance. They'd talked about Jason last night after Mark's phone call, worried about both boys, wondering if they should reach out. And now here he was, looking exhausted and lost and like he was barely holding himself together.

"You okay?" Jim asked.

"Yeah. Fine." The automatic response came out, but his voice cracked on the second word.

"Jason." David's voice was soft. "You don't look fine. And after what Mark told us about what's been happening at school—"

"He told you?" Jason's face flushed.

"He's worried about both of you," Jim said. "We all are."

Jason looked away, jaw tight.

Jim stepped closer, his voice dropping. "Listen. It's cold out here, you look like you haven't slept all week, and you're clearly dealing with something heavy. David and I were just heading out for the day, but honestly? That can wait. Why don't you come back to our place for a bit? Just to warm up. Talk if you want to. Or just sit. Whatever you need."

"I need to see Christopher," Jason said, but his voice was wavering now.

"We can help you with that," David said. "But first, let's just... take a breath. Get warm. Figure out what you want to say to him. Sound good?"

Jason looked between them. Last week felt like a lifetime ago—that dinner where he'd broken down, where they'd welcomed him like family, where Jim had shown him what it looked like when two men loved each other openly.

"Okay," he whispered.

———

Ten minutes later, Jason sat on Jim and David's couch, hands wrapped around a mug of hot cocoa he wasn't drinking.

He'd been here before—that quick stop last week when he and Christopher had met Jim for the first time, standing awkwardly in the kitchen before they all headed to the Averys for dinner. But this was different. Now he was actually sitting in their living room, really seeing the place. It was even nicer than he'd glimpsed from the kitchen —tastefully decorated, comfortable furniture, framed photos on the walls—but it didn't feel like some art gallery or showroom. It felt lived-in. Welcoming. Like a real home.

Jim and David sat nearby, patient, waiting.

"I don't know where to start," Jason said finally.

"Start anywhere," Jim said gently. "We've got time."

And then it just... came out. Fast and tumbling and barely coherent, like a valve had been opened and everything he'd been holding back came flooding through.

"Christopher thinks I don't love him anymore and I do, I fucking love him so much it's killing me, but everything's falling apart and it's my fault. Rick—my mom's boyfriend—he found out I'm gay and he went to Burkhart's and shot his mouth off and now the whole goddamn school knows and people are calling us fags in the hallway and Christopher's getting shit and it's because of me, because I couldn't just keep my fucking mouth shut—"

"Jason—" David started.

But Jason couldn't stop. The words kept coming, faster, more desperate. "And my mom found my notebook where I write stuff and she knows now and she won't fucking talk to me about it, she just knows and won't say anything and I don't know if she hates me or if she's ashamed or what the fuck is going on, and she got this promotion which is great but we have to move, we're moving to fucking Indianapolis in two weeks and I haven't told Christopher because how do I tell him that? How do I say I'm leaving when he already thinks I'm pulling away and I am, I'm doing exactly what William did—"

"Who's William?" Jim asked gently.

Jason's breath hitched. He'd mentioned the name without thinking. "The... there's these boys. From like a hundred years ago. I've been dreaming about them for weeks and Christopher and I, we've been researching them at the library and the historical society and we found out that William, he... he killed himself on the railroad tracks because he thought it would protect Daniel, his... his boyfriend or whatever they called it back then. William's family found out he was queer and they were going to send him away or beat it out of him or something, and he thought if he just died, Daniel would be safe from being associated with him."

Jason was talking so fast he was almost hyperventilating. "And in my dream last night I was William and Christopher was Daniel and I was standing on those tracks with my foot caught and the train was coming and I thought I was protecting him but right before it hit I realized I wasn't protecting shit, I was just abandoning him, doing to him what my—"

He stopped abruptly, the words catching in his throat.

Jim remembered last week at dinner—the way Jason had broken

down when they were saying goodbye, begging them not to leave. He'd suspected then there was something deeper, some wound that hadn't healed. Now he understood.

"What your father did," Jim said quietly.

Jason looked up, tears streaming down his face. "I was eight."

————

Jason sat at the kitchen table doing his multiplication tables—the homework assignment Mr. Peterson had given the class. Six times seven equals... he paused, counting on his fingers. Forty-two. He wrote it down carefully.

In the other room, the TV was on—Channel 4 playing afternoon cartoons. Scooby-Doo. He could hear Shaggy's voice saying "Zoinks!" but he couldn't watch until his homework was done.

His mom was still at work. She always worked late on Thursdays at the drive-thru window.

His dad was moving around the house. Jason could hear him rummaging through drawers in the bedroom, opening and closing them. Then footsteps going down to the basement. Coming back up. More opening and closing.

Jason looked up from his homework and saw his dad walk past carrying an old duffel bag, stuffing clothes into it. A pair of jeans. Some shirts. His dad opened another drawer, pulled out socks and underwear, shoved them in.

Jason watched, curious. His dad disappeared into the bathroom. Came out a minute later with his razor and toothbrush—Jason could see them between working on his next problem.

"Are you going on a trip, Daddy?"

His father didn't respond. Just kept packing. Zipped the bag. Went back to the bedroom for more.

Jason found it odd. His dad had always been a stern man—didn't talk much, didn't smile much. Jason had secretly wished he'd be like some of the other daddies he saw when they picked up their kids at school: picking them up and swinging them around and giving them big kisses, asking about their days. His daddy never did that. Never picked him up from school. Never asked about his day.

Jason's thought was interrupted by his father carrying his bags through the house toward the front door and outside to the car. Jason watched curiously, then got up from the table and walked to the open doorway.

Through the screen door he could see his daddy throwing his stuff into the trunk. Then slamming it down hard.

The loud SLAM made Jason jump.

His father came back toward the porch. Jason heard his footsteps on the wooden steps. The screen door opened.

Jason stepped back and looked up at his daddy.

He looked... weird. Different. Like he didn't recognize Jason. Like Jason was a stranger standing in his house.

"Daddy?"

His father reached into his jacket pocket and pulled out a wrinkled envelope.

"Give this to your mother."

Jason took it in his small hands. The paper felt thin, but important.

His father turned and opened the screen door to leave.

"Daddy? Where you going?"

His father paused, his back still to his son. "Out."

Then he let the screen door slam on its hinges.

Jason jumped again at the sound.

He walked to the screen and pressed his hand against the mesh, watching his father get into the car. The engine started. Jason raised his hand in a small wave.

But his daddy acted like he didn't see. Just backed the car down the driveway fast and pulled away.

Jason watched it turn the corner at the end of the street.

That was the last time he ever saw him.

Sarah got home around six. Jason was sitting in front of the TV watching a rerun of The Brady Bunch.

"Hi Jace! Miss your momma?"

She came over and picked him up, making a groaning sound. "Oh, you're getting so big! I won't be able to pick you up much longer. You're gonna grow taller than me!" She laughed as she set him down.

She headed toward the bedroom, still talking. "It was a long day at work today, but I'm home now. I was thinking we might go out for dinner tonight because—"

She got quiet.

Jason stood by the sofa looking down the hallway toward his parents' bedroom. A commercial was blaring on the TV.

Then his mother came quickly down the hall, her face changed. Worried.

"Jace—what happened to your Daddy? Where is he?"

Jason shrugged. Then he remembered the envelope. He ran to the kitchen table where his completed homework sat and picked it up.

"Daddy told me to give this to you."

His mom took it, turning it over in her hands. She opened it slowly.

A single hundred-dollar bill fell onto the table.

She pulled out a small piece of paper—handwritten, just a few lines. Jason watched her face as she read it. Watched the color drain from her cheeks. Watched her read it again, like maybe she'd gotten it wrong.

Then she sat down at the table and covered her face with her hands.

"What's wrong, Mommy?" Jason ran to her side.

But she couldn't speak. How do you tell your eight-year-old son that his Daddy left them? Said he couldn't take it anymore. That it was better for everyone. And signed it "Good luck" like they were a lottery ticket.

She pulled Jason close and held him, her body shaking even though she was trying to hide it.

That evening she opened a can of SpaghettiOs for Jason's dinner instead of going out like she'd planned. She skipped bath time and sent him straight to bed.

Jason lay in the dark listening. After a while, he heard it—his momma crying behind her bedroom door. Quiet at first, then harder.

He snuck out into the dark dining room. The letter was still sitting on the table where his mom had left it.

He picked it up carefully and took it into the bathroom, closing the door behind him. Turned on the light.

He was still learning his reading, but it was a simple enough note:

Sarah—

Here's $100. It's all I had in my wallet. I can't do this anymore. You and Jason are better off this way.

Good luck.

Jason stared at the words. He could read most of them. "Can't do this anymore."

Do what? Was his daddy doing something he wasn't supposed to? Was he in trouble?

Or... was it Jason? Was Jason the thing he couldn't do anymore?

Jason turned off the light and put the letter back exactly where he'd found it. He ran quietly back to his dark bedroom and hid under the covers.

What couldn't his daddy do? Would he come back? Was it something Jason did? Did he do something wrong?

The more he thought about it, the worse he felt.

It was his fault. It had to be. Daddies didn't just leave unless there was a reason.

And the reason was him.

The weeks that followed blurred together. His mom crying when she thought Jason was asleep—except now he knew she was crying, heard it through the thin walls. Bills piling up on the kitchen counter —red envelopes that his mom would stare at with her hand over her mouth. His mom taking extra shifts at the bank, leaving before Jason woke up, coming home after he'd made himself dinner.

Two months later, they had to move out of their house—the one with Jason's room and the tire swing in the backyard and the neighbor's dog he'd play with. They moved to an apartment. Smaller.

Darker. In a worse part of town where police sirens woke him up at night.

At school, kids found out. Found out Jason's dad had left, found out they didn't have money anymore, found out Jason was on free lunch now.

"Your dad didn't want you," David Keller said one day on the playground, loud enough for everyone to hear. "That's why he left. Because you're a loser."

Jason punched him. Hard. Kept punching him until a teacher pulled him off.

He got suspended for three days. His mom had to leave work early to pick him up from the principal's office.

She didn't yell at him on the drive home. She just looked exhausted. Defeated. So tired.

"I'm sorry," Jason said, his knuckles still throbbing.

"It's not your fault, honey."

But it felt like his fault. If he'd been better, smarter, less annoying —if he'd been worth staying for—maybe his dad wouldn't have left. Maybe his mom wouldn't have to work so much. Maybe they wouldn't be poor and struggling and living in a shitty apartment where the heat barely worked.

He learned to be tougher after that. Learned to look mean so kids would leave him alone. Learned to swear and act like he didn't give a shit about anything because if you don't care, people can't hurt you.

He learned to build walls so high nobody could see over them.

And at night, alone in his small bedroom in that shitty apartment, he'd cry into his pillow where nobody could hear him. Tell himself that at least they weren't homeless. At least he wasn't in foster care. Other people had it worse.

He just had to toughen up. Deal with it. Stop being weak.

Stop hoping his dad would come back.

Stop hoping anyone would ever love him.

———

Jason was sobbing now, the words still pouring out between gasps. "And I told myself I dealt with it, I told myself I was over it, it was years ago, whatever, my dad's a piece of shit and I don't need him. But I haven't dealt with shit, I just pushed it down and now I'm doing the same fucking thing to Christopher that my dad did to us, I'm abandoning him and telling myself it's to protect him but really I'm just—"

David was crying too, not bothering to hide it. His hands were clenched tight in his lap.

Jim's voice was steady but his eyes were bright. "Jason, you're not abandoning Christopher. Not yet. You're here, trying to figure out how to make this right. That's the opposite of what your father did."

"But I've been such an asshole to him all week—"

"Because you're scared," Jim said. "Because you're carrying too much and you don't know how to share it. But that's different from choosing to walk away without explanation."

Jason wiped his face with his sleeve. "But I am walking away. My mom's taking that job in Indy and I'm going with her and Christopher doesn't even know yet and—"

"Are you going to tell him?" Jim asked carefully.

Jason nodded miserably.

"Then that's where you start," David said, his voice rough with emotion. "You tell him the truth. All of it. Let him decide how he feels instead of deciding for him."

"But then he'll hate me—"

"He won't hate you," Jim said firmly. "He might be hurt. Might be angry. But Jason, he loves you. And love means working through the hard stuff together, not protecting each other from the truth."

Jason stared at his untouched cocoa. "William thought he was protecting Daniel by leaving. And I've been thinking the same thing—that if I pull away, if I make Christopher hate me a little, it'll hurt less when I leave. That maybe people will stop targeting him if they don't think we're together anymore."

David leaned forward. "Jason, look at me."

Jason looked up.

"I've spent my entire adult life hiding," David said, and there was anger in his voice—but directed at himself. "Pretending, being afraid, keeping Jim a secret, acting like half of who I am doesn't exist. And I told myself I was being smart, being safe, being practical." His voice broke. "But all I've really been doing is teaching kids like you to do the same thing. To hide. To be ashamed. To be afraid."

Jason saw Jim shift closer to David, offering support without touch.

"You and Christopher," David continued, "you took a chance. You were brave enough to be honest about how you felt. To be together even knowing it was risky. And I've been over here thinking I was some kind of role model when really I've just been showing you how to live scared." He wiped his eyes. "I'm so sorry, Jason. I should have done better."

"You didn't do anything wrong," Jason said.

"Neither did you," David said firmly. "People being cruel—that's on them. Not you. Not Christopher. Never on you."

Jason felt something shift in his chest, just slightly. The weight didn't disappear, but it felt... different. Less crushing.

"That dream," Jason said quietly. "The one I told you about. I can't stop thinking about it. William thought he was helping. But he wasn't. He was just... leaving. Like my dad."

"But you woke up," Jim said gently. "You had the dream and you woke up and the first thing you did was get on your bike to go find Christopher. That's not abandonment. That's the opposite."

Jason looked up. "But what do I say to him?"

"The truth," David said. "That you're scared. That you love him. That you don't have all the answers but you want to figure it out together."

Jim pieced together everything Jason had spilled out. "You were heading to Christopher's house when we saw you on 8th Street, weren't you?"

"Yeah." Jason's voice was small.

"Why don't you give him a call?" Jim suggested. "Let him know you're coming. That you want to talk."

Jason nodded and stood, moving to the kitchen phone. His hands shook as he dialed. He knew Christopher's number by heart—had since the first time Christopher had written it down for him weeks ago.

The phone rang. Once. Twice. Three times.

"Avery residence." Mark's voice.

"Mr. Avery? It's Jason."

There was a pause—surprise, then something that sounded like relief. "Jason. I'm glad you called. Christopher's been... we've all been worried."

"Is he there? I really need to talk to him."

"He went out for a bike ride this morning. Left a few hours ago, actually." Mark's voice shifted toward concern. "He seemed pretty down when he left."

Jason's stomach dropped. "Do you know... did he say anything about where he might go?"

"No. Just that he needed to get out, clear his head." Mark hesitated. "Jason, should I be worried? Is something—"

"No," Jason said quickly. "I mean... I've just been a real asshole this week. I'm sorry, Mr. Avery, I didn't mean to—"

"I know what you meant," Mark said, and his voice was gentler. "Jason, listen. I hate seeing Christopher the way he's been. And I know you're dealing with something too. If there's anything Diane and I can do to help—"

"I'm actually at Mr. Barnes and Jim's house right now," Jason said. "They've been... they're helping me sort some stuff out."

"You are?" Mark sounded genuinely pleased. "I'm glad. I'm really glad you have people looking out for you, Jason. You know... if it would help, I'm happy to listen too. Help you work through whatever's going on. Or I'm sure David and Jim are—"

"They are," Jason said. "They're being really great."

"Good. Because you should know—you have people who love and care about you. A lot of people."

The words hit Jason harder than he expected. His throat closed up. It was hard to hear sometimes when people said they loved you. Made him want to trust them but scared him at the same time.

"Thanks," he managed.

"Why don't you come over for dinner tonight?" Mark suggested. "You and Christopher could use some time together."

"Yeah. That would be good."

"Do you have any idea where he might have gone?"

Jason hesitated. "The farmhouses, maybe. The ones we've been researching."

"Out west? I can come get you, drive you out there—"

"Farmhouses?" Jim asked from across the room, catching the word.

Jason covered the receiver. "It's where Christopher and I have been going. For that research project. I think he might be there."

"We'll take you," Jim said immediately. "It'll be dark soon."

Jason uncovered the phone. "Mr. Avery? Jim and Mr. Barnes are here—they said they'll drive me out there."

"I heard." Mark's voice was hesitant. "Jason, he's been gone a while. I'm getting worried."

"He's probably just clearing his head. You know how he gets." Jason tried to sound reassuring. "I don't want to make a big thing out of it."

"I don't know..."

Jim held out his hand for the phone. Jason passed it to him.

"Mark? It's Jim. Listen, Jason seems pretty sure he knows where Christopher is. David and I will drive him out there right now. We'll find him and bring them both back to your place. You have my word."

A pause. Then Mark's voice, steadier now: "Alright. But if you don't find him within the hour, call me. I'll come out myself."

"Understood. We'll have them home safe."

Jim hung up and grabbed his keys. "Let's go. We'll put your bike in the trunk."

They got Jason's bike secured—it stuck out but they tied the trunk down—and headed west. Jason sat in the back, his knee bouncing anxiously.

"These farmhouses you mentioned," Jim said, glancing at Jason in the rearview mirror. "Tell us about them."

"One's on top of a hill overlooking everything," Jason said. "White paint but it's all peeling now. Has this tower thing—a widow's peak—

on top. The other one's smaller, down the road with an old barn behind it that's half collapsed."

"And this William and Daniel," David said. "You said you and Christopher researched them?"

"Yeah. At the library and the historical society. William lived in the big house on the hill—his family had money. Daniel lived in the smaller one across the road. His family worked the farm. They were... they were together. In love. Back in like 1889, 1890."

"And William's family found out?" Jim asked gently.

"Jesus. Can you imagine *back then*?" David spurted out.

"Yeah. We found newspaper articles, death records, all this stuff. William died on the railroad tracks—the article said it was an accident but we..."

Jason paused. He couldn't tell them he saw it one night played out by ghosts. "Uh, we... found Daniel's journal entry at the historical society." Jason's voice dropped. That seemed realistic. "I don't think it was an accident. William put his foot between the rails on purpose. He thought if he was gone, Daniel would be safe. No one could connect them anymore. No one could hurt Daniel for loving him."

"Jesus," David breathed out again.

"Daniel never got over it," Jason continued. "We don't think he ever loved anyone else. Died alone in 1931." Jason wiped his eyes. "And in my dreams, I keep seeing William make that choice. And last night I was him and I finally understood—he thought he was being noble but he was just... he was just destroying Daniel."

They drove in silence for a moment, the weight of the story settling over them.

Jim was quiet for a moment, choosing his words. "These are just dreams, right? I mean, you haven't actually seen—"

"There." Jason pointed. "That's them."

They rounded the curve and there they were—exactly as Jason had described. The white farmhouse perched on its hill, the widow's peak jutting up against the darkening sky. The smaller farmhouse across the road, vines growing up the walls. The leaning barn behind it.

David pulled over onto the shoulder. "Holy shit. They're real."

"I told you they were real," Jason said, already unbuckling his seatbelt.

He scanned the area. No sign of Christopher at first. Then he spotted it—Christopher's bike lying in the grass near the old barn.

"He's here," Jason said, pointing.

They got out. Jason led the way around the smaller farmhouse, through the woods. Jim and David followed, picking their way through dead undergrowth and bare branches.

They emerged at the railroad tracks.

And there, maybe fifty yards down the line, sitting on the ground with his back against the rail—

"Christopher!" Jason shouted.

Christopher's head snapped up, disbelief crossing his face. Then he was scrambling to his feet.

Jason ran.

He ran like his life depended on it, like everything that mattered was in those fifty yards. He knew the path through the old cornfield, the fastest route. Behind him he could hear Jim and David trying to keep up but he didn't wait.

He crashed into Christopher with enough force to nearly knock them both over, arms wrapping tight around him.

"I'm sorry," Jason gasped between sobs. "I'm so sorry, I've been such an asshole, I'm so sorry—"

"I thought you didn't want me anymore," Christopher choked out, clinging to him. "I thought—"

"No. God, no. I love you. I fucking love you so much. I'm sorry. I'm sorry."

They held each other as the sun sank lower, painting the sky in shades of purple and green—that strange twilight color when everything feels suspended between worlds.

From the edge of the woods where they'd just emerged, breathing hard from trying to keep up, David and Jim stopped. They stood there watching the two boys hold each other, listening to their voices carry on the wind—words tumbling out between sobs, apologies and reassurances and broken explanations.

They couldn't make out everything being said—they were still far enough away, and the wind was picking up as the sun set. But they could see enough. Could see two boys who loved each other finding their way back.

Jim put his hands in his pockets, watching silently.

David stood beside him, and as the twilight deepened, something caught his eye. Movement down the tracks beyond where Jason and Christopher stood.

He blinked, sure he'd imagined it. But no—there was something there. Two figures, translucent in the fading light. Not quite solid. Not quite there.

"Jim," David whispered. "Do you see—"

"Yeah," Jim breathed, his eyes fixed on the same spot. "I see them."

Chapter 19

Courage

Jason and Christopher sat on the cold ground by the railroad tracks, arms wrapped around each other, rocking slightly like they were trying to create warmth where none existed.

"I'm sorry," Jason kept saying between ragged breaths. "I'm so sorry. I thought I was helping, I thought if I just stayed away it would be easier for you, I thought—"

"Stop." Christopher's voice was thick with tears. "Just stop. You're here now. That's all I care about."

"But I hurt you. I made you think I didn't—"

"I know you love me." Christopher pulled back just enough to look at Jason's face in the fading light. "I was scared you didn't, but I know you do. I can see it."

Jason's face crumpled and he buried it against Christopher's shoulder again. "I fucked everything up."

"No you didn't. You didn't fuck anything up!"

Neither of them believed it, but saying it out loud felt important somehow. Like if they said it enough times it might become true.

They didn't notice the two figures standing a couple of yards down the track, translucent in the gathering dusk. Didn't see Daniel tug at

William's sleeve and point toward the woods where Jim and David stood frozen.

———

David couldn't move. Couldn't breathe. Couldn't look away.

The two figures—boys, ghosts, whatever they were—stood there on the tracks clear as day even as the sun dropped below the horizon. The taller one with sandy hair. The shorter one holding that unlit lantern.

And they were looking right at them.

"David," Jim whispered, his voice barely audible. "Tell me you're seeing this too."

"I see them."

Daniel raised his hand slowly. Not quite a wave. More like an acknowledgment. *We see you. You see us. We're all here.*

Then, as the last sliver of sun disappeared and cold night air rushed in to fill the space where warmth had been, they faded. Not all at once, but gradually—like watching smoke dissipate until there was nothing left but empty track and two living boys holding each other in the dark.

Jim finally broke his paralysis, his attention shifting to Jason and Christopher. They were huddled together on the ground, rocking, Christopher's hand stroking Jason's hair while Jason's shoulders shook with quiet sobs.

"Come on," Jim said, his voice steadier than he felt. He started walking through the dead cornfield toward them.

David shook his head, trying to dispel the fear and wonder and impossibility of what he'd just witnessed. Then he followed Jim.

———

They led the boys back toward the car slowly. Both were so wrung out, so emotionally exhausted from weeks of pressure and fear and navigating impossible situations. Jason tried to start explaining, words tumbling out between hitching breaths, but Jim gently interrupted.

"Hey. Not right now. Let yourself just... be. Be gentle with yourself." Jim's voice was calm, grounding. "We're going to get you both home. Plenty of time to talk later. For now, let's just go."

David found himself with his arm around Jason's shoulders, guiding him through the woods, past the leaning barn, down toward where they'd parked. Jason leaned into him slightly, like he needed the physical support to keep moving.

Christopher led Jim to where his bike lay in the grass behind the barn.

"Shit," Jim muttered, looking at it. "Jason's bike is still tied in the trunk."

"It's okay—" Christopher started.

"No, you'll need it. Tell you what—I'll stash it behind the barn where nobody'll notice, come back for it later. Okay?"

Christopher nodded. Jim maneuvered the bike into the shadows behind the collapsed structure, then placed his hand on Christopher's shoulder and walked him down the road toward the car where David and Jason were waiting.

———

The drive back was quiet. Jim turned off the radio—even the low hum felt like too much. The only sound was the fan heater blowing warm air that slowly thawed their frozen hands and faces.

From the backseat, Jason started to speak. "Christopher," he said between silent sobs, "there's something you need to know."

"Jason." David's voice was gentle but firm. "Maybe we should get back to our place first. Get properly warm. Then you two can talk."

Christopher looked at Jason in the dim light from passing street lamps. There was so much Jason was holding inside. So much Christopher didn't know. He wanted to know all of it. Wanted to help. Wanted to stop feeling like he was on the outside looking in.

As soon as they pulled into the driveway, Jim headed for the kitchen phone while David ushered the boys into the living room.

"Make yourselves comfortable on the sofa. I'll get the kettle on."

Jason and Christopher sank onto the couch, still sitting close, Christopher's hand finding Jason's and holding tight.

Jim came back from the kitchen. "I'm going to run back and get Christopher's bike. Mark and Diane know you're both safe."

"Wait." Jason's voice was small. "Can you... can you stay? Please?"

Jim paused, studying Jason's face. It wasn't the same desperate panic from that dinner last week, but there was something there—a need for stability, for presence, for someone to help anchor him while everything felt like it was spinning out of control.

"Yeah," Jim said softly. "I can stay. The bike can wait."

David brought mugs of hot cocoa and set them on the coffee table. He looked at Jim with a question in his eyes: *Should we give them space?*

But Christopher spoke up before they could leave. "Could you... could you both stay? Please?"

David looked at Jim, concerned. Jim's expression said: *Just be there. Listen.*

They sat in chairs across the room—close enough to be present, far enough to give the boys space.

For a long time, nobody spoke. The house was quiet except for the ticking of the clock on the mantel and the occasional sound of someone shifting position.

Finally, Jason broke the silence. He turned to Christopher, his voice flat and defeated.

"Mom got her promotion."

Christopher blinked. "That's... that's good, right?"

"Yeah. I guess. But..." Jason's throat worked. "It's in Indy."

Christopher's face went through a progression of emotions—confusion, then understanding, then fear, then grief. Jason watched it happen, watched Christopher's brain register what that meant, and felt his own carefully constructed walls crumble.

"You... you have to move?" Christopher's voice was barely a whisper.

Jason could only nod.

"When? After graduation? Next year?"

"Thanksgiving."

The word landed like a bomb.

"That's..." Christopher couldn't finish.

"Not even two weeks," Jason said.

They both looked like they'd been hit by a train. Like William's train had finally caught up to them after all.

David surprised himself by standing and moving to the sofa. He sat down next to Jason, tentative at first, then slowly placed his hand on Jason's back and rubbed gentle circles.

Jason was crying again—not the violent sobs from earlier, just quiet tears that wouldn't stop. He'd cried too hard at the tracks. Now he was just... empty. Broken.

Christopher looked at his boyfriend through his own tears. Jason wasn't breaking down. He was already broken.

"We can still be boyfriends, right?" Christopher's voice was desperate, grasping for something to hold onto. "I mean, I can come visit and maybe you can come back here sometimes, right?"

Jason just stared at the lamp on the side table, not really seeing it, and nodded.

"And we can make it work. People do long distance all the time. We can write letters and call and—"

They both knew it was impossible. Neither had a car. They couldn't ride bikes nearly fifty miles each way. They hadn't even finished Driver's Ed yet.

There was nothing more to say. Nothing to do. Just sit there holding hands while their future collapsed around them.

———

After some time—maybe twenty minutes, maybe an hour—Jim quietly excused himself.

"I'm going to grab Christopher's bike and drop both at the Averys'. Won't be long."

The boys barely acknowledged him, still sitting close together in the dim living room, holding on like they might drift apart if they let go.

David tried to be helpful—brought them damp washcloths to freshen their faces, offered snacks neither wanted. Finally he just let them be, retreating to the kitchen to give them privacy.

He sat at the kitchen table, his mind spinning through everything that had happened. The harassment at school. Jason's father leaving. The move to Indianapolis. Two boys in love facing an impossible situation.

And those figures on the tracks.

David's rational mind tried to explain it away. He'd been talking with Jason about the research, about William and Daniel. Everything had been so emotional, happening so fast. It was cold. Getting dark. He'd been out of breath chasing Jason through the woods. He must have conjured it up. Some trick of fading light and exhausted brain.

Right?

The kitchen door opened and David jumped.

Jim came in, pulling off his cap. David could feel the cold radiating off him, his coat still buttoned.

"Get the bike okay?" David asked.

Jim sat down heavily at the table. "Yeah. I got it."

Something in his voice made David's stomach clench. "What happened?"

"I'm probably just tired. This whole day has been..." Jim shook his head. "Too much."

"Jim. What happened?"

"I saw a light."

David's eyes widened.

"I propped the bike behind that barn like I said. And when I went back to get it, I didn't have a flashlight—forgot to grab one. But the moon's out, so I could see well enough. I was worried about tripping, you know? So I was watching the ground. But then..." He paused. "Then I saw light coming from inside the barn."

"Jim—"

"I know how it sounds. I know I'm tired and this day has been insane and I'm probably seeing things—"

"What did you see?" David leaned forward.

Jim met his eyes. "Them. The two we saw earlier. What did Jason say those boys names were? The one's they'd been researching. Daniel and William? It had to be them."

The names felt strange in the kitchen, in their normal house, under normal lights. Like speaking a spell that might make something appear.

"What were they doing?"

"That's the thing." Jim's voice dropped. "They looked like they were arguing. I couldn't hear anything, but their body language—the taller one was agitated, the shorter one was trying to calm him down. And then..."

"What?"

"The taller one—William?—he stormed out." Jim's eyes were wide, remembering. "Carrying the lantern. And he walked right through me."

"Through you?"

"Through me. I felt..." Jim struggled for words. "Cold. Like every bit of warmth got sucked out for a second. And then he was past me, heading toward the tracks."

David's mouth had gone dry.

"Daniel stayed in the barn for a moment. I just stood there—I couldn't move, couldn't think. Then Daniel ran after William, and I jumped out of the way but..." Jim shook his head. "He stopped. Right next to me. Looked at me."

"Looked at you."

"Like he could see me. Like he was asking for something." Jim's hands were shaking. "Help, maybe. I don't know. But he wanted something from me."

"What did you do?"

"Nothing. I froze. And then he just... disappeared. Gone. Like he'd never been there."

They sat in silence for a long moment.

"I haven't been drinking," Jim said. "I know what it sounds like, but I swear—"

"I believe you." David took Jim's cold hands in his. They were trembling. "We both saw them. At the tracks. We both saw them."

"What the hell is happening, David?"

"I don't know."

They sat there holding hands across the kitchen table, trying to

324

process the impossible, until David realized how much time had passed.

"We should probably get the boys over to Mark and Diane's."

Jim nodded. "Yeah. They need to eat. Need to..." He trailed off. What did they need? Everything they needed was being ripped away in less than two weeks.

David stood, taking charge in a way that surprised him. "I'll get their coats. You warm up the car."

———

Mark opened the door to find Christopher looking utterly defeated, Jason behind him like a soldier who knows he's lost the war and can't figure out how to surrender with dignity. Jim followed, then David who seemed to have found some inner reserve of strength.

"Hi David." Mark reached out and surprised David with a hug. It felt good—solid and real and grounding.

Diane appeared and immediately pulled both boys into a motherly embrace. "Why don't you both head upstairs and wash up a bit? It'll help you feel better. Okay?"

They nodded and disappeared up the stairs without a word.

Diane hugged Jim, who seemed to slowly return to himself, then David, who had been holding everyone together all evening but now sagged slightly in her arms.

"Come sit," Diane said. "What happened?"

Around the kitchen table, David and Jim explained what they knew. Sarah's promotion. The move to Indianapolis. The impossibly short timeline. Christopher's devastated reaction.

"He tried to be positive about it," David said quietly. "Back at our house. Suggesting they could stay together, work out visits. But everyone knows..."

"It's impossible," Mark finished, his jaw tight with anger. "And that Rick bastard—I've never even met the guy but I'd like to punch him in the face for starting all this."

"A lot of people are like Rick," David said heavily. "More than we want to admit."

"Jason must be going through hell," Diane said. "All this... and that business with his father..."

David had quietly shared what Jason had told them about his dad leaving when he was eight. The abandoned note. The hundred dollars. The years of poverty and bullying that followed.

Mark's hands clenched into fists on the table. "Jesus Christ. Everyone that kid has ever loved has shit on him. No wonder he was pulling away from Christopher—he didn't want to drag him down too."

"Drag him down," Jim repeated thoughtfully. "That's exactly what he said. Like he was falling into oblivion and didn't want Christopher to fall with him."

"I'm worried about him," Diane said. "After everything..." She didn't finish the thought. Didn't need to.

"If only they didn't have to move," Jim said.

"But there's still the harassment at school," Mark pointed out. "The bullying. The gossip around town. Even if they didn't move, they'd still be dealing with that shit."

"And their ignorant parents," Mark added, clearly frustrated. "People thrive on making others miserable."

The four of them sat there—a clover of anxiety, anger, sorrow, and growing determination.

David's face suddenly changed. His eyes widened slightly, then narrowed as he worked through something in his head.

"What's that look?" Jim asked, noticing immediately.

Diane leaned forward, studying David's face. "You're thinking something."

"It's crazy," David said. "Probably completely insane."

"What?" Diane pressed.

David turned to Jim. "Hear me out before you tell me it's wrong."

Jim looked like he might protest that he'd never do that, then realized he probably would and nodded instead.

"What if..." David took a breath. "What if Jason didn't have to move?"

"How would that work?" Diane asked carefully. "Sarah has this promotion. Why wouldn't she take it?"

"Oh, she should take it. From what Jason said, they need the money. It would help them a lot."

"Then I don't get it," Jim said. "How would Jason not move if Sarah takes the job in Indianapolis?"

David turned to Jim fully now. "Don't freak out."

"Oh god," Jim muttered.

"What if we let Jason stay with us? Let him finish the semester—it's only a month until Christmas break. Then they could work out what happens after."

"That would give Jason and Christopher more time," Diane finished, understanding dawning.

"And maybe give us time to..." Mark started.

"But even if Sarah agreed," Jim interrupted, "he'd still have to move eventually. And what about the bullying?"

"At school and in town," Mark added. "That's not going away."

Diane looked between them, then settled on David. A small smile crept across her face as she realized what he was really proposing.

"Gentlemen," she said, interrupting their back-and-forth. "I think David is saying he would..."

"Come out." David said it like he was sixteen himself, scared to speak the words aloud, but willing them anyway.

Jim whipped around to stare at him. Mark's eyes went wide.

"I'd come out," David said more firmly. "At school. In town. Stop hiding."

The room went silent, three sets of eyes locked on him.

Diane smiled. She understood.

"You're sacrificing yourself?" Mark asked.

"No," Jim said on David's behalf, his voice thick with emotion. "No one's being sacrificed. He's—"

"Going to be myself," David finished. "My true self."

Another silence.

"David," Mark said carefully. "No offense, and I respect the hell out of you for even thinking this, but... what good would that do for our boys?"

"I can help by being out in the open. Show people it's okay. Take the heat for them. Get people off their backs."

"By starting an uproar over having a gay teacher?" Mark's voice rose despite himself. "They'd crucify you!"

David visibly flinched. Mark immediately regretted his volume.

"I'm sorry, I didn't mean—"

"No, you're right," David said. "It would cause problems. Probably big ones. But Mark..." He leaned forward. "These are kids. They're sixteen years old. They shouldn't have to suffer because we're too afraid to rock the boat."

Diane put her hand on Mark's arm. "There's another benefit. David, you could talk to Sarah. She must be going through hell herself right now. Can you imagine? Her boyfriend leaves, her son is suddenly outed, she's dealing with gossip and judgment and trying to do this all alone." She looked at Mark. "We're lucky to have David and Jim. We have people we can talk to, people who understand. Sarah probably doesn't have anyone. She's trying to handle all of this by herself while dealing with some... assholes..." She said the word with emphasis. "Who want to make things harder."

She was building momentum now. "If David is willing to take some of that heat—and I don't wish it on him, but at least he and Jim and us, we're adults. We can stand up for what's right. We can't expect these kids to just suffer in silence while we hide!"

Mark stared at his wife, slightly stunned. Jim was reminded why being open mattered—people like Diane existed. Allies who understood.

David felt his insecurities crumbling. Whatever happened, Diane would be there with him.

"David," Diane said, "I think it's a wonderful idea for Jason to stay with you both to finish the semester. And I think you should absolutely be yourself. But I have a suggestion."

"What's that?"

"I wouldn't call an assembly or make some big announcement. I'd just... be normal about it." She smiled. "Have Jim come to your classroom one day. Drop off your lunch or something small. Something I'd do at Mark's office."

Jim's smile began to creep upward as understanding dawned.

Mark visualized the last time Diane had stopped by his office—

bringing a folder he'd forgotten at home. Quick kiss goodbye, then left. The guys at work had said hi to her, asked about their Memorial Day plans. Normal stuff.

Then he imagined Jim doing the same thing in David's classroom.

"I think Jim should come to my classroom, not the office," David said thoughtfully. "That way more students would see."

"You could stop by just before first period starts," Diane suggested. "By lunch, the whole school would know."

"Think that will cause any trouble?" Mark asked, knowing full well it would.

"Oh, definitely. But probably not from who we expect."

"You might want to let Principal Morrison know I was there," Jim said. "He and I met once a few years ago. Seemed decent enough."

"I will. But after you show up." David was working it through. "When I drop off my weekly student report, I'll mention I'd accidentally left it at home—busy with the holidays coming up—and you were kind enough to bring it by."

"That's perfect," Diane said. "Nonchalant. Nothing unusual. It's up to him to ask questions if he wants."

"The holiday weekend is coming up," Mark added, getting into the planning. "You could blame it on that. Too busy shopping..."

"You're willing to do that?" David asked.

"The real question is, are you willing to do it?"

David looked at Diane and Mark, then at Jim. "I'm scared. I'll admit it. But yes."

Everyone smiled. Jim leaned over and kissed David's cheek, making Mark blush slightly and Diane beam.

"There's an issue though," Jim said suddenly.

"What?" Diane asked.

"We need to ask Jason and Christopher about all this."

"And David," Diane added, "I think you should talk to Sarah directly. I know I'd want to speak face-to-face, not over the phone."

"Of course. But maybe I should call from school—"

"No." Diane was firm. "What you and Jim are proposing is personal. This is her son, not just a student. She doesn't know you. Why would she let Jason stay with you? You know?"

They nodded. The idea seemed good on paper, but...

"On second thought," Diane said, "I think I should call her first."

David looked at her questioningly.

"I'm a mother. I'm also the mother of her son's boyfriend. I should have called her before now, honestly. I think I can talk to her about what's happening, and just... listen. Then I'll introduce you. Does that make sense?"

"That's perfect," David said.

"I think I'll call now, actually."

"Now?" Mark looked at the clock. It was almost eight.

"There's no time to waste." Diane stood. "I'll just call to set up a time for us to meet. Maybe dinner. Just the two of us."

"Do you want to talk to the boys first?" Mark asked.

"I think..." A smile crept across Diane's face, like she knew something they didn't. "I think the three of you might handle that. I'm fairly certain they'll be excited about delaying the move."

She disappeared down the hallway toward their bedroom and closed the door.

Mark stood. David and Jim followed. Mark walked to the bottom of the stairs and called up in his best dad voice:

"Christopher? Could you and Jason come down, please?"

David looked at Jim.

"You scared?" Jim asked.

"Like you don't know."

Chapter 20

Family Does

The boys came down the stairs looking completely wiped out —eyes red-rimmed, movements slow, like they'd run a marathon and barely made it to the finish line.

Mark took one look at them and checked his watch. Almost eight. "You know what? On second-thought, I think we should table any more heavy conversation until everyone's had some rest. It's late."

"We can give you a ride home, Jason," David offered. "We can pop your bike back in the trunk."

"Can I come?" Christopher asked immediately, his voice small and hopeful.

Mark started to object—it was a school night, Christopher needed sleep—but Jim spoke up first, looking to Mark with eyes saying more than his lips. "If it's okay with you, Mark, we can drop him back here on our way home. Won't take long."

Mark looked at his son, then at Jason. Both boys looked run through the wringer—exhausted, emotionally spent, barely holding themselves upright. But he saw they needed this. Needed a few more minutes together.

"Alright," Mark said softly.

"Thanks, Dad." Christopher's relief was apparent to everyone.

The ride to Jason's house was quiet. Christopher sat in the back with Jason, their hands linked between them on the seat where the adults couldn't see from the front. Neither boy spoke, but they didn't need to. Just being together, knowing there might be a way forward, was enough for now.

When they pulled up to the small house on 24th, Jim got out and helped Jason retrieve his bike from the trunk. Christopher followed, lingering near the car.

"I'll see you in the morning," Jason said quietly, but he didn't move toward the house. Just stood there holding his bike, not ready to let go yet.

"Yeah. 1st period." Christopher looked toward the front window where a light glowed. Jason's mom was home. He wanted to hug Jason, kiss him, hold onto him. But out here in the open, even in the dark...

Jim, reading the moment perfectly, said quietly, "Christopher, why don't you help Jason put his bike away? Around the side there, out of the wind."

He nodded toward the darkened space along the side of the house, away from the street, away from windows.

Christopher didn't understand at first, but Jason did. He wheeled his bike up the walk and around the corner. Christopher followed.

Jim returned to the car, where David was watching in the rearview mirror.

"Where are they going?" David asked.

Then he saw them disappear around the side of the house into the shadows, and he understood.

From the car, Jim and David tried to look away—tried to give the boys their privacy. But they caught a glimpse anyway. Two silhouettes pressed together against the side of the house. Jason leaning his bike against the siding. Christopher stepping close. The unmistakable shape of a kiss—real and proper and needed.

Young love.

Jim felt something tighten in his chest. David reached over and took his hand.

"We have to help them," Jim whispered. "We have to find a way."

"We will," David promised.

A moment later Christopher came jogging back to the car, his face flushed, a small smile playing at his lips despite everything.

They drove back to the Averys' in silence, Christopher in the back-seat looking out the window at the dark houses sliding past, holding onto that kiss like a talisman.

———

Jason wheeled his bike the rest of the way around back and leaned it in its usual spot. The porch light flickered—still needed a new bulb—and cast strange shadows across the overgrown lawn.

He touched his lips, still feeling Christopher there.

Then he went inside. His mom was asleep on the couch, Channel 13 news on low volume. Jason turned it off, grabbed the afghan from the back of the sofa, and draped it over her carefully.

She stirred slightly but didn't wake.

He stood there for a moment looking at her. She looked tired even in sleep. Lines around her eyes and mouth that hadn't been there when he was younger. Gray streaks in her hair she covered with drugstore color every few weeks.

She'd been doing this alone for eight years. Raising him, working as much as she could, keeping them afloat. And he'd been so wrapped up in his own shit lately he hadn't even thought about how hard this must be for her too.

"Love you, Mom," he whispered.

Then he went to his room and closed the door. Kicked off his shoes but didn't bother changing. Just collapsed onto his bed fully clothed and stared at the ceiling.

So much had happened. So much might happen. His brain couldn't process it all.

Eventually exhaustion dragged him under into dreamless sleep.

Around three AM, Sarah woke with a start.

The afghan was draped over her. The TV was off. The house was dark and quiet.

She sat up slowly, her neck stiff from sleeping at an odd angle.

Jason must have come home and covered her up. She'd meant to wait up for him, to talk, but exhaustion had won.

She stood and stretched, then made her way down the hall toward her bedroom. Paused outside Jason's closed door.

Quietly, carefully, she opened it just a crack.

Moonlight trickled through his curtains, illuminating him curled against his pillow the way he used to when he was little. One arm tucked under the pillow, the other hanging off the side of the bed. Still fully dressed.

Sarah felt her heart clench.

He'd been so joyful as a young boy. So full of life. Always laughing, always curious, always running and playing and filling the house with noise.

And now... now he was so serious. So guarded. Carrying too much weight on those thin shoulders.

They'd been through a lot. Both of them. And she wanted to make it better. Wanted to fix it somehow.

For both of them.

She pulled his door closed gently and went to bed, her mind already spinning through everything that needed to happen. Everything she needed to figure out.

———

Sarah pulled into the parking lot of Rax, up on 30th Street Tuesday after work. The restaurant was busy—families grabbing dinner, teenagers clustered at tables laughing too loud. The neon sign glowed red and orange in the twilight.

She checked her makeup in the rearview mirror one more time, then made herself get out of the car before she could change her mind.

Diane was already inside near the entrance, waving. "Sarah! I'm so glad you came."

They hugged briefly, and Sarah felt some of her anxiety ease. Diane had such a warm, genuine presence. No pretense, no judgment. Just... kindness.

"Thank you for inviting me," Sarah said. "I'll admit, I wasn't sure what to expect."

"Just two moms trying to figure out how to help our boys," Diane said with a smile. "Come on, let's order. The salad bar here is actually pretty good."

"I told Jason it was 'girl's night out' and he had to make do with PB&J tonight," she laughed.

"I think Christopher look absolutely frightened at the prospect of his father cooking," Diane shared joining in her banter.

They made their way to the counter, ordered two salad bar meals, then found a booth in the corner away from the other diners. The curved glass windows offered a view of the parking lot and the street beyond—far enough from traffic that they could talk.

For a few minutes they just made small talk while building their salads. The weather. The holidays coming up. How fast the semester was going.

But then they settled into the booth with their plates, and Diane set down her fork and looked at Sarah directly.

"How are you doing? Really?"

The question, asked with such genuine concern, nearly broke Sarah's composure. "I'm... managing."

"That's not what I asked."

Sarah took a shaky breath. "I'm terrified. For Jason. For myself. I don't know what I'm doing. I feel like I'm failing him."

"You're not failing him," Diane said firmly. "Sarah, you've raised that boy on your own for how long?"

"Eight years. Since his father..." She couldn't finish.

"Eight years. Working, keeping a roof over his head, getting him through school. That's not failing. That's surviving. That's being strong for him even when it's hard."

Sarah wiped at her eyes. "But now this. With him being... with Christopher. And people talking. And Rick running his mouth all over town." Her voice dropped to barely a whisper. "I just wanted to protect him. I thought moving to Indianapolis would give us a fresh start where nobody knows. But Jason's been pulling away and I don't know if he hates me or blames me or thinks I'm ashamed of him—"

"He doesn't hate you," Diane interrupted gently. "He's scared. He thinks you're disappointed in him."

"But I'm not!" Sarah's voice cracked. "I don't have a problem with Jason and Christopher being together. They're sweet together. It's the first time since his father left that I've seen Jason actually happy. Really, truly happy." Tears spilled over. "But I'm scared for him—what people will do, how hard his life is going to be. I can't protect him from all of that."

"No," Diane agreed softly. "You can't. None of us can. But you can support him. Love him. Make sure he knows you're on his side."

"I want to. I do. I just don't know how to talk to him about this. I don't know what to say. I don't know..." She trailed off helplessly. "I don't know if I even fit in your world, Diane. You and Mark, you're educated, successful, I'm sure you have a beautiful home and wonderful life, and I'm just... I'm just trying to keep us afloat. I've never even had anyone to talk to about any of this. I feel so alone."

"You're not alone," Diane said, reaching across the table to squeeze Sarah's hand. "Not anymore. Because we're in this together now. Your son and my son love each other. That makes us family, whether we planned it or not."

Sarah felt fresh tears well up. "I've been so alone with this. I didn't know who to talk to. Didn't know who would understand."

"Then let me help," Diane said. "Let us help. Mark and me. And there are some other people in our corner who've been incredibly helpful. People I'd like you to meet."

"Who?"

Diane leaned in closer, lowering her voice. "David Barnes. Jason's guidance counselor? He teaches Driver's Ed."

"I know Mr. Barnes. Jason speaks highly of him."

"Well," Diane said carefully, her voice dropping to a whisper even though no one was nearby, "David is gay. He and his partner Jim have been together for years. And before I say more—I asked David's permission to share this with you. He said yes because he wants to help Jason. He wants to help both boys."

Sarah blinked, processing. "Mr. Barnes is... I had no idea."

"Most people don't. He's kept it quiet for obvious reasons. But

Sarah, he and Jim are some of the kindest, most genuine people you'll ever meet. They've been helping us navigate this—helping us understand what the boys are going through, what they need from us. And they care about Jason. Really care about him."

Sarah's mind was spinning. There was so much Diane was saying —not just about David and Jim, but about conversations that had clearly already happened. Decisions being discussed. A whole group of people she didn't know who were apparently invested in her son's wellbeing.

"Why?" she finally asked. "Why do they all care so much? They don't even know Jason. Don't know us."

"Because they see themselves in him," Diane said simply. "David especially. He knows what it's like to be young and scared and feeling like you have to hide who you are. And he doesn't want Jason and Christopher to go through what he went through. None of us do."

"But what can anyone do?" Sarah asked, her voice breaking again. "It's why I'm moving us to Indianapolis in a couple of weeks. To give us a fresh start. It's the only solution I can see. Get us away from the poison here, away from all the gossip, give Jason a chance somewhere new."

"I understand," Diane said. "But what if there was another way? A way that helped Jason and gave you the fresh start you need?"

"I don't understand."

"Come to dinner," Diane said. "At our house. You and Jason. We'll invite David and Jim too. You can meet them properly, get to know them both. And we can talk about some ideas we've had. Ideas that might help everyone."

Sarah wiped her eyes and managed a small smile. "Okay. When?"

"How about Thursday? That gives you a couple days to think about everything. And Sarah?" Diane squeezed her hand again. "You're not alone anymore. We're all in this together now."

Sarah felt something loosen in her chest—something that had been wound tight for eight years. "Thank you," she whispered. "I can't remember the last time anyone..." She couldn't finish.

"I know," Diane said softly. "I know."

They finished their salads talking about lighter things—Christopher's terrible singing voice that somehow got him into choir, Jason's dry sense of humor, the ridiculousness of teenage boys in general.

But as Sarah drove home that night, she felt something she hadn't felt in longer than she could remember.

Hope.

Maybe there was a way forward. Maybe she didn't have to do this alone.

Was that impossible to ask for?

———

David had intentionally saved Jason and Christopher for the last in-car practice group of the period. While other students worked with his teaching assistant in the simulators, David led them out to the parking lot.

"Christopher, you take the wheel first."

Christopher looked surprised—Jason usually went first since he was more nervous and needed more time—but slid into the driver's seat without argument.

David got in passenger side. Jason climbed in back.

Diane had called David late the night before, after her dinner with Sarah. Filled him in on their conversation—Sarah's fears, her loneliness, her genuine love for Jason mixed with terror about his future. Her tentative agreement to dinner Thursday night.

"Before we start," David said as Christopher adjusted the mirrors, "I need to talk to you both about something."

Both boys went still.

"Your mom had dinner with Mrs. Avery last night," David said, looking at Jason in the rearview mirror. "They talked. About every-thing. About you two, about the move, about all of it."

Jason's face went pale. He knew she was going out with her, but hadn't said a word when she got home. Just looked like she was think-ing. "What did she say?"

"She loves you. She's scared for you. She wants to help but doesn't know how." David's voice was gentle. "And we have some ideas—Jim and me. Ways we might be able to help. But Jason, I need to know something first."

"What?"

"Do you want to stay here? Finish the semester instead of moving to Indianapolis right away?"

Jason's breath caught. Christopher's hands tightened on the steering wheel.

"I... yes. Of course I want to stay. But my mom—"

"Would still take the job," David said. "She needs it. You both need it. But what if you could stay here with Jim and me until Christmas break? Finish Driver's Ed, finish your semester, have more time with Christopher. Then move to Indianapolis after the holidays when your mom's settled."

"You'd let me stay with you?" Jason's voice was barely a whisper.

"If your mom agrees. If you want to. Yes."

"But..." Jason struggled. "What about the bullshit here at school? For Christopher and me. I mean..." he tried correct his language. David looked turned in his seat to look at him, but gave no indication of calling him out.

"I don't want to drag you into my shit," he continued. "And my mom—would she be okay by herself? I mean, would I be abandoning her, all alone up there?"

"Jason," David said firmly. "First, you're not dragging me into anything. I'm making my own choices. Second, your mom wouldn't be alone—she'd be building a new life in Indianapolis, which is easier to do without worrying about you changing schools mid-year. And third, you wouldn't be abandoning her. You'd be taking care of yourself, which is what she wants."

"What would I have to do?" Jason asked.

"Nothing yet. Just think about it. We're all having dinner tomorrow night at Christopher's home—you, your mom, the Averys, Jim and me. We'll talk more then. But I wanted to know how you felt about it first. No sense getting everyone worked up if you don't even want this."

"Should I tell my mom? Before dinner?"

David considered. "You could. But she's bound to have a lot of questions. I think she'd like to get to know Jim and me a bit better before agreeing to let you stay with us. Don't you think?"

Jason nodded slowly. "Yeah. That makes sense."

"So just think about it. We'll all talk tomorrow."

"Okay." Jason's voice was stronger now. "Thank you. For even thinking about this."

"Of course." David shifted in his seat. "Now Christopher, let's work on your three-point turns. Jason, you're up after. And in this car, it's still Mr. Barnes. Can't have you two getting too comfortable with me. Not at school, at least."

Both boys smiled, the tension breaking slightly.

They spent the rest of the period actually driving, but the whole time Jason kept thinking about tomorrow night. About his mom meeting David and Jim. About whether this might actually work.

About maybe, possibly, not losing everything after all.

———

After finishing the in-car practice session with Jason and Christopher, David watched them head off to their next classes before returning to his own classroom. He stood at his desk watching the parking lot through the window, waiting. Second period students were starting to trickle in, but his eyes stayed fixed on the lot, searching for Jim's car. His hands were shaking slightly.

Jim had been called out for a couple of flights Monday morning— back-to-back routes to Boston, then London, returning to Chicago. Their original plan to do this after Thanksgiving had felt too far off. David had decided Sunday night, lying in bed trying to read while his mind spun, that they needed to act sooner.

So they'd agreed: Jim would come to school after his flight. Given the time he landed in Indy, he'd arrive around second period, if his schedule held.

Plenty of students would see. Word would spread.

David's heart hammered as he spotted Jim's car pulling into the lot. He'd driven straight from the Indianapolis airport, still in his pilot's uniform, making it just in time.

This was it. No turning back.

Students were filing in, claiming seats, talking amongst themselves. David pretended to organize papers on his desk, but his eyes kept flicking to the door.

A knock on the doorframe made everyone look up.

Jim stood there in full uniform—crisp, commanding, undeniably handsome. Half the girls in class visibly swooned.

David's voice almost cracked but he held it together. "Jim. Hey."

"Hey David." Jim walked over like this was the most natural thing in the world. "Here's that file you forgot at home." He held out a manila folder. "Good thing I wasn't flying out again today!"

He turned slightly toward the class, taking them in with an easy smile. They were absolutely soaking it in—the tall pilot, the casual familiarity, the way he called Mr. Barnes by his first name.

"Thanks, Jim. I really appreciate it." David took the folder, their fingers brushing briefly.

"Anytime, hon."

The endearment dropped into the room like a stone in still water.

The bell rang.

Jim checked his watch. "There's the bell. I should let you get started." He gave the class another warm smile and a small wave. "See you tonight after school. I'm making meatloaf. Have a good day, everyone!"

Then he was gone.

David didn't let the moment linger. He launched immediately into his usual pre-class joke—something about a student driver and a stop sign—and dove into the day's lesson.

But he could feel it. The buzz in the room. The whispers that would start the second the period ended and explode by lunchtime.

By fifth period, the entire school would know.

———

David walked to Principal Morrison's office before lunch, his weekly report folder in hand. His heart was still racing from Jim's appearance, but he made himself walk in like nothing unusual had happened.

He knocked on the doorframe. "Hey Peter, just wanted to drop off this week's report."

Peter looked up from his paperwork. "Thanks, David. Come on in."

David set the folder on the desk. "Sorry it's a bit late. I almost forgot it at home this morning—busy week, you know, trying to get ready for Thanksgiving and everything—but thank God Jim wasn't flying out again today and could swing by to drop it off. Otherwise I'd have had to drive all the way back home."

He was rambling. He knew he was rambling.

Peter picked up the folder, but his eyes were on David. "Jim?"

"Yeah, you met last year. After the Christmas party? He picked me up afterward and you were heading out at the same time. Tall guy, beard, pilot for United?"

Peter's face was carefully neutral. "Right. I think I remember."

David shifted topics quickly, launching into a discussion about another student who needed intervention. But he could see Peter wasn't fully listening. Could see the wheels turning.

Jim. Home. The file from home.

Those rumors Peter had heard were true.

"So," David finished, "would you prefer I handle it or refer directly to you?"

"What? Oh." Peter refocused. "You handle it. My trust is in you, David. Always has been."

Something loosened in David's chest. "Thanks. I appreciate that."

He started to leave, then Peter's voice stopped him.

"David?"

He turned. "Yeah?"

"Tell Jim thanks. For bringing the report over. It's... I appreciate him doing that."

David felt his knees go weak. He took a breath. "I'll let him know. Tonight. When I get home."

He made it back to his office, closed the door, and sat heavily in his chair.

He'd done it. Made it real and public. Put himself out there.

And Peter Morrison had just acknowledged Jim. Had thanked him. Had made it okay.

David put his face in his hands and took several deep, shaky breaths.

Some people would surprise you, Jim had said. Would show up when it mattered.

Maybe there were more of them than David had thought.

———

Sarah pulled up to the Avery house with Jason, exactly on time. She'd changed clothes three times before settling on slacks and a nice sweater—nothing too formal, nothing too casual. Still, as she got out of the car, she felt inadequate somehow. This house was beautiful. Larger than anywhere she'd ever lived. The neighborhood was nicer than anywhere she could afford.

These people were sophisticated, successful, had good lives. And she was just...

"Mom?" Jason was watching her with concern. "You okay?"

"I'm fine, honey." She forced a smile. "Let's go."

Diane opened the door before they even knocked. "Sarah! Jason! Come in, come in."

Inside was warm and welcoming—tasteful furniture, family photos on the walls, the smell of something delicious cooking.

Christopher appeared at the top of the stairs and practically flew down. Before Sarah could process it, he'd wrapped Jason in a tight hug right there in the entryway.

Sarah felt her breath catch. She'd known they were together, but seeing it—seeing her son held like that, seeing him hug back with equal need—

"Hi, Mrs. Reynolds," Christopher said, finally releasing Jason and turning to her with a bright smile. "It's really good to see you again."

"You too, Christopher." Sarah managed a smile. "And please, call me Sarah."

Mark appeared and took Sarah's coat. "Boys, why don't you head to the kitchen and grab the plates? Set the table for us?"

343

As they headed toward the kitchen, Diane gently took Sarah's arm. "Come with me for a minute before dinner. There are some people I'd like you to meet."

She led Sarah into the formal living room—clearly a space reserved for special occasions. Two men stood when they entered.

The taller one stepped forward first, his presence immediately calming. "Sarah? I'm Jim. It's wonderful to finally meet you."

His handshake was warm, firm, genuine. He had kind eyes and an easy smile.

Then the other man approached. "Mrs. Reynolds. I'm David Barnes, though I suppose you already know that from school. Please, call me David."

"Mr. Barnes—David." Sarah shook his hand. "Jason speaks very highly of you."

"He's a remarkable young man. You should be very proud."

Mark appeared with wine glasses on a tray. "Why don't we all sit? Get comfortable?"

Sarah took the wine glass Mark offered—her hands trembling slightly. She couldn't recall the last time she'd had wine with anyone. The men she'd known were beer drinkers at best, usually whiskey straight from the bottle down at whatever bar they frequented.

This felt... civilized. Like she was Eliza Doolittle being brought into high society.

But that wasn't fair to them. They genuinely seemed to like her. Seemed to want her here.

They settled into seats—Sarah on the sofa, Diane beside her, the men in chairs around them.

"Boys," Mark called toward the kitchen, "why don't you hang out in Christopher's room while we talk? We'll call you down for dinner."

Jason appeared in the doorway, looking uncertain. Christopher behind him.

"We're not in trouble or anything, right?" Jason's voice was guarded, defensive in that way Sarah recognized—expecting the worst, always.

"No trouble at all," Mark said gently. "We just want to talk with your mom first. Give us a bit, okay?"

As the boys headed for the stairs, Mark added with a grin, "And don't get too carried away making out up there!"

"DAD!" Christopher's face went scarlet.

Jason burst out laughing—a real, genuine laugh that made Sarah's heart clench. When was the last time she'd heard him laugh like that?

Sarah found herself smiling too. The joke had been so casual, so normal—just a dad teasing his son the way any dad might. Except it acknowledged that Christopher was dating another boy, and nobody was hiding it or whispering it or treating it like something shameful.

It was just... normal. Accepted. The way Mark said it with such obvious love for his son, everyone sharing in the gentle teasing—

Sarah had never seen anything like it. The word "gay" was something people rarely said aloud unless they were speaking in hushed, judgmental tones. But here it was, right out in the open, treated with the same casual affection as any other aspect of who these boys were.

It felt oddly welcoming. And deeply, surprisingly nice.

———

Upstairs, Jason and Christopher sat on Christopher's bed, the door closed, both feeling anxious and uncertain.

"What do you think they're saying down there?" Jason asked, bouncing his knee nervously.

"Probably just talking," Christopher tried to reassure him. "Getting to know each other."

"But what if they're ambushing her? Trying to convince her of something she doesn't want?" Jason's voice rose slightly. "What if she feels pressured—"

"Jason." Christopher took his hand. "Take a breath."

"I can't. I'm always worried about something. You know that."

"I know. But sometimes you worry about things that aren't actually problems. Your mom agreed to come here, right? Nobody forced her."

"Yeah, but—"

"And David and Jim, they've been nothing but kind to you. To both of us. You don't actually think they'd hurt your mom, do you?"

"No." Jason deflated slightly. "No, I don't think that."

"So maybe it'll work out for the best."

Jason looked at him, something sad and resigned in his eyes. "It's hard to feel that way when things never seem to work out for the best in my world, Christopher. Good things don't happen to people like me."

Christopher's heart broke a little. "Do you think meeting me was a good thing?"

Jason's expression softened immediately. "Of course I do. You're the best thing that ever happened to me."

"Then maybe that's the start. Maybe good things are finally coming your way." Christopher leaned closer. "And maybe you've just been so wound up trying to protect yourself from hurt that you've forgotten there are people who love you. Who want good things for you."

"Just you."

"No." Christopher squeezed his hand. "Not just me. Maybe not the same way I love you—" He kissed Jason softly, feeling him melt slightly into it. "But everyone downstairs loves you too. David and Jim, my parents, even your mom. They're all down there right now trying to figure out how to help you. How to make things better."

Jason felt tears prick his eyes. "When did you get so smart?"

"I learned from you." Christopher kissed him again. "Now stop worrying. At least for a few minutes."

"I'm trying, but it's hard not knowing..."

Christopher reached over and pulled Jason into another long kiss. "Let me help distract you," he teased after coming up for breath.

———

Downstairs, Diane was catching Jim, David, and Mark up on her conversation with Sarah at Rax. Sarah listened, occasionally adding details—her fears about Jason's safety, her worries about Rick's poison spreading, her conviction that moving to Indianapolis was the only way to protect her son.

But also her loneliness. Her feeling of inadequacy. Her sense that she didn't belong in their world.

"I've been doing this alone for eight years," Sarah said quietly. "Ever since Jason's father walked out. I've had to be strong for Jason, couldn't let him see me fall apart. But inside..." Her voice broke. "Inside I've been drowning. And I realize now that I taught Jason to do the same thing—to bottle everything up, to sacrifice himself for everyone else, to never ask for help because asking for help means you're weak."

She wiped her eyes. "I've been so worried about the harassment and the bullying that I didn't see I was teaching him to hide. To think he was the problem. To believe that if he just toughened up and pulled away from Christopher, everything would be fine. Just like I've been telling myself that if I just work hard enough, sacrifice enough, eventually things will get better."

Diane reached over and squeezed her hand. "But you can't sacrifice yourself into happiness, Sarah. Not you, not Jason. All that does is teach him that love means suffering alone."

"I know." Sarah's voice was barely a whisper. "And I hate that I did that to him."

David set down his wine glass and moved to a chair closer to Sarah.

"Sarah, if you don't mind, I'd like to tell you about myself. About my life. I think it might help you understand what we're proposing and why."

Sarah looked over at him, unsure of what he was about to say.

David took a breath. "I grew up here in Connersville. Mark and I actually went to school together." Sarah glanced his way before returning to David. "I've known I was gay since I was about Christopher and Jason's age. But this was the 60's—there was no way to be open about it. No way to be honest. So I hid. Dated girls I didn't have feelings for. Pretended to be someone I wasn't."

Sarah listened, fascinated.

"I met Jim about fifteen years ago. And for the first time in my life, I felt like I could breathe. Like I could be myself. We've built a good life together—a real life. But we kept it quiet. Separate. I never brought Jim to school functions. Never mentioned him as anything but a friend or roommate. I was terrified of losing my job, my home, everything."

"That must have been so hard," Sarah said softly.

"It was. But recently I realized something." David leaned forward. "I was teaching kids like Jason and Christopher to do the same thing. To hide. To be ashamed. To live half a life out of fear. And I don't want that for them."

"So you came out," Sarah said. "At school."

"Sort of. Jim stopped by class." David smiled at the memory, still fresh and nerve-wracking. "Dropped off a file I'd 'forgotten.' We didn't have to say much, but I'm sure by lunch everyone knew. Probably half the parents by now."

"Aren't you scared?" Sarah asked. "About losing everything?"

"Terrified," David admitted. "But this is important. Jason and Christopher are important. And there are other kids out there—kids who feel different, who don't fit in—who need to see that it's possible to be yourself and survive. That you don't have to hide forever."

"I've talked to Principal Morrison," David continued. "And most of the teachers. Some will have problems with it, I'm sure. But more people have been supportive than I expected. And I have people who will stand with me—like Peter, and these wonderful people here, and..." He paused. "And I hope you."

All eyes turned to Sarah.

She felt the weight of it—their hope, their expectation, their genuine desire to help.

"Of course, David." Her voice was stronger than she felt. "I just... I don't know how to help. Honestly, I'm barely keeping us afloat as it is. And I don't really understand why you all care so much. You don't even know us."

Jim leaned forward, his calm presence immediately soothing. "But we'd like to. And we think we might be able to help. But only if you're comfortable with it. This is about what's best for Jason—and for you."

He gestured to include Mark and Diane. "We're all in this together."

"I don't understand what you mean," Sarah said.

"Without getting too much into your personal business," Jim said gently, "we're aware of the promotion. And first—congratulations! That's wonderful!"

Sarah blinked, caught completely off guard. Aside from her boss— whose congratulations had felt hollow and transactional—no one had acknowledged her achievement. She'd worked so hard for this. Had endured so much just to keep her and Jason alive, let alone get ahead. She was proud of earning that promotion. Proud of proving she could do it.

"Thank you," she said, her voice catching. "I... I know I shouldn't boast, but I worked really hard for this. Really hard. And I've had to endure so much just to... well." She lifted her chin. "I'm proud of myself. There. I said it."

"You should be proud!" Diane leaned over and gave her a warm side-hug. "God, I'd be proud too! I don't think I could have done half of what you've done. Are you running the show now?"

Sarah blushed. "I'm going to take over the branch on 38th just north of downtown. They've been looking for a new bank manager and..."

"That's wonderful!" Diane practically cheered.

Mark raised his wine glass. "To Sarah. And her very well-earned promotion."

"To Sarah," everyone echoed.

They clinked glasses, and Sarah felt tears streaming down her face. She couldn't remember the last time anyone had celebrated her. Recognized her accomplishments. Made her feel like she mattered.

She'd never had wine like this before—sitting with people who seemed to genuinely like her, toasting her success, treating her like she belonged.

It felt civilized. Warm. Like she'd stepped into a world she'd only seen on television.

"Thank you," she whispered, overcome. "This is... this is really nice."

Jim set down his glass and traded places with David, sitting next to her. "There is one complication with the promotion. A timing issue. But we think we might be able to help with that—buy you some time. But we need to know what you think first."

He explained the plan: Jason staying with them until semester's end. He had a personal friend in Indianapolis with a beautiful remodeled Victorian homes off Massachusetts Avenue and needing a good tenant. Now that he knew she was going to be managing a bank up off 38th, it'd be even more perfect, close by. He'd ensure she got the 'friends-and-family' discount. He even thought of helping with the moving plans.

"I've had to move so many times I should have started a moving company instead of becoming a pilot," Jim said with a self-deprecating smile.

Sarah was overwhelmed. "Why would you do this for us? What's the catch?"

No one had ever been this nice to her. Not without wanting something.

Jim reached over and gently took her hand. She felt the sincerity in his touch, the genuine warmth.

"Because family helps family, Sarah. Jason is family to us now. We may not be his fathers, and I know you're just getting to know us. But Jason and Christopher love each other. That makes us family."

Sarah looked around—at Diane, who met her eyes with warm understanding. At Mark, who smiled gently. At David, holding Jim's arm with obvious affection.

Then back to Jim, who squeezed her hand once before letting go.

"Besides, David and I both have had help getting ourselves started, especially when our families... couldn't."

Sarah caught the tinge of sorrow in his voice and wondered if he had meant to say 'wouldn't'.

"Does Jason know about this?" she asked.

"Actually," David said carefully, "he was more worried about you. About leaving you alone. He's been trying to figure out how to help everyone—you, Christopher, all of us—and carrying it all inside. Thinking that maybe if he just pulled away, cut things off with Christopher, the pain would go away faster. For everyone."

Sarah's hand flew to her heart. "He thought... he thought he was protecting us?"

"By letting go of Christopher, yes. The way his father... well, if you'll forgive my intrusion, abandoned you both."

Sarah felt like she'd been punched. "Oh my God. I didn't... I didn't see it."

"None of us did until recently," Diane said gently. "But Sarah, that's why we want to help. You've got so much going on, trying to handle everything alone—"

"And we'd like to help, give something back, as it were," Jim finished simply.

Sarah couldn't speak. Could only cry quietly while these people— these strangers who'd somehow become something more—waited patiently.

"I should talk to Jason," she finally managed.

"Of course," Diane said, standing. "I'll get him."

"Diane?" Sarah stopped her. "Could Christopher join us too? I think... I think he should hear this."

"Absolutely." Diane smiled. "I'll get them both."

A moment later, Jason appeared in the doorway, Christopher right behind him. Both looked nervous.

"Mom? Everything okay?"

"Come sit, honey. Both of you."

"Why don't we give you some time?" Diane ushered everyone out towards the kitchen.

They settled on the floor in front of her chair—easier than trying to find space on the furniture. Sarah noticed how naturally Christopher reached for Jason's hand. How they fit together.

"I wanted to talk to you about what everyone's been discussing," Sarah began. "About the promotion, about the house in Indianapolis that Jim's friend has, about you potentially staying here until Christmas with David and Jim."

The boys nodded—they knew most of this already.

"But there's something else I need to say first." Sarah's voice caught. "I need you to understand what your father's departure did to me. How much it hurt. I never talked about it because I didn't want to burden you—you were just a child. But you're not a child anymore, Jason. You're growing up. Becoming a man."

Jason blinked, startled. He'd never thought of himself that way. "Man" seemed like something for older people. He'd always just seen himself as some stupid kid.

But looking at Christopher beside him—both of them figuring out love and prejudice and so many fucked up choices—maybe they were further along than he'd realized.

"When your father left," Sarah continued, "I felt like I was drowning. Felt like I wasn't good enough, wasn't pretty enough, wasn't smart enough. Felt like if I'd just been better somehow, he would have stayed. And I've carried that shame and pain for eight years, never talking about it, never dealing with it, just pushing it down and working harder and telling myself that if I just sacrificed enough, eventually things would be better."

Her voice broke. "And I taught you to do the same thing. Taught you that love means suffering in silence. That asking for help means you're weak. That you should sacrifice yourself to protect the people you care about."

She looked at Christopher. "I understand now that you've been withdrawing from this wonderful boy because you thought you were helping. Thought that if you just pulled away, he'd be safer. You wouldn't drag him down with you."

Jason couldn't speak, could only nod. How did she know all of this?

"But honey, that's not helping. That's hurting. And it hurts so much." Sarah wiped her eyes. "I still hurt from your father leaving. We had good times. We had you—the best thing that ever came from that relationship. And I could never imagine walking out on you. Never."

She leaned forward, her voice fierce. "So I need you to promise me something, Jace. I need you to let Christopher love you. You hear me?"

"Jace," Christopher whispered, trying out the nickname. He liked it.

Sarah smiled through her tears. "Let him love you, especially when everything's falling apart. Because if you don't, you might as well just leave like your—"

She couldn't finish. Eight years of held-back grief came flooding out.

Jason was off the floor in an instant, kneeling beside her chair, holding her.

Christopher hesitated only a second before joining, his arms around both of them.

"I'm sorry," Sarah sobbed. "I shouldn't—"

"I won't leave him, Mom," Jason said, his own tears falling. "I promise. I won't leave him. And I won't leave you either."

"I know you won't, honey. I know." She pulled herself together slowly. "No mother wants things to be hard for her child. But I also don't want you to be alone the way I've been alone."

She wiped her eyes and looked down at them—these two boys kneeling on her floor, looking up at her with such trust.

They were so young. But also somehow not as young as she'd thought. Christopher's hand was covering Jason's protectively. Both of them had lived through things no teenager should have to face.

"Your father leaving nearly destroyed me," Sarah said quietly. "But I never dealt with it. Just pushed it down, told myself to be strong, to provide, to not burden you with my pain. And in doing that, I taught you the same thing—that real strength means suffering alone." She shook her head. "But that's not strength, Jace. That's just... survival. And I don't want either of us just surviving anymore."

Jason looked at Christopher and wiped his eyes with the back of his sleeve.

"We're going to move to Indianapolis," Sarah said, her voice steadier now. "I'm going to take that job and talk to Jim's friend about that house. It sounds wonderful. But..." She turned to Christopher. "I want Jason to finish his semester here. With David and Jim. And I expect to see you up at our new house in Indianapolis. You hear me?"

"Yes, ma'am," Christopher said seriously.

"Good." Sarah managed a smile. "Now come here and give me a hug before we have dinner."

Jason stood and fell into her arms. She held him tight, feeling him shake with relief and emotion.

Then she pulled back and opened her arms to Christopher. "Well, where's my hug, son?"

Christopher looked at Jason, who had tears streaming down his face at hearing his mother call Christopher "son." Christopher stepped into her embrace, and Sarah held him just as tight.

She leaned down and whispered in his ear: "Take care of him for me when I'm gone. Love him when he won't let anyone else close. Can you do that?"

"Yes," Christopher whispered back. "I promise", but then his face changed as if he suddenly remembered something. "Do you think I can come stay over the weekend with Jason sometimes?"

Sarah pulled back and smiled at both of them. "I think we can make that work." She winked at Jason. "Now let's go have dinner before everything gets cold."

She stood, keeping one arm around Christopher's shoulders as they walked toward the dining room. Jason followed, still trying to figure out what they'd whispered about.

"What did you say to him?" he asked.

"Never you mind," Sarah said mysteriously. "You'll figure it out eventually."

———

Over dinner, Sarah and the boys shared her decision. Everyone was thrilled. They talked logistics—Jason's room, moving plans, driving lessons.

Jim joked about having moved so often he could do it blindfolded. Diane and Sarah started planning decorating trips for her new house she knew nothing about yet. Mark groaned about having two teenage drivers on the road.

"Think of it this way," Jim said with a grin. "They can drive themselves to Indianapolis and back. No more hauling them around."

"Count me in!"

Everyone laughed.

David teased that they still had to pass his class and the boys suddenly looked worried.

"Maybe there's hope after all?" Mark teased to another round of laughter.

"I can't wait to come up and see your new place," Christopher exclaimed.

"I can't wait to see it either!" Jason teased back.

In a lull, Diane caught Sarah's eye. "You know, speaking of Christopher visiting, we should probably talk about boundaries. With these two. Regarding..." She trailed off meaningfully.

Sarah's eyes widened. "Oh. Yes. We should definitely talk about that."

Both boys went crimson.

"We can discuss it later—" Diane started diplomatically.

"You might as well get it out now," Jason said bluntly, his face still red. "Everyone knows you're talking about our sex life."

The table went silent for a beat, then erupted in laughter.

Sarah stared at her son, shocked he'd just said that so openly. But then she started laughing too. She'd told him to be honest with her, to not hold back. This was what she'd asked for.

And watching him—seeing how he said it without shame, without hiding—she realized he was more mature than she'd given him credit for. Still young, still figuring things out, but growing into himself. Becoming his own person.

It made her uncomfortable thinking about him and Christopher being sexual together. But she also recognized she shouldn't be surprised. And his honesty, difficult as it was to hear, was better than lies and secrets.

She caught his eye and gave him a small nod—*it's okay*. He looked relieved, if still embarrassed.

They did discuss boundaries then—appropriate and reasonable ones that both mothers agreed on. Then moved to lighter topics. Holiday plans. Driving tests. The upcoming Thanksgiving break.

"Two sixteen-year-olds with licenses," Mark groaned. "God help us."

"Dad! We're good drivers!" Christopher protested with a smile, even though he knew his father was just giving him shit.

"I think it's perfect," Jim said. "They can finally drive themselves."

"I'm just teasing," Mark replied. "And, I'm sure you both will be just fine," he added, relenting to his son and Jason.

"I'll be the judge of that," David teased and gave his best 'teacher' face.

More laughter.

"Still," Sarah said quietly. "I worry about the boys. There's a lot of assholes out there." She caught herself. "Sorry. But not just drivers—people who..."

David understood her worries about how the boys were being treated and shared more about his conversations at school. With teachers. With Principal Morrison. Even with Christopher's science teacher who unfairly separated him in lab last week.

"They'll still be out there," David acknowledged. "But we're doing what we can to make it better. To show people it's okay. And we'll keep protecting them however we can."

"I want to help too," Mark said. "Next summer, company picnic—I'm bringing both boys. Introducing Jason as Christopher's boyfriend. Proudly."

"One step at a time," Diane cautioned gently.

"True," Jim agreed. "This won't be easy. Probably never will be completely easy. But it'll get easier. And you build your family—the people who support you, who love you, who show up when it matters." He looked around the table. "Like all of you."

Mark raised his glass. "To family."

"To family," everyone echoed.

They clinked glasses—Sarah included, feeling the warmth of the wine and the warmth of these people who'd somehow become her people too.

She didn't know what the future held. Didn't know if Indianapolis would be the fresh start she hoped for. Didn't know if Jason and Christopher would be okay in a world that didn't always make space for love like theirs.

But she knew she wasn't alone anymore.

Chapter 21

Something Called Home

The days that followed blurred together in a rush of activity and change.

Thanksgiving weekend, Jim orchestrated Sarah's move from the small rental on 24th Street to her new home in Indianapolis. The house was in Chatham Arch—a five-bedroom Victorian that Jim's friends Marty and Stephen had spent the last two years completely renovating. Exposed brick, original hardwood floors, modern kitchen, updated bathrooms. It was stunning.

Jim had convinced them to rent it to Sarah sight unseen. "Friends and family discount," he'd insisted.

When Marty and Stephen heard Jason's story—heard about Christopher, about the harassment, about two boys trying to love each other—they'd agreed immediately.

"She can have it for a dollar a month for all we care," Stephen had declared dramatically. "Those boys need protecting."

Marty had been more practical. "We'll give her a fair rate. But we're absolutely throwing in free interior decorating services."

Sarah had been overwhelmed when she first saw it. The house was beautiful—far nicer than anywhere she'd ever lived. One of the upstairs bathrooms was still being finished, tile work in progress, but everything else was move-in ready.

"I can't afford this," she'd said, her voice breaking.

"Yes you can," Jim had said firmly. "We worked out the numbers. Trust me."

Marty and Stephen had been there for move-in day, helping unpack boxes, making Sarah laugh with their banter, immediately adopting her as the sister they'd never had.

Jason and Christopher rode up with David and Jim, ready to help haul boxes and furniture. When they walked through the front door, they found Marty directing furniture placement like a general commanding troops while Stephen followed behind, critiquing every choice with cutting commentary.

"That credenza absolutely cannot go there, Martin. It throws off the entire flow of the room."

"It's a credenza, Stephen. It doesn't flow. It sits."

"Everything flows. Haven't you learned anything from Feng Shui?"

"I've learned that you're impossible when you've been reading design magazines."

Jason and Christopher had stood in the doorway with boxes in their arms, trying not to laugh. Marty spotted them first.

"Boys! Thank God. Come settle an argument. Does this credenza work here or does Stephen need new glasses?"

"I have perfect vision, thank you very much," Stephen had said, then turned to Christopher with a dramatic once-over. "Well hello there, handsome. You must be Christopher. I'm Stephen, purveyor of good taste and excellent cocktails. This is my partner Marty, who has neither."

"Charmed," Marty had said dryly, extending his hand for a firm shake. "Don't mind Stephen. He knows not what he does."

Christopher had been a little nervous—these were Jim's friends, gay men who were out and open and unapologetically themselves in a way he'd never seen before. But their warmth was immediate and genuine.

"And you must be Jason," Marty had said, pulling him into a hug. "We've heard so much about you. Jim talks about you constantly."

"He does?"

"Oh honey," Stephen had said, "you have no idea. You and your charming boyfriend here have basically become Jim and David's entire personality. It's adorable and slightly nauseating."

Sarah had appeared from the kitchen. "Boys, you're here! Did you eat? I can make sandwiches—"

"Mom, we're fine."

"Are you sure? Because I have—"

"We're helping her get settled," Marty had interrupted gently. "She's already trying to feed everyone. We may have to stage an intervention."

That first night, sleeping in Sarah's new house, Jason and Christopher had stayed up late talking in Jason's new room—easily the nicest bedroom Jason had ever had. Two windows looking out over the tree-lined street. A real closet. His own bathroom.

"This is amazing," Christopher had whispered, lying on Jason's new bed. "Your room back in Connersville is nice, but this..."

"You're being polite," Jason said with a laugh. "Our old place was shit and you know it."

Christopher grinned. "Okay, yeah. But I was trying to be nice."

"I know." Jason lay down beside him. "But you don't have to with me, you know that. It was a fucking dump. Admit it. This place though... I still can't believe this is real."

"You deserve it, babe" Christopher said softly. "Both of you do."

———

Sunday afternoon meant it was time for Jason to head back to Connersville with Christopher. School wasn't over yet—still a few more weeks until Christmas break. His "temporary" arrangement with David and Jim would continue until then.

Sarah had cried saying goodbye, holding him tight. "Call me every day. Be good. Mind your Uncle David and Jim."

The "uncle" title had stuck after the first time Sarah used it jokingly. Both David and Jim loved it.

"We'll take good care of him," Jim had promised.

"I know you will." Sarah had hugged them both. "Thank you. For everything."

Marty and Stephen had swooped in then, pulling Sarah back toward the house. "Come on, honey. You're going to be too busy to miss him anyway. We need to pick out curtains for the downstairs. And Stephen has opinions about throw pillows that you absolutely need to hear."

David and Jim gave them both a look of appreciation while Jason pulled Christopher's hand to the car.

"I have correct opinions," Stephen had clarified and winked at the two before turning to guide Sarah into the house.

Christopher held Jason's hand, both of them quiet in the backseat of David's car. It was a school night—Christopher needed to get home. But leaving Indianapolis, leaving that brief weekend of normal domesticity, felt harder than either of them had expected.

They dropped Christopher off first. Diane and Mark met them at the door, welcoming everyone in for a few minutes. The adults talked in the kitchen—something about Christmas plans—while Jason and Christopher went upstairs to Christopher's room for a moment alone.

"I hate this," Christopher said quietly, sitting on his bed. "Having to keep saying goodbye."

"I know." Jason sat beside him, their shoulders touching. "But it's only two more weeks. Then Christmas break. Then..."

"Then you're back in Indianapolis for good."

Jason didn't know what to say.

They sat in silence, both thinking about what that meant. Jason would be moving up to Indianapolis after the semester ended. Christopher was welcomed, he knew, but Indy was a long way.

"We'll figure it out," Jason said, not sure if he believed it.

"Yeah," Christopher echoed. "We will." Another problem for another day, he resolved.

———

"Come on," Jim said, leading Jason towards the back of their home. "We want to show you something."

They stopped at a closed door halfway down the hall.

"Your room," David said, opening it. "We've been working on it since you said yes to staying with us."

He stepped inside and froze.

"We wanted it to feel like home," Jim said.

The room was overwhelming. A proper desk with a computer—an actual computer, the kind other kids had but Jason never dreamed of owning. Bookshelves along one wall. His own walk-in closet, bigger than his entire bedroom at the rental house had been. A bathroom with a shower that didn't leak, thick fluffy towels that matched, everything coordinated and beautiful.

The bed had a classic nautical comforter with matching curtains. The walls were painted a calming blue-gray with crisp white trim. Professional. Elegant. Like something from a magazine.

"This is..." Jason couldn't finish. His throat had closed up.

"Is it okay?" David asked, suddenly worried. "We can change anything you don't like. Paint, decorations, whatever. It's your room. We just wanted—"

"It's perfect," Jason choked out. "It's... I can't believe this is for me."

"Of course it's for you," Jim said gently. "Who else would it be for?"

Jason looked around at the room—at the care they'd taken, the thought they'd put into every detail. The room back in Indianapolis was nice. The nicest he'd ever had. But this... this was something else entirely.

He felt almost afraid to touch anything. Afraid to ruin the newness, the perfection of it.

"Don't you like it?" Jim asked, reading his hesitation.

"I love it. I just... I can't believe you did all this. For me."

"Jason." David stepped closer. "You're part of our family now. This is your home. We want you to feel at home."

"You can change anything you want," Jim added. "Put up posters, rearrange furniture, make it yours. That's what home means."

Jason couldn't hold it in anymore. He grabbed them both in a hug, tears streaming down his face. "Thank you. Thank you so much."

They held him, and Jim said quietly, "Stuff doesn't matter, Jason. People do. And you matter to us."

———

The next day at school, Christopher couldn't wait to hear all about it. They'd taken to eating lunch with Allison in the dressing room behind the auditorium stage—a space that was technically off-limits but that nobody bothered checking. They'd bring sandwiches from home and hide out there, away from the cafeteria, away from everyone else.

Things had mostly died down for them. The harassment had shifted—people were more interested in gossiping about Mr. Barnes and his "hot pilot boyfriend" than they were about two sophomores. Some girls had taken to calling Jim "Mr. Barnes' boy toy"—David turned bright red the first time he overheard it.

"So?" Allison demanded as soon as Jason sat down. "Tell me everything. The house, the move, did you meet Jim's friends? Are they fabulous? I bet they're fabulous."

"They're pretty great," Jason admitted. "Marty and Stephen. They're funny. Stephen especially—he's got this whole camp thing going on. Makes you laugh constantly."

"I want to meet them," Allison declared. "Are they single?"

"Allison, they're together. Partners."

"Well obviously. But do they have single friends? Gay men always know the best straight guys."

Christopher choked on his sandwich, laughing. "Where do you even get this stuff?"

"I read," Allison said primly. Then her eyes went wicked. "Speaking of which. You two. Spill."

"Spill what?" Jason asked warily.

"Don't play dumb. You spent the weekend together. At Jason's new house. With bedrooms. And privacy." She leaned forward. "Did you...?"

"Allison!" Christopher's face went scarlet.

"What? I'm curious! Gay sex is hot."

"Oh my God," Christopher buried his face in his hands, his shoulders shaking with mortified laughter.

"You're such a bitch," Jason said, but he was grinning.

"So? Did you?"

"Not as much as you think," Jason finally admitted. "But... we've done some stuff."

"JASON!" Christopher looked like he wanted to sink through the floor.

"That's all you're getting," Jason said firmly to Allison. "And you're straight anyway. Why do you even care?"

"Because guy-on-guy action is hot," Allison said matter-of-factly. "Woof."

Christopher made a strangled sound. "I cannot believe we're having this conversation."

"I can't believe you're so uptight about it," Allison shot back. "It's 1989, Christopher. Get with the program."

Jason and Christopher looked at each other and burst out laughing. It felt good—normal and silly and exactly what they needed.

———

The days passed with relatively few problems. A few parents called Principal Morrison to complain about Mr. Barnes, asking if "what they'd heard" was true. Peter listened patiently, neither confirming nor denying, diplomatically redirecting them toward actual concerns about their children's education.

Most of the complaints came from parents whose kids were already in trouble—failing classes, racking up detentions, in danger of not graduating. Peter noted the pattern and filed it away.

"David, got a minute?"

"Of course. What's up?"

Peter leaned against the doorframe to his office. "The Christmas party Tuesday. You're coming, right?"

"Planning on it." David had always attended.

"Good. I wanted to make sure Jim knows he's invited too." Peter said it matter-of-factly, like it was the most obvious thing in the world. "It's for all the staff and their spouses, significant others, you know? I think Jim qualifies."

David looked up from his paperwork, stunned. "You... you want Jim there?"

363

"Of course I do. I'd like to get to know him better. I only met him briefly that once." Peter smiled. "Just tell him not to stress about it. It's casual."

"I... thank you, Peter."

"Don't thank me. Just bring him." Peter straightened. "See you Tuesday."

After he left, David sat there for a long moment, staring at nothing.

Peter had gone out of his way to personally invite Jim. To make sure David knew he was welcome. That they were welcome.

It mattered more than Peter probably realized.

———

Tuesday evening, they drove to Miller's Cafeteria—a local institution where Peter always held his Christmas parties. Jim wore his pilot's uniform, not to impress but because he'd literally driven straight from the Indianapolis airport where he'd landed barely an hour and a half before, collecting David on the way.

David was nervous. More nervous than he'd been the day Jim showed up at school.

"Relax," Jim said, squeezing his hand in the car before they went in. "It'll be fine."

"What if people—"

"Then they're assholes. And you don't need them anyway."

Most of the faculty was already there when they arrived. Several teachers looked up as Jim walked in—tall, commanding in his uniform, undeniably handsome. A few faces went carefully neutral. A few smiled warmly.

Peter made a beeline over. "Jim! Glad you could make it. Thanks for coming."

"Happy to be here," Jim said, shaking his hand.

Peter introduced him around. Most teachers were polite, curious. A few asked about flying—where he'd been recently, what routes he flew, whether he'd been affected by the recent pilot strike.

Jim was a natural. Warm, funny, self-deprecating in just the right ways. He told stories about mishaps at airports, about eccentric passengers, about the time turbulence caused coffee to spill all over the cockpit instruments.

David watched him work the room and felt something loosen in his chest. Jim belonged here. Was welcome here.

A few teachers left not long after Jim arrived—made their excuses and headed out early. David noticed. Noted their names. Fuck them, he thought viciously. I didn't have much in common with them anyway.

What surprised him was Mr. Delaney.

Of all the teachers David expected support from, Frank wasn't even on the list. They'd gotten along professionally, but they'd never been close—and Frank's reputation as the school's sternest enforcer didn't exactly scream "ally."

Frank approached them near the punch bowl, his wife at his side.

"David. I wanted to introduce myself properly to your partner." He extended his hand to Jim. "Frank Delaney. I teach history. This is my wife Margaret."

Jim shook hands with both of them. "Nice to meet you. I've heard good things."

"I wanted to say," Frank continued, his voice low enough not to carry, "what you both are doing—being open, being yourselves—it matters. It takes courage. And I respect the hell out of it."

David blinked, stunned. "Thank you, Frank. That... that means a lot."

"Not everyone will be kind about it," Margaret added gently. "But you've got allies. More than you might think."

They chatted for a few more minutes—normal conversation about Christmas plans and the snow forecast and whether Miller's coffee was getting worse or if they were all just getting older. Then Frank and Margaret moved on to talk to other colleagues, and David stood there feeling slightly dazed.

"See?" Jim said quietly. "I told you."

"Yeah," David managed. "You did."

The weekend of December 15th, Christopher came to stay at David and Jim's house. Officially to "hang out." Realistically because it was the last weekend before Jason would move to Indianapolis for Christmas break, and everyone knew they needed this time together.

Christopher marveled at Jason's room. "You're so lucky. This is amazing."

"It's pretty great," Jason admitted. He felt a little awkward—proud that for once he was the one with the nice space, but also slightly embarrassed that Christopher seemed impressed.

"I mean, my room's fine," Christopher continued, looking around. "But this? It's like a hotel."

"A good hotel," Jason corrected, grinning.

"The best hotel."

They spent most of Friday evening just existing together—playing Nintendo in the living room, helping Jim make dinner, screwing around on Jason's new computer. Normal, domestic things that felt impossibly precious.

Saturday morning, David and Jim made themselves scarce. They'd had a quiet conversation with Diane and Mark earlier in the week, acknowledging the boundaries they'd set but also recognizing this was the boys' last weekend together for a while.

"We'll be in and out," David had promised. "But we'll give them privacy. They need this."

"Thank you," Diane had said. "For understanding. For caring about them."

"They're good kids," Jim had said simply. "They deserve support."

Saturday night, the house was quiet. David and Jim were Christmas shopping in Cincinnati that would conveniently take several hours. The boys had the house to themselves.

Jason showed Christopher what he'd found in the bathroom medicine cabinet earlier in the week—a box of condoms and a small bottle of lubricant tucked behind the first aid supplies.

Christopher's face went bright red. "They... they put those there?"

"I guess so." Jason felt his own face heating up. "I mean, they know we're... you know."

"Yeah, but..." Christopher stared at the items like they might bite him. "That means they think we're going to..."

"Yeah."

They'd fooled around before. Done stuff. But not that. Not yet. Neither had been quite sure how to bring it up—whether it was too soon, too much, too awkward. But the thought had been there, lurking, impossible to ignore.

"We don't have to," Jason said quickly. "I mean, just because they're there doesn't mean—"

"I know." Christopher looked at him. "But... do you want to?"

Jason's mouth went dry. "I... yeah. Maybe. If you do."

"I think I do. I just don't really know..." He trailed off, embarrassed.

"Me neither," Jason admitted. "But we could... figure it out? Together?"

"Yeah," Christopher said softly stepping closer to him. "I'd... like to."

————

The first snowfall of the holiday season began Tuesday night, December 19th—fat, lazy flakes drifting down through the darkness, coating Connersville in white just in time for the last day of school.

Wednesday would be a half day. And more importantly, it was the day both Christopher and Jason had scheduled their driving tests, back-to-back appointments at the BMV across from the fire station.

Jason was nervous. Anyone could see it.

It had already been three weeks since he'd moved in with David and Jim, and breakfast that morning was quiet—Jason pushing his eggs around his plate, barely eating. Jim tried to make conversation about the snow, about Christmas plans, about anything to distract him. But David could see the tension in Jason's shoulders, the way his knee bounced under the table.

David had given Jason an A in Driver's Ed for his written work and simulator practice. But only a B for in-car driving. It wasn't that Jason didn't know what to do—he knew all the rules, understood vehicle operation, could recite proper procedure in his sleep. He just didn't trust himself yet. And that lack of confidence showed in how he drove: overly cautious, hesitant, second-guessing every decision.

He'd get there eventually. David was sure of it.

Christopher, on the other hand, was a sure bet. Confident without being cocky, comfortable behind the wheel, the kind of driver who made it look easy.

"I'll give you both a ride after school," David had offered. "We can head straight over."

"Thanks, Mr. Barnes," Christopher had said with a grin, knowing full well to use David's teacher name at school even though they were past that everywhere else.

But now, watching the snow come down harder, David felt his own nerves kick in. Driving tests in fresh snow. With Jason already anxious.

This would be interesting.

———

School let out at noon. David met both boys at the front entrance of the building, car keys in hand.

"Ready?"

"Born ready," Christopher said confidently.

Jason just nodded, his face pale.

The drive to the BMV was quiet. Christopher tried to make conversation from the backseat—something about Christmas shopping, about the forecast calling for more snow overnight—but Jason barely responded.

"You'll be fine," David said as they pulled into the parking lot. "Just breathe. Drive like you've been practicing. You know this."

"Yeah," Jason said, but his voice was thin.

Christopher went first. His examiner was a young man—probably late-twenties—who looked vaguely familiar. When he introduced himself, David recognized him: Tommy Brennan, a former student from several years back.

And unless David was very mistaken, Tommy was one of the kids who he'd wondered about back in school, reminding him of the boys.

It'd been awhile since they'd spoken. He looked like he was doing well for himself.

David and Jason waited in the lobby, making small talk about nothing in particular while Jason fidgeted.

Twenty minutes later, Christopher came through the front doors grinning from ear to ear.

"Passed!" He held it up triumphantly.

"Congratulations," David said, genuinely pleased. "I had no doubt."

Jason managed a smile. "That's great, bab.. I mean, Christopher."

"You're up," Christopher said, squeezing Jason's shoulder. "You got this."

Jason looked like he was going to hyperventilate.

Tommy caught David's eye and gave a small nod. *I've got him.*

They headed out to the car. David and Christopher returned to the lobby to wait.

"He's going to be okay, right?" Christopher asked, bouncing his leg anxiously.

"He'll be fine," David said with more confidence than he felt.

———

Inside the car, Jason's hands were shaking as he adjusted the mirrors.

"Take your time," Tommy said calmly. "No need to rush, especially since it's snowing."

Jason looked at the flakes falling and gulped before pulling out of the parking lot, hyper-focused on every movement. Check mirrors. Signal. Look both ways. Ease into traffic.

Everything was fine until the turn onto Fifth Street.

Jason signaled looked right then left and started to turn, almost hitting a pedestrian stepping off the curb who ran up from out of nowhere.

"Brake!" Tommy said sharply.

Jason slammed the brake. The car jerked to a stop. The pedestrian —a guy in his twenties wearing a Connersville Spartans jacket—glared at them and kept running, flipping them off as he crossed.

Jason's face went white. "I'm sorry. I'm so sorry. I didn't see—"

"It's okay," Tommy said evenly. "I didn't see him either. But you need to check for pedestrians before you commit to a turn. Always. Even if they're crossing against the light."

Jason nodded, his throat tight. That was it. He'd failed. He knew it.

But Tommy just gestured forward. "Let's keep going."

They finished the rest of the test. Jason was so nervous he overcompensated on everything—stopped too far from stop signs, turned too slowly, drove five under the speed limit the whole way.

When they pulled back in front of the BMV, Jason was certain he'd bombed it.

Tommy made notes on his clipboard, then looked up. "You passed."

Jason blinked. "What?"

"You passed. You're a little too cautious, which is better than being reckless, especially in this weather. And you followed all my instructions. Just work on your confidence, okay? You know what you're doing. Trust yourself."

"I... thank you." Jason felt tears prick his eyes, relief flooding through him.

"And hey," Tommy added quietly as he opened the door. "Tell Mr. Barnes thanks. For everything he's been doing. It matters. To me."

Jason eyes went wide before he nodded, understanding. Tommy smiled and stepped out.

————

When Jason walked through the front doors of the BMV, David could see it in his face immediately—the relief, the disbelief, the joy.

"You passed," David said, grinning.

"I passed!" Jason's voice cracked. "I can't believe I passed!"

Christopher grabbed him in a hug, lifting him off his feet for a second. "I told you! I told you you'd be fine!"

Tommy followed them in, looking a bit haggard but smiling. He caught David's eye. "He'll be fine. Just needs more practice. Build that confidence."

"Thank you, Tommy," David said meaningfully.

Tommy nodded and headed to his next appointment.

That evening, Mark and Diane insisted on taking everyone out for a celebration dinner. "Boys' choice," Mark had declared.

"Pizza King," Jason and Christopher said in unison, then looked at each other and laughed.

"Pizza King it is," Diane said.

The restaurant on Western Avenue was busy, but they managed to find a large table and ordered an embarrassing amount of food.

Jason called his mom from the payphone near the bathrooms, feeding quarters into the slot.

"Mom? I passed!"

"Oh honey, that's wonderful! I'm so proud of you!"

"I almost hit a guy crossing the street," Jason admitted. "But the examiner let me keep going and I passed anyway."

"Well, I'm sure you were nervous. But you did it! I wish I could be there to celebrate with you."

"It's okay. We're at Pizza King with everyone. David and Jim, the Averys."

"Good. You have fun, okay? And Jace?"

"Yeah?"

"I'm counting down the days until you come home for Christmas."

"Me too, Mom. Love you."

"Love you too, honey."

Back at the table, Jim was telling some story about a near-disaster landing in Chicago during a storm, making it funny even though it had probably been terrifying at the time. Christopher was leaning against Jason's shoulder, both of them exhausted from the stress of the day but happy.

David watched them all—this makeshift family they'd built—and felt something settle in his chest.

They were doing it. Against all odds, against harassment and fear and uncertainty, they were carving out something good.

And it was only the beginning.

Saturday, December 23rd arrived faster than anyone expected.

David and Jim drove to the Averys' house that morning to help load up for the trip to Indianapolis. Jason's things were already mostly packed—clothes, some books, his Walkman, small gifts he'd wrapped for his mom and for Christopher.

Mark was outside loading suitcases into the trunk when they pulled up. Jason hopped out almost before the car stopped, not waiting to knock or be invited. He was family now. Could walk right in.

"Christopher?" he called up the stairs.

Christopher appeared at the top, his duffel bag in hand, looking bittersweet. Happy they'd get the weekend together but sad knowing he'd have to come home Christmas Eve.

"You okay?" Jason asked, coming up to meet him.

"Yeah. I'm fine."

"You don't look fine." Jason came up behind him and wrapped his arms around him. Christopher melted into the embrace, closing his eyes.

"Boys!" Diane called from downstairs. "Let's get moving or we'll be late!"

"Coming!" Christopher yelled back.

"You have everything?" Diane continued. "Your Christmas sweater for your grandma tomorrow night?"

"Yes."

"Change of socks and underwear?"

Christopher gave him a look. Jason grinned and ran to Christopher's dresser, snatching a pair of briefs before Christopher could stop him.

"I grabbed a pair for him!" Jason yelled from the top of the stairs waving them like a flag.

Diane's laughter echoed up. "Thank you, Jason!"

Christopher's face went scarlet. He grabbed the briefs and shoved them in his duffel. "I'm going to kill you in your sleep."

"Looking forward to it," Jason said sweetly.

Outside, Jim and Mark stood by the cars holding keys.

"You're driving us up."

Jason froze. "Me?"

"Yes, you. Who else? Frosty the Snowman?" Jim laughed.

"But—"

"You've got your license. And who better than your Driver's Ed instructor to help if you need it?" Jim nodded toward David, who was leaning against the car grinning.

"I'm off duty," David announced. "It's Christmas break!"

Everyone laughed.

Mark handed his keys to Christopher. "You're driving us. Just follow Jason."

Christopher's face lit up. "This is the coolest thing ever!" He jogged to the car, then turned back and ran to Jason. "You'll be fine. I'll be right behind you, babe."

"You just want to look at my ass," Jason teased.

Christopher stopped him cold. "You're right. And it's a pretty nice ass too." He made a show of checking out Jason's rear.

David hadn't seen that coming and nearly doubled over laughing.

"Touché," Diane said to her son, grinning as she got in the car.

Mark slid into the passenger seat, confused. "What did I miss?"

"Tell you later, dear," Diane said.

"Come on, Hot Ass," Jim said, pushing Jason toward the car. "Let's hit the road."

David laughed so hard he had to lean against the car for support. Jason was completely gobsmacked, his face bright red.

————

The drive to Indianapolis went smoothly. Jason was nervous at first, hyper-aware of Jim in the passenger seat and David in the back, but after the first few miles he settled in. Checked his mirrors. Maintained speed. Signaled properly.

Behind them, Christopher followed at a safe distance, occasionally waving when they stopped at lights.

By the time they pulled onto Sarah's street in Chatham Arch, Jason felt almost confident.

Then he saw the house.

"Holy shit," he breathed.

The entire Victorian was decorated for Christmas. Lights strung along every roofline and portico, down the iron fence, lining the sidewalk. Tasteful wreaths hung in every window with white candles. And the Christmas tree in the front window—massive, perfectly decorated, glowing—looked like something from a Norman Rockwell painting.

"Mom did all this?" Jason asked, stunned.

"Not alone," Jim said, grinning.

Sarah appeared on the front porch wearing an apron that said "Tis the Season... to be Mary." She ran down the steps through the light snow and pulled Jason into a fierce hug.

"Look at you! Already driving"

"How did you do all this?" Diane asked, getting out of the other car and gesturing at the decorations.

"Oh, I have my in-house elves." Sarah smiled just as Marty and Stephen emerged from the front door carrying a box of ornaments.

"Guilty!" Stephen called out when he saw everyone staring.

Jason ran over to help them. "What are you guys doing?"

"Finishing touches," Marty said. "Your mother has excellent taste but needed a professional hand."

"A professional hand," Stephen corrected, "and my impeccable sense of style."

"Christopher, dear, can you help us too?" Stephen asked, eyeing Christopher appreciatively. "We need someone tall for the lights."

They were finishing decorations on a small birch tree in the front yard, stringing white lights through the bare branches.

"Something tasteful," Marty said to no one in particular.

"Go on inside, everyone," Stephen called toward the adults. "It's much warmer. The boys will help us."

He leaned in toward Mark and Diane, stage-whispering, "Besides, the eggnog is extra extra this year, if you know what I mean." He winked.

Diane laughed. Mark grinned. They already loved these two.

Inside, the house was warm and smelled like cinnamon and pine.

The decorations were perfect—sophisticated but welcoming, elegant without being stuffy.

Sarah gave tours, showing off what Marty and Stephen had helped her accomplish. The kitchen was fully stocked, the living room furniture arranged just right, the upstairs bedrooms each decorated in their own style.

Jason's room—his Indianapolis room—looked like it belonged to someone else. Someone who had money. Someone whose mother could afford nice things.

"You like it?" Sarah asked, watching his face.

"Mom, it's... it's amazing."

"Marty and Stephen helped. But I picked out your comforter. That dark blue. I thought you'd like it."

"I love it." Jason hugged her. "Thank you."

———

By late afternoon, everyone had gathered around the dining room table for an early dinner. Sarah had cooked—a proper meal with pot roast and potatoes and vegetables. Marty opened wine. Stephen made a show of mixing cocktails.

After dinner, Marty suggested a game. "Monopoly!"

"Oh God," Stephen groaned. "This will only end in tears."

"I love tears," Marty said cheerfully. "Makes it interesting."

They set up the game in the dining room. Jason, Christopher, Jim, Marty, and Mark played while David and Stephen sat on the sidelines.

"I know better than to play," David announced. "It always ends in arguments."

"Told you," Stephen said, sipping his drink.

An hour in, Mark landed on Park Place—which Jim owned, along with Boardwalk, both loaded with hotels.

"That'll be one thousand dollars," Jim said pleasantly.

"What?! No! It's Christmas!"

"Told you!" Stephen yelled from the couch, then took a dramatic sip of his cocktail.

Everyone burst out laughing. Even Mark, despite losing, was grinning.

"You're ruthless," Mark said, handing over his fake money.

"Thanks for flying with us today!" Jim replied in his best pilot voice.

Jason and Christopher nearly fell out of their chairs laughing.

———

In the living room, Sarah and Diane sat together near the window, wine glasses in hand, watching the snow fall outside.

"How's the new job?" Diane asked.

"Busy. So busy. There's so much to learn." Sarah sipped her wine. "But I think I can do it. I really do."

"I know you can," Diane said firmly. "You're stronger than you give yourself credit for."

"I miss Jason though. Miss having him around." Sarah's voice caught. "But I can see he's happy. Really happy. That helps."

"He is happy," Diane agreed. "And David and Jim are wonderful with him."

They both turned to look into the dining room where David was standing behind Jason, leaning down to give him advice on which property to buy while Jim was fully absorbed in the game, treating Jason like his own son.

"Look at them," Sarah said softly. "They've really taken to each other, haven't they?"

"They have." Diane smiled. "David and Jim needed Jason as much as he needed them, I think. They're a family now."

Sarah felt tears prick her eyes. Jason had been missing something —some stability, some male presence, some sense of being valued—for so long. And now he had it. Had two men who genuinely cared about him, who wanted him to succeed, who weren't going anywhere.

"How are you doing?" Diane asked gently, turning back to Sarah. "Really? At night, when it's quiet?"

Sarah knew what she was asking. Knew Diane understood the loneliness, the silence of an empty house.

"I'm okay," Sarah said. "I will be. It's quiet here sometimes. But I can't complain."

"You can complain to me," Diane said. "Anytime. We're friends now."

"Thank you." Sarah squeezed her hand.

"Besides," Diane added with a grin, "sounds like you've got Tuesday night Bingo with Marty and Stephen's crew. That'll keep you busy."

Sarah laughed, her face flushing slightly. "They've invited me to join their group. All these... well, men like Stephen. Very theatrical. Very funny. I've never met people like them before."

"Sounds perfect," Diane said warmly.

A crash from the dining room made them both look over. Jim was demanding rent from Marty, who was dramatically protesting. Stephen was cackling from the couch.

"Should we break it up?" Sarah asked.

"Probably," Diane said, but neither of them moved.

It was nice, sitting here. Watching their boys laugh. Watching everyone be together. Chosen family, messy and loud and imperfect but real.

———

Finally, Sarah called everyone into the living room. "Time for gifts!"

"Thank God," Stephen said, refilling his cocktail and sauntering toward the Christmas tree. "That game is far too dramatic for my delicate constitution."

Christopher looked at Stephen, fascinated. Everything about him was so different from anyone Christopher had ever known—campy, theatrical, unapologetically himself. It was mesmerizing.

Jason pulled Christopher onto the couch and snuggled close. Christopher fit perfectly against his side.

Mark and Jim were still play-arguing about Park Place. David gave Diane a look that said *Want to trade?*

"No," Diane said aloud with a grin. "You keep him!"

Everyone laughed.

Sarah asked Marty to play Santa. Stephen immediately protested. "I should have worn my tights!"

More laughter.

"Our gift first," Marty said, handing Sarah a beautifully wrapped box. "For you."

"Me? Oh, you two didn't need to—you've done so much already!"

"Have we?" Stephen looked at Marty with exaggerated innocence. "See! I told you!"

"Shut it, Stephen," Marty said affectionately.

Sarah opened the box slowly. Inside was a gorgeous winter coat from L.S. Ayres—the department store downtown, expensive and elegant. She held it up, speechless.

"And there are matching gloves in the box, honey!" Stephen added before taking another sip. "Merry Ho Ho!"

Sarah stood and kissed both of them on the cheek. "It's wonderful. Thank you so much."

Marty took a playful swipe at Stephen. "That's the closest you'll ever get to making out with a woman!"

Jason nearly fainted from laughing so hard. Sarah beamed. Diane couldn't remember having this much fun in years.

"Who's next?" Marty grabbed another box, this one labeled "From Santa."

David read it aloud and added, "Ooooh! I just love a man with a beard!"

Jim smacked his arm playfully. The boys absolutely lost it—they'd never seen David camp before. It was hilarious.

Inside was a small photo frame with a picture of Sarah and Jason when he was little—both of them smiling, genuine and happy.

"Awww," everyone chorused.

"Jim said something last month," Sarah explained, her voice thick. "About family helping family. That really resonated with me. Made me trust you all. So I wanted you to have something to remember your contribution to our family."

Jim hugged her tight. David followed.

"How old was he here?" Jim asked, studying the photo.

"Seven or eight, I think."

Christopher asked to see it. Jason passed it over, and Christopher leaned back into Jason's arms, studying the picture.

"You were such a cute little boy," Christopher said softly.

"Cute?" Jason protested.

"So adorable," Christopher continued, making Jason blush. "Look at you, Jace."

Only his mom had ever called him that. Sarah heard it and smiled, catching Jason's eye. She nodded slightly—it was okay. Christopher could use that name now.

Jason felt something shift in his chest. He leaned in and kissed Christopher—longer than a peck, sweet and genuine and unashamed.

The room erupted in a collective "awww."

"Get a room!" Stephen yelled.

Everyone laughed again, the moment perfect and imperfect and exactly what it needed to be.

Marty pulled out another box. "This one's hard to read..."

"It's for you both, you big 'mo's!" Jim called out. "Get some glasses!"

Jason sniggered. Stephen gasped dramatically, clutching his cocktail. "I'll have you know, I may be a big 'mo, but I look fabulous!"

The room erupted again.

"Well, are you gonna open it or am I going to refresh my drink?" Stephen chastised Marty.

Marty tore at the wrapping, opened the box, then suddenly closed it, eyes wide, staring at Jim and David.

Everyone leaned forward, curious.

"What is it?" Diane asked.

"Oh, I'll let Marty decide if he wants to show you," Jim said with a smirk. "Ho ho ho."

David elbowed him, his own face bright red.

"Well?" Christopher finally asked for everyone.

"For God's sake, Marty dear," Stephen sighed. "Open it already!"

Marty gave Jim and David a look that said *I'll get you back*, then opened the box and tilted it for everyone to see.

Inside, nestled in silk lining, was a life-size dildo with a red Christmas bow tied around the base and a card that read "Jingle Balls!"

The room erupted.

"OH MY GOD!" Diane yelled, pointing. "Is that what I think it is?"

Sarah was laughing so hard she could barely breathe, her face bright red.

"Cover your eyes!" she told Jason.

"Oh honey," Stephen deadpanned. "He probably wrapped it."

Marty quickly closed the box, staring at Jim and David. "I wonder who THIS came from."

Jason and Christopher were dying—they couldn't believe how naughty everyone was being. But it was all in good fun, and Jason had never imagined being at a Christmas party like this, especially with his mom.

Marty rummaged for the next gift. "Only a few left. Let's see... this one's for the Averys. From Frosty."

Diane took the small box—barely wallet-sized—and sat back down next to Mark. She opened the envelope inside and her face went puzzled, then her eyes went wide.

Mark smiled. He knew.

"What is it?" Sarah asked.

"It's... cruise tickets. Out of Miami. Five days to the Bahamas!" Diane looked around the room. "Who's Frosty?"

David raised his hand slowly.

"David! What?!"

"Jim and I thought... well, with everything that's happened this year—"

"And who doesn't love a little drama, honey?" Stephen interrupted.

Marty swatted him. Christopher snickered.

"We figured you two might like a break," David finished. "Escape the snow. Relax a little."

"But when are we...?" Diane looked at the tickets.

Mark spoke up. "Tomorrow. After we drop off Christopher."

"Drop me off where?"

Jason looked equally confused.

"Jim, David, and I have been coordinating," Mark explained. "I thought we could use a little second honeymoon. A few days away. Just us."

"And we absolutely insisted on getting the tickets," Jim added. "Wouldn't let him say no."

Diane remembered Mark mentioning he needed to stop by David's house last week. That had been the planning session.

"You little stinkers!" She was grinning now. "I can't believe... wait. Where is Christopher going?"

Mark looked at his son. "You don't mind if we drop you off at the Reynolds' house while we're gone, do you?"

Christopher paused, processing. "The Reynolds?"

Jason's grin spread wider than the Cheshire cat. He nudged Christopher. "Hello! What's our last name?"

Christopher's eyes went huge. "Really?! I get to stay here?"

"All week," Sarah confirmed.

Jason turned to his mom. "Wait—you were in on this too?"

Sarah gave him an innocent look.

"I can't believe you all!" Diane swatted Mark's hand, then squeezed it tight. "Thank you. Thank you so much."

"Girl, get that bikini ready," Stephen said, snapping his fingers. "Hot mama is coming to town!"

More laughter. Diane protested modestly. "I haven't worn a bikini since Mark and I started dating!"

"Always time to start again, honey!" Stephen shot back.

Christopher was thrilled. He'd thought he had to leave tomorrow. Now he got almost a whole week with Jason.

Jason was already mentally planning everything they'd do.

"Thank you," Diane said, looking at Jim, David, and Sarah. "This means so much."

"What about my parents?" Diane suddenly remembered. "And your folks, Mark?"

"Already taken care of," Mark said. "They're all in on it."

"How did you coordinate all this without me knowing? You can't even coordinate changing your clothes!"

David and Jim fell back laughing at Mark's expression. Priceless.

———

As things settled, Marty searched for the remaining gifts. Jason and Christopher were still empty-handed.

But there was only one box left. Fairly large, nicely wrapped in old-fashioned paper. Addressed to Christopher.

Everyone looked at each other, confused. Nobody remembered this gift.

Christopher carefully peeled at the tape, trying to preserve the paper. Jason finally told him to just tear it already before they started collecting social security.

Stephen choked on his drink. Marty grinned.

"Well done!" Marty said.

"See what you've created, Stephen?" David said. "He's turning into a little you!"

"You mean perfect?" Stephen replied.

The family loved the banter, the Christmas music playing softly, the laughter. They were making memories and they all knew it.

Christopher opened the box. His eyes went wide. He stopped, staring.

Jason smiled, knowing.

"What is it, Christopher?" Diane asked.

"Pull it out," Jason encouraged softly.

Christopher reached in slowly and extracted a worn lantern. Paint flaking, a few dents, clearly old but held together. It looked like something from a film set.

"Is that from a railroad car?" Jim asked, curious.

"It's... interesting, honey," Diane said, glancing at Sarah, who shrugged—she didn't know the significance.

David saw Christopher's face and went pale. He remembered. He knew.

Christopher looked at Jason, then back at the lantern. "It's... it's perfect." He fought to keep his voice steady, knowing this meant so much more than anyone else in the room could understand.

"I didn't know you two were into antiques," Marty said. "There's this fabulous shop I should take you to."

"Oh God, Marty," Stephen groaned. "We've got so much crap at our house already we might as well be called Sanford & Son!"

Everyone laughed, the moment moving on.

"Thank you, Santa," Christopher said quietly to Jason, and kissed him.

Diane made a mental note to ask about the lantern later. But Marty was already looking for the last gift.

"Jason's... I don't see it." He searched under the tree, by the credenza. "Oh dear. Did we forget?"

"No," Sarah said, her voice cutting through the noise. "Jason's gift isn't in a box."

Everyone turned to look at her.

She stood, moving closer to where Jason sat on the sofa with Christopher leaning back against him.

"Jace... I was going to give this to you later. But I've been thinking, and I want to give it to you here. With everyone."

Jason's head tilted, curious. Christopher leaned forward slightly, but Jason pulled him back, filling the space with his warmth.

Sarah smiled and caught Diane's eye. Diane didn't know what was coming, but she could tell it would be significant.

"Jace... Christopher... I'm still figuring things out. Getting settled here. And thanks to Marty and Stephen—" she looked their way and they smiled warmly, Stephen holding Marty's arm, quiet for once —"I'm getting there."

"And thanks to you, David and Jim, for encouraging me. And Mark, for helping with my boy, for not giving up on him. Or your son." She looked at Christopher. "Whom I'm proud to call my own."

Christopher beamed. Jason bit his lip, smiling harder than he had in forever.

"But it's been you, Diane, who've really helped me see things in myself I never realized. Or believed I could do. Or be. I'll always appreciate our talks."

Diane's eyes filled with tears. "You have plenty to give, Sarah."

Sarah nodded, then turned to Jason. "But I've also been thinking a lot about you, Jace. And Christopher. And growing up. And... needing..." She paused, the word heavy. "A father."

Jason felt pressure build in his chest. The mention of his dad—or *a* father—hit like a physical weight.

"I've spoken with David earlier this week."

Jim looked at David, surprised. He didn't remember Sarah coming by. The others looked equally curious.

David sat quietly, a small smile of acknowledgment on his face.

"And if you would like," Sarah continued, her voice steady now, "I think you should finish school in Connersville."

Jason's face went puzzled. So did Christopher's.

"But Mom... school finished Wednesday."

"No. I mean the rest of school. Through graduation."

"This May?"

Sarah smiled and looked at David for help.

He shifted, glancing up at Jim before turning to the boys. "Sarah asked if we'd be willing to have you stay with us through *your* graduation. The next two years. And I said yes. If Jim's okay with it."

Jason's mouth dropped open. Christopher looked like he might faint.

Diane and Mark appeared more surprised than they'd been about the cruise tickets.

Sarah was beaming, though tears threatened.

Jason turned to his mom. "You... you mean it? Like... really?"

Sarah nodded, fighting back happiness and melancholy mixed together. She was releasing him. Letting him finish school, explore his relationship with Christopher, figure out who he was meant to be. With father figures he needed. Especially as he grew into a man. Especially as he navigated being gay.

It would be hard. She had conditions: at least one weekend a month in Indianapolis. Christopher was welcome, but she didn't want Jason out of her life. And summers—she expected him home for summers. His room would always be his. He'd have two homes now.

"You've literally got a country estate and a city home, Your Highness!" Stephen said dramatically.

Jason couldn't find words.

"So what do you say, Jace?" Sarah asked.

Christopher moved aside so Jason could jump into his mother's arms. No words needed. She knew. Everyone knew.

Christopher didn't know what to do with himself until Sarah pulled back and opened her arms to him too.

"Come here, son."

Christopher fell into the hug, Sarah holding him just as tight as she'd held Jason.

"Our family," Jim said quietly, and everyone nodded.

"Our family," they echoed.

Jason and Sarah held on for a long moment, both crying now— happy tears, grateful tears, tears for all they'd survived and all that was still ahead.

And around them, this makeshift family they'd built—David and Jim, Marty and Stephen, Mark and Diane—watched and smiled and knew they'd all found something rare.

Something worth fighting for.

Something called home.

Epilogue

loved

The first signs of spring were approaching. Some of the snow had melted a few weeks ago, though forecasters kept threatening another winter storm. Still, sunshine in March felt like water to someone lost in the desert.

Jason had grown accustomed to living with his dads—that's what he'd started calling them, though it had happened by accident.

One afternoon, David had gotten after him for forgetting laundry in the washer overnight. It had started to mildew, and David wasn't happy about it.

"Okay, *dad!*" Jason had shot back, trying to sound both funny and sarcastic.

David paused mid-sentence.

Jason heard himself. *Dad?*

"Sorry," Jason said quickly, turning back to restart the washer. "I was trying to be funny. It's stupid."

David remained standing there.

"Dad?" he asked quietly.

Jason didn't know how to respond.

David let it go. He wasn't upset—not even perturbed by the sarcasm. From the look on Jason's face once he'd realized what he'd said, David knew something profound was changing. Jason was opening up. Letting them in.

That night before bed, David told Jim, who nearly cried.

"But let's not push him," Jim said, wiping his eyes. "We're not his dads. Not really."

"We're the closest thing he's got," David replied softly.

The next morning at breakfast, Jason gathered his courage. He was following David out to the garage when he gave Jim his usual morning hug.

"Have a great day at school," Jim said, like always.

"You too, Dad."

Jason said it matter-of-factly, then closed the door before Jim could respond. Inside, his heart raced. He wasn't sure if it was okay, but he'd said it and now he just wanted it to not be a big deal.

It was a big deal to Jim.

Dad.

He had to call Marty and Stephen immediately.

———

Jason had picked up Christopher in Jim's car. He was off on a flight to Frankfurt and wouldn't be back until Monday, but he'd practically forced Jason to use the car while he was gone. The only condition was that Jason had to drive him to the Indianapolis airport Thursday after school in time for his night flight to Chicago.

Which meant Jason would be driving back alone. At night. In winter.

He'd been extremely nervous, but he'd taken his time, stayed focused, and done fine. When he pulled into the garage that night, he'd felt genuinely proud of himself.

David hadn't acted worried—just kept grading papers at the kitchen table like it was no big deal. But Jason could tell his body seemed less tense once Jason walked through the door. Jason gave him a quick hug as he passed and hung the keys by the doorway.

Now it was Saturday morning, and Christopher had jumped in

the car practically before Jason finished pulling into the Averys' driveway.

"Be careful!" Diane called from the porch. "And button your coat! It's still cold!"

"I will, Mom!"

Christopher slid into the passenger seat, grinning. "I still can't get over the fact that you're picking me up. You were the one who was nervous about getting your license!"

"Yeah, well. Jim's schedule works out sometimes." Jason leaned over and kissed him. "So where to?"

"I thought you knew what we were doing."

Jason shrugged. "It's sunny out. Finally. I just wanted to get out of the house."

"Even though it's barely forty-eight degrees?"

"Better than twenty."

"Wanna go to DQ?"

"Are you buying?"

"I've got like five bucks," Christopher pleaded.

Jason grinned. "I'm just fucking with you. Dad gave me some money."

"Which one?" Christopher laughed. "You're so lucky. Double the dads!"

"Lucky how?"

"Double the allowance!"

"I wish. More like double the people making me take out the garbage."

"Yeah, but you love them."

Jason did.

———

They sat at Dairy Queen eating sandwiches and ice cream, staring out at the Park Road traffic through the windows.

"You know what's funny?" Jason said, dipping a fry into his Blizzard. "We're sitting here bitching about how cold it is, but we're still eating ice cream."

"You're such a dork," Christopher said.

"Salty and sweet." Jason held up the ice cream-covered fry. "Best combination ever."

"I'll give you salty and sweet." Christopher wiggled his eyebrows.

Jason burst out laughing, then took a huge bite of ice cream and opened his mouth to gross Christopher out.

Christopher slapped at his arm. "You're disgusting."

"Yeah, but you love me."

"I do."

The words hung there for a moment, warm and solid and real.

"Come on," Jason said, standing. "Let's go walk around Roberts Park. We're already up here."

———

It was deserted. Too cold for most people, not enough snow for sledding. Jason parked by the back amphitheater and they walked down the hillside toward the horse track, then into the woods.

The ground hadn't thawed yet. The trees were still bare. But the sound of the Whitewater River—normally muffled by leaves in summer—was loud and clear as they got close.

They talked about school. About finishing sophomore year in a few months. Summer plans—Christopher coming to Indianapolis for a few weeks in June, Jason coming back for the carnival in July. Christopher's parents, Jason's mom, random bullshit.

All the while, they shivered slightly despite their winter coats. Direct sunlight warmed them, but they froze the moment a cloud passed over.

Still, the sky was beautiful—that deep blue that promised spring was trying to break through.

They followed the riverbank south, winding past the spots where kids fished and waded in summer. Jason wondered how many boys like them had come down here over the years, looking for privacy. A chance to be alone. To be themselves.

Christopher saw it first.

He put his hand out in front of Jason, who'd been looking down at the rocky creekside trying not to step on ice.

"What?" Jason started to ask, but Christopher put his finger to his lips.

Jason looked where Christopher was pointing—toward the river just as it curved around a bend.

At first, he didn't see anything.

Then—

It was as if something had poked through the cold winter landscape. The river still flowed. The trees were still there. The blue sky, the light breeze. But a vignette had formed—edges slightly cloudy and indistinct—and through it, they could see the same scene, only different.

Inside the vignette, the trees were green. Full of leaves that rustled in the same breeze they felt outside. The sky held the same clouds. The river had bits of melting ice at their feet but inside the portal it flowed free and clear—warm, summer water.

And at the edge of the riverbank—

Two boys. Playing. Shirts off, barefoot, trousers rolled up to their knees.

Jason recognized them instantly: William and Daniel.

But they seemed different somehow. Back at the farms, they'd always seen them in nightshirts, sneaking between houses or arguing near the tracks. Here they were in regular clothes, laughing, splashing each other in the water.

Christopher noticed their shirts and shoes piled on a log. Outside the vignette, that same log was covered in snow.

It was fascinating. No longer the desperate, tragic figures they'd seen before. This was another time. A happier time. Summer days and river play and laughter.

Laughter.

Jason could hear them. Christopher could too. Daniel's voice was higher-pitched, gentle. William's was deeper than they'd expected—a rich baritone that seemed at odds with his thin frame.

Jason laughed a little in surprise. Christopher joined him.

Suddenly the boys in the river froze. Turned.

They had heard Jason and Christopher.

Heard them. Saw them.

Christopher tensed. Jason reached around and held him close, both of them huddled in their winter coats against the cold air.

William began wading through the river toward them. Daniel followed, looking curious, then breaking into a smile once they got close enough to see properly.

Jason and Christopher were freezing, but that's not what kept them rooted in place. This wasn't a memory. Wasn't some ghostly projection. William and Daniel were *there*—solid, real, no translucence or otherworldly glow. It was like someone had wiped the world with a magical cloth and in that one spot cleaned away a hundred years.

"You made it," William said, his voice clear and strong.

Jason looked at Christopher, wondering if William was talking to them or to someone they couldn't see.

Daniel came closer. The warm water he'd been wading through splashed up onto Christopher's pant legs—Jason could see it hit, could see the wet spots form, though it began to freeze almost immediately in the cold air.

"Wh-what?" Jason whispered.

"You made it," William said again, smiling. "We'd been waiting."

Jason stared at him, trying to process. They were actually speaking to them. Not just some image or memory or whatever ghosts were supposed to be.

Daniel giggled. "I think he's scared of us, Willy."

Willy.

Christopher latched onto the endearment. They'd never found nicknames in the old documents. But hearing it made these two suddenly more real—not just photographs and newspaper articles, but people who'd loved each other. Who'd had their own private language.

William smiled, and Jason could see how attractive he really was. No wonder Daniel had fallen for him.

Daniel looked at Jason as if he'd read his mind, cocking his head with a slightly jealous expression.

Jason laughed despite himself.

"What's funny?" Daniel asked.

"Funny?" Jason found himself responding.

"Yeah?" William was still smiling, clearly amused.

"You... you can hear me?"

"Course we can. You're standing right there."

Jason shot Christopher a glance.

"You two are hopeless," Daniel said with another giggle, turning his attention to Christopher.

"D-Daniel?" Christopher found his voice finally.

"Yeah? You're Chris, right?"

"Christopher," he replied automatically, then realized he'd just corrected a ghost.

"Christopher," William repeated, letting it sink in. "You wanna join us?"

Jason suddenly wondered if he meant the river or something more permanent.

William laughed, catching the thought. "No—I mean in the river. You two have a long time before..." He trailed off meaningfully.

Jason let out a visible breath of relief. Christopher's grip on his hand was so tight it was cutting off circulation.

"What's wrong with you both?" William asked. "You look like you've seen a ghost!" He laughed at his own joke. Daniel joined in.

Some of the warm river water splashed onto their jackets. Jason and Christopher both realized this was no figment of their imagination. William and Daniel were *there*.

But how?

"Are you real?" Christopher asked finally.

Both boys in the river looked puzzled.

"Real? Course we are." William's expression shifted. "You're the ones who keep showing up like ghosts."

"Us?" Jason said.

"Yeah. Daniel saw you following him from my house last year. Damn near scared me to pieces. Almost fell off the roof."

"Me?" Jason exclaimed.

"Yeah, you! Out at night sneaking around. I thought you were some kid who'd climbed the parapet before you suddenly vanished."

Daniel stayed slightly behind William, curious about Christopher but wary of Jason.

"I didn't vanish. You did."

"I do no such thing. One minute I'm looking down at Daniel and I see you staring at me, but soon as I turn back you're gone. Right, Daniel?"

"Scared the shit outta me!" Daniel's higher voice backed him up. Then he looked at Christopher again.

"Why do you keep looking at me?" Christopher finally asked.

Daniel became shy. William looked back at him, then turned to Christopher.

"Because you've been walking by him. On our road. I'd seen you. Daniel's been too afraid to come down at night after that. It's why I got him his lantern—so he didn't have to walk in the dark."

Christopher went pale. "The lantern?"

Daniel looked a little sheepish but also curious.

"I... I didn't mean to scare you," Christopher said.

Daniel nodded and walked out in front of William, who remained in the river, water clearly flowing from the icy banks across the foggy barrier and warm across his feet.

"Are you a real ghost?" Daniel reached out as if to touch Christopher.

"I'm not a ghost," Christopher said firmly.

Daniel flinched, retracting his hand and stepping back into William, who looked around as if scouting whether they were alone before pulling his arms around Daniel's smaller frame.

"We've..." Jason tried to explain. "We've been dreaming. Or seeing you both. Or..." How did you explain this to ghosts who thought *you were the specters?*

William smiled slightly and looked down at Daniel's head, hair almost touching his chin. His gaze traveled to where Jason's hand held Christopher's tightly.

"You boys..." William said quietly. "Are you like us?"

Daniel was staring at their intertwined hands, then at Jason, then back to Christopher.

They knew.

"This is Jason," Christopher said. "My boyfriend."

William looked at them without significant reaction.

"Do you know what that means?" Jason asked carefully.

"Course. We ain't dumb. He's your buddy. Everyone's got a boyfriend or two."

Jason looked at Christopher, wondering if that word meant something different in their time.

"Christopher and I are in love," Jason said clearly.

William's expression changed. A slow smile crept across his face. "You mean... like me and Daniel?" he whispered.

Christopher nodded, relaxing slightly. Daniel squirmed shyly, but William held him tighter.

"Why you dressed in those funny coats?" Daniel finally asked. He and William were still shirtless, still sweating from playing in the summer sun.

"It's cold where we're at," Christopher answered.

"Where you at? Ain't you here?" William asked, curious.

"No," Jason realized. "We're not."

Daniel's eyes went wide. "So you both *are* ghosts?"

"We're..." Jason began, but then squeezed Christopher's hand, giving him a look. "Something like that. But we're not gonna scare you or hurt you."

Daniel pulled back into William's chest. Something about Jason seemed to frighten him, though curiosity kept winning out.

William, for his part, didn't seem fazed. In fact, he was drawn to Jason for some reason.

"I weren't scared of you before," William said. "You just looked spooky."

Jason understood. To them, he and Christopher were the mysterious beings drifting in and out of their world.

"You said earlier we'd made it," Christopher spoke up. "What did you mean?"

"We heard you coming. Splashing down the river. Figured someone was heading our way. Then we looked over and there you were."

Christopher looked at Jason, confused.

Almost to himself, Christopher whispered, "What about the railroad track? And the accident?"

"What accident?" Daniel asked, stepping forward. "When?"

Jason realized they'd somehow stepped into a time before the tragedy. Before William's family found out. Before everything fell apart. Before William made that terrible choice on the tracks.

"Nothing," Jason said quickly, giving Christopher a *follow my lead* look. "Just... nothing."

"You sure?" Daniel turned to Jason with curious blue eyes. Shiny, real eyes.

Jason could only see the years ahead of him. The loneliness that awaited. The hurt and ultimately the danger. He knew he needed to let these two have their moments together without talk of impending doom. Without trying to warn them of something that had already happened—or would happen—or however time worked in this impossible place.

Instead, Jason stepped forward into the water. The warm water. He reached out to Daniel slowly and patted his shoulder lightly.

"We're just here to look out for you both."

Daniel shuddered slightly, like Jason's hand was very cold, and instinctively pulled back into William's embrace. Jason stepped back onto shore, his foot suddenly freezing as he left the summer warmth.

Christopher looked amazed but nodded to them both. "We're here to help you."

"Help us?" William questioned. "With what?"

Jason wasn't sure what to say.

"To know you're loved," Christopher finally answered.

"You *are* loved," Jason agreed, his voice firm.

The vignette began to shrink. Colors started to fade. The cold winter world came breezing through stronger now—bare trees, icy banks, gray sky.

And then they were gone.

Christopher and Jason stood on the banks looking at the cold river, ice forming along the shoreline, snow on the log where clothes had once been piled.

They were alone.

They turned to each other. No words were needed. Neither frightened nor sad. Just... accepting.

They realized that had been the message all along.

You are loved.

And perhaps—just perhaps—that small gift they'd given to two boys from another time might change something. Might give William and Daniel the strength to hold on a little longer. To believe their love mattered. To know they weren't alone.

Or perhaps not.

Perhaps the past was fixed and unchangeable, and all they'd done was give two doomed boys a moment of comfort before the darkness closed in.

But standing there on that riverbank, Christopher's hand warm in his, Jason chose to believe in them.

They were loved.

About the Author

Michael Manosca first pursued a career in the arts, studying in Chicago, but storytelling has always been at the heart of his creative expression. His travels across the world have shaped his perspective, infusing his writing with the depth and nuance of the people and cultures he has encountered.

Michael writes in a deeply personal format, inspired by the relationships and experiences that shaped his upbringing. He explores the intricacies of friendship, the search for identity, and the quiet moments that define us. Through vivid characters and emotional depth, he hopes to craft stories that linger in readers' minds long after the final page.

When not writing, he can be found wandering the northern woods, exploring new cities, or enjoying a lively conversation in a tucked-away café. He currently resides along the western coast of the United States and is already working on his next story.

Also by Michael Manosca

Beyond Ties that Bind

Treffen

Bloodlines

Prism

Almost Always

Reflections at the Window

Flickering

A Language of Water

Static & Signals